# THE HORRIFIC SUFFERINGS OF THE MIND-READING MONSTER HERCULES BAREFOOT HIS WONDERFUL LOVE AND HIS TERRIBLE HATRED

Carl-Johan Vallgren

# THE HORRIFIC SUFFERINGS OF THE MIND-READING MONSTER HERCULES BAREFOOT

## HIS WONDERFUL LOVE AND HIS TERRIBLE HATRED

*Translated from the Swedish by*
*Paul and Veronica Britten-Austin*

THE HARVILL PRESS
LONDON

Published by The Harvill Press, 2005

2 4 6 8 10 9 7 5 3

© Carl-Johan Vallgren, 2002, 2005
English translation © Paul and Veronica Britten-Austin, 2005

Carl-Johan Vallgren has asserted his right under the Copyright, Designs and
Patents Act 1988 to be identified as the author of this work

First published with the title *Den vidunderliga kärlekens historia*
by Albert Bonniers Förlag AB, Stockholm

First published in Great Britain in 2005 by
The Harvill Press
Random House
20 Vauxhall Bridge Road
London SW1V 2SA

Random House Australia (Pty) Limited
20 Alfred Street, Milsons Point, Sydney,
New South Wales 2061, Australia

Random House New Zealand Limited
18 Poland Road, Glenfield,
Auckland 10, New Zealand

Random House South Africa (Pty) Limited
Endulini, 5A Jubilee Road, Parktown 2193, South Africa

The Random House Group Limited Reg. No. 954009
www.randomhouse.co.uk

A CIP catalogue record for this book is available from the British Library

ISBN 1 84343 1513

Typeset by SX Composing DTP, Rayleigh, Essex
Printed in Great Britain by Clays Ltd, St Ives plc

# THE HORRIFIC SUFFERINGS OF THE MIND-READING MONSTER HERCULES BAREFOOT HIS WONDERFUL LOVE AND HIS TERRIBLE HATRED

. . . from a closer relative, Miss V, than you may suppose

West Tisbury
Martha's Vineyard, Mass., USA
July 15, 1994

Dear Miss Vogel,

First I would like to thank you for your visit, which has left me many precious memories, and which has also, I hope, answered some of your questions. Genealogy is for me an uncharted area, but in your case, it would be hard not to draw the same conclusions as you have done: namely, that while you have kept the woman's surname, mine is, as you so rightly guessed, the anglicised form of our ancestor's German name.

I am old now, as the first Barefoot came to be in his day, and the price I'm paying for extreme old age is loneliness. If your guesses prove correct, then you are my closest living relative on my father's side.

In Chilmark parish I am the only one left who remembers him. He died in 1914, from the after-effects of mumps, shortly before the outbreak of World War I.

By then he had reached the grand age of 101. That was the same summer as I turned eight, long before mass tourism transformed Martha's Vineyard into the outdoor museum you encountered during your, alas, far too brief stay on the island. I

3

called him Grandfather, though this was inaccurate: he had outlived all his children and was in fact my great-grandfather.

The attached memoranda are a record of what he told my relatives, in particular my older sisters and myself. The rest is the result of my own research more than half a century ago. Information derived from the archives in Germany is naturally at your disposal. You may find the material from Königsberg of particular interest, the original records, as you know, having disappeared during the chaos of the war years.

When he was still alive I was too young to understand the details of his story: mainly I remember him as a kind-hearted little man, his face concealed behind a cloth mask, an expert at the grammar of sign language who, one day when I was visiting, whispered clear as can be, but without moving his lips: *Better to hold your tongue and be taken for a jester, than to speak and dispense with all doubt of it!* The quote, I later learned, came from Lincoln, whom he had once met.

The first deaf people came to Martha's Vineyard in the 1790s. Intermarriage caused the handicap to spread throughout the area. In my youth there were deaf people in every family. In Tisbury and Chilmark parishes they made up about a third of the population, in some of the villages all the inhabitants had hearing defects, so in the end the whole island learned sign language. Those of us who could hear grew up bilingual. Indeed I learned sign language even before English, since both my mother and my father had hearing disabilities. Put it this way: the handicap was so common that the idea of deafness didn't even exist. We never regarded them as "deaf". It was *we* who lived among *them*, not the other way round. They were the ones who set the cultural climate on the island; their world was our world.

The recessive gene had disappeared by the early fifties, but the old people among us still cling to sign language; not to tell dirty jokes (though that does sometimes happen) or in order to exclude visitors and tourists from our private conversations (which, as you probably noticed, also sometimes happens), but for the simple reason that it was the island's lingua franca. It was used as often as English. Besides which, it is a more expressive idiom than spoken language. Only recently I read in *National Geographic* about Providence Island in the West Indies, where the population, in much the same way, use an old form of Maya sign language when speaking among themselves. I could send you a copy of the article, you might find it helpful.

For obvious reasons I am most familiar personally with the American episode of Barefoot's story, though I chose to focus my research on the earlier years of his life, in Europe. According to family legend he mourned your great-great-grandmother so deeply he never again truly loved another woman. This notwithstanding, he had four children with two local women. My sisters and I were the first in our family to be born without handicaps.

Have you ever really asked yourself what *sound* is all about, Miss Vogel? This is a matter of interest for several different reasons, but above all because it indicates blind spots in our relationship to consciousness.

Sounds are vibrations which set the molecules in the air in motion. People who can hear apprehend sound on a scale of twenty to twenty thousand Hertz. Sound waves made up of fewer than twenty vibrations a second are called infrasonic; those made up of more than twenty thousand vibrations are called ultrasonic. Bats live exclusively in ultrasonic spheres; clinically speaking, they can't hear sound, they sense it. It is in this infrasonic world that alligators, whales, the Pampas ostrich and the cassowary live. Here, too, the idea of hearing is meaningless, since none of these animals can "hear" in the ordinary sense of the word. The alligator, for example, lacks ears. It listens with its body, that is to say, it registers vibrations from the outside world with a sensory nerve under an abdominal layer of skin.

During your stay, you asked which of these worlds Barefoot lived in. I would like to pose the hypothesis that he lived outside of our known hearing index, and that he "heard" on another frequency, hitherto scientifically unknown.

Moreover, during the autopsies carried out immediately after his death, a number of puzzling physical paradoxes arose. His heart, for instance, was over-dimensioned, twice the size of a normal human heart, despite his being a dwarf. When I came across this curious detail in his medical journal, I interpreted it symbolically: his life, just as that of your great-great-grandmother, is a love story. The doctor wrote that he "lived against all the odds", with a heart that ought to have stopped in early childhood, only

5

one kidney, only one functioning lung and an abdomen eaten away by tumours which, according to the expertise of the day, were at least half a century old by the time of his death. But the most fascinating of the post-mortem findings were the auditory organs: the vestibule of the inner ear, which in humans makes up the centre of equilibrium, was missing altogether. He ought not, in fact, have been able to walk or move about at all.

A month after his death a more extensive post-mortem was carried out on his corpse at a teratological clinic in Boston. The post-mortem dissector – a specialist on deformities – maintained that the right ear, apart from a slight petrification of the malleus, must have been as good as intact during the earliest years of his childhood, "up to the age of two" was his guess. This contradicted the evidence produced by the first autopsy. For it meant that he must have been able to hear, however slightly, during his infancy.

This could explain his musical talent – the eternal enigma in his biography: how can someone who has been deaf from birth understand and play music? Maybe, as the dissection suggested, during his earliest childhood – before the handicap took over completely – he had been able to discern notes and sounds?

It is extremely difficult for a hearing person to imagine the world of the deaf. You would have to imagine a world in which no sounds exist, no sough of the wind, no voices, no sound of a loved one's laughter, perhaps no comprehension of what sound is. Someone who is born deaf never speaks of silence, or lack of sound; nor do they complain about being deaf, any more than someone born blind complains about a lack of visual information, since they can't even imagine what seeing is like. Just as you, Miss Vogel, cannot miss a phenomenon you have never experienced, or a person of whose existence you are unaware, or a place to which you have never been. All this – deafness, blindness – is at best a metaphor.

Lew Wygotski, the renowned defectologist wrote: "Words die giving birth to thoughts, implying thereby that thought and speech transcend one another." This is along much the same lines as Schopenhauer's assertion that thoughts die the minute they are dressed in words. Words are but reference points for our experiences, the idea of conversation being to evoke common ground through associations between people. But maybe there are other ways of arriving at the same result. It is sometimes said that a picture says more than a thousand words. So does music, it is a method of conveying emotional states of mind from the creator to the listener.

One thing we can be sure of: a deaf person who has never learned any language at all lives in limbo. People and objects lack names, existence becomes chaotic, a mass of non sequiturs. The idea of questions and answers loses all meaning, abstractions do not exist, such people's intelligence remains on the level of a two-year-old. For it is through language that the child is introduced into the symbolic sphere of history and the future, it is through language that the small child learns to abstract and classify.

My parents used a language richer by far than English: sign language. Contrary to spoken language, sign language is four dimensional, occurring simultaneously in time and three-dimensional space, thereby conveying an enormous amount of information in a very short time. At only three months a child can learn signs, long before it is mature enough to attempt expressing its emotions in gurgles and words. The first sign I learned was the one for milk. According to my parents I was four months old at the time, that is to say at an age when normal children in normal families are capable only of expressing their hunger and need for breast milk by screaming. My first dreams were of hands communicating by signing, words without sounds, words as visual information, the mute movement of lips, mobile symbols. I still sometimes dream in sign language.

My uncle, Henry Russell-Price, was one of the foremost poets in America, but completely unknown outside a small circle of initiates. He was a sign-language poet. I remember meeting him when I was young, and how his body would start twitching and spontaneously producing signs when a moment of inspiration fell on him. He was a divinely gifted poet, the old people on the island talk about him to this day; I've met people from various sign-language groups all over America who can "recite" his verses for hours on end without tiring.

There is so much that hearing people don't know about deaf people's culture. About the humour and irony in sign language, about choirs who "sing" using signs, about how it feels to enter a restaurant where all the diners are deaf, the fantastic atmosphere at the tables where hands are signing at lightning speed, strange silences broken only by loud outbursts of laughter when someone has "said" something funny. Or what a breach of etiquette it is to put yourself between two people engaged in sign language, or how *ugly* it is to listen to others' conversation, that is to say, by staring at their hands.

As I grew up in this culture, it doesn't feel a bit odd, but when I try to explain it to outsiders I am forced to use similes. It's the same thing with Barefoot; any attempt to talk about his extraordinary gift and life has always to be in a figurative sense.

Some neurologists maintain that our conscious minds are not in sync with the world around us, and that we experience reality with a slight retardation, with the time it takes for the brain to screen off irrelevant impressions. And maybe it is in the light of this that we should see our forefather's gift? That he, contrary to people he met, was in tune with the sense impressions, that he lost no time screening off facts, so that, not only did he have access to a greater amount of information, but he was also so quick on the uptake that he seemed to be able to predict what people were thinking?

Again, this is all speculation, impossible to verify. The ego is but a map of a larger consciousness, just as language is a map of the terrain and must not be confused with the terrain itself.

As you may have noticed, Miss Vogel, it is only with a great effort that I am able to ring in the object of your interest, and only through these paraphrases, similes and related examples. But one thing is for sure, and that is that Barefoot's extraordinary gift functioned as a substitute for sensory shortcomings.

Every person has his own unique understanding of the world. A missing sense is compensated by another. The deaf hear with their eyes and speak through signing. Through the Tadoma method, Helen Keller developed a way for those who are both deaf and blind to understand the world through touch. By laying fingertips against another person's lips and larynx, the person who is deaf and blind can "feel" a fellow human speaking; by tracing letters or signs in the hand he can also make himself understood.

Our ancestors were born into a Europe that still looked on the deaf as idiots, and where sign language had not as yet spread, long before Alexander Graham Bell and Helen Keller succeeded in altering our attitude to this handicap. Nature herself compensated Barefoot for his lack of hearing, but in so radical a manner that it does not lend itself to science's landmarks. That is why my notes have assumed the form of a similitude, in order to try and get to the root of *our* enigma.

Let us not be hypocrites, Miss Vogel, I use this formula *our* consciously. At our very first meeting it was quite clear to me that you were one of us, the small group of initiates. And what you are searching for is not Barefoot, our ancestor, but for yourself, and the gift that frightens you because there is no rational explanation for it. In Martha's Vineyard you noticed that I knew and tried to shield you.

I believe those moments when you "hear beyond hearing" occur more seldom for me than for you; you have quite simply inherited more of his gift. With me, it occurs sporadically, when I'm least expecting it, but it no longer frightens me. (Just now, as I was writing these lines, the maid was on her way to my study to throw a glance at the one functioning clock in the house, I "heard" her formulating her query in her thoughts long before she reached the door, and so as not to be disturbed, I called out "almost four". "Thank you," she called back. After more than twenty years' employment here she has ceased to be astonished.)

I am almost as old now as Barefoot was when first he spoke to me on his inexplicable wavelength. I don't know if my father had the gift – anyway he never showed any signs of it – but one of my paternal aunts had it and tried to conceal it from the world until her dying day.

Now that I am nearing the end of a long and full life, the fiery cross must carry on. You, Miss Vogel, strike me as being the perfect choice. I am going to tell you Barefoot's tale, because who could understand it better than you? We are both late-comers, fruit of a monster's love, and today you are my closest living relative on my father's side (even though you live on the other side of the Atlantic in a small, Nordic country).

Above all, you have the gift. So I leave his tale in your keeping.

Jonathan Barefoot

I

One evening in February 1813 Dr Johan Götz was in his surgery sorting the bottles in his medicine cupboard when he came across the simple silver ring set with amber, which his wife had given him on their first day of marriage fourteen years before. That was when he opened his practice in Königsberg after finishing his medical studies at the famous Albertina university; that is to say, before the arrival of his children, before he employed two maids and before the somewhat disparaging military title of "barber-surgeon" had been added to those qualifications he already possessed. His fingertips, softened from a day spent palpating his patients, had discovered the ring in a crack in the wooden shelf he reserved for liniments and laxatives, next to a jar of congealed cream of mercury that he, in the course of the week's treatments, had put back in the wrong place. He moved to the window, beyond whose pane a snowstorm had been raging for forty-eight hours. He was unable to recall when last he had seen this piece of jewellery. It must have disappeared during one of the ritual transformations of the old merchant house when the surgery had been moved from a smaller room to a larger to keep pace with his growing practice. He lit the argand oil lamp above the examination bench and held the ring up to the light. Encased in the amber was a scarab, an insect of a kind related to the Egyptians' sacred beetle. Fetching a magnifying glass from his instrument cupboard, Götz, being the physician he was, noticed coldly how death must have overtaken this creature shortly after it had emerged from the pupa, for it was seriously deformed. The head was twice as long as the body. Only one of its three pairs of legs had developed. It also lacked jaws and antennae. When the resin had caught it in its glassy trap its life had already been over.

Slipping the ring on to his finger, the doctor was pleased to notice it still fitted, despite the detrimental effects of good living on his physiognomy. I'm a lucky man, he thought, I have a wife who still throws me the same impassioned glances she did fourteen years ago. I have two beautiful daughters. My surgery is thriving to the point where I am grateful to every snowstorm that grants me some much needed rest. My name is respected even by my few enemies, and my studies in Lavoisier's chemistry have won acclaim far beyond the borders of East Prussia.

From upstairs his children's noisy laughter, followed by the sound of his wife's stern admonishments delivered in the tones of all-embracing maternal love, confirmed the family's bliss.

Götz put the last of the liniment bottles back in the cupboard and locked it. On the laboratory bench, beside the vertical volta batteries he'd recently purchased for curing Königsberg's middle-class wives of their migraines, stood his pocket lupp from his years at the faculty. On impulse he placed the ring under its lens and laid it on the reflector. A miniature world stood revealed. Grains of sand, dust particles, microscopic air bubbles, the insect's larvae so minute he could only now detect it with the naked eye. Two thousand years had passed, he thought, since, melted by a merciless neolithic sun, the amber had trickled down a tree trunk, bearing with it into the future a fragment of the past, a beetle. And this prehistoric hostage had borne witness to the fact that there had at least been no change in nature's struggle for fundamental harmony. Enthralled by the beauty of the amber, the doctor allowed himself to sink into a daydream – of threatening Viking ships, of horse-borne Crusaders and Hanseatic Coggs on their way up the River Pregel to trade their amber with the savage Prussians. There was my cradle, he thought, the world where I – a direct descendant of the Astias, Prussians or Russ settlers on whom the scholar in me cannot but have its reflections – was born into a family of merchants and doctors; an offspring of amber collectors brought to the Christian faith in the final moments of the Middle Ages by Adalbert of Prague, Bruno von Querfort, Hermann von Salsa or some other crusading knight of the legendary Order of the Sword. My ancestors, thought Götz with a blasphemous shiver, worshipped animals and ancestral spirits, bent the knee to trees, idolising them in sacred groves, chanting ecstatically over the bodies of sacrificed slaves who might well have hung from the offspring of the very same tree whose resin is now lying there in its silver setting and revealing itself under my pocket lens. They had also sacrificed the misshapen, the deformed, the hare-lipped, the deaf and the blind, even the younger of each pair of male twins.

At the back of his mind he also smiled at love's sublime music coming from upstairs as his wife and her chambermaid began putting the children to bed. Pomerania, Galinden, Natangen, his mental excursion went on; in those legendary lands my forefathers were collectors of amber, great hunters and horsemen, spoken of with dread by Gallus Anonymus, with longing by Ibrahim ibn Jakub (he who travelled to the land of Slavonians on behalf of the Spanish Moors and had fallen in love with one of the big-bosomed women the savages had made him a present of), who had earned respectful mention in the Madgeburg Annals, been mystically revered in Thietmar von Merseburg's *Cronica* and been accorded a crusader's frigid military salute by Peter von Duisburg in the documents of his Order.

Amazed by the wealth of detail in these overwhelming dreamy historical images, Dr Götz's attention drifted from the inner to the outer vision as he came back to reality – the missing jaw, the over-dimensioned skull section of a monstrous insect – magnified twenty times over by the optics of his pocket lens. They made him shudder.

Lifting his gaze from the lens, he let the last traces of his daydream disperse. In the street the sound of hooves could just be heard, followed by a sleigh bell. "Anyone who presents himself in such a gale at this hour," he thought, "must be out on an urgent errand indeed."


It was Franzceska Beyer, the Götz's maid-cum-nanny since the arrival of their youngest daughter Elizabeth seven years earlier, who opened the front door into the night. As far as she would later recall, she had instantly realised – despite being half blinded by the Arctic winds, advancing from their cradle in the Gulf of Bothnia and howling and roaring like a wolfpack down the central quarters of the ancient city of Königsbert – it was a very young girl, moreover one of easy virtue. Yet she was clad as if for mid-May, wore saffron yellow shoes, a colonel's plume in her hat, and over her shoulders only a loosely buttoned Venetian cloak.

"Can I speak to Dr Götz?" she asked, shivering. "It's urgent. A matter of life and death."

Franzceska felt sorry for the girl's light clothing and her face's deathly pallor. Amid a perfumed cloud of musks and ambergris soaps she admitted her to the hallway, and saw through a gap in her outdoor garments that, save for a lace corset, she was virtually naked.

"In Jesu name," she said, pointing to the hall tabouret, "do sit down. I'll fetch the doctor and get you some tea to warm yourself."

Two minutes later when Dr Götz appeared, together with the maid and likewise his wife Catherine, whose sixth sense never failed to pick up anything of note happening in the house, the girl had collapsed in sobs on the floor. Together they lifted her up. But scarcely had they placed her on the seat than she jumped up again, shouting, "There's nothing wrong with me! It's the Polish girl! She's dying in childbed, and as Miss Vogel's having a baby too and Madam Schall asked me to take the sledge to the doctor's, and seeing as how you two are old acquaintances and known for saving the lives of both rich and poor without taking them in any special order . . ."

The girl's hysteria released the doctor from his recollections of that part of his youth he believed was forever kept secretly screened off by a shield of family love. For it was his wife who bade him run and get his bag while she tried to calm the girl.

Taking the steps down to his surgery two at a time, Götz retrieved his emergency bag from its brass hook behind the door, and since it was a question of a delivery, supplemented its contents with two lancets, his tongs, styptic ointments, a dozen bandages and cotton wool compresses, plus a newly purchased and hitherto unopened bottle of laudanum. While he was busy with all this, he noticed the ring was still on his finger and – without being able to explain it or put up the slightest resistance – again let himself succumb to the kind of shameful excitement he had enjoyed in the distant past in the Sackhenin district as a regular client of Madam Schall's love nest, known in those days as: *Your House of Desires.*

That had been during his student years in Albertina, before the ball arranged by Königsberg's cavalry officers at which he first met Catherine Mahlsdorf and behind the dinner hall's damask curtain had given her the clandestine kiss which deprived him for ever of any desire for the kind of love one pays for. He recalled the women of six nationalities who travelled with the army's baggage train who, between the wars, had been taken on at Madam Schall's and who had let their daughters run amok in that enormous building, until such time as they were considered old enough to be sold to the highest bidder. He recalled a negress from the French colonies with cocoa-coloured skin and hair fuzzy as steel wool. Allegedly a Yoruba princess, one rumour had it she had been sold as a slave to the Russian tsarina before running away with a Dutch adventurer, who eventually lost her at dice to Madam Schall. He recalled with distaste the auctioning off of a weeping nine year old whose maidenhead was won in the end by a sailor. With similar excitement he called to mind the enormous grey-haired Agrafena Nehludova, a Russian woman who, surrounded by an endless array of soaps, perfumes, eaux de cologne and smelling salts, had lain, naked and audibly hissing, on a divan that was a sea of satins and linen, in an undergrowth of flower vases, jewellery, hairpins, mirrors, obscene prints and love letters written on vanilla paper by ecstatic admirers of every age and class of society, and had received clients young enough to be her children, or, come to that, grandchildren. One evening, bewitched by the deep-red rose behind her ear and the sanctimonious smile that, after their copulation, seemed to promise him eternal life, Götz had himself boarded her ship of Olympian lechery, no less inebriated by a bottle of Malvoisie than by her odour of Havana snuff and debauchery. It was said she had not got up from her encampment for more than two decades – a rumour, culled from love's mythologies, which Götz had never found reason to disbelieve. For never among all the evenings he had visited the establishment had he once seen her lift her massive anatomy from that erotic divan where, between amorous interludes, her goose quill replied to

17

love letters or else she languorously vegetated with a pinch of snuff. Together with gonorrhoea, she had been the most unchanging feature of that establishment, where the girls came and went like migrant birds.

The doctor let his recollections of past excitements evaporate, again took hold of his professional self and found he had put the ring down, though he couldn't recall where. When he left his surgery it was with the strange conviction that he would never find it again, and that Fate, in some inexplicable way, had linked this with the delivery awaiting him in Königsberg's most celebrated whorehouse.


In the hallway, meanwhile, Catherine Götz, assisted by the maid, had given the girl a glass of linden tea and wrapped her in a woollen shawl. The colour had returned to her cheeks. Now she was sitting hunched up on the tabouret, the glass of tea cupped in her hands, her gaze fixed on some spot on the carpet that could equally have been a point on her inner horizon.

Drawing her husband aside as she helped him on with his fur coat and fox-fur gloves, Catherine Götz whispered as she buttoned up his intricate bootlaces and handed him his walking stick, "You'll have to explain all this about the Schall woman's establishment, Johan, as soon as you get home. I didn't think we had any secrets between us, either from our life together or the past."

Götz noticed a tear in the corner of her eye; a tear she brushed his hand from when he tried to wipe it away.

"A whore!" she said in a voice meant to sound contemptuous but which failed to hide an innate sympathy for the vulnerable. "Thank goodness the children are in bed. If you weren't bound by your Hippocratic oath I shouldn't let you go there."

Götz let her button up his fur coat right to the collar and put on his hat and lawn scarf before picking up his bag and going over to the girl. "Hurry," he said, "or we'll have the coachman's life on our conscience in addition to the rest of this miserable business . . ."

The snowstorm was the worst within living memory; worse than the winter gales from Siberia that had ravaged the Bay of Danzig around the turn of the century. A flurry of snowflakes the size of half-crowns was blowing in with full gale force from the

Baltic. So thickly wrapped up was the coachman that only the tip of his nose stuck out from under the sleigh's leather hood. The horses, Götz noticed as they drove off, had lost all sense of direction, and it was only through instinct that they didn't trot straight off into the wall of the next house. The girl, buried under a heap of rugs, her hair sprinkled with snow, sat opposite him.

"Tell me," he demanded, "what has happened?"

As the sleigh moved along Königsberg's snow-covered alleys, the doctor heard in outline of the misfortune that had driven the girl into the gale. One of Madam Schall's girls had been in labour for more than forty hours, and her strength was giving out. From this account of the labour pains Götz realised that birth spasms had set in, but couldn't be clear as to whether the birth itself was overdue.

"The head's too big," the girl said, in a voice that seemed not to trust its message. "The head's too big, I saw it with my own eyes."

Götz found it hard to believe the birth could have gone that far and then stopped. Probably the severity of the woman's pains, he told himself, was due to a narrow pelvis. It transpired that this was her first childbirth. At the same time, the girl explained, shouting to make herself heard above the wind's diabolical howling, another girl was giving birth in the next room. So it was a question of two deliveries, one normal, one with complications. Apparently the establishment had had no-one else to turn to.

Götz recalled an older woman who acted as a midwife and maybe even, in secret, as a baby farmer, though on that point he might be deceiving himself. Despite everything, his memories from those days lay blessedly in fallow, in a fifteen-year deep soil of premarital urges he had no desire to dig any deeper into than he'd already done this evening. When had the waters broken, he asked. The girl wasn't sure. "The head's too big," was all she could volunteer, as if the words kept going round and round in her mind.

As far as Götz could make out, the sleigh was moving southwards, along Langgasse. The snow had eased up a little, but there was no change in the gale's force. In Schloss strasse a lamplighter was fighting an heroic battle to carry out his duty, and further down from Kneiphof Island bells could be heard tolling in the cathedral tower. The doctor wondered what the reason could be

19

for ringing bells at the height of a snowstorm. Baffled by his own question, he leaned forward and asked the driver.

"Ain't ye heard, sir?" the driver shouted back. "The Provincial Council has decided to go to war against Bonaparte. Which means more bloodbaths, and that's for sure."

Götz sank back into his rugs, and for a while his attention strayed from the call of duty and the girl in the sleigh, sobbing at the thought of her friend's plight. It was a rumour Götz had heard a week ago, but hardly credited. Encouraged by the Russian successes, the Prussian nobility had decided to revolt against the Frenchman's new order of things.

Painful shudders passed through the doctor when he thought back to the three campaigns he had served in, and which he'd only just come through alive, the worst of them being Austerlitz, where the East Prussian grenadiers had been crushed by Marshal Davout's divisions. He was still being tormented by nightmares from that battlefield, the terrible wounds caused by the French guns, the bayonet wounds, punctured lungs and entrails, limbs shot away, legs blown to pieces, burns that had made full-grown men cry like babies, scream for their mothers, suck their thumbs and die. In the field ambulances they'd worked in shifts carrying out operations, waded up to their ankles in an indescribable slush of blood, excrement and amputated limbs, all in an unbearable atmosphere of lethal anxiety and meaningless prayers that could cause the most hardbitten to faint. Yet it was true, what his immediate superior had afterwards said to him over a glass of port wine in a Berlin officers' club: without all those deaths and our faithful body snatchers we wouldn't be saving so many lives today.

They had become masters at staunching bleedings, sewing up cuts and slashes, removing shattered arms and flinging them on to a heap, at amputating with only a shot of brandy and a quiet prayer to numb the pain. But the price, Götz now understood from his nightmares, was a terror that wouldn't leave them until the day when they themselves said goodbye to life. For terror it was that shadowed them after all these wars.

And now, he thought, seated in the sleigh bound for his youth's happy-go-lucky love nest, the church bells ringing in his ears, now they were all set to go to war again, if only to reinstate their Prussian honour. That was why they – Count Yorck, Alexander zu

Dohna-Schobitten and Baron Hardenberg – had ordered the bells to ring out through this blizzard, to get the King, hiding with his court at Memel, to show some courage.

In a cloud of whirling snow they drove on down Prinsenstrasse, Götz winning his duel with his horrific memories by thinking about Immanuel Kant, who had lived in a house on this street during his student years, and always been so punctual to the minute that people had set their watches by him. Awakened by his servant, who had one leg shorter than the other, and who, so rumour had it, was under strict orders not to let his master go back to sleep even for ten minutes, even if he begged, Kant had risen at exactly a quarter to five every morning. In the evening, so another rumour went, this same servant would roll him ingeniously up in four patchwork quilts for him to pass the night, motionless as a mummy. This procedure, the philosopher had maintained, enriched his dreams and stimulated his imagination. At nine o'clock sharp the light went out.

Affected by the thought of Kant's chronomania, Götz took out his silver watch and saw that it was past ten o'clock. They should reach the establishment in about a quarter of an hour at most.

Brushing some snowflakes from his face, he stared out at the row of façades behind which the city's wealthier businessmen sat counting their day's takings; men who had also visited Madam Schall's establishment in years gone by, and whose sons might possibly have fathered the infants he was now being called out to deliver. Could there be some connection, he wondered, between objects and events? As between the amber with the beetle in it, this uprising against Bonaparte and the delivery just now awaiting him in the House of Desires, for instance?

Madam Schall received him without a flicker of recognition. A characteristic piece of discretion, Götz assumed, developed over more than three decades in her trade, first as a common prostitute, then as a hostess and, finally, after many diligent intrigues and much saving up, as proprietress of the establishment and all its chattels, and with half a dozen girls in her debt for the rest of their lives. She had aged more than he might have imagined. In his day she'd been a striking woman who could as easily have been thirty as fifty, dressed in bustles and forever busy with her household accounts or calling in cash due from those who had enjoyed her services on tick. Now she was, at best, an ageless old woman.

"Thank goodness you could come, doctor," she said. "The girl's in a bad way. I hope you don't think it inappropriate, but we've sent for a priest."

Götz gave an embarrassed nod. "Just show me the way," he said. "Science can't wait for the supreme unction."

They passed through a hall where time had stood still since his last visit. Its wallpapers were painted with the same frivolous Pompeiian motifs where everyone was hard at it with everyone else. In the windows hung the same white satin curtains, intended to create an atmosphere of cleanliness and luxury. But it was gloomier now than it had been. Before the turn of the century the brothel had been a battlefield for unmarried men in delirious mood. Laughter had echoed as a myriad customers hailed each other in a dozen tongues. In the doorways to their rooms half-naked women had whispered to their clients in the language of love, promising with indecent gestures to satisfy their most secret desires, assuage their gnawing hunger, their burning thirst, undressing them with their eyes and teasing them like children by snatching at their hats. On summer evenings Madam Schall had arranged masquerade balls. In the garden where Chinese lanterns, likewise painted with obscene motifs, had hung from the fruit trees, grown men had played hide-and-seek in the dark, naked men chased girls across the lawns, all in a spirit of joyful abandon, as if life consisted of suffering and humanity's ultimate consolation lay in escaping unclothed into a game of hide-and-seek. Now only a gloom of inverse strength prevailed. Or was it he himself who had changed? Seeing everything now clear-sightedly – the furniture that had seen better days; the grubby tablecloths; the parlour table formerly laid with Meissen china, but now more likely populated with germs – as if through a newly acquired lens?

Upstairs he took in at a glance the room that was to etch itself for ever on his memory. On the bedside table lay the morocco jewellery box with its cheap trinkets, the enamel washbasin, the water tap and the folded napkins which constituted every prostitute's basic accoutrements.

In a bowl by the bed lay some oiled satin condoms, not to prevent pregnancy – on this point the girls still preferred *coitus interruptus* and herbal ointments from the Lithuanian market women – but to prevent diseases, some absolutely incurable and others that brought with them a slow putrefaction but spread such irritation to the brain that the victim died at one of the city's lunatic asylums in a purgatory of indescribable itchings. In a wardrobe hung sinfully low-cut nightdresses. In a drawer lay clothes in cambrics of seven different colours. On the dressing table stood a battery of soaps, perfumes, oils and pomades, and in the middle of the room, pale unto death, in a bed where sheets covered her bulging stomach, lay the girl.

Götz set her age at about twenty though his unconscious conferred on her the qualities of an angel beyond her years. She was blonde, but of the Slavonic kind, with red streaks in her untidy knot of hair. Putting down his bag, he felt her pulse. She was hardly alive. Her breath came in intermittent gasps. Her feverish forehead was burning hot.

A movement from the other side of the room made him turn. It was the clergyman.

"Prepare yourself for a shock, doctor," he said. "I've never seen anything like it. Whatever it may be, it won't live long, thank God."

Götz noticed the priest's bag was like his own, filled, presumably, with implements for deliverance of the soul rather than the flesh: biblical words, sacramental wafers and bottles containing oils for the supreme unction. The man's presence irritated him. Not just because he regarded himself as defending – as he often put it – the island of science against the stormy ocean of superstitions and metaphysics; or because he embodied the opposite of the commonsense atheism he, qua doctor, cultivated, albeit in secret so as not to scare the daylights out of Catherine Götz or confuse his children and fill them with anxiety at a sensitive age. But more out of a feeling that he shouldn't commit a breach of etiquette vis-à-vis this man in black who spent his life wishing to high heaven what he, Götz, wanted to keep firmly planted on earth.

Lifting the sheet, he recoiled instinctively from a sight that in all its monstrous detail was to haunt him to his dying day half a century later in the Age of Steam.

The child, which by some miracle had succeeded in getting itself halfway out into the world, was nothing but a quintessence of human deformity. So grotesquely large was the skull emerging from the birth canal that it had split the woman's pelvis. He could scarcely bring himself to look at the face turned towards him. The harelip was such that neither nose nor nostrils existed. In the centre of the child's face leered a dark red cavity, like a bowl whose lacerated edge ended at eye level. On the bald head were strange protruberances reminiscent of black fossilised snails. The tongue was split like a snake's. Bumps and swellings disfigured the temples, the mottled skin was scaly like a lizard's. It was a monster.

Götz had to close his eyes to keep his composure. The girl was probably beyond saving. Judging by the sheets, she must already have lost several litres of blood. Her deep unconsciousness bordered on coma. Her pelvis and stomach muscles had ceased to function, so there was no chance of getting the delivery going by natural spasms. For a moment Götz thought of delivering the child with the scalpel, but rejected the idea since, in her weakened state, it would put the mother beyond saving.

He took out lancets and scissors, disinfected his instruments. The girl's heartbeat was so faint that at least it would not cause yet more excessive bleeding. Drenched in his own sweat, Götz cut open her vagina. His only thought was to at least save the life of this creature that, by its own force, had thrust its head out into the world. It was a miracle, he thought, the birth even having got this far, that the head could have left the womb without killing the girl instantly. All the time he worked, her pulse was growing weaker, but by now the vagina entrance was so large he could pull the child out without having to use the tongs. As if from far away in another world he heard the clergyman mumbling a prayer, preparing to bless this whore about whom neither of them knew a thing, but whom everyone realised was lost.

Slowly, centimetre by centimetre, he pulled out the child. What was supposed to be a face, he noticed, had a bluish flush, the umbilical cord having wound itself several times round the child's neck as if nature had at the last moment opted for a mercy killing.

Götz cut it and went on easing the body this way and that, the woman's breathing meanwhile sinking so low it could barely support life. The deformities revealed themselves successively as he drew the child into the world.

Exterior ears there were none, and the auditory channels were overgrown by layers of some kind of petrified skin. The child was probably deaf.

Since the child had shown no sign of life, the doctor was struck by the thought that it might already be dead. The closed eyelids did not stir. It did not cry. Now he could see the child's whole body. On its shoulders were protuberances he took for arms and hands, but which reminded him rather of parboiled roots from a very small plant. In a jumble of thoughts which banished his disgust but put pressure on his medical ethic, Dr Götz worked on. Should he make an intentional mistake? Why not? What good would this life be, and if allowed to live, what future did it have? And for how long; and at what cost of suffering?

His hands' tactile sense took up the thought his mind refused to grasp: the protruberances, the lumps, the deformed chest indicative of underdeveloped lungs. The infant's back, he noticed, was covered with black hair as thick as a kid goat's. It's more animal, he thought, than human being.

By now the body was quite free, and he could see it was a boy. So far only the genitals seemed, almost unrealistically so, without deformities. Someone behind him was talking about the girl. The poor creature was an orphan from some Slavonic minority, whatever that meant after Poland's partition. On a trip to Danzig Madam Schall had found her begging in the streets and taken pity on her. In the three years she'd been working in the brothel she had managed to save up a little money, intending sooner or later to return to her home village. Who was the father? Uncertain. Probably an officer; they used to like her way of surrendering to their whims. Not that Götz heard any of this, or that they were already speaking of her in the past tense. He was working feverishly.

The legs, he saw with a certain relief, were better developed than the arms. A dwarf's legs, but if he survived he'd be able to walk on them. He lifted up the boy, held him close and slapped the furry backside, hoping for a scream from the horrific orifice that was both nose and mouth, gullet and windpipe. The breathing did in fact start up, though there was still no gurgle or scream.

Götz became aware of the murmurs of the girls now gathered in the room. Laying the child down on the bed beside its mother, he put his ear to her mouth and listened. No breathing. Gently, he pressed his fingertips against the carotid artery. Quite still. He became aware of the clergyman standing beside him:

"It's too late," he said. "We can only hope the Lord will receive her."

"Why wasn't I called earlier?"

Götz was surprised by the anger in his own voice, an anger nourished by the fact that we always arrive too late for our most crucial encounters, as if fate intentionally delays sending out invitation cards. If only I'd been sent for ten hours earlier, he thought, perhaps I could have saved the girl.

The clergyman did not disguise his revulsion as he contemplated the boy.

"I can't say a prayer over her," he said. "Nor can I do an emergency baptism of this . . . whatever it is."

"Why not?"

"You can see for yourself why not. Would the good Lord make fun of His own creation thus?"

Götz too looked at the boy: the furry back, the split face, the grotesque overgrown head, as large as the rest of the body. Though he was breathing, the eyes remained closed as if afraid to see the world that awaited them.

"What we have before us, doctor, is the fruit of Satan's concubine. This creature isn't begotten by man. It isn't human at all." Picking up his bag the priest went to the door. "Believe me," he said. "This isn't the first time. Only a month ago a boy was born in Lemberg that was half-human, half-wolf. He lived for exactly four minutes. Four minutes too long, in my opinion."

The priest left the room, and in the ensuing silence the doctor turned to Madam Schall.

"Where's the other girl?" he asked. "I was told there were two births."

\*

Two doors away the other birth had been without complication in the room that had once housed the great Agrafena Nehludova who, seven years ago, had suddenly and inexplicably arisen from her encampment and disappeared without trace. Though the doctor knew nothing of that particular story. As he stepped over the threshold the baby was already lying at its mother's breast, washed and wrapped in linens. It was a plump girl with nut-brown eyes and downy hair. He asked a few questions about the mother's condition, comforted her when she started to weep over the fate of her unfortunate sister. It was then he noticed that the bells still tolled on Kneiphof Island.

"At least this little girl has come into this world in high style," he said with an effort, to lighten the mood. "It's for her the cathedral bells are chiming."

He gave the newborn a routine examination. How unfair it seemed that Fortune should scatter her gifts so randomly. That this child could be so fully formed and healthy, while the boy in the next room, born this same night, in the same house, of the same sort of woman, had been denied even the most basic anatomical harmony. He wondered who would care for the orphan during the brief spell of life he assumed was left to it? Would anyone give him the breast? He doubted it. They'd just take him to the baby farmer. The thought gave Götz a feeling of relief quite devoid of guilt, implying as it did an end to a life that would otherwise be only pain and suffering.

He devoted a few minutes more to the woman until he was sure her condition was stable and had given instruction on how to wash and feed the infant. Then Götz went back to the boy's room.

He found the boy panting in Madam Schall's arms, his eyes still closed. Some of the girls had already started to wrap the mother's corpse in a winding sheet. A window, wide open, aired the unmistakable smell of death.

"What will happen to the boy?" he asked.

"We'll look after him," said Madam Schall, rocking the child, "for as long as he's allowed to live."

Only now did Götz fully take in the life he had brought into the world. He recalled the anatomy hall at Albertina. In glass jars filled with alcohol, the professors had kept deformed foetuses: Siamese twins, stillborn in the sixth month; a girl with hydrocephalus and on her back a birthmark shaped like a dragon; a boy with lockjaw and another with five rows of teeth and a brain showing growth failure in the fontanelle. All this monstrosity, this collection of grotesque jokes staged by heartless Nature, neatly numbered and arranged on shelves above charts of the circulatory and muscular systems, bones and intestines, had stuck in his memory. There were mongoloids and albinos, some of them seemingly mere fortuitous collections of bones and flesh, lives that had mercifully been rejected in good time, together with animal foetuses of every kind, two-headed calves, an incredibly misshapen pig, a lamb with its head growing from its stomach. But what he saw in front of him – this enormous skull with lumps like stones, the split face, the furry body and the inadequate protruberances standing for arms – seemed the most cruel, because the child was still alive, cursed with a life against which it could not defend itself.

"Isn't there anything you can do, doctor?" Schall asked.

"No," he said. "The cleft palate is too severe to operate on."

He took the bottle of laudanum from his bag.

"Give him a few drops of this for the pain. We can only hope he won't use up too much of it."

He waited while the girls washed away the blood and vernix. Wasn't there something he had overlooked? He realised what it was. He had yet to look into the boy's eyes.

He asked to hold him.

Amazed that this reflex could be missing, Götz gently prised the eyelids open with his fingertips. The eyes were grey and seemed clouded by an infection or cataract. But the boy, without a blink or so much as a shudder, and with a gaze so steady it seemed able to support a collapsing wall, ceased to gasp for breath.

Götz would never be able to explain exactly what had happened that evening as the snow flurried and the bells' clangour rang out over Königsberg. Suddenly, as the boy fixed his ageless eyes on him, it was as if he was at a central point inside Götz's mind.

In some way the boy stared – or stepped – right into Götz, got inside him as a parasite intrudes unnoticed into a human body. Without language, scarcely aware he even existed, he flouted all scientific laws; and, worst of all, could read the doctor's most secret thoughts.

This boy, Götz knew, could see into all the evasions and half-repressed thoughts and desires that were his self; was aware of what he was feeling at this moment, was an observer of his childhood's long-forgotten emotional storms – the unquenched longing for breast milk and bodily warmth – his wordless death wish, his suppressed desire to exact revenge upon a cruel world, the shameful teenage excitements and the red-hot passion still seeking an outlet and auguring the day, two decades later, when he would leave his wife for a woman of a lower class. This boy saw his forbidden attraction to his youngest daughter, like a smell of rotting flowers; his crazy dream of crossing the Atlantic to the New World which reason had long ago rejected, but which he was amazed to find still alive in him with undiminished force.

The boy knew how he longed to run from the room and yet linger in it and watch him die, while at the same time hoping he'd survive; was listening to his secret thoughts at this moment, some having already taken shape in words, others not quite, rough drafts only, hewn out of consciousness' marble. Tiny though the boy was, the doctor knew he could see all of these things at the centre of the mind that was himself.

Shuddering to the marrow of his bones, he handed the infant back to Madam Schall.

"The priest is right," he mumbled. "This is no human being. It's the Devil's offspring."

The bells that rang out over Königsberg the night the boy was born did indeed augur a new era. A decade of calamitous conflicts went into the grave at Leipzig and Waterloo, and the town on the River Pregel entered a new era of greatness. Madam Schall contrived to make the most of the general boom; for demand rose in every sphere, not least where love was for sale. Six evenings a week, Sundays as holy days apart, her house filled with clients. Calèches and landaus jostled with cabs in its courtyard. There was more laughter than tears, though the latter weren't uncommon either. Madam Schall made it her business to win over the new-rich bourgeoisie for her establishment: provincial councillors specialising in Prussian land reform, influential judges, musicians and copyists; the city's young snobs who preferred von Kleist to Goethe and Hoffmann to Jean Paul, as well as their Freemason fathers who had a craze for all manner of secret societies; and then, of course, young squires on leave, as much at a loss in peacetime as martial in war, sighing unconsolably for their fallen steeds and dead comrades. Under the new chandeliers captains from Uhlan regiments and cuirassiers in gala uniforms strove to outshine one another – until their clothes came off and left them as naked as the Lord had created them and the girls could admire the enigma of their battle scars' fantastical sutures, the work of drunken barber-surgeons a hair's breadth from semi-mythical battlefields, or shriek with horror as porcelain eyes were plucked out and held up like war trophies from some foreign land. Schall even succeeded in recruiting clients among employees of the new semaphore telegraph, secretly hoping they'd spread her brothel's reputation far and wide by means of the complex light signals used on cloudless nights.

The economy blossomed. Some of her girls earned so much money they went home to their native villages, until within a few years nearly half Madam Schall's tribe had been exchanged for new girls, some from as far away as Berlin, where Madam Schall had discreetly advertised in a supplement to the weekly news-sheet for "gentlemen's companions".

Now the same frivolous light-heartedness reigned as in her youth, notwithstanding all the sailors arriving from foreign shores with novel diseases almost impossible to stem, causing Schall to impose a special fee on anyone refusing to use the precautions she otherwise provided free of charge – a fee so high only the wealthiest merchants could afford this prophylactic measure, a hundred years before its time, to hinder the spreading of syphilis.

Her new girls were dear little things dressed in the latest fashions, and Schall, who in her youth had had governesses in a long-since ruined Bavarian business house, let several of them be taught the arts of poetry-reading and piano-playing, thus still further enhancing her establishment's status.

The tradition of holding masked balls in the garden on summer evenings was also resumed, and likewise on Saturday afternoons, in the everlasting minor key of autumnal rains, poetry com-petitions in praise of love. During the last years of the decade some celebrities appeared, leaving behind them memories and anecdotes – or leaving a girl in the family way so she had to be handed over to an old wise woman Madam Schall had brought all the way from Kiev against a promise to look after her in her old age. The *luminatus* Jung-Stilling from the Palatinate, for example, who one evening demonstrated his magical skills in the room normally reserved for private parties; or Goethe's miserable son August who, having bitten off in a single bite the nipple of a newly arrived girl, who then defended herself by stabbing him between the eyes with a hairpin, had caused a scandal by leaving the establishment, in broad daylight, in an open landau, naked save for a plaster on his forehead. Or Alexander von Humboldt, recently back from a long journey in a country no-one had ever heard of, and some even doubted existed, with a bunch of treacherous diseases which almost cost the pro tem mistress of his affections her life and which, by love's free circumambulations, was spread to four others.

Madam Schall was tolerant when it came to odd lusts and had a magistrate's sense of justice when it came to disputes. "Everyone has the right to be happy in his own way," she would say standing behind her desk upstairs meticulously totting up accounts for all the house's services. "But it's up to my girls to set the price."

She would boast that there was no desire in this world her girls couldn't satisfy, and in more serious moments would even intimate that society held no other institution so useful to it as the brothel, adducing as evidence the half-dozen attempted suicides her girls were said to have fended off at the last moment with their irresistibly seductive arts. Or again, all those men who, broken down by life's adversities, had turned up at six in the afternoon with what little was left of their lost fortunes, their souls in a sorry state of dissolution, and left at midnight, laughing and ready to tackle whatever trials the morrow may bring. Even cases where marriages on the brink of the abyss had been saved she would cite to support her line of reasoning, the men, and they not few, at least in her imagination, who'd found relief on her girls' bosoms and been so thoroughly re-educated lovewise that they'd been able to inject new life into a marital bed dead as the timber it was made of, creating a sensation in better halves who had ceased to love them a quarter of a century ago.

In a word, she said that the shipwrecked heart did not exist that hadn't taken refuge in her house. Only one thing irritated her – that she could not open an institution where the town's ladies might be similarly served by young men wise to their hearts' anguish and clairvoyant of their desires, thus sagely realising that not for another century would the time be ripe for such an experiment.


It was in this peculiar environment that the boy grew up. On the night he was born to an accompaniment of church bells and whirling snowflakes most doubted he would live to see his first dawn, but even those who had turned their compassion into doubt saw their merciful hopes dashed. He had obstinately refused to surrender to death.

What few knew, but some suspected, was that some individuals are born with a will to live so strong it can defy the laws of nature. Not merely did the boy survive the dawn, but the following day, week and month too, until there could be no doubt of his intention to survive, if not his entire childhood, then at the very least his first year. And this he did, but under such torments as could have broken the most hardened of hearts.

From the first day he was fever-ridden. Pains in his malformed body made him shudder until loss of consciousness freed him of them. In the third month, weakened by his duel with death's emissaries, he was assailed by a suppurating pox that burst and left scars, disfiguring the few square centimetres of his body which until then had seemed normal. Armed only with an iron will he defied death in battles that lasted for weeks at a time, and when the pains retreated, he smiled a smile that brought tears to the girls' eyes.

For four weeks he struggled against a brain fever and won right at the finishing line, when his temperature, which had reached forty-three degrees, at long last began to subside. He clung to life like a capsized sailor to a raft, without compass or chart. All with only one aim – to ride out the storms and survive at all costs. The stunted arms were racked by growing pains. The deformed parts of the ill-grown skeleton threatened to puncture him from within. Yet he refused to surrender to the pains. After sanguinary civil wars with legions of bacteria the sores in the cloven face healed. Not until his first birthday would the monstrous orifice cease to suppurate and give off a stink of crude vulcanised rubber that would make a corpse gasp for breath. Though his guardians did not quite understand it at the time, this was in fact the final battle. Death, to its own amazement, was forced to haul its ensign and, having spent all its powder on a single adversary far more obstinate than anyone could have guessed, sail away to new shores.

Two weeks after this decisive victory the boy was christened. It was done in a simple ceremony under the auspices of a Polish chaplain in the same room where first he had looked out on the world. By then no-one could recall the mother's Slavonic surname, nor whether she'd expressed any wish as to what her child's name should be. But Madam Schall, who had a weakness for heroic deeds and a penchant for antiquity, decided he should be called Hercule, spelled the French way; and said that, in view of the nature of his hands, it was obvious he would have to do most things with his feet, and so bound him to that role with the sur-name Barfuss, which is German for Barefoot. This improvised sacrament not withstanding, he was registered under these heroic-sounding names with the Prussian tax collector, as an orphan adhering to the Catholic faith, under Madam Schall's guardian-ship. From that time forward life had acknowledged him.

No-one could have believed that under such circumstances Hercule Barfuss could develop like a normal boy. Yet he did. The girls thought he must submit to his handicaps, that he must be retarded. He also seemed to be deaf and dumb. During his first two years of life he never reacted to sounds or voices. Half-hearted efforts were made using the so-called Büchner staves. Long auditory pipes were thrust into his sealed auditory channels to amplify sounds; but no-one ever saw him react or heard him utter anything more than a sob or a whine when overcome by the pain. Yet these misgivings, too, were frustrated, as death's designs on him had been. Behind the corrosive façade lay a lucid intelligence.

When he was older Hercule seemed to understand everything that was said to him. At first taken for a miracle, it was afterwards explained away by saying he didn't wholly lack hearing, despite the lack of conchae.

It was hard to find any other explanation. When asked to sit still, for instance, he obeyed without hesitation. When urged to go to sleep, he closed his eyes. And when asked a question he would sometimes, if not always, respond with a nod or a shake of his head. The girls supposed he must somehow be able to lip-read, or that their voices' vibrations must somehow be forming intelligible sentences within him. Very few of them ever suspected he could read their thoughts.

Later on, when he had learned to interpret the girls' gestures, of which some had been notated by Wilhelm Kerger, the famous teacher of the deaf and dumb, he also learned to read and write, not only in German but also in French. Then Madam Schall, out of a sentimentality for her own past, had taken on a governess for him. But by that time no-one gave his silence a thought. When he wanted to communicate something important he would quite simply write it down on a slip of paper, and the circumstance of his never speaking fell, as it were, out of the picture.

Clever as he was at compensating for his supposed deafness, Hercule became just as smart at compensating for his other handicaps. For lack of properly formed arms and hands, he became quite remarkable at using his feet instead, thus living up to his surname. Over time he became a veritable orthopaedic conjurer, until in the end there was no task an ordinary person carries out with his fingers Hercule couldn't do with his sensitive toes.

Aged one he could walk. At three he could use a knife and fork. At four he could open doors. At six he could force all kinds of locks and at seven was able to write. Later he would learn to play the organ with his masterly feet, though this takes us far on into our story.

The woman who looked after Hercule Barfuss up to his second birthday was called Magdalena Holt. Living on the Danish island of Bornholm at the time of Hercule's birth, she had been in dire straits, and was obliged to place her own six-month-old boy in an orphanage and take work at Madam Schall's establishment not to starve. She cared for Hercule as if he was her own son, transferred all her pent-up maternal feelings on to him, badly chipped at the edges though he was. When he was in agony she wept with him. When in feverish spasms, she was indefatigably at his side in an almost saintly way. It was she who breast-fed him, not from the breast, his mouth being what it was, but from a bottle with her own milk. It was she who tended his sores, eased his pains and rocked him to sleep. It was also she who first became aware of his unique gift.

This gift, supernatural if one dare call it that, did not always function, and during his first years of life Hercule was too small to understand it himself. When gradually he did become aware of it, not only would he learn to master, but also instinctively to conceal it, for his own self-preservation.

The first time Magdalena Holt experienced the way he could rummage around a person's mind was one afternoon about a year after his birth. At that moment she was sitting on a stool in the

35

servants' room with the little boy in her arms, bottle-feeding him from her breasts' immense reservoir. Suddenly, he stopped drinking and stared at her. Unnerved, she met his eyes.

It wasn't the gaze of a child, but of a whole destiny. And suddenly she knew, with the same dizzy feeling that had assailed Dr Götz, that the boy could see through her.

It was as if he had stepped inside her and revealed to her her own long-forgotten longings. Afterwards she would remember it as if he could read not only her conscious thoughts but also her subconscious ones, thus revealing her to herself in her soul's mirror. What the boy first evoked in her was a feeling of disorientation, a queer, colourless mist that gradually assumed the shape of images, or rather whole sequences of them. On this inner canvas she was amazed to see painted a little row of fishing huts on her native island – with thatched roofs and whitewashed walls – and herself walking arm in arm with a man she recognised, a relative. Only then did she understand, with a violent contraction of the roots of her heart, that she had loved this man all her life, but never dared admit it. In the same instant she knew she must one day go back and marry him and fetch her son from the orphanage, and so make up the sum of her happiness. All this she knew with such certainty that for a moment she thought she had lost her mind. She had always looked on the man as any other relative, or so she thought. He was a skinny fellow with a slight squint and freckles who stammered. In his youth he had been a common seaman aboard English warships. Now she realised with a lucidity that threatened to burst her apart that she had loved him above all else ever since she was a little girl, but, aware that her love was forbidden, she had banished it to the cellar of her unconscious, tried to efface it altogether so as to believe she had outwitted it. Or else, if ever it had peered out, she had taken it for something else. Yet with undiminished strength it had gone on living, even though she'd had a child with another man, a drunken good-for-nothing who left her when she got in trouble. With a shudder she accepted all she now saw inside herself – the hallucinations which, aided by the boy, laid bare her most secret yearnings – to be true. In this knowledge there was as much terror as joy. Then in a trice he vanished from that place inside her where she had clearly felt him to be. Looking down she saw he was asleep in her arms.

Years later Magdalena Holt, knowing her experience that winter day was the simple truth, a distillation of her own longings, would turn it into reality. She never told a soul, but until the day she left the brothel she saw the boy through different eyes and would be grateful to him for the rest of her life.

Fancying there was some connection between her strange experience and the boy's appetite, she became particularly observant when giving him the bottle. More often than not when she tried to catch his attention by passing a finger to and fro before his eyes he would lift up his deformed face, but nothing remarkable would happen. And indeed, she would only be exposed to his gift on three more occasions, the last time in association with a catastrophe.

The second time, too, was when she was giving him his milk. Suddenly, with a gaze as ancient as bedrock, he looked up at her, and again she felt how he stirred her thoughts, all the while making a slight gurgling sound, which she understood to be the beginnings of speech.

Out of the sludge of oblivion her forgotten desires again began to rise up, faintly at first, then ever more pictorially, until once again they appeared as a vision in her mind.

She saw herself sitting bent over a thick volume with a magnifying glass in her hand. On the table lay a quill pen and an ink pot. She realised she herself had made the ink from camphor and pulverised oak apples. This too was an old dream that had been put to flight by life's realities. A dream of looking for God. In the autumn of her years she would be re-baptised by a wandering Mennonite, and devote the last years of her widowhood to studying the Scriptures. At the time of this vision, though, the idea seemed to her ridiculous, it then being many years since she had closed her heart to any belief in God.

On the third occasion – the most banal, but which she would always remember as the first time she heard the boy actually speaking inside her – Hercule had just learned to walk. It was a Sunday afternoon in springtime when the girls had a day off. Unobserved he had wandered perilously close to the waterlily pond with the spouting nymphs, which Madam Schall, after several years of the accounts looking increasingly healthy, had installed in a corner of the garden. Magdalena spotted him just as he was standing on the brink, delightedly flapping his little stumps of arms, entranced by the Chinese goldfish popping up to the surface for a nip of air, and was waving to Henriette Vogel, the girl who was born the same night as himself and whom he never wanted to be away from. Terrified he would fall in, Magdalena ran over and grabbed him, frightening him and making him cry.

Rocking him in her arms, she felt how the fur on his back stood on end, how his body trembled, how his tears wetted her stay-less bodice. She stroked the huge, grotesque head that swayed clumsily on its neck in such a way that she was fearful he might one day suffocate. Whereupon it happened again, without him even looking at her. Taking his stance right in the middle of her anxious stream of consciousness, he said very clearly and in a sort of ghost voice: *Put me down!*

Which she did, more out of shock than because of the force of his command; and instinctively she replied, in her thoughts: *What did you say?*

Then it happened again, without his lips stirring or him looking at her, the goldfish having recaptured his attention. Inside her mind she heard him say, quite clearly: *You scared me! Let me be!*

Years later she would note that the boy had actually spoken to her in Danish; and she had sensibly tumbled to it that most probably he sounded different depending on who he was communicating with as he made himself understood, so to speak, beyond the confines of language, and therefore what she heard as a voice was in fact a thought. Yet one so personal she had instantly known it to be his and no-one else's, just a shade more toneless than if he'd actually spoken out loud, as if the coustics were worse inside her head.

Though all likenesses were inadequate, Magdalena accepted that the boy not only read her thoughts, conscious or subconscious, but with all the ease in the world could suddenly start to speak inside her.

The fourth and final occasion was shortly before Magdalena, determined to make up for past horrors with a happier future, left Königsberg for good in a little lateen-rigged fishing boat that flew the Danish ensign.

The terrible mutilation of her breast was by then a fact, and Hercule had come into her room to comfort her, because in those days she was crying nearly all the time. The pain had made her close up like a clam. She had wanted him to go away. But before she knew what was happening he started singing inside her in that strange ghost-voice of his: a simple, children's ditty she herself had sung to him during his earliest years at the time when she imagined he would at least be able to respond to her voice's vibration. Now she could hear his voice clearly inside her, how he was speaking loving words of comfort to her mingled with a child's innocent sympathy.

*Don't be sad*, he was saying, *everything will be all right, you'll soon be leaving here.*

Many years later she would look back at him in a religious light and, shortly before her death, write to a woman friend in Odense: "Nothing could be hidden from him, and that was a relief. It was like making a great confession."


Hercule Barfuss' talent wasn't to everyone's liking, however. And it would be even less so after he had learned to control it.

People who experienced it during his first half-dozen years at Madam Schall's were in the habit of blaming their experiences on something else, to the general relief of their common sense, their sanity.

In her second year there one of the girls, Anke Strittmater, suffered a nervous breakdown after being bitten by an adder that had somehow got into the house. Once, when Hercule happened to be in her room, she cried out so loudly before she lost consciousness it could have shattered the crystal glasses in Madam Schall's display cabinet. Later, when asked what had happened, she explained she had heard the ghostly voices of dead children; and after that had dreamed her father was coming to rape her.

This was not altogether far from the truth. Several of the girls, especially those who had not been driven to prostitution by war or by hunger, or been thrown out of their homes after some scandal involving their honour, had been victimised by their fathers or brothers. Some were conscious of what incest was, others were not. Fräulein Strittmater was one of the latter. Never in her life would she admit that the mental image which came to her in the boy's presence was an exact reenactment of the scene within her home's four walls, staged not once but repeatedly from her sixth birthday until, one night in an August thunderstorm, aged fourteen, she had run away. That scene her conscious mind had rejected, had thrown overboard like bulky ballast to save her from going under. Instead she had blamed it all on her weak nerves after the snake bite, and thereafter, to be on the safe side, had avoided being alone in the same room with Hercule.

Other girls claimed they heard strange voices of ghosts or the "little people", blaming it on the brothel lying so close to a church-yard known for accepting suicides. Yet others, again, realised it was Hercule speaking inside themselves, or else put it down to idle imaginings due to fatigue after a whole night in the service of love. And though some had their suspicions, most hadn't the least inkling of Hercule's gift since he learned as time moved on that it was not merely dangerous, but also fraught with responsibility.

From the time of his christening, when death had granted him a reprieve of uncertain duration, Hercule Barfuss became the exception in a house where love had to be paid for. It was on him, on the altar of unconditional love, that Madam Schall's girls lavished their purest feelings. His appearance didn't frighten them, for they had learned from experience to fear the monstrosity of the soul, not of the body. On the contrary, he fortified them. Now they knew for certain there was someone whose lot in life was worse than their own. He could come and go as he pleased, and from the day Magdalena Holt ceased bottle-feeding him he was no longer tied to any girl in particular, except Henriette Vogel.

For Hercule, Madam Schall had only one rule: from six p.m., when the first clients began to arrive, he had to keep out of sight.

Everyone understood why, though she gave no reason. He was such a terrifying sight she was afraid he would deter customers. So from six p.m. until late at night when the last of her guests had gone he was kept locked in one of the servants' rooms on the top floor.

During those hours the house became businesslike, filled with a singular atmosphere. Lovesick men turned up looking shame-faced or passionate. In one of the halls where the girls sat in a row, perfumed and scantily clad in honour of love, each chose the lady of his heart and disappeared with her into one of the meagre private rooms, with its washbasin, towels and bunk. The house turned into a ship with a cargo of dreams. There were times when Hercule had a weird sensation of being rocked to sleep on the bosom of the ocean.

At the end of his extraordinary career Hercule would think back on the atmosphere he had inhaled in his room late at night. On his inner wavelength he would listen to every secret: a student's nervousness on his first amorous night, gentlemen's murmured declarations of love, the latent fear in the girls' giggles, the sabre duel of two sergeant majors out in the garden as they fought over some new arrival. All the thoughts in seventeen languages. He would recall the sad odours of loveless affection, of the soul's wilting flowers and the heart's frozen watercourse; the pain as champagne glasses clinked in hollow toasts. The excitement of quarrels and fights. The light from fireworks. Drunks' mindlessness, fiascos and defeats. Sorrow in its every aspect, and a thousand different wishes which floated up to him from every corner of the establishment.

Alone in his room he traced these thoughts back to where they had first taken shape, to the mind in which they had first sprung up, all manner of thoughts and passions he, Hercule Barfuss, had the peculiar talent of divining. In this house were assembled all the longings for affection, for pain, for ecstasy, for forbidden fruits – and to inflict suffering on others.

This last desire, emanating from the soul's darkness, from years of bitterness and hatred, was what frightened him most, realising as he did it was part of human nature. He could trace it back to its source, look into sick lechery, not of people in themselves but their terrible fantasies. When the tragic incident occurred with Magdalena Holt he already knew who the perpetrator was for he had already sensed him, years earlier, in this throng of impulses.


As far back as he could remember Hercule had adored Henriette, ever since she was a little girl. Fate, for some inscrutable reason, had brought her into the world on the same night as himself. His was a love whose beginnings were lost in time's first narrow passage, before the world had taken shape. He had no first memory of her. She had always been there, as taken for granted as the air he breathed, as night and day. They had been fed their milk in the same room, slept in the same bed, been put in the same playpen, cared for by the same sisters in misfortune who shared a common fate. Children of the same establishment, fathers unknown, they were bound to each other by love's manifold mystery.

That February night when the bells had pealed and thundered, Henriette's mother had asked herself, just as Dr Götz had, about Fate's lack of justice. But at the same time she'd had a feeling that everything was already written down in life's book, whose text no man on earth can alter and whose author finds it beyond him to own up to his own mistakes. In tragic conformity with some law, her sister in misfortune had to die so that she herself could live, and a boy had to be born so deformed that her daughter might be healthy. To such a degree had she been filled with these thoughts that shortly after her delivery she'd had a sensation of being dangerously in debt to Providence. She would have liked to come to terms with a happiness she did not consider that she deserved by adopting the boy; but Madam Schall, whose word was law in this autocratic kingdom of price-tagged delights, had delegated all maternal duties to Magdalena Holt, the new arrival.

For the newborns to be bonded together as brother and sister would in any case have been a supererogatory formality. They were twinned souls beyond any blood-tie. From the age when they started to crawl they turned to each other. Neither of them could imagine doing anything in their waking hours without the other. And on more than one occasion they had literally been dragged apart at bedtime. They were hungry and thirsty at the same moment, laughed at the same things and cried for identical reasons. Some found it eerie when their first milk teeth appeared on the very same Friday afternoon in July, or when they each took their first steps as a thunderstorm shook the building to its foundations one spring morning. People were amazed by their seeming to understand each other wordlessly, that they played soundlessly and hardly had to exchange glances to know what the other wanted. In the same extraordinary way one always seemed to know where the other was or was intending to go.

This child couple – the one so perfectly formed, the other so crippled – moved the girls to tears, and the incompatibility of the match became more evident with the years as Hercule never grew to be more than a metre in height, whereas Henriette grew to be a tall girl.

Sheltered not only from insight, but also from others' eyes, Hercule led a quiet life. Madam Schall's girls being the only people he ever met, he knew nothing of the outside word. In the daytime he never transgressed the boundary between the two worlds and it was an unwritten rule that no-one took him with them on outings or errands into town. For girls who took money for their dishonour this had nothing to do with a lack of courage; on the contrary, they well understood the necessity of protecting him from a world that rarely accepts deviates. So his dismay was all the greater the day he encountered it for the first time.

This incident occurred at Easter in the seventh year of his life. One Maundy Thursday, to be exact. It was mild for the time of the year, but windy, and he was in the garden with Henriette where the girls were busy pruning fruit trees, when a sudden gust of wind caught her printed calico cap and tossed it high above the privet hedge into the neighbouring yard, enclosed by four walls, which belonged to an old stablemaster. Taken aback, the girl stood looking after it and Hercule Barfuss did not hesitate for one moment to take his first historic steps away from love's sheltered realm; he scraped off his left shoe with his right foot, opened the gate with his toes and, without so much as a thought, without any further consideration, without hearing any alarm bells, but filled with a sense of excitement for which he had no name, Hercule ran with one bare foot out on to the potholed road, weathered by the winter storms.

He didn't stop until he got to the stablemaster's house, by the wall of which lay the cap, alongside a budding daffodil. Picking up the cap with his foot and putting it between his teeth – as he usually did with things he wanted to move – and glorying in being at Henriette's service, not until that moment did he notice he was being watched.

In front of him stood a boy, horrorstricken at seeing, for the first time in his life, a figure out of a fairy tale, of the kind that edifies children by scaring them out of their wits. Hercule himself,

43

sensing the boy's terror, became equally frightened and dropped the cap. But when he tried to calm him by smiling, the boy started to scream, which brought more people to the spot.

Surrounded by an outraged crowd of men, women, children and old folk, he heard the buzzing of their thoughts – *an abortion . . . what is Satan doing here on our road on Maundy Thursday?* – filled with such fear and hatred that for a split second he was afraid he might drown in it.

No-one would remember who cast the first stone, and for Hercule it was all a muddle – the uproar, the strangers – so nothing of all this left him any memory of the faces.

Afterwards, when Henriette Vogel comforted him up in the servants' room, she told him – in the remarkable way in which they had learned to communicate – that the hairs on his back had stood on end. He himself had no memory of how he'd managed to get back into the house with her cap in his mouth. Where he lay, curled up close to her, he was still too upset to be reconciled with an evil world, so he barely noticed the pain in his head where the stones had struck him. Only when she held the cap up for him to see did he smile, comforted by the thought that his suffering had been for love.


This event was significant. No sacrifice was too great for Hercule to make for this girl, the inexplicable object of his affection, whom he loved without a second thought, limitlessly, and without asking for anything in return. In summertime he picked flowers for her in the garden and tied them up in silken bouquets. In the autumn of her years Madam Schall, who saw him on one occasion tottering along in the flower bed, carefully breaking off the flowers' stem between two toes and gathering a bunch of them in his mouth, would commission an artist to depict this ontological love she had devoutly preserved in her ever more confused memory. Hercule carved wooden figures for Henriette, also, of course, with his feet. He made up stories he knew would amuse her, combed her hair and undid her plaits – all with his toes but with such dexterity it became a legend in the establishment. When Henriette was troubled he would caress her with his feet until she fell asleep, when she was sad and cried he would put his leg around her waist.

On her side, Henriette loved Hercule as unreservedly as he loved her. He had always been there. His aspect was so familiar to her she never saw it as deformed. On the contrary, she found it pleasing beyond words just because it was unmistakably his. No more than he did she need any explanation for feelings so strong they lived a life of their own. From as far back as she could remember he had spoken to her through what might, for simplicity's sake, be termed thoughts, something she had grown so used to she didn't find it in the least odd. When she wanted to ask him a question she posed it within herself, and heard him answer in a voice so personal that it seemed no different from people's ordinary voices.

Later, aware that she bore the same name as Heinrich von Kleist's unfortunate lady love, she would relate that she had kept secret his special gift, even from her own mother, not out of fear, but because she knew intuitively, as he himself did, that it would frighten people even more than his deformed appearance.

She couldn't conceive of a world without him, and childlike imagined it had been created solely for the two of them, which was why she defended all his actions, even when they broke the house rules. The year she turned eight Henriette campaigned to have the rules concerning his nightly quarantine changed, and, when she realised her efforts were doomed to fail, insisted on being with him in the room from when the first client arrived until the last had left. She got her wish, for nobody dared challenge a love bordering on fanaticism.

Shortly after Hercule and Henriette's tenth birthday, the tragic event came about that would later be interpreted as an omen of the misfortunes that would befall the house. The catastrophe occurred one February night when no-one except our hero was awake. By this stage his gift of foresight had developed to a point where it worked even in his sleep. Nothing escaped its sensors and by the time the villain was in the garden he was already awake.

As surely as if he had seen him in broad daylight Hercule knew this individual was out there. He knew also that it was a man, one of the establishment's clients.

Henriette Vogel was sleeping like an angel beside him, but everywhere he could sense the fantasies of someone whose only wish was to cause suffering. In his mind they took shape as elaborately detailed illustrations, images so dreadful that he had to drive them off not to burst into tears.

Like a hunter the man crept through the garden, climbed a wall, dashed towards the storage shed then on along the house's façade before jumping up on to the terrace. At one point Hercule imagined a picklock. At another an ever more hectic rising pulse, a cold calculation, a lock broken open, a hand clasping a door handle.

Now the person was in the house, downstairs, moving stealthily in the dark so as not to wake anyone.

A fit of shivering shook Hercule when he realised that the man had stopped right beneath him, two floors down, and when this seeming human fount of hatred began moving again – along a corridor, up the stairs to the second floor where the girls slept, transgressing one internal boundary after the other – he felt sure he would die of terror. Whereupon the movement ceased and he knew exactly where the man was: outside Magdalena Holt's room.

He didn't know where he found the strength to get up and leave his own room. He had crept along the top floor, to the staircase. Everything was still. For a split second he hoped it was just his imagination playing a macabre trick on him, but in that same instant he was wrenched from his pious hopes. Now, as clearly as any person would sense the taste of salt or the smell of smoke, he sensed that the person who had woken him was standing by Magdalena Holt's bed intent on carrying out a hideous and gruesome fantasy. It took Hercule several minutes to pluck up the courage to go downstairs, and later he'd reproach himself for not knocking over a china cupboard or banging on a door to waken the whole house and drive the criminal to flight, for only a few minutes later the deed had been done.

Silence reigned in Magdalena Holt's moonlit chamber. The door stood open. She lay on the mattress, tied to the bedposts, unconscious, with a rag stuffed into her mouth. She was bathed in her own blood. Her left breast had been cut off and taken by the villain.

*

In the spring the police began to look into the matter. But the sparse evidence led nowhere. The girls were of little help. Interrogated in private, they were questioned about clients with unusual desires, but this, as one of the gendarmes summarised the matter, seemed to be the rule rather than the exception. Nor did Magdalena remember anything about the event, having been knocked unconscious in her sleep. The constable in charge of the interrogations observed that the girls' memories, not only of the clients' names, but also of their physical appearances, was poor. Fear was a prevalent fact of their existence, weakening their memory more than was good for them. Hercule Barfuss wasn't interrogated, since he, in the normal course of things, was always kept out of sight when the house had visitors. His testimony would in any case probably have led more to confusion than to clarity.

In late May Magdalena Holt left the establishment, marked for life. Yet hopeful of returning to her childhood island and marrying the man whom, with Hercule's help, she had realised she loved and a few years earlier had become engaged to by correspondence, she was sure she would find happiness. Her long, drawn-out convalescence, which she barely survived and then only with the aid of Providence, left with her departure a feeling that all this was only the beginning of the house's misfortune. It had become poisoned with suspicion. The girls grew cautious and reserved. Some refused to sleep with clients they didn't know, others adopted an old wartime habit of sleeping with a dagger under their pillow. Rumours of the bloody deed spread and frightened off some clients. Others didn't relish the thought of a brothel that had been visited by inquisitive gendarmes. By early summer the establishment had lost half its trade. The clients became ever fewer, and several of the girls stole away in the dead of night without giving notice, leaving only a hastily scribbled farewell note.

It was in these difficult times that the decision was made to auction off Henriette Vogel on the open market of love.

Henriette had grown to be an unusually well-developed girl, tall for her age and looking older than was attested by her birth certificate. Several men had already cast languishing glances in her direction, and more than one client had asked Madam Schall in a whisper whether the girl wasn't a little old to be still wearing her hair in plaits. In a house where everything was for sale and fidelity was at best a daydream nurtured on lazy Sunday afternoons, there was no moral obstacle to selling off a ten-year-old girl's maidenhead to the highest bidder. The *Jus primae noctis* was at that time an oft-used item of merchandise in the town's brothels, and could fetch a considerable sum, invaluable for an establishment teetering on the brink of ruin. Anyway, the girl had been brought up to follow in her mother's footsteps, the profession, then as now, being one that was handed down from generation to generation.

Even so, it was the failing economy that drove her mother and Madam Schall to the difficult decision. The girls did their best to prepare Henriette for her ordeal by means of an informal initiation rite made up of a thousand words of good advice and various admonitions. They gave her knowledge of tricks to bring the man to his bliss as quickly as possible and with minimum trouble; the surest manipulations, the least painful positions, how forgetfulness could help, and how by means of a brew of cloves, wine and camphor she could drive away recurrent attacks of nausea. They explained the simplest way to get rid of men after the act, how to negotiate a price and how far it could be bartered down. They told her never to fall in love, though that could sometimes be the easiest way to avoid humiliation, and never to go along with something her instinct contradicted, at least not unless the price had been fixed to her satisfaction. Kisses cost extra. They asked her to keep certain of love's words and gestures to herself so they should not be worn out the day she, against all odds, found a man to take her to a happier existence as a married woman in a middle-class home – most of the girls' dream. They taught her to protect herself against pregnancy and disease. How best to defend herself against sailors who'd had one over the eight. They also gave her little gifts, accessories, jewellery, perfumes and amulets that would protect her from shameful diseases and bring her luck.

Henriette put up with all this in so carefree a way it seemed to verge on indifference. She delved into the musk-scented ambience of bedroom antics, accepted the ritual gifts, tried on suitable garments – hats with cockades in them, cordwainers' ladies' shoes, and frilly underwear – all the time heroically fighting off her fear of the

48

evening of the auction. At moments she even managed to forget all about her coming ordeal. Her thoughts were with Hercule Barfuss.

He was in despair. Stricken to the ground by life's injustice, he scarcely ate. He knew her future had long ago been sealed, but love refused to take facts into consideration. He couldn't imagine any injustice more hideous than that she should be sold to nameless men. For the first time in his life he understood that a future awaited them, and it was blacker than night. Looking into it he saw nothing; it had no room for creatures such as he. Unable to envisage himself in so alien a place, he saw his life had been a provisional arrangement, protected by a sisterhood that before long would start questioning who he was and what he was doing here. It was like looking down into the grave.

Two weeks before the evening of the auction, to all appearances fatally weakened by his despair, Hercule was assailed by feverish cramps. After a night when all hope seemed to have fled and his heart could almost be heard grinding to a halt, with a deep sigh, as when a cork is pulled out of a bottle, the old wise woman employed by Madam Schall had to draw on all her professional skills to resuscitate him. Only slowly and with the help of Henriette's care did he recover. She sat at his bedside from early morning to late at night. In the end, overcome by tiredness, she was found seated on the edge of his bed, one hand on his furry back and the other in an open Bible. She fed him with spoonfuls of meat broth, laid on mustard compresses, and calmed his fever with ice packs.

Delirious, he saw her face floating around the room, but it was a mask ripped off by an invisible hand, and underneath was a sheet of paper scribbled over with an obscure future filled with misfortune. Adrift in the floating ice of his subconscious, he was surrounded by a grief so strong that it could undoubtedly have changed the course of history. Hercule awaited the end.


So came the evening of the auction. The ground floor was filled with guests and the sound of clinking glasses and girls exchanging businesslike jokes. The bidding for an hour's pleasure could begin.

There was crunching on the gravel as new cabs arrived. Lusts and desires spread throughout the establishment like a dense fog. Around this way of life there were no mitigating circumstances.

Each evening demanded that happiness be reinvented and die as each succesive client climbed into one of the girls' beds.

From his attic room Hercule inhaled the loveless air. He cursed the deadly irony of Henriette from now on having to share it with the man who was shortly to take possession of her. Sobbing, he banged his head against the wall, again and again, trying in vain to knock himself out.

By the time he ceased doing so, an atmosphere of tense excitement had fallen over the house, and Hercule realised the auction had begun. He felt the madness spin round the room like a leaf in an autumn gale. Half choked by his sobs, he wondered what unforgivable sin he must have committed to be punished with such terrible grief. Yet somewhere in the midst of his despair, it must be, with the image of Henriette Vogel in his mind, standing in her underclothes in a corner of the large salon, surrounded by faceless men, he passed out. Suddenly he awoke, an evil hand at his throat that could well have killed him. The man who had all but murdered Magdalena Holt was now alone with Henriette.

Years later, sitting on the windowsill of a burgher house in Danzig and staring out through the eyes of a stray cat, Hercule would recall in detail all that ensued that evening and which in less than a week would lead to his being torn up by the roots and ruthlessly flung into orbit around an extinct sun. He had run along the corridor and down the stairs. The clients turned round, astonished, and stared at him in disgust, revulsion writ large on their faces. Some of the girls had tried to bar his way. There was an eruption of horror from someone who was scared out of his wits by the mere sight of him. Tracking down the pulsating sick lust, Hercule prayed to God that there had not yet been time for anything to happen to Henriette. Opening a door to one of the rooms, he saw a man dressed in women's clothing turn towards him and smile – but in an instant the smile turned into a disgusted grimace.

The instincts raging in the house confused him. They were everywhere: the bitterest longings of souls and bodies. Consumed by fear, he went on running, staggering and limping on his short legs, weighed down by the burden of his enormous head, the image of Henriette Vogel engraved on his retina.

In one room some naked clients leaned drunkenly over a blindfolded girl who had collapsed on the floor. Opening the door to another room he saw two men sharing the same girl, her features so distorted by shame that he didn't recognise her. A group of sailors pointed at him, and burst into nervous laughter, two of them calling to mind their deformed sister. He rushed on, determinedly pursuing his trail.

At the far end of the wing he came to the bridal chamber. Tried to open it. Found it locked. The noise brought people to the scene: the sailors who had been laughing at him; a gold-braided officer wearing his jacket, but neither trousers nor shoes. Girls he knew, scantily clad with whatever had lain to hand.

Somebody spoke: "What's going on, what's all the noise about?" But the boy seemed not to hear. Just went on hammering the door with his head and feet. All around him he heard people's thoughts: *hideous child . . . so deformed . . . should never have been allowed to be born . . .* In the midst of all this commotion, Madam Schall arrived. Someone thought: *the bidding's over, young cripple. The girl's already been sold. One hundred and eighty gold marks! For a price like that one could stay here a whole year, loving and breakfast thrown in.*

He continued beating at the door until the key turned on the inside.

Never would he forget the look of the man who was yet to have the last word in his life's drama: the searching blue eyes, the moustache glistening with sweat, the well-pressed velvet coat, the unbuttoned breeches. The man looked at the crowd, one by one, coldly. Finally his glance fell on the deformed boy.

"What kind of a freak is that?" he asked, turning to Madam Schall. "Is this a brothel you're running or a madhouse?"

"I beg your pardon, Herr Court Magistrate," she answered. "But the boy was carrying on so, we were afraid there had been some accident."

Through a crack in the door Hercule saw Henriette. She was sitting on the edge of the bed, still clothed, her face white as a sheet. This time, he told himself, I'm not too late.

"Be sure to lock that animal away and leave us in peace."

The gathered crowd withdrew to the salons and private rooms, and Madam Schall apologised for what had happened. She would look after the boy, she said; he had recently been ill and was not quite recovered. The man with the moustache nodded and made a gesture indicating that he wanted to shut the door. But at that moment Hercule forced his way into the room.

A new uproar began. He clung to Henriette, who had started weeping heart-rendingly. Once again people came running to see what was going on. Madam Schall tried to tear him away from the girl. But then, as if paralysed, a deathly pallor on her face, she stopped short, as if afraid she was going mad; for she heard a voice, like a ghost inside her, which she knew to be Hercule. The voice said clearly, *He's the one who cut off Magdalena Holt's breast!*

Above the murmur of voices and Henriette's lamentations the magistrate yelled, "Get that damned abortion out of here before there's an accident!"

But even if Hercule had been able to hear such ruthless language it wouldn't have affected him. So focused was his mind on saving Henriette that he didn't even notice the violent kick that landed on his back. But Madam Schall – still shaken by the haunted voice that had spoken up inside her and which she was sure was inspired by the Holy Ghost – did notice it, and put an end to the tumult by thrusting the official personage to one side.

"Enough!" she said, in an icy-cold voice acquired over a lifetime spent on the brink of disaster. "Herr von Kiesingen may collect his money from my office. The girl is no longer for sale!"


Less than a week later, the establishment was closed down. No amount of protesting availed. No petitions from influential gentlemen who had been protecting Madam Schall's activities for years. No pleas for mercy. The order to raid the place had been made by Klaus von Kiesingen, president of the Königsberg Divisional Court of Appeal.

Madam Schall herself was put on the first boat to Tallinn, where an elderly admirer had paid a small fortune to have her acquitted from the charges of procuring. Several of the girls were interned in the notorious Danzig spinning house, where more than one of them died of its hardships. The others were scattered to the winds. Rumour had it that Henriette Vogel and her mother managed to escape to relatives in Saxony, though other rumours had them separated under stormy circumstances and the girl ending up in a Berlin brothel.

For our hero, years of darkness and humiliation were in store.

II

One Sunday afternoon in the dog days Julian Schuster, a Jesuit monk in the monastery at Heisterbach in the hills of Upper Silesia, stopped at its refectory window, and, unable to conceal an expression of profound surprise, looked around him. What had drawn his attention? Not the small crowd that was settled outside the monastery gates hoping to witness a miracle. Not the two novices sitting in the yard, absorbed in Loyola's spiritual exercises. Nor yet the abbot Johann Kippenberg, who was walking around the gallery, his forehead deeply furrowed by dark thoughts in which Schuster himself played a certain part. What had drawn his attention was nothing he could even see. It was a voice, a voice that seemed to be speaking inside him, in a way he had never experienced before.

To Schuster it sounded like the voice of a confused boy. And he wondered whether it wasn't his own voice, speaking from some murky recess of his mind.

*How long*, the scarcely audible voice said, *have I lived in the valley of death* . . .

Then, in a hum which made it impossible to catch any more words, it disappeared again.

"Odd," Schuster mumbled, looking up at the abbot, who was whispering something to one of the novices. "Why does old age invariably set in with talking to oneself? And what's worse, and as if that's not bad enough, believing the person you pretend you're listening so attentively to is someone else."

Quite right. In the context of his own epoch, Schuster was already old. Though his name suggested otherwise, just like Ignatius Loyola, founder of the Order, he was of Iberian birth. But from his steel-grey lion mane, his massive body and an iron physique built up during the adventurous years of his novitiate, not many people would have guessed he was turning eighty-four.

Again he heard that voice inside himself, and even though he couldn't quite catch what it said, he understood intuitively it was connected with some kind of loss.

A little perturbed by the merciless ravages of old age, he did his best to concentrate on the murmur of the crowd at the gates.

"They're crazy," he muttered to himself. "If those peasants had their way the boy would be canonised at once. This will end in a catastrophe."

The words, with their hint of a prophecy, relieved his unrest. His thoughts were interrupted by someone speaking to him. Not the ghost-voice this time, nor yet his own, from the depths of his mass of memories, but the abbot's through the open window.

"What shall we do, Schuster?" Kippenberg sighed. "We can't just drive them away."

The abbot, Austrian by birth and educated in Rome under Cardinal Teobaldi, was half Schuster's age. During the difficult years when the Jesuit Order had been excommunicated, he'd helped build it up on Prussian soil. Behind the gentle eyes lay an organisational talent quite out of the ordinary, which, Schuster guessed, would by and by see him one of the congregation's leaders.

"Why not let the boy go out there to them awhile?" he replied. "It could hardly make things worse. The peasants aren't asking for much. It's all about some heifer that's escaped, or a charm that's been lost. They imagine the boy can peer into hidden realms. We can only meet superstition with knowledge."

"We haven't the right to," said Kippenberg. "Not in the name of our Society. Not on monastic ground, before we've confirmed whether he . . ."

The abbot fell silent. And again Schuster heard the voice inside his head: *search*, it was saying, very clearly, before becoming incomprehensible again: *I must find . . .*

"You know, Kippenberg," he said, "in my youth we used to lure the Indians out of the Music State's rainforest with an organ. To them, the savages, it was a miracle. And short of producing a miracle we couldn't get them to believe."

"But this lot aren't savages," the abbot retorted. "We don't need to preach the gospel to them. This region is Catholic. I'm worried, and so ought you to be, Schuster. Yesterday I was afraid the mob might storm the monastery. Haven't you noticed how the crowd has been growing daily? There are hundreds of people out there, maybe thousands . . . How is the boy anyway, is he still refusing to speak?"

"It's not certain that he can speak," Schuster said. "Besides which, he seems not to hear. I'll have a doctor examine him. We can't exclude the possibility of his being deaf."

"It's not possible to learn to play the organ, Schuster, if you are deaf. You must know that."

"The handicap could have come on later in life. A result of shock, maybe. The boy could be an army child from the war."

"What about his lights, his intelligence?"

"Strangely enough, he seems to understand almost everything one says to him. Lip-reading, perhaps. I just can't understand why I was moved to pick him out. He's no good at anything except playing the organ. Work helping in the kitchen is too heavy for him, and you can't carry water or sort turnips with your feet . . ."

Again Schuster lost track of his thoughts. Since the boy had come to the monastery he'd been finding it hard to concentrate, had been affected by morbid broodings, woken up by nightmares that kept sleep at bay until the dawn light could be seen over the mountains. He couldn't even play instruments any more; the joy had gone out of it as that boy began to delve ever deeper into the world of music. He was beset by doubt, but couldn't understand where it came from or the reason behind it.

"I'm as anxious about him as about these recurrent sieges," Kippenberg went on. "And you're right, Schuster. No-one can learn to play the organ so quickly. He must have learned before they put him in the asylum. Where does he come from? That's what we must find out."

"Someone seems to have dumped him on the asylum steps,"

Schuster said. "At least, so I was told. In the dead of night, during a snowstorm."

"Poor creature . . ." The abbot lowered his voice. "We have every reason to worry about our novices. Only yesterday another disappeared without so much as leaving a letter of resignation. And you wouldn't believe the things I'm being told in confession. Even our purest souls are losing their faith. Schuster, are you listening to me?"

He had broken out in a sweat. It was mid-August and the heat was unbearable, insufferable. Taking a handkerchief out of his girdle pocket, he mopped the nape of his neck. A smell of freshly baked bread was coming from somewhere. The crowd's murmurings had died down. It was true, he thought, what the abbot had pointed out: the novices were losing their faith, and this too he knew was because of the boy, though he didn't understand how.

"Forgive me," he said with a slight bow. "Permit me to withdraw to my room. I've neglected both the hours and the Mass. It is time for me to have a private conversation with our Lord."


On his way to the dormitories Julian Schuster pondered whether there could be a link between the boy's dumbness and the years he had spent in the asylum; and whether the explanation was to be found in the desperate harmonies he would extort from the organ pipes. It wasn't unthinkable. Modern-day institutions defied description, and it was from among the Ratibor asylum's idiots, those considered sane enough to carry out simple tasks, that the monastery was getting its kitchen boys. Schuster had gone there himself that April morning to find a replacement for a halfwit who had died of a stroke while preparing the unleavened bread for Easter.

Never would he forget that scene in one of the madhouse cellars. The boy was shackled like a wild beast to a hook in the wall. Beside him lay a wooden platter with leftovers unfit for the monastery's pigs. The little bunch of straw he sat on was caked with faeces, its stench so foul it kept off even lice.

Once before, in Venice, he had seen a human monster, among the participants in a procession at Carnival time; and on another occasion, on an island in the Aegean to which the Greeks sent their poor. But never as horrific a creature as this.

"Why do you keep him chained up?" he had asked.

"He frightens the inmates," the guard answered. But something told Schuster it was the warders who were really afraid.

Releasing him, Schuster asked himself what special plan the Lord could have had for this creation of His. The boy's body was so deformed he did not at first notice the violent bruises, the gaping wounds, the scars, the putrefied sores where the manacles had dug so deep he could almost see bone. He had clearly been assaulted daily and Schuster breathed an Ave Maria, so upset was he by such brutality.

"What is your name?" he had asked him, in a whisper, there in the darkness. But the boy had merely shaken his head. When Schuster had questioned the management about the boy's origins, he could only conclude that he had no history. An itinerant copper-smith was said to have found him starving to death on a country road outside Breslau, and sent him to the asylum. Noticing he lacked ear conchae, Schuster had assumed he could not hear at all; but later, when the boy had shown proof of musical talent, had supposed he couldn't be completely deaf, or at least not from birth. Maybe this shortcoming was indeed an asset? He seemed to hear what others could not.

For almost an hour, as the crowds outside the monastery gates continued to grow, Schuster spoke in private with his God. And when the conversation was at an end, leaving him none the wiser, he remained sitting at his desk, leafing absent-mindedly through the pages of *The Golden Legend*, a text he'd been absorbed in during the past month, but now laid it aside with a sigh, and went over to the bookshelves.

For a while he stood in front of the volumes trying to pick out some work that could divert his attention from recent events: Ludolf of Saxony's *Vita Christi*, Thomas à Kempis' *The Imitation of Christ*. But before he could select anything, weariness overcame him again. Sitting down on his bunk he looked around at the simple table, the stool, the crucifix on the wall.

The distant sound of organ music came from the chapel. It was the boy playing. When the bell rang for vespers he hardly noticed it: *prime, tierce . . .* he didn't even register which of the hours it was ringing for.

Now he stood at the window of his cell. The crowds had settled on the slope beneath the kitchen building, hoping the boy would show himself. It was mainly young women, but there were also old people and cripples who had come believing the boy, in addition to his alleged second sight, could cure their aches and pains. By the well some children were playing. A cow strayed off to the brook. Some of the peasant families had brought along baskets with food. Enterprising local men were selling beer and pretzels. Over the last month the monastery had become a resort for pilgrims.

These people, Schuster thought, sweat running down the back of his neck, could not grasp the notion of a transcendent God. They demanded miracles if they were to believe. Over the years he himself, contemplating flowers, a river, a tree, had come to know how the soul could merge into and become one with the divine. In South America he had heard God's voice in the jungle, had glimpsed His plan for creation in termite hills, in a jaguar's eyes, in the Guaraní Indians' wonder at musical instruments. But for *these* people it was utterly impossible to experience God in a tree, or to trace the kingdom of heaven in a watercourse. All they saw in a tree was timber for a shack. In a river, fish for food. In a cornfield only a loaf of bread. To win them over you had to teach them to read and write, or feed them during crop failures. It was through adaptability and practical work that the Society had won souls for the faith.

Suddenly he gave a start so violent he almost lost his balance. Clearer than ever he heard the ghost-voice.

*Henriette*, it said. Just that one word, *Henriette*!


To find a link between what was now happening here in the monastery and what he himself had witnessed half a generation ago at the other end of the world, Julian Schuster had of late more and more frequently returned to the years of his youth. The story had begun shortly after his twelfth birthday when he had joined the Order's brethren as a novice at Jerez in Spain (then under the Bourbon monarchy). And since he'd been thought to be musical he'd been trained as choirmaster and organ builder by Santiago de Castellón, the famous musician-priest, regarded in his own day by the whole known world as master of the organ. During his novitiate, secretly wearying of the monotony of a monastic life, Schuster had applied to do missionary work, and been sent out on an Indiaman to the Spanish dominions overseas. But he hadn't sailed alone. Also on board was an organ, dismantled but complete with its stops and stop-heads, ivory keyboards and gilded frontal pipes, a gift from Ferdinand IV to help the brethren win over the souls of the last of the Guaraní warriors.

Never would Schuster forget that May evening when, at the height of the monsoon, he had put into Asunción by riverboat and a drunken oarsman, whose Spanish was so mixed up with the Indian lingo that Schuster could hardly understand a word he said, had ferried him over to the quay. The red-hot bunk. The dust that seemed to make the air glow. The stench from the marshes where liberated slaves lived in huts raised on poles. Vultures and dogs fighting over the waste in the open sewers. Rats dashing in and out between the carriage wheels as he had made his way up to the Jesuit monastery in the company of Father Sepp. Formerly a member of the royal orchestra in Vienna it was he who, with his four decades of missionary experience, was to teach Schuster the trick of using music as a landing-net when catching souls.

Five nights he had stayed in the town while the organ was being shipped over to a smaller riverboat, resting up from a journey that had lasted almost three months, first wafted on by trade-winds across the Atlantic, then by mule caravans until they'd reached Paraguay, God's own state in the heart of Spanish America.

The experience was unreal. He had never been homesick during the years of his novitiate, but the longing he felt then for the monastery's ascetic comforts, for the ritual of the hours, for Santiago de Castellón's diffident lectures on the organ's harmonics, had been unbearable. Mosquitoes turned his nights into an inferno of itching and scratching. The daytime heat threatened to drive him out of his mind. The stink of carcasses and human corpses and the winds blowing in putrefaction from the marshes took away his appetite. He saw the town, with its fathomless poverty, its sick dying in gutters, its Spaniards the jungle had turned into savages and the Indians' drummings and ecstatic cries that filled his sleep with nightmares, as a limbo, an antechamber to hell. And when at last Father Sepp and he had boarded the riverboat that was to take them up the Rio Apa to the primaeval forests of the north-east, he was seized by panic that he would never see the Old World again. Everything, the town, the jungle, the people, all was a premonition of the evil fortunes awaiting him at the end of his life.

Those first days, sitting on deck under a canvas awning, they had still seen villages and human life. Rowing boats lay moored by the bridges. Tame sasypodoids were tethered to huts. Naked children were at play in the lagoons and had waved to them. But on the fourth day all humankind had suddenly vanished, and during the rest of their upriver voyage the only signs of life had been the caymans sunning themselves on sandbanks, catching butterflies in their wide-open jaws.

Three weeks it had taken them to reach their destination – a missionary station in the province of Concepción, west of the crumbling mass of the Maracaju Mountains. The settlement consisted of a few timber shacks with roofs made of banana leaves and a church built of rough palmwood, embraced by jungle on three quarters of the compass. By then Schuster had lost ten kilos in body weight, and the humidity had rotted his linen shirts.

Another priest, Father Leander, met them at the pile bridge. Further up the slope, under a colourful canopy, stood a group of Indians, holding what he at first took to be blowpipes. But as the priest led the way up to the mission house the savages had begun playing a piece popular in Europe a few years before, in four-part harmony. What he had taken for blowpipes were in fact flutes. He couldn't believe his ears. To hear music here, at Christianity's last outpost, seemed to go against the grain of nature.

That same day the organ had been unloaded, then the riverboat and its crew of twenty-four Indian oarsmen, paid off in brandy, had continued upstream towards Asunción. Apart from a few iron fittings that had been attacked by rust most of the instrument was in good repair. There, in their huge cases, were the *rückpositiv*, the wooden manuals, the soundboards, the *haupt-, brust-* and *oberwerk*, the pipes, the pedals and two dozen Italian olivewood windchests which in a fortnight would be sending labial tones echoing out over the jungle to frighten the howlers and silence its parrots' bellicose arrogance.

At that time Schuster was about to turn twenty. But sitting on the crates containing the Florentine bass-pipes in the shade of the dilapidated chapel, where the naked savages were taking their siesta, arrows laid across their chests, and with the jungle inching forward before his eyes like a huge green huntsman, he realised that his life was nothing he could take for granted. Ten miles inland began the area still controlled by the last of the Guaraní warriors. Three generations had gone by since the first Jesuits had begun tempting these savages out of the jungle. The heads of the Guaranís, who loved music, had been turned by the notes coming from spinets, violins and wind instruments. Some were said to have fallen into a trance at the sound of the Spanish trumpets, and certain tribes had taken the missionaries, who mastered all these instruments, whose sonorities no creature of the jungle could emulate, for gods. With music for bait, and by promising to teach the savages to play these instruments of paradise, the brethren had managed to baptise them and had founded hundreds of model villages along the water-courses. Large areas of jungle had been felled and turned into fertile arable land. Each village came to have its own – often exceptional – Indian orchestra. Further along the Paraguay River the clearings had grown into small towns, all presided over by Jesuit missionaries like Fathers Sepp or Leander, courageous men who feared nothing but their own terror during supernatural thunderstorms. The slave-hunters, so-called Mamelukes, had been forbidden to set foot on missionary soil. In this musical land across the ocean, the ideas of Louis Blanc and Karl Marx, which wouldn't burgeon in Europe for another hundred years, were already in practice. No private ownership existed in the compounds. All property was held in common.

It had been Schuster's job to build the huge instrument whose harmonies were to convert the last savage souls to the true faith, and he fell to his task with a dedication inspired as much by his fear of the wilderness as by God. During his second week there, aided by a dozen natives who had turned up in canoes from a compound a day's journey further downstream – and who handled their machetes as skilfully as they did the instruments they had brought on which to play celestial music in the starry nights, or as skilfully as they caught the parrots they kept in cane cages and sold to German merchants – he cleared a four-kilometre pathway through the jungle up to the high plateau. Their mellifluous singing and their way of decorating their faces with colour from red bark to keep the jungle spirits at bay amazed him. But when he asked them about some savage Indians said to be still living in the district, they merely smiled their enigmatic smiles.

At the end of the pathway a glade was cleared. The heavier sections of the organ that could not be carried without risk of dropping them caused a certain amount of trouble, until Father Sepp suggested they be put back into their boxes and rolled along on logs, using ropes and tackle where the slopes were too steep. It took yet another week to get the parts into place and assembled under Schuster's supervision, the whole beneath a roof of plaited bast matting. By then the Indians had gone quiet, and their silence as they squatted at the forest fringe whisking away mosquitoes with palm leaves was so foreboding it brought him out in goose pimples.

Here, sheltered somewhere behind a wall of verdure, in an area that for centuries had been a blank spot on the Viceroy's maps, lived the last of the Guaraní warriors. In Asunción Schuster had heard drunken mestizos talking about savages whose magical tricks bent the minds of even the most hardened soldiers, and about others who preserved human flesh in snake poison and grilled missionaries' hearts over an open fire, spicing them with chilli fruits. Not that he believed them, except during the night when the jungle filled with ominous noises and jaguars' eyes gleamed out of vegetation, and the weeping of persons drowned long ago could be heard down by the river.

The day the organ was finished the Indians abruptly vanished: something Schuster could never explain. He turned round, and they were gone, seemingly swallowed up by the jungle. Father Sepp had gone back to Asunción to receive a delegation from the Vatican, and Leander was at the missionary station with two women who had gone down with malaria. All he heard was the squawking of parrots, the insects' symphony, the eerie knocking sound from the jungle that never ceased swelling and contracting. And it was at that moment, faced with the magnificence of Creation, he sat himself down at the organ and began to play – played for hours on end, tramping wind into the windchests, improvising fugues and chorales up and down the manuals' aliquots, mixtures, reeds and flue stops. Even a minuet. He tried to imagine what this strange object might look like to a pair of eyes that from their jungle hideout might never have seen a white man before. Like a strange throne? Or a rumbling monster with a woman on its back, as in the last hours of the Apocalypse? By the time he stopped playing darkness had fallen, and the jungle seemed suddenly emptied of sound.

Schuster fell to his knees and prayed his way through the entire rosary. Then, after committing himself to God's mercy, after quenching his thirst from a jug of molasses, he had fallen asleep in a hammock strung beween two rubber trees.

When he opened his eyes it was dawn and the howlers were performing their lascivious serenade. He got out of his hammock, before falling to his knees and praying for courage to endure his fear.

At the forest edge, around the organ, a group of naked Guaraní warriors were standing with blowpipes in their hands.


That morning sixty years ago had remained in his mind with a clarity of detail rare in his later memories. Defying his secret homesickness, Schuster had stayed in the jungle for almost fifteen years. Becoming a legend in the Jesuits' missionary strivings, he founded four thriving compounds, the largest counting three thousand souls. So perfectly had he taught himself the savages' languages, he'd been appointed editor of the two-volume dictionary put together at the request of the Congregation, in which each word, even from the remotest Indian dialects, had been transcribed and translated into Latin. Only a man of his constitution could have withstood life at this last outpost of Christianity. He survived two cholera epidemics, one bloodthirsty Indian uprising, a severe bout of scurvy, jungle fevers that had lasted for months at a time, four poisonous snake bites and half a year's enslavement by the Mamelukes after they burned down his last compound and he elected to yield himself up, a captive to the slave-hunters together with the savages he loved as dearly as the children he would never have. When the Brotherhood was gradually forced out of the state to which they'd brought the light, hidden it under a bushel and so painstakingly protected, his grief was all consuming. Power-crazed kings drove them away from their Terra Divina in the depths of the primitive jungle, scotched their attempt to build a new Eden from a fresh shoot of the tree of mankind: create an Adam and Eve of the Indian race.

Schuster felt that somehow there was a link between this boy and the savages. And that was why, this Sunday evening in late summer, having neglected his hourly prayers, he listened anxiously to this strange ghost-voice that had begun haunting him, and was trying to work out what it could be.

His thoughts turned to the boy. The first event that, in popular belief, had been declared a miracle had concerned a shepherd by the name of Dietmar Fromm who maintained he had only to take one look at the boy to learn the whereabouts of a runaway ewe – in a ravine where she'd gone astray while he, neglecting his pastoral duties, had been visiting a girl. The cripple, he asserted, had given him a lucid mental picture of where his runaway sheep was to be found. "It was absolutely clear," he said. "I stared at the cripple, just wishing to find her, and suddenly I knew everything."

Shortly afterwards, also with the boy's foresight, another peasant had succeeded in finding a silver plate that had vanished some thirty years earlier. In the boy's presence he had been vouchsafed a vision. It was in fact this peasant himself who had buried the plate in an apple orchard during one of the wars, when raids had been everyday affairs, but had afterwards forgotten where. He swore the boy had shown him the exact spot. His inner vision had been under the aegis of the Blessed Virgin holding a golden sceptre in her hand, her halo of mechanical butterflies glowing so strongly he was momentarily blinded by it.

A woman, Konstantine Paul – admittedly a known hysteric – had insisted he was a kind of mirror in which one could see one's unknown self. She maintained she had been cured of vague heart ailments merely by sitting outside the monastery gates and listening to him play the organ. "He helps me look into myself," she said when questioned by the village priest, "God bless him!"

Then there were people who saw he could read their thoughts and was a mesmerist, others who claimed he had cured them at a distance of all sorts of ailments: toothache, ringings in the ears, bad breath, constipation, lameness, lung trouble. A blind man even claimed to have had his sight restored, though Schuster was sceptical about this, and rightly so.

But what worried Schuster most was the novices. No fewer than seven had disappeared since the boy had come. One had declared with the confidence of an adult that God was an invention of the authorities to oppress the masses, and that Christ's sacrificial death was a myth. The man who had been crucified was actually a Greek highwayman, whereas the Galilean carpenter's son on whom they had built their bogus faith had fled with his mother to Assyria, as was proven by the apostle Paul – then still called Saul – having met him on the road to Damascus.

The interesting thing about this novice, Schuster noticed, was that shortly before these events he had been alone with the boy for nearly a whole week, encouraging him to lend a hand – or rather a foot – in the monastery kitchen.

Another novice had admitted in the confessional to no longer being able to keep his vows of chastity. Two more had quite simply disappeared without leaving any explanation. Yet others had been overcome by inexplicable bouts of weeping. One would wake in the middle of the night crying like a lost soul, straying about the corridors, mumbling prayers to be forgiven for some nameless sin.

The boy was rumoured to be possessed. On their own initiative some of the older brethren had sent a spokesman to Abbot Kippenberg and, citing the rules of the house, asked him to return this "devil's child" to the madhouse.

In all these thoughts Schuster was trying to find some link between the recent unexplained events in the monastery and a twilight hour forty-five years earlier during his time in America, when with a sense of wordless insight he had at last stood in front of a certain Tihuan – or Juan as the Spaniards called him – a medicine man, blind from birth, from one of the villages in the north of the country. He had been called in to find a cure for a dysentery that was assailing Schuster's sensitive European entrails.

The experience taught Schuster not to underestimate the healing arts the Indians had developed through the necessities imposed by the jungle: the feverish realities of a snake bite, poisonous plants, stinging thorns, bloodthirsty vampire bats and hungry parasites. This was why he had gone to him, tempted by his reputation for being able to cure all the illnesses the Spaniards hadn't brought with them to a continent which already had enough of its own.

He had found himself outside a hut set apart from the village by a grove of agave cactuses. Blind though Tihuan was, in some amazing way he could, even so, "see" Schuster. With astounding self-assurance he'd held out his hand, grasped his arm, and drawn him into his hut.

Lying down on the floor, Schuster ignored the half-dozen shrunken heads of one-time enemies whose eyes stared indignantly down at him from the ceiling. In the dark the man's own eyes had seemed luminous as he muttered an invocation that, besides the names of the legions of spirits that – according to the Indian way of seeing things – had beset him, comprehended the name of God's Mother. Half hypnotised, Schuster closed his eyes.

Never would he find words to adequately express what he'd experienced that day, nor any explanation for his journey inside himself. Later, he was to describe it as taking on the shape of the wind or a draught, and of his being sucked, by some gastroscopic miracle, into his own mouth, the hot moist cave where his tongue lay, swollen and blue as a dead whale, and travelling down the rough shaft of his gullet until he found himself hovering over a turbulent, splashing internal sea.

It was true. He had descended into his own belly, looked at the lumps of sweet potatoes, maize cakes and the recently ingested river mussels drifting about in semi-dissolved platforms on the surface. To his own great surprise, he had dived below the surface of this stinking marsh, which was so murky it was almost impossible to see, until he reached the drain, the roaring cesspool which he understood to be the beginning of his large intestine. He had plunged into this ghostly tunnel through bloody catacombs, a gushing stream of bodily waste, past flocks of intestinal parasites that were attacking the walls of his guts where he felt how Tihuan, through his power, was locating and annihilating them.

And so it went on, mile after mile, hour after hour as it seemed, through the dark winding tunnel – grooved, bleeding, with a stench that defied description – until it tapered off and squeezed with convulsions, like seismic quakes from his physical geology, pushing him through his rectum and out into the darkness of Tihuan's hut.

Shaken to the core, he had managed to rise to his knees, rub his eyes and then open them, sure he'd emerged from an hallucination. What he had experienced at first aroused his suspicion that the medicine man had decided to drive him mad as punishment for colonial crimes; for now, through a point in his own consciousness, he could hear him clearly: *The jungle spirits have deserted Schuster, they hate the White God, but I have spoken to them . . . all Tihuan asks for his services is a tankard of brandy . . .*

With his soul in a state of dissolution, and a distinct feeling in his diaphragm of his diarrhoea really being cured, he stood up and with a silent prayer to the holy Franciscus Xavier, patron saint of missionaries, left the hut.

So this was how the events were connected, he understood it now, this evening hour in the Silesian monastery: the medicine man and the deformed boy. Maybe it was true what Konstantine Paul had whispered to the village priest in a sudden overwhelming eagerness to confess: the boy – like Tihuan – had the key to let them into their own souls, could himself pass into them, was actually capable of speaking to them through their own thoughts.

The years in the asylum had all but robbed Hercule Barfuss of his sanity. He didn't even know how long he had been there. Had only a diffuse memory of the magistrate von Kiesingen personally having him chained up and ordering the coachman to take him away from Königsberg. After which had followed the mad stagecoach journey along snowed-up roads at nights with neither food nor water, until at dawn, half dead of starvation, he'd been dumped on a Silesian country road. And when he'd recovered consciousness he found himself in an institutional hell.

Memories from the lunatic asylum would haunt him far into his old age; memories of living corpses dragging themselves about the halls, drooling, wailing, sobbing, more prisoners in their own confused minds than ever they were behind the asylum's locked doors. Souls of the dead were doomed to endless wanderings, the horrors they had endured in life having so deprived them of any sense of direction that they couldn't find their way to the heavenly realms they invariably deserved.

Here were all kinds of lunatics. Idiots, mongoloids and epileptics. There were hysterical women, ranting and deranged, and others suffering from fainting fits and painful bouts of nervous fever. Human life was as easily snuffed out as a candle's flame. Behind these locked doors women and men of all ages lived and died, children too, unfortunate victims of a fate that knows no mercy. Some, the fruit of nocturnal meetings between two confused people on a straw-covered floor, had been born in the institution. Others' fathers were the very men who guarded them, their mothers chained to the walls of the women's wing.

For seven years he had lived in this shadowland that could surely have spurred even Dante to greater achievements.

He had never been afraid of the inmates. In a world where all the rules were inverted they had seemed almost sane. It was the guards he feared.

One night during his first month in the asylum, they had picked at random on a victim to avenge an unsolved theft: a ten-year-old girl. They had beaten her with canes and handcuffs until, long after their victim had given up the ghost, exhausted, they had taken a break, laughing themselves silly on wine before having another go at the corpse, until all that was left was a bundle of ragged clothes, blood, bones and lacerated flesh.

It was such men who ruled over this inner circle of hell, and Hercule had seen straight into their souls, blacker than the blackest night. In their depths lurked only one desire: to inflict suffering on others. To be able to do so gave them as much pleasure as if it had been a gift from heaven. Such people, he knew, existed everywhere in the world, made up of the same dark matter in which evil had its source. Amazing, that mankind had even survived, hadn't long ago succeeded in destroying itself.

The wing of the asylum he was in was under the command of two brothers named Moosbrugger. The younger, a short stocky man who never expressed himself in anything but grunts, used to beat his victims unconscious. The older, a pock-marked tyrant who had lost one ear in a duel, had made it his habit to steal their food. On one occasion the brothers were said to have strangled a boy after raping him. It was only a rumour, but Hercule had never had reason to doubt it, for these monsters, as he was to know from his own experience, were capable of anything.

When rescue came and he, to his astonishment, found himself at the Jesuit monastery, absorbed in music's circle of fifths and its interrelationships between thirds, under the supervision of Julian Schuster, beyond the reach of his tormentors, and still unsure whether he was dreaming, he couldn't understand how he had survived. It was Fate, he thought, that must have selected him blindly.

Perhaps his gift, too, with whose help he could anticipate and influence people's actions, had kept him alive. He had been able to make the guards thirsty by planting the idea of a pitcher of beer in their heads, or setting their entrails itching, so that instead of assaulting him or stealing his food they would sit down on a bench, to drink or to scratch imaginary louse bites.

The thought of Henriette Vogel had also helped him to go on living. Her memory had prevented him from capitulating unconditionally to madness and surrendering himself to a fate dictated even before he'd been born, but with which he had called an indefinite truce: death. At such times, when he'd been amazed at each new beat of a heart living on borrowed time, he had evoked the image of her in his gloomy cellar. Where could she be?

Was she with her mother or had they been separated? Had she inherited her mother's profession? He had to remind himself that she was now a grown woman, no longer a child; and he had imagined her as being beautiful as ever, or more so, if such a thing were possible. Love filled every corner of his consciousness over which madness did not stand sentry. Just to meet her for a single moment he was prepared to renounce everything. This longing became so strong he forgot his own horrible predicament. He knew she was waiting for him. All he lived for was to find her again. He had entertained fantasies of escaping, impossible though it was, the lunatic asylum being as heavily guarded as if it were the repository of state secrets. He saw others try but fail before they'd even breathed the fresh air, only to be sent down five metres underground to a place, the horrors of which no-one had lived to tell the tale of.

Little by little, surprised by the strength of his dark feelings, Hercule turned his hatred on to the guards. Hate, he realised, was a force infinitely more powerful than his gift, a force of nature that could oppose even the fiercest resistance; a concentrated beam of hatred, capable of destroying everything in its path, but also of corroding its own bearer. He had hated the guards with a strength that could only measure itself against his love for Henriette. At the same time he was careful not to provoke them, for he knew he was defenceless against their innate ruthlessness, and they needed no more than a whiff of a pretext to knock him, with one deft blow of their canes, senseless.

It could well have been the last year of his life, had Julian Schuster not intervened. With a distilled horror dawning inside him, Hercule had begun to feel his strength was giving way. The slightest glance at his surroundings told him the inmates weren't here to be hidden away, as the insane, the mad and the misshapen always have been down the ages. They were here to be killed off. The guards beat them bloodily for the slightest misdemeanour, stole their food so as to hasten their departure from this life. Some of those who ranted and raved were kept in cages. Others were exhibited for money, the curious, for a ha'penny, being given leave to peep through the bars of their prison.

That last winter had been so dreadfully cold. Not a morning had gone by without one of the inmates being found dead of hypothermia, huddled up on the floor next to some fellow sufferer in hope of sharing a little warmth. Sometimes an almost blissful smile intimated that death had come as a saviour, inviting them to a heavenly banquet with kind words, words they had never heard in life.

Since longings and dreams were the last to leave these human wrecks, Hercule could see right into their most secret selves. He saw their simplest desires: to eat their fill; to move, just once, freely among other people. He heard their confused thoughts, their mute cries for dignity, felt their vain yearning for love, their feverish desires in summer's heat, the dumb man's longing for language. He traced in a Czech woman who was in the asylum, not "andromania", virginal hysteria – the excuse her guardian had given in order to get rid of her – but simply a desperate need for sleep; she had not slept a wink in ten years.

When the Jesuits had found him that freezing Easter morning, chained to the wall, scrofulous and covered in purulent sores, Hercule wasn't sure whether what he saw was real or yet another of the hallucinations – his own or others' – that had been making up his everyday existence. He was in such a bad state they had begun counting his days. He'd felt death's angel breathing down his neck when it had come creeping through the darkness to collect someone who looked as though they deserved to be out of their misery.

Throughout those last days in the asylum it had been the

thought of revenge that, against all odds, had kept Hercule's heart beating, each beat more hesitant than the one before, a bit closer to death in each widening pause between despairing pulse beats, when even the memory of the girl he loved above all else lay buried in the stinking straw, next to the dead, who lay there in the darkness, losing their warmth like bread brought out of an oven to cool. Livid, his white-hot hatred was a guerrilla fight against death's henchmen, and above all against the Moosbrugger brothers who had made his life a living hell for seven years. He revelled in fantasies of repaying everyone who had ever inflicted suffering on him, swore they would all get more than their share of his revenge.

Not until he arrived at the monastery had he realised the nightmare was over. He thought the Jesuits should really have chosen someone else, some able-bodied boy who could work as a servant. He saw his deliverance as a random act of Fate.

In music he discovered his wounds' first bandage, and devoted himself to it with all the joy of his new-found freedom. On the afternoon that Julian Schuster, still unsure as to whether his protégé really was deaf and dumb, instructed him with signs and gestures on the fundaments of organ point, it struck him that music was somehow linked to this gift he'd been born with. Was not music, too, a systematic expression of the people's innermost longing?

He heard it in the mystical sphere where it had its origin. The acoustic sounds had their counterparts in ideas he, with the help of his gift and the vibrations flowing through his body, could apprehend. He grasped it in the key system, in the Neapolitan sixth that made the abbot frown in consternation, reminding him as it did of some forgotten youthful sin, and which spoiled the monks' concentration during Whitsun's ninth prayer of jubilation, in the harmonies that pierced the brethren to the marrow of their bones and made them tremble to their extremities with subconscious longing. He was surprised by the progress he made and that he was in fact hearing the music, albeit freely turning it internally into his gift's tonalities. He was surprised his toes hadn't been destroyed by seven winters in an icy cellar. But though still tormented by those repulsive memories, by his hatred for the guards, by his hatred of mankind, he pushed on in every spare moment, indifferent to the commotion he was causing all around him and quite unaware he was making the novices doubt their faith or that the district's peasants were beginning to regard him as a miracle worker. He went on playing, healed more and more by each modulation in the name of love, every dominant masked in a dominant seventh being tuned to beauty's key note, or each time he dissolved a chromatic scale into an intoxication of ideas or joined together two remote keys, both built on the same longing: for Henriette Vogel.

U naware that a knot was about to be tied in this deformed boy's destiny, Schuster fell asleep on his bunk in his cell. The crowd outside the monastery in the village of Heisterbach, Upper Silesia, had grown and been joined by folk from other widely scattered mountain villages. For the rumours about the miracle worker had, at a given point in time, crossed the boundary at which temptation becomes mass hysteria.

He was woken at dawn by knocking at his door. Opening it, he found Kippenberg standing outside in the corridor, clad only in his nightshirt.

"What's up?" he asked.

The abbot, deathly pale, was holding a candle in his hand.

"Hurry," he hissed, "for God's sake! They're storming the building!"

Schuster dressed swiftly, stuffed his rosary into his breeches pocket and sent a guilty prayer excusing himself for neglecting the paternosters he'd sworn to say first thing that morning. In the novices' dormitory, where half-dressed men were running around looking for their belongings, total chaos reigned. Schuster sensed the terror in their prayers, one was sobbing, another weeping. Panic was rife. A glance at the window made him stiffen. Outside were so many dirty, emaciated people. Peasant women half out of their wits were pounding their fists against the walls and doors.

Beside him he heard the abbot yelling at the top of his voice to make himself heard, "Where's the boy, Schuster? We must get him out of harm's way. Can't you see they're out of their wits?"

"Isn't he in his cell?"

"No, I've given orders to search for him."

Somewhere from the direction of the refectory came the ominous sound of a windowpane breaking. The crowd's roar came in even louder from outside.

"They're breaking in," the abbot gasped. "The boy has bewitched them."

In a corner to Schuster's left was crouched a young novice, trembling in fear, a scapular pressed against his chest. Further down the corridor a group of boys had gathered with spades in their hands, to all appearances prepared to defend the monastery to the last. But when one of them yelled "Where's that child of Satan? Let's get rid of him, once and for all!" he realised he had mistaken their intention.

Turning to the abbot, he shouted, "If the peasants don't tear him to pieces, the brethren will. We've got to find him."

Leaving the dormitory with Kippenberg at his heels, he followed the passage that led to the west wing. It was just getting light. Through the windows he saw the sun rising over the limestone mountains that in the dawn of time had assumed the shape of a group of slumbering Amazons. In the foreground the mob was swaying to and fro. Everywhere were people. They had surrounded the entire building, their clenched fists hammering on the doors and windows. Howling with excitement they were after the monster, screaming out their wretchedness, their bondage, all their humiliations: the bread they had to eke out with bark from young birch trees, the eternal childbirths, the starvation, the trials and tribulations sent to them by an arrogant God who never heeded their prayers. They needed this monster, their existence being so miserable they were prepared to stake their last hope on a mere miracle worker.

Neither in the west wing nor in the kitchen was he to be found. They searched the storage rooms, the lavatory, and again the cell where he slept, all with no result. Steadying himself against Schuster, Kippenberg whispered feverishly, "In the chapel. We haven't looked in chapel."

To a sinister accompaniment of a human battering-ram beating violently on the monastery gates they hurried along the corridors. If the sluice gate doesn't hold, Schuster thought, they'll all drown, God-a-mercy.

Rounding a corner, they halted at the chapel door. In there, almost drowned by the din outside, sounds of the organ could be heard, desperate ancient harmonies, a lachrymose melody of unhappy love.

Opening the door, Schuster stepped into a darkness more constricting than in the passage. The crowds were banging against the windows with their clenched fists and everywhere ghostly faces with wide-open mouths and feverish eyes were screaming at them to hand over the monster.

They found him sitting on the bench at the organ, staring blankly in front of him, his feet a blur on the keyboard. Julian Schuster discovered miracles can repeat themselves; for now, just as he had that time in Tihuan's hut half a lifetime ago, he heard a phantom voice inside him; the very same as had been pursuing him all day, and which he now realised was the boy's.

*Help me*, it pleaded, *for God's sake . . . I've got to get out of here . . .*

Dizzy, as if a plug had been pulled out and all the blood was leaving his head, Schuster sank to the floor, his face the greyish yellow of the splinter from Jesus' cross the house kept in a reliquary. Unmistakably he felt the boy's presence inside himself, in the confusion rummaging about in his own mind, reading his every thought as clearly as if it were printed in a book.

"Holy Mary Mother of God," he whispered. "The boy's possessed."

But he got no further. For now the very thing he most feared happened. A dull crash as the gates gave way. It was like the Flood, he'd recall later, a sea of shouting, screaming people pouring into the chapel. And somewhere amid the flailing arms and hysterical faces the boy, terrified, being carried aloft like driftwood afloat on the undulating surface of upstretched hands.

# III

G roping with his sixth sense's antennae for this mysterious invisible person who, in an unmistakably provocative tone of voice, kept speaking to him, beside the church on the Piazza Navona where God in His active days had allowed the blessed St Agnes' hair to grow so long it covered her private parts, to be exact on the square metre where, according to legend, the martyr had halted and generously prayed for her executioners' salvation, exactly there, was Hercule Barfuss.

*Well, young man*, the voice inside Hercule now said, *why so jittery? Isn't this what you do all day long, climb shamelessly in and out of people, listen to their most hidden thoughts, the snakepit of remorse, search out their anguished hearts, the thorny thickets of their blazing megalomania and inferiority complexes, their mis-givings at a world being declared round though as far as the eye can see it's as flat as a frying pan, all their congenital pettinesses, so trivial they'd die of shame if they knew you knew about them. Sooner or later you'll have to allow for their contrary, that's to say, the likes of me!*

He looked around, hoping for a glimpse of whomever was addressing him; but due to his own insignificant stature all he could see, at waist level, were billowing crowds shouting, laugh-ing, children crying, women blushing, men in breeches and filthy horsehair shirts guzzling wine from leather flasks and gesturing obscenely to some actors who were performing on a stage on wheels to one side of the market place.

*Who are you?* he asked, a trifle nervously, unsure whether this intruder wished him ill or was just making fun of him to pass the time.

*I'm made of the same stuff as you are, unfortunate man, and our gift is the most terrible thing imaginable, is it not? What excitement is there in a life where nothing's hidden any more? You see a beautiful woman and think how sweet creation is, and the next minute her entrails are revealed to you, the darkness of her soul, the swamp of stupidity and ill will as she looks at you with disgust. You see a little boy and think, what an uncorrupted human being. And before you've even had time to finish your thought and your ridiculous attempt to see youth as something glorious, you hear the same old tune from the depths of his childish soul: "I'm going to be a soldier when I grow up, and kill everyone in sight!" Behind the most delightful smile lurks an assassin. Behind the priesthood's love of mankind lurks only contempt and love of power. With the passing of the years our gifts make us cynical, and that's for sure . . .*

Right in front of Hercule, a woman, horrified by the sight of him, crossed herself, and snatched up her little daughter in her arms to protect her from whatever misfortune might be heralded by so hateful a spectacle. He tried to read her lips, but she was too quick for him, and instead, like a faint crackling sound, he heard her think: *A monster . . . bad luck. Alessandro said they put the Evil Eye on folk . . .* He calmed her with a brief negation of her fear, sending a sense of harmony through her instead; at which the woman, infused suddenly with a sense of security of whose source she had no idea, gave a cautious smile.

*You can see for yourself!* the voice inside him said. *The likes of us must always be a step ahead, open up a back door into men's hearts, whisper a few hurried words of reassurance, but take care to shut it behind us before they have time even to realise we've been there, because if they catch us at it they'll burn us at the stake as sorcerers, or throw us in the lunatic asylum, something of which you yourself, if I'm not mistaken, have the most ghastly memories . . .*

The phantom voice gave another laugh, this time not at all unfriendly, but rather sad, compassionate, reminiscent to Hercule of Schuster.

*What do you know about that?* he asked.

*I know most things. What did you think? That you're the only person in the world to be possessed of these faculties? There are more of us than you might believe, the age of sibyls and mind readers isn't over yet, no matter how hard the men of the Enlightenment try to bury us in formulas, or how the priesthood wants nothing better than to have us put to death. I'm one of those clairvoyants in the service of truth, and in a way I've come further than you. After all, you can't see me, you don't know who I am; whereas I, on the contrary, have had my eyes on you for several days or weeks, to be precise, ever since you arrived here in Rome in the company of that sceptical old Jesuit and started your wide-eyed tour of the Eternal City, a free man for the first time, lucky fellow!*

Up on the stage Il Dottore was in the act of reproaching the young Pulcinella for his foolishness and lack of initiative in a love affair, and a man in a black mask was approaching Colombina with a knife in his hand. But the crowds were melting away. "Malocchio, Malocchio!" (the Evil Eye) someone shouted, and had our hero been able to hear it, he might have shuddered at being the object of such an accusation, before realising that the warning was directed up on the stage at Colombina, whose life was in mortal danger but who, oblivious to this wicked world, had lost herself in the memory of her beloved and, looking wholly unconcerned, was sniffing his handkerchief perfumed with snuff.

*People love theatre and spectacles*, the voice inside him sighed, *and that's generally how we make our livings. Has it never occurred to you to make yours as a seer? Believe you me, you'll strike them dumb, they'll shower you with gifts and eulogies. There's nothing more flatters a man than having his innermost self presented in a favourable light, especially if he's sad and full of self-hatred. Use your talents, your phantom gift, join our association, dance with us in our Festival of Fools. Before you can say knife some mentally retarded prince will be rewarding you with your weight in gold, all because you've got him to swallow some brilliant prophecy based on petty secrets he imagines he has managed to keep, but which you've seen right through all the time!*

The mob began jeering at the stage where Colombina, having been so ingeniously stabbed from behind, was bathing in her virgin blood, and the final line was being delivered by a tearful Harlequin holding up the murderer's dagger.

*You poor thing,* the phantom voice went on, *you seem quite lost. So many people, so many thoughts and feelings, all so confusing! But beware, young man, all too often the likes of us end up in trouble. And considering what your face looks like, why don't you wear a mask like Harlequin and Il Dottore up there? It'd spare you all the shame and cries of horror and facilitate an incognito . . .*

Hercule Barfuss was intent on trying to locate whomever it was, somewhere amid this sea of people, playing hide-and-seek with him. And by and by, albeit very faintly, he managed to trace the outline of his observer, perhaps only because he was being allowed to do so. Never before had he encountered so cleverly closed a mind.

He searched at waist level, between men's legs, amid the belts on women's skirts, instinct telling him that the man who was addressing him stood at the same lowly altitude as himself, was perhaps squatting down, or leaning over, the better to survey him.

*Not bad,* he heard the phantom voice say. *You're getting closer, bird or fish or something in between! Anyway, what are you doing here all by yourself? Where's that guardian of yours, that Jesuit brother?*

*At the Vatican*, he replied, on the same wavelength the other was speaking on, as he shut out the stench of rotten fish, of horse droppings and rubbish barrels, the sweet sickly smell from spice vendors and florists' shops, ignoring a shove from a drunk in the crowd, who a moment later, staring down horrified at this grotesque apparition, crossed himself. He shut off all four of his other senses so as to focus wholly on his search for the source of this petulant voice inside his head.

*At the Vatican? Do you have the least inkling of what plans are being concocted over your head? Doesn't it occur to you that the abbot had some special design in sending you all this way? If I were you I'd watch my step. And what about the girl you're searching for, have you found any traces of her? There there, don't forget I'm as familiar with your thoughts as I am with the contents of my own trouser pocket, you simply haven't learned to shield them. I've been following you for two weeks now and you've noticed nothing.*

*Following me, why?* he asked, surprised.

*People like you interest me. For professional reasons. You might be useful to me, but everyone has to go through a trial period . . . I've checked up on you, put you to certain tests, to see what you're made of. The problem here appears to be the girl, you simply don't seem able to get her out of your mind.*

*What do you know about Henriette?* he asked nervously.

*No more than your unending obsessions have revealed. Anyway, how was your journey? From what I understand, you've come as a pilgrim from afar.*

How was my journey? he thought. Each day had been like Creation's first. Not a moment had passed since he'd left the monastery without his experiencing something for the very first time. Unfamiliar smells, the landscape, changing as he and Schuster had travelled south, the plains, rivers, the stupendous Alps; people they had met or looked at through the carriage windows, the colours and tastes, the pines and olive groves that as twilight fell over the fields looked like sleeping animals. The world's sheer size and wealth had filled him with amazement. But on another score the voice was right: a thousand times on his journey he'd bowed his head amid all these people. Somewhere out there, in this continent called Europe, he kept thinking, *she* must be. Somewhere in this complex weave of time and events that links people together she must have left her imprint, dropped a stitch. Such was the hope he had nurtured ever since they had left Silesia. If only he could come across a memory of her in the mind of someone who had seen her, whether recently or long ago made no odds. Encounter someone who'd glanced at her if only for a brief instant yet retained the image of this girl for whom he never gave up searching, and whom he loved with a force able to defy the laws of nature.

In the gloom of taverns he had fumbled in the innermost psyches of chance encounters, floated adrift in their memories, been shipwrecked in an archipelago of sorrows, gone astray in a nautical chart of dreams. In draughty attic rooms shared with travelling salesmen and pilgrims, in the transient atmosphere of post houses, in godforsaken villages, at the gates of clamorous cities, by waysides, changing horses at the post stations, in the unassuaged longings of men in whom painful memories suddenly flared up like torches, in the pasts of beggars that struck him like sad melodies as they stretched out their hands to passers-by, engrossed in a happier past that had been sunnier, warmer, better.

Day and night he had gone on searching in his mad hope that the age of miracles was not yet over. But nowhere had he found any trace of her.

*Get a hold of yourself,* the voice interrupted his ruminations. *Stop thinking about that girl and look behind you!*

He gave a start. Up on the stage the actors were taking a final bow after their last act.

Slowly the crowd dispersed, clearing his view. Now, in the light of the Roman sun, Hercule saw him very clearly. His instinct that had told him to look for his observer at eye level had been correct. The person in question was standing only a few yards away, beckoning eagerly to him to follow. Not bent double, as he'd guessed at first, or squatting down to get a good look at a real-life monster. It was a boy, dressed in a tatty black coat, his face hidden behind a Venetian-style carnival mask.

It was in the October following the storming of its gates that the head of the monastery had decided to send Hercule to Jesuit head-quarters at the Borgo Santo Spirito in Rome, there to be examined by the Inquisition's special committee on demonology, which had only recently, after some years lying fallow, retrieved its authority.

According to the version Abbot Kippenberg had given Schuster, what they wanted to ascertain was the source of the boy's gifts. Did these derive from a brighter or a darker source? Were they subject to some rational explanation in line with those modern Enlightenment ideas that, to the horror of some and the secret delight of others, were gradually gaining ground even in the venerable Society of Jesus.

Naturally the object of this interest had not himself been consulted, and in any case Hercule was so absorbed in his new-found freedom that nothing else interested him.

That night when the monastery had been stormed by the Silesian peasantry he – for the first time – had come to appreciate the full extent of his gift. He had stirred up people's minds to such a degree they'd taken him for a miracle worker; and only pure luck and Julian Schuster's intervention, pacifying the agitated mob with threats and promises, had prevented them from tearing him to pieces. This had placed him doubly in the elderly priest's debt.

Their journey to Rome had taken over a month; firstly through the German countries by mail coach, then on foot and by sleigh over the Alps, and finally astride the mules provided by the Jesuit houses along the pilgrim route into Italy.

Hercule was a beginner in the *refugium* of existence. His whole life had been spent behind locked doors, so he knew little of the outside world. Nor had he grown a centimetre taller since his eighth birthday. But he'd matured, until he seemed to be four times his real age. From his chin sprouted a goatee beard and on his cheeks grew lynx-like side whiskers. At the same time his cranium had lost the little tuft of hair it had once had. But the thick fur on his neck and back was still there, as were the cleft, snakelike tongue and the monstrous cavity in the middle of his face that could scare the living daylights even out of a rabble of soldiers, and which would pursue them in their nightmares to the end of their days. Unchanged too were his dwarf legs, his arms that resembled parboiled roots from some rare medicinal plant. With these attributes, and from the rustling suit of pleated linen the brethren had sewn for him before he'd left on his journey, it was hardly surprising if he'd been an object for all eyes, drawn everyone's attention.

One Sunday afternoon after Mass at Innsbruck he had played a piano with his bare feet in an inn, and so stirred up the music-loving landlord's feelings that he'd wept like a child. Chins dropped when people saw him scratch a louse bite with the tip of his shoe or, seated on the floor, fasten the top button of his ruffled shirt with one foot while holding up a mirror and critically looking at himself with the other. On one occasion even the horses had turned pale in wonder as he, standing on one leg, had helped the coachman change the canisters, and while silently whispering to them in animal language, with the other foot had groomed their tails.

Probably the journey would have been easier had he – precisely as the voice on the Piazza Navona would later reproach him for not doing – worn a mask. It happened that children burst into tears at the mere sight of him, and on more than one occasion Julian Schuster had had to muster up all his authority for them to be allowed to spend the night at some hostel whose very pigsty the landlord declared to be full, though actually terrified of bringing down God's wrath for putting up what they were sure was a child of Satan, one thereto "rigged out in carnival costume".

Accusations of this kind weren't new to Hercule. But not until the autumn of his years, when wisdom had taught him to brace himself against all manner of insults, would their poison cease to hurt him. Meanwhile, he stored it up, until he could no longer stand being consumed by it.

In one Tyrolean village they had visited the market and almost been lynched while waiting for the coachman to repair two broken wheels. It was early morning and a pregnant woman at one of the flower stalls had let out a shriek at the sight of our hero and fallen senseless to the ground in a shower of pine needles from a funeral wreath. Folk had come running from all directions and soon Schuster and Barfuss were surrounded by menacing villagers accusing them of putting the Evil Eye on an unborn child. One market salesman claimed the fruit in his baskets had turned rotten at the very moment the stagecoach had drawn up on the highway, and another that he'd had dreams auguring a divine visitation on the region. Once again it had been Schuster who'd saved them by displaying the elegant missive he'd received, impressively sealed and stamped with seven authoritative stamps after leaving Cardinal Rivero at the Jesuit Congregation, declaring this boy to be a famous miracle worker under papal protection. Only then, and most dubiously, had the crowd withdrawn.

Apart from these mishaps the journey had gone better than expected, without their being confronted by any of the ever more brutal highwaymen typical of that time and who were seldom known to spare their victims, even less so if they turned out to be ecclesiastics. They'd crossed the Alps in a snowstorm of Olympian force no less fierce than the one that had ravaged Königsberg the night Hercule had been born. A rumour would reach them that it had cost twenty-four pilgrims their lives when their horses had panicked at the wind's terrible howling and taken nine sledges with them over a precipice. When they arrived in the Po plain it was summer again and at each roadside altar Julian Schuster had fallen to his knees and kissed the little statues of the Blessed Virgin.

The only really black cloud had been the Jesuit's waning spirits. He had seemed happy enough during the journey's first weeks.

He'd been positively affected by a badly needed waft of the adventurous years of his youth as he had struck up aquaintance with other travellers, played cards with the coachmen and drunk cider in the taverns, where he was surprised to hear the same old travellers' yarns he'd heard in his youth. In a word, he had enjoyed this escape from monastic routines and from feeling stifled by incense, from the refectory's sepulchral silence, from Abbot Kippenberg's air of misunderstood sainthood, and, not least, by the doomsday atmosphere that had prevailed in the monastery since Hercule's arrival.

But gradually, as they neared their destination, his spirits had failed him and his joviality given way to worry.

Ever since the night when he had received conclusive proof of his protégé's gift, Schuster had begun to see the boy through a new and sharper lens. Instinct told him the boy's powers were not demonic, but something else, something inexplicable. Allowing for his still being confused, he'd taken care not to frighten him.

Rightly. Marked by his experiences, it was taking Hercule time to overcome his feelings of mistrust. Not until the fourth week of the journey did he begin speaking to his friend with the aid of his strange gift. At first not often, but gradually, as Schuster won his confidence more. And though he was never to confide in him to the extent he deserved, he became more and more candid.

Hercule knew what he owed Schuster. And it pained him to see his saviour fretting, plagued by misgivings that in short measure had come to command his entire life, the only life he knew, and question every choice he'd ever made, to become the person he now was. A terrible fate for a man who'd spent a lifetime in the services of the brethren. The fact was, Schuster had started to doubt the existence of a God who rarely heeded prayer, so seldom in fact that when it did happen, it seemed more like a stroke of luck. Schuster had come to doubt the value of a monastic life and suspected Fate of really having had another life in store for him, of which it had already written out the score, though by some stroke of ill luck, and because he had heeded the call of his heart, he had condemned himself to suffering, and been fooled into choosing another path. Tormented by a celibacy he was too old to revoke, he was haunted by the voices of children and grandchildren he'd never had, by the happy laughter of a family in whose bosom he would never grow old, unquestioned patriarch of the family estate between Jerez and Seville, whose monastic substitute seemed ever more hollow and poverty-stricken. As they'd approached the Holy City he was also filled with another, more diffuse, cause for concern, whose motives, since they were unknown to him, escaped not only our hero but also Schuster himself. The priest's apprehensions had hourly grown stronger as they had drawn nearer to the city. So obviously beset was he by these worries that on the evening they arrived in Rome at the assembly's seat of honour at the Borgo Santo Spirito, Hercule had half expected Schuster to break down and weep.

It was in this mood they had settled into their quarters – a guest room in an annexe to the brethren's Hospital del Santo Spirito, a humble chamber in the quarters closest to St Peter's Church, furnished like a monastery cell and whose only window looked out on to a backyard in everlasting shadow.

In the daytime Schuster had disappeared to attend meetings. After spending hours with clerical officials in the Vatican offices, he would return late at night, depressed and restless. Hercule could awake to find him lying sleepless on his bunk, staring at a damp spot on the ceiling. Not until dawn did sleep take him by surprise amid his guilty feelings at not being able to gather his thoughts into a prayer.

Of the plans Abbot Kippenberg had made over their heads, Hercule still knew nothing. But Schuster, with antennae honed by a long and dangerous life, seemed to intuit them. Hercule, on the contrary, was still swept up by the *joie de vivre* that had finally liberated him, and by the belief that, if he was patient enough, he would sooner or later find his Henriette.

That afternoon it was with a child's curiosity about existence and a feeling of invulnerability that he went to the Piazza Navona, where the Holy St Agnes had once prayed for her persecutors. It was there the phantom voice, for a reason he still didn't understand, had started speaking to him.


Driven by an overwhelming curiosity, Hercule had followed on through alleys of the Ponte Parlone quarter. Dusk was falling. Far away over the Alban hills a storm was brewing as they passed through passages so narrow and so densely crowded that their inhabitants had ceased to interest themselves in each other's secrets. Zigzagging through the trade quarters, they passed butchers' shops and tanneries, taverns where drunks were playing cards, prostitutes on the lookout for the night's first customers. Agile as a cat, the boy he was following had slipped through the throngs, climbing over sleeping drunks, slinking in between carriage wheels and mules and pushing on ahead in so matter-of-fact a manner that the city could well have been a part of his own clothing. Twice Hercule lost sight of him, but at the very moment he'd given up hope of again seeing his guide, he found him waiting at the next street corner.

At the Piazza Farnese their path was barred by a funeral procession. Hercule was just about to catch up with his diminutive cicerone when the latter suddenly raised his hand in a gesture that told him not to come close and in his mind whispered very clearly to him: *Keep your distance, it isn't good for creatures like us to draw too much attention to ourselves!*

He obeyed, but without understanding why this rule should make them play cat-and-mouse like this.

They went on along the wall until they got to the Jewish ghetto, whose gates were guarded by soldiers, its inhabitants being forbidden to leave the area after sundown. Turning left at the via Giulia, they followed the Tiber's bank with its shellfish stalls, its lotteries, its invalids and ragamuffins holding out their begging bowls to passers-by, and so carried on eastwards until they got to the Forum.

Here, among the ruins of ancient Rome, cows were grazing, shepherds lay sleeping on the plinths of Corinthian columns, and an unnatural fog hung over everything, as if in a painting by some befuddled artist. Darkness fell abruptly. Once more, by the remains of an antique villa below the Palatine Hill, the other boy stopped to wait for him. They were alone now, no-one else was in sight, and he beckoned to Hercule to follow. Thrown aside on the floor of what had once been a mosaic-inlaid patio of a consular palace lay the cover from a well. His guide disappeared into the darkness and Hercule heard him say: *Creatures like us are better off underground. Don't be afraid . . . follow me . . . but keep close, or you'll be lost.*

Later he was to realise that it was down into Rome's catacombs they'd climbed, though at the time he had supposed them to be a widely ramified, multi-layered cellar. He was astonished by the maze, corridors going off to right and left, the smell of thousand-year-old mildew and woodlice fleeing at the sound of footfall. The boy had lit a lantern, and Hercule followed without asking any questions.

At one point in these subterranean halls, where the dead exhaled hoarse whispers in Latin and the ghosts of Roman soldiers roamed in hope of finding a way out, they came to a crypt filled with human bones. Cowled skeletons stretched out bony hands to them, clung to yellowing scythes fitted together of vertebrae; held out worm-eaten hourglasses fashioned from infants' collarbones. All this reminded Hercule of his own mortality; he would never find his way out again if he lost sight of his guide. Chandeliers made of human jawbones hung from the ceiling, enormous ornaments likewise made of vertebrae covered the walls, reassembled skeletons of children rested peacefully under the vaults of prehistoric thigh bones.

Delving ever deeper into this labyrinth they took a left turn, then a right, until after wandering for half an hour along humid tunnels filled with mysterious shadows cast by non-existent creatures, and where times and epochs criss-crossed in utmost confusion, Hercule found himself standing in a hall illuminated by oil lamps. When his eyes had adjusted to this sudden gleam, Hercule saw that he was standing in the midst of a troupe of extraordinary-looking people.

*We're all monsters*, his enigmatic cicerone whispered inside him. And with a theatrical gesture, as if on stage in front of a many-headed audience, removed his mask.

It wasn't a boy who faced them after all. It was a full-grown man, albeit of exceedingly short stature. And Hercule understood immediately why he wore a mask. Right in the middle of this little man's forehead was one single eye, as on the mythological cyclops.


The man who had led the way down through Rome's meandering catacombs was a cyclops. His name was Barnaby Wilson. The single eye in the centre of his forehead was a result of some congenital human deformity, proving he wasn't a descendant of the monsters who ate humans for breakfast in Homer's verses. A native of the Welsh village of Llanerchymedd, Wilson, since losing his family at the age of seven in the great Cardiff fire, had been blown like a leaf in the winds of fortune, hither and thither throughout Europe. Just now he was the leader of one of Italy's more obscure variety shows, a travelling troupe of more than thirty people who kept starvation at bay by exhibiting their hideous abnormalities for money.

In his later years Hercule would write about Wilson in connection with the unification of Italy; a period when Wilson acted as counsellor to Garibaldi himself, a position that suited him perfectly, since he, possessing as he did an inexplicable foreknowledge of the enemy's secret plans, was able to disclose them even before they'd had time to be dispatched by courier. But all that was much later on, and at the time when Hercule first made his aquaintance Wilson was fully occupied with his travelling show.

What Hercule witnessed that evening in Rome moved him deeply, inasmuch as he for some reason had always lived in the belief that he was unique, alone not only with his gift, but also in his appearance. Judging by people's reactions to him, he'd had no reason to believe otherwise than that such misfortune really was his alone. Never before had he met another real-life monster, but all this changed in the lamplight as one by one he was introduced to Barnaby Wilson's protégés.

They surpassed anything Hercule could ever have imagined. There was a hermaphrodite, inspiringly named Gandalalfo Bonaparte and said to be Emperor Napoleon's bastard child, and a girl with yellow curls named Miranda Bellaflor, in whose mouth four tongues vied for space. There were the twins Louis and Louise who had been joined at the waist since birth, who always spoke simultaneously and were often at furious odds with each other. And then, of course, there was Barnaby Wilson himself, the cyclops who, like Hercule, was endowed with the gift of mind-reading.

There were quite a few in the group who possessed unusual and unexplained talents and who, with the passage of time, had added greatly to the troupe's reputation as it travelled throughout Italy from one market place to the next. Leon Montebianco, for example, was said to see as far back in history as ten thousand years and thus was able to search for the lost city of Troy. His testimony had proved to be so exact that on the one occasion when the German geographer-to-be Schliemann witnessed, as a child, a performance, he'd taken him at his word, and half a century later, after only a single thrust of his spade into an insignificant hill by the Hellespont, had discovered the site as predicted by Montebianco. There was Signora Ramona who every month since her fifteenth birthday had taught herself to speak a new language fluently, and was therefore able to write love letters in 116 known languages. There was the woman who could turn any type of base material into gold, and the Turkish poet whose single leg was covered in a scorching hot snakeskin, so hot you could light your cigar on it! Another member of this company was the Provençal dwarf Lucretius III, self-taught master of the art of handling a magic lantern, who by using a complex system of mirrors could display the most lifelike phantasmagoria of famous historical figures. But all these people's gifts, Barnaby Wilson explained with great authority, were no more than nature's compensation for their physical defects.

Years later, looking back on that night and at its subsequent tragic epilogue in Genoa, Hercule would understand that for the first time in his life he had come home. These were his fellow beings, brothers and sisters whose misfortunes were only relative and inspired in each other a melancholy sense of affinity. They too had been sacrificed on nature's callous altar and existed for no weightier reason than as a warning to an age that believed the seed could be accursed for seven generations should some forefather have signed a contract with the powers of darkness.

As the hours went by, Barnaby Wilson told him about his wards, about their experiences of life on the outskirts of human existence; about their humiliations, sufferings and persecutions, about lunatic asylums; but also of the happiness they had found in one another, and of the fantastic laurels they had won by placing their gifts at the disposal of his travelling company.

Inspired by their story, Hercule gave a complete account of his own life. In the telepathic manner commanded by both of them from earliest childhood, he told Wilson of his childhood, his years in the asylum, his stay in the Jesuit monastery and everything that had happened there; about the peasants who'd taken him for a miracle worker and the monks who had suddenly been beset by doubt; in short, all the events that, in accordance with life's implacable consequences and its refusal to cite any alternatives, had brought him to Rome. And, not least, he told of Henriette Vogel, the girl-child he hadn't seen since their eleventh year of life, but who had not been out of his thoughts for a single moment, who gave his life true meaning, who was the alphabet of his dreams and the meridian of his longing.

Moved by his tale, Barnaby Wilson invited him to join their troupe. That very morning they would be setting off with their appalling deformities and magical talents in fifteen canvas-covered wagons to bring joy to Calabrian villages, all for an entrance fee of two centesimi a head. This, the circus director guessed, would increase Hercule's chances of finding the girl by several hundred per cent.

Hercule thought long and hard over this generous offer from a man he'd met for the first time only a few hours before and who seemed motivated by nothing but compassion for his brothers and sisters in misfortune. But in the end, feeling himself indebted to Schuster, he declined.

That same morning, with a deep sense of melancholy, he left the remarkable group of people. As they emerged from beneath the earth at the Forum the light of dawn could already be discerned behind the Colosseum. Holding up a finger no bigger than a child's, Barnaby Wilson pointed him in the direction of Borgo Santo Spirito on the other side of the river. The cockerels of the Eternal City had united in a song that Hercule interpreted as signifying a final separation. But he was mistaken.

I n the same twilight hour as the phantom voice had begun talking to Hercule on the Piazza Navona, Julian Schuster had found himself in the Vatican in a papal stateroom in a magnificent building between the Belvedere palace and the Ethiopian College. He was listening with growing anxiety to what Cardinal Aurelio Rivero had to say about his protégé.

"This, Schuster, is undoubtedly a sensitive matter, and it must be solved in a manner satisfactory to all concerned. The general of your Order of brethren is following our investigations with great interest, and trusts us to bring the whole matter to a satisfactory conclusion. I suggest we as soon as possible carry out an examination of the boy in accordance with the rules laid down by Martín del Río."

Cardinal Rivero, responsible for the brethren's special commission in the fight against heresies, topped up Schuster's wine glass, to remind him of the differences between the monastic way of life and that of their representatives in the Vatican.

"We are, even so, living in the nineteenth century," Schuster made so bold as to say. "Not even in America did we cling to the *Recherche de Magique!*"

"New times, admittedly. But personally I draw quite other conclusions from this so-called 'development'. With all due respect to reason, was it not the men of the Enlightenment who had us excommunicated? Let me be honest: we must consolidate the power restored to us by the politicians, as a result of the Restoration."

Schuster picked up an olive from the tray the Cardinal pushed over to him, but then, feeling he'd just overcome the temptation, replaced it.

"Your Eminence, what do you mean when you say the problem must be solved?"

"Hasn't Abbot Kippenberg told you of our plans?"

"My task was to bring the boy to Rome for you to take a look at him. There was never any mention of *plans*."

Rivero gave him a look that laid claim to a knowledge of details beyond an outsider's horizon.

"In any case, it's nothing for you to trouble your conscience with," he said. "You're free to return to Silesia tomorrow if you wish, I've ordered a carriage for you, with two changes of horses. Heisterbach needs your presence as oldest in your house. Considering recent events there, a moral inquisition ought to be initiated as soon as possible. I would suggest you take over Kippenberg's duties as father confessor. A monastery dissolving into anarchy! Novices disappearing or breaking their vows – and all for the sake of an organ-playing monster who's said to be able to read minds and, what's more, is deaf and dumb!"

"With your permission, my Lord Cardinal, I'll stay until the investigation is completed. It could be interesting to observe your methods."

Rivero spat out an olive stone on to a gilded plate, and wiped his mouth with a silk handkerchief.

"The end justifies the means," he said. "That is what outsiders think the brethren's motto is, do they not?"

"Only so far as the means used are in accordance with the will of God," Schuster replied.

"And if, as rumour has it, the boy is a mind reader, or worse, can read people's hidden thoughts, how shall we proceed?"

"With all due respect, Your Eminence, I still don't understand what you are trying to say."

The Cardinal gave a curt laugh, then let his features settle back into a parody of the Holy St Christopher, who watched them protectively from an oil painting on the wall.

"There's a reason why people repress certain thoughts and

reflexes," Rivero said tersely, "and keep them a secret even to themselves. Otherwise what would become of us? Besides, it isn't only God who whispers to us. In moments of weakness other voices can worm their way in . . ."

Rising from his armchair, the Cardinal started pacing the room with his hands behind his back. Stopping at the little altar where a Bible lay open, he touched it with a beautifully manicured finger-nail.

"You mean the boy could be a spokesman for the Devil?" Schuster said.

"Please, spare me your ironies, my dear brother. Kippenberg has been keeping me informed of the goings on in your house. Already eight novices have broken their vows, half a dozen have uttered blasphemies, to put it mildly. Let us suppose it's the boy who is behind all this, and that he, all by himself, is capable of throwing a whole monastery into chaos . . . does that seem reasonable: alone?"

Rivero broke off mid-sentence as a Swiss guard entered with a silver casket and placed it on the table underneath the enormous crucifix adorning the wall. Casting a guilty glance at Our Saviour, Schuster reflected: *It's this suffering, O bleeding God, which scares people away. Why couldn't we have found a more beautiful symbol for our faith?*

"Desire is in itself innocent enough," he said. "It's our attitude to the desire that's sinful."

"Most ingenious. Tell me, Schuster, are you preoccupied with false doctrines?"

"All that preoccupies me are your so-called *plans*."

The Cardinal sat down again in his armchair.

"So how do you explain that the boy taught himself to play the organ with his feet in less than half a year, like any Conservatory student? Deaf as he is?"

"Musicality is a gift from above. In the Americas I saw savages learn to play the flute in four days."

"And it never occurred to you that it was unnatural? You never asked yourself: how could it be possible for a savage to suddenly blow a trombone?" The Cardinal was touching on a raw nerve with Schuster.

"To be honest, I never have fully understood our theological stance in this matter. If you permit me, Your Eminence, music has been both embraced and developed by Christians, at the same time as the very same Christians exclude it as being something demonic; a paradox I've never been able to come to terms with. Mediaeval monks transformed song into an instrument by developing harmony and counterpoint. Music became an ecclesiastical concern, but then when least we expect it, it is turned against us. In the transition from one harmonious chord to the next it suddenly becomes demonic, and no-one has ever been able to explain to me how this feat is accomplished. Perhaps you can enlighten me?"

The Cardinal sighed.

"From what I've heard, you're a headstrong man, Schuster. It must be your Spanish-German temperament. Your Habsburgian temperament, one might almost say. So I shall pretend not to have heard your sophistries. But how about you yourself, don't you have any opinions on this matter?"

"Which matter?"

"Have you had any personal experience of the boy's so-called gift?"

Schuster hesitated. Something told him not to expose too much of what he knew.

"No," he said. "If one overlooks the fact that he learned to play the organ in so short a time, despite his apparently being deaf and indeed, in the physiological sense, lacking ears, which I admit is hard to explain. But since it's not been possible to make any medical diagnosis, we're none the wiser. It's possible he can hear more than we think."

"My view precisely," the Cardinal answered, smiling. "Some people hear more than we think."

Rivero opened the casket and took out a key. He got up, his costly cardinal's gown with its gold brocades rustling slightly against the marble floor as he did so.

"I believe", he said, "the time has come for a brief change of scene. I think perhaps you'll understand things better if you allow me to show you some illustrations . . ."


For no fewer than three generations Julian Schuster had instilled in his novices the brethren's conviction that the world could, in principle, be made a better place if one admitted to the possibility of a hidden, divine plan. Armed with the ingenious medium provided by a rock-steady *ratio studium*, he had infused into his pupils' minds such ideas as *discrécion, prudencia* and *caridad discreta*, pleading for the *regnum humanitatis*, or the crystalline humanism he believed was the foundation of the Order's belief system. But in this twilight hour, standing in a cellar beneath the brethren's chancery as Cardinal Rivero inserted the key into the lock of an ancient oak door, he felt the convictions of a lifetime beginning to crumble. They had just walked past a dozen armed guards stationed in disconsolate backyards. Three times, notwithstanding his high rank, Rivero had had to show papers permitting Schuster to pass in his company.

"If you'd tried to get in here by yourself", he said, pushing the door open, "you'd have had to wait four months for a permit, fill in some fifteen forms so bureaucratic that the procedure in itself would have put your nerves to a severe trial. An extensive investigation would have been made into all your doings since the day you entered the Order, you'd have had to get three high-ranking officials to vouch for you, and even then it's by no means certain a dispensation would have been issued, even for one afternoon."

They came into a hall-like area lit by candles mounted in brackets on the walls. By one of the reading desks a monk was leaning over a folio volume. Rivero turned off into an almost invisible path, bordered by heaps of books and shelves stacked with documents. With a shudder Schuster realised they were in the inquisitor's library of forbidden books.

"Alas, Schuster! We're almost the same age, you and I, yet fate has found fit to treat us so very differently. You have had the adventures, I a career. That you've had no promotions has of course nothing to do with your talents; you have all the qualities needed for a higher position in the Order. In fact, I'm surprised you haven't been offered a position already. You've had a classical education, and shown great competence in your practical work, not least in the Americas. You have been an example to the Freemasons and the men of the Enlightenment during an epoch when it could cost a man his life to publicly declare himself a member of your Order.

"Did you know, there has been some hint of a position for you in Spain? Our old allies, the Bourbons, are back on the throne. Only yesterday I was speaking with the Bishop of Córdoba at the Concilium, there's a post vacant as abbot of a monastery in Granada, your home district, Schuster. But it must be filled forthwith."

Schuster threw his superior a look of surprise.

"What do you mean?" he asked.

"There's a ship leaving for Málaga the day after tomorrow. You can be on it, on the condition, naturally, that you hand over all responsibility for the boy to me. The case may take some time."

"This comes a little suddenly. Only moments ago you were saying they expect me back in Silesia."

Rivero laid a fraternal hand on his shoulder, smiling a little too quickly, a little too amiably, for Schuster not to be suspicious of his intentions.

"On closer consideration, I do believe Granada is in greater need of your services. I would advise you to seize the opportunity while you can. Let us look after the boy here in peace and quiet, while you attend to your compatriots' salvation."

By now they had come to a room the size of the novices' dormitory in Heisterbach. Confronted by this enormous collection of forbidden books that had been spared being burned at the stake, Schuster was filled with awe and fear in equal measure. Thousands of volumes filled the shelves, voluminous tomes bound in calfskin and morocco, dusty folios, printed matter in demy and quarto. Yellowing parchments lay heaped up atop locked cabinets, illustrated works and encyclopedias filled entire sections. Ladders were needed to get at the ones highest up.

"We're standing amid a sea of blasphemies," Rivero said solemnly, "which would threaten to drown us were it not for this dam: the *Index Tridentinus*. Do you know how many years it has taken the Church to collect this mass of unbelief? Five centuries! Thousands upon thousands of our Christian brethren have dedicated their lives to this end, since it's widely acknowledged that the Devil writes books faster than man can read them."

The dust hung static in the candlelight. Schuster had a vague feeling of having experienced this moment many times before, though he'd forgotten just where and when and for what reason.

"Look around you," Rivero muttered. "Profanations of the

papacy and the Holy Scriptures, the most absurd accusations ever aimed at our faith; *Solomon's Key, The Lucifer Letters*, the *Kabbala*, Satanic manuals all. Centuries of *censura subsequens* that have saved men from God's punishment. I tell you, were these writings to be released, there would be a second Flood."

With a ringed finger the Cardinal pointed at a section of manuscripts locked into a huge glass cupboard.

"The writings of Cathars and spiritualists, disrespectful interpretations of the Bible by Beguines and Beghards, instruction books in unjustifiable self-mutilation written by flagellants. Books by Moors, Jews and Calvinists. Donatists' liturgies for the worship of demons, satanic bibles by Arians and Bogomils, collections of letters that confuse God with the snake in paradise. All this heathen ingenuity is enough to make one lose one's mind!"

Unconsciously, Rivero placed his hand on his heart, as if the simple act of listing them was a malignant blasphemy.

"There are spiritual paths here that no man should ever tread. Paths over abysses that lead deep into the most unfathomable darkness, into the most bitter loneliness imaginable!"

Schuster got the feeling of being in the middle of an enlarged human brain stuffed full with perilous information; and this led his thoughts back to the boy, his ward. What plans were they discussing? What were they intending to do to him? Ponderings were interrupted as the Cardinal took a step towards another section.

"Have you ever leafed through the spurious *Gospel of Peter*? It's enough to raise the hairs on the arms of a child murderer. Or the *Bible of the Manichees*? These envoys of the Devil are trying to prove that it wasn't Our Lord who died on the cross, but one of the common thieves. That his body was nothing but an illusion of the demiurge, and that for him to have died an agonising death on the cross would be beneath the dignity of their supposed God. They maintain that Christ was pure spirit!"

Rivero went on to mutter something about lost souls before going over to a folio that lay open on a desk affixed to the wall.

"Published in Bologna in 1661. Designs for machinery and automatic machines that we hope will never see the light of day."

The open volume showed a picture of something resembling an insect, crowned with a rotating metal blade, in the shape of a four-leafed clover.

"A helixapteron or dragonfly machine," Rivero said disdainfully. "I wish I could experience this upward striving as an innocent longing for the kingdom of heaven, but it's the other way round: they want to put themselves in God's place, be His equal instead of His servant."

He turned the page to another design, a winged construction surrounding a kind of cylinder.

"In the beginning God created only four types of being capable of flight: angels, birds, bats and insects. The day man carries out his perverse fantasies about flying machines, we'll be done for. It'll be the ultimate revolt against the plan of Creation before Our Lord has our earth laid waste."

"Can they in fact be constructed?" Schuster asked, looking at a draft for what would become a twentieth-century aircraft.

"In theory: yes. And look at this; still more machines, ideas that can only have been inspired by the darkest of powers."

Rivero turned another page, a woodcut illustrating a self-acting machine with pistons and tubes with dense smoke rising from their vents, as from a minor volcano.

"A steam engine, of course," he said. "The technique was known as far back as in antiquity, but the Greeks were more interested in experiments on the mind than in engineering. As you know, the English have started mass-producing these engines."

They crossed the threshold to another room, not quite so big as the last. Here were no bookshelves, only oaken cupboards locked with iron bolts. A vague premonition told Schuster that this was where the most renegade writings were kept, and when Rivero unlocked one cupboard Schuster glimpsed a row of black Devil's bibles with Roman numerals on them.

Still muttering, the Cardinal picked out a leather-bound volume and blew the dust off its covers.

"This is a very useful book," he said, "in the right hands, that's to say."

Schuster read the yellowing title page: SPIRITUS SUCUBA E INCUBU.

"This folio contains illustrations of the fruits of the Devil's concubine," Rivero muttered, "as well as case descriptions of monsters. Look at this: Printed at Avignon, under the pontificate of Benedictus XII!" He pointed at a woodcut representing a boy with a horn in the middle of his forehead. "A well-known case. The mother was a dissident nun, the father an incubus."

Some lectures on the subject of demonology he'd heard shortly before leaving for the New World more than sixty years ago flashed through Schuster's memory: in the category of demons a sucubas was a female sexual partner, incubus a male one. The sperm was said to be cold as ice; but in most cases the supposed fruits of these unnatural unions between a human and a demon did not survive. They were eaten up, or so it was said, during the orgies following a black mass.

He could not help but laugh.

"If you were to believe half of what man has made up, inspired by his nightmares, the world would be a dreadful place to live in."

"How can you be so sure about that, my dear brother?"

"No-one could believe this!" Schuster pointed at another illustration, showing a boy with a pig's tail and a demon's face growing out of his stomach. "That these beings could be the fruit of a devil's concubine are imaginings of sick souls."

"And how do you explain the boy's monstrosity?"

"You mean that he came into this world during a black mass? Accompanied by seven sputtering black candles, steeped in fat from unbaptised infants? If he was born deformed, it wasn't to expiate innate sins, or because his mother had invited an incubus into her bedchamber. It was because God, whose ways are inscrutable, wished it to be so."

Rivero passed the tip of his tongue across his teeth.

"Judging by your tone of voice, Schuster, you sometimes seem to forget I'm your superior . . . Look! This is most interesting."

A new page showed a picture of an adult monster. The deformities were much the same as those of Hercule Barfuss: the furry back, the calluses, the bumps, the cloven tongue, an abnormally cavernous face.

"This man was called Silvester de Costa. He lived in Lisbon in the sixteenth century. The odd thing was although he was both deaf and dumb he had certain gifts; it was said he had second sight. The Inquisition investigated him and found him guilty of sorcery. He was executed during an auto-da-fé at Burgos."

The Cardinal regarded the illustrations with a look so full of contempt that Schuster shuddered.

"I assume nothing of the sort will occur in this case," he said.

The Cardinal slammed the folio shut.

"Of course not. I only want to impress upon you the gravity of the situation. Let me just say that there are functionaries within our field who are not quite as enlightened as you or I, and you must have no Rousseauesque expectations as to their methods."

"Permit me, Your Eminence . . ." Schuster fumbled for words, "I stand on the right side vis-à-vis our former enemies, just as you do. There's every reason for us to praise the work of the Congress of Vienna. I'm no supporter of Freemasons or Jacobites; but the fact is that we're living in a new era. The steam engine's here to stay, and if I correctly understand our Order's strivings, we too will enjoy the benefits of this new age. Not everything that happened in the dark years was bad. There was a power in the Enlightenment that has contributed to the good of man; new sciences, research, technique . . ."

Cardinal Rivero threw him a peculiar look.

"I appreciate your being so forthright!" he said. "But whether or not the steam engine is to our benefit is not for you to judge. Allow others to draw conclusions in these matters. This is not what you have come to Rome for. I want you to bring the boy to my office tomorrow morning. We have experts on these matters. The examination is exhaustive and will leave nothing to be desired. We must establish, once and for all, the source of his supposed gifts."

The Cardinal made a gesture towards the exit.

"Meanwhile," he said, "I really think you should consider the Granada offer. The boy's in good hands, and as soon as the investigation is over, we shall see to it that he is given a place in one of our monasteries. He must be of some use. Take my advice and board the ship to Málaga. They need you in Spain."

In a heavy mood, Julian Schuster left the library of forbidden books, and although the Cardinal tried to mitigate the unspoken misgivings growing within his fellow Jesuit, he was not very successful. Under the pretext of having some letters to write before the bell rang for vespers Schuster declined an invitation to dine that same evening with a bishop. After promising to appear with the boy at the ordained hour tomorrow, he left the Cardinal on the via della Conciliazione, in a shadow cast by the dome of St Peter's.

A mirror covering the examination chamber's shorter wall, in front of which exorcists of old used to place suspected witches in order to ascertain whether they showed up on the foil, made the room seem larger than in fact it was.

There was only one window and it was covered by Spanish-style shutters. On the walls hung pictures of the Virgin, a painting portraying Loyola receiving his divine vision on the road outside La Storta, and a processional cross that had once belonged to the Knights of Malta.

In a corner stood a laboratory bench with a wide range of instruments. Enthroned in the middle of the floor was a spinet, and further away a strange piece of furniture reminiscent of a barber's chair.

Apart from Hercule and Julian Schuster, only the Cardinal and an inquisitor, Sebastian del Moro, were in the room.

Del Moro was a skinny man, dressed in the robes of the Dominican order. A pair of rimless spectacles gave him a scholarly air. The complicated ritual he was responsible for was part of a plan drawn up long ago and intended to be executed in accordance with Martin del Río's guidelines for establishing whether or not a person was in alliance with the Devil.

"Is the monster retarded?" he asked, turning Schuster.

"The boy's intellectual powers are completely normal, unless deafness counts as idiocy."

Del Moro ignored Schuster's ironical tone of voice. Out of a leather bag he had brought with him he soundlessly – with an air of sitting on dark secrets, as he'd entered the room through a back door – took out a notebook and a piece of charcoal which he wetted with an uncommonly pink tongue.

"I hear he's able to read minds?" he continued amiably.

"He might simply be lip-reading."

"What do you believe?"

Schuster sighed, "You're the one who's been entrusted with this examination, not I."

"But as an intellectual experiment. It seems inexplicable, does it not? Our innermost thoughts are hidden from everyone but Our Lord, are they not?"

"Confession shows us a way out of the bondage of sin," Schuster said.

"I happen to be of the opinion that there are exceptions," del Moro continued, jotting something down in his notebook. "And that there may be those, other than Our Lord, capable of apprehending our thoughts. To start with, what are thoughts? Have you any opinion on this matter?"

"Primarily they're an expression of our longing for God."

"Thoughts are the voice of our conscience," del Moro said. "The soul gives rise to consciousness, consciousness to conscience, and from our conscience comes thought. I surmise your exile in Germany brought you into contact with the new philosophers? What is it Kant says? We can never grasp the world as it is, only the way it seems to us."

The inquisitor smiled enigmatically and returned to the matter in hand.

"When was the monster born?" he asked

"Our guess is around the year 1810. I thought you'd got all the information from Abbot Kippenberg's letters. Besides . . . if we are to suppose that the boy can hear even though he's deaf, that he's the exception to the rule, *a priori* it could only be reasonable to call him by his name."

"How do you know his name?"

Schuster bit his lip to stop himself from letting out any more ill-considered remarks.

"He can communicate in writing," he said. "Even in French, should that prove necessary. The boy is surprisingly well educated considering he's an idiot."

"Come come, Schuster," the Cardinal broke in. "Let the inquisitor ask such questions as he deems necessary. We're not here to quarrel."

"Is the family Catholic?" del Moro continued in the same amiable tone.

"The boy's an orphan, but was probably baptised a Catholic. He had a crucifix around his neck when we found him in the asylum."

"And confirmed?"

"He'd been put into the lunatic asylum at the time when he would have taken his first communion."

Now, for the first time, the inquisitor turned towards Hercule Barfuss. Contemplated him with a look that reflected no feelings whatsoever. It was as if he were standing in front of an inanimate object – had we been able to put ourselves inside Hercule's world, if only for a brief moment, we would have been utterly astounded. For Inquisitor del Moro's innermost being had surrounded itself with an impenetrable wall, a kind of watertight mental bulkhead which formed an integral part of the demonological method. Not that the exorcist wasn't acting wholly in accordance with the ritual. From the moment the examination commenced he had transformed himself into an instrument in God's hands, and so as not to risk going out of his mind, maybe even losing his life, in a traumatic confrontation with the forces of darkness, not allowed himself any thoughts or feelings whatsoever.

"Have you been able to find out anything about the mother?" he went on, in the same toneless voice.

"No, but our guess is she was an army prostitute."

"How so?"

"The war years saw an illegitimate child to every second soldier. If they didn't starve to death they were just abandoned. Especially the idiots."

"And where did he learn to play the organ?"

"In the monastery."

Del Moro took off his glasses, wiped them meticulously with a handkerchief.

"I would be interested to partake of the boy's skills," he said. "A deaf and dumb monster who plays the organ! To tell you the truth, I've never heard the likes of it."

Hercule positioned himself at the spinet and the inquisitor placed a sheet of music in front of him, gesturing that he wanted to hear him play; and Hercule, whose confusion had been steadily mounting ever since he'd entered the examination room, played the piece flawlessly at only the second time through.

"That was by Clementi," muttered the inquisitor. "Spectacular, and with his feet at that! Who has he got all this from?"

"From me," said Schuster. "And I hope I won't be on the list of lost souls because I had the bad taste to allow a monster into the realms of music."

Del Moro smiled a curt military smile, then, recomposing his facial expression into that of his professional persona, led Hercule over to the strange chair that stood in the middle of the floor. Calm as any medico, he removed Hercule's clothes, examined the grey hat's sweatband, gave the chequered piping a shake, turned the underwear inside out and regarded the flat-heeled buckled shoes as if they bore some cryptic message he was disappointed to find he couldn't decipher.

"That is all for the time being," he said, turning to Schuster. "The examination will take no more than twenty-four hours. But in order for it to succeed it must be carried out under controlled conditions. I must ask you to leave us alone with your protégé until tomorrow. Even demonology demands a certain empirical procedure in order to obtain results. Go back to your room, Schuster. We'll call for you as soon as we're finished."

Shortly after Schuster had gone, the Roman sun went behind a cloud, and from far away could be heard an ominous rumble of thunder. Hercule, naturally, noticed nothing of this, nor did he note the inquisitor's dry voice as he turned to Cardinal Rivero.

"Your Eminence, it is of vital importance that we understand each other if we are to succeed. You must have no thoughts at all while I am examining this creature. Under no circumstances whatsoever may you allow your mind to wander."

"And why not?" the Cardinal asked

"Believe you me, this creature possesses powers you couldn't imagine exist."

Del Moro opened his bag and picked out some strangely shaped bits of metal that he proceeded to join together in a most precise fashion until they took on an appearance reminiscent of a medical instrument.

"Are you familiar with the *Asio otus*?" he asked. "The long-eared owl. It can hear the movements of a dormouse at a distance of two hundred metres. Or hear a mole breathing a metre underground. The bird has an extremely well-developed sense of hearing. And even though it hunts at night, its vision is poor. When it moves it makes almost no sound at all, its thick coat of feathers renders its flight soundless. Its prey – the mole, the mouse – doesn't stand a chance, doesn't have time to notice anything before the hunter has it in its clutches."

The inquisitor lit an oil lamp that was hanging above the examination chair, and held the otoscope up to the light.

"Bats are said to be specialised in the same way," he went on. "Blind, no sense of smell, a reduced sense of touch. But their hearing is excellent. One sense has effectively been developed at the expense of the others."

The Cardinal gave him a baffled look.

"Do you mean that the boy, because of his lack of speech and hearing, has developed another sense?"

"What I mean is, that we must take all necessary precautions. This monster is capable of exploiting the least weakness in our soul. Seal off your innermost being, Your Eminence. Pray, if you need to."

The inquisitor put the instrument to his eye and stared into Hercule's all but overgrown auditory channels.

"Extraordinary!" he said. "The eardrums are missing!" He twisted the lamp to one side to let the light fall on the ear at a better angle. "The boy's deaf. But the sacculus which allows for gravitational orientation seems to be intact. I hope we'll have the opportunity to do an autopsy."

He took the instrument out and wiped it on a piece of lint.

"Your Eminence is of course acquainted", he said solemnly, "with what the so-called evolutionists maintain? That man and beast have the same progenitor, who comes from the sea. And as evidence they adduce the ear. In animals and man alike the inner ear is filled with water. A remarkable anachronism, they say, that our auditory faculty should still be governed by submarine rules. Only through a filter of water can we transform sounds and render them comprehensible to the mind."

Rivero stood up, clearly agitated.

"What are you trying to say?" he asked.

"Nothing in particular. This monster has in any case quite a different genealogical table. His ears contain no water whatsoever!"

Del Moro proceeded to take out a pair of scissors from his bag and cleaned them in a basin filled with alcohol.

"I'm going to remove his hair growth," he said. "Nothing must be left to chance. I want you to examine the hair. Pay especial attention to the knots and tangles, that's where they hide their amulets! And whatever you do, seal off your innermost being, so that the monster cannot possess you."

And with two deft movements of his hands, so swift that in his confusion Hercule scarcely noticed what was happening, del Moro fastened his legs and what little he had of arms with leather straps to the chair and started the demonological examination.


It took the inquisitor an hour to relieve Hercule of all his hair. The furry back, in particular, offered resistance, and del Moro was forced to sharpen his razor no fewer than four times before the procedure could be concluded by exposing this part of Hercule's body. He could hardly believe his eyes. The back was covered with large calluses; the skin was porous and tinted slightly green, as though overgrown with lichen. In between the shoulder blades he discovered to his amazement a deep cavity, the bottom of which lay somewhere in the region of the front of the monster's chest. Here and there bones, wrongly grown, strained the overlying skin like a tent. Peculiar birthmarks had petrified to the point where they looked like stones.

All the while mumbling conjurations, del Moro rid Hercule of his downy beard and unruly whiskers. So fascinated was he by the young monster's physiognomy that he failed to notice how the bulkheads that sealed off his consciousness were beginning to leak, the palisade beginning to crack, to the point where his thoughts became an easy prey for the object of his interest.

*. . . attempting to find the witch's mark . . . Satan is always a step ahead . . . why hasn't this symptom had time to change . . . for every new method we develop, the Evil One serves up a new defence . . . a similar case was discovered in Paris a year or two ago . . . a boy picked up on everything everyone around him was thinking . . . could tell you where you'd lost things . . .*

Hercule could make nothing of this, and his confusion mounted still further when he saw the demonologist open his bag and take out an awl-like object and, still mumbling conjurations, kiss it as if it were a chalice filled with sacramental wine.

*. . . according to del Río one should be on the lookout for warts, or birthmarks . . . how can one do that on a body as deformed as this, it's nothing but a heap of abnormalities and calluses . . . let us with God's help put an end to this . . .*

And just as Hercule had intimated from this jumble of thoughts, del Moro set about a scrutinising search for a witch's mark on Hercule's body, a hidden wart or birthmark which, according to the great witch-hunter Martin del Río, is insensitive to pain and does not bleed no matter how deeply the needle is inserted, thus proving, beyond any doubt, that what they were dealing with was one of Satan's innumerable henchmen.

Hercule was only fragmentarily aware of his surroundings – the rain beginning to fall against the window, the Cardinal digging his fingers into the hair which had been cut off him and which lay in a thick mat at the foot of the examination chair.

*. . . to find an amulet, a black relic, a chicken's claw, a snake replica . . . he could have got this gift of his from just about anywhere, and even if the men of the Enlightenment rationalise the whole thing with formulas and prove the Evil One to be a fiction, it still doesn't explain the fact that he has thrown a whole monastery into anarchy. . .*

By now del Moro was stabbing needles into him with all the force he could muster; into his back, his armpits, the soles of his feet. Blood was oozing from dozens of sores all over his body. The pain was excruciating. He started to cry and jerk convulsively against the straps as the needles dug half a centimetre deep into his flesh. Very calmly del Moro fastened Hercule's head to the back of the chair and turned to the Cardinal, "Can you find anything, Rivero . . . an amulet, a devil's cross?"

"Nothing so far."

With a sense of horror that near rendered him unconscious, Hercule watched the inquisitor walk over to the laboratory bench, and clearly heard his thoughts: *This bit of theatre will soon be over . . . the men ought to be with Schuster at any moment . . .*

That was when he knew they intended to kill him. And not only him, but his benefactor Schuster, too. In a moment of devastating lucidity he understood it all: that, in this context, his gift was of no import, whether it could be explained or not wasn't of the least consequence. The important thing was not even whether it existed. But that it existed as a possibility.

*Let me go!* he screamed right into del Moro's gaping mind.

On hearing this soundless cry that echoed inside him seven times as loud as an ordinary scream, the inquisitor almost fell to the floor. During his thirty years of working as an exorcist he had never experienced anything like it. With the sweat pouring down his face, he turned to Rivero, "There's no doubt about it, the monster is possessed! Let us, in the name of God, put an end to this!"

Hercule lost consciousness. And this, as it turned out, saved his life. For it was his unconscious body that afforded del Moro and Rivero the brief respite they needed in order to find out what was happening, a matter of extreme importance. In a building a street away, four novices – forerunners of the late-nineteenth-century *sapinieri* or *Sodalitiorum Pium*, the name later given to the Vatican's secret service – had just been sent out on a mission to silence the chief witness to this affair.

**L**ying on the bunk in his cell, Julian Schuster opened his eyes and looked around to see where the voice that had woken him up was coming from. There was no-one there. Just his own doubts lurking treacherously in the dark.

But then he heard it again: the phantom voice.

*Hercule?* he asked. *Are you there?*

*Soon dead . . .* came the reply.

The message he received was scarcely louder than a hum. He listened intently, but now all he could hear was a faint murmur rising from one of the downstairs corridors where the Order's officials had their offices.

Then he heard the voice again, much clearer this time.

*Schuster*, it said, *we must get out of here . . .*

*Hercule*, he replied, *is that really you?*

The answer was instantaneous. *Hurry . . . the men are closing in . . .*

Schuster got up, on legs so shaky he could barely stand.

*What men?*

*Four of them . . . in this building . . .*

Again the brother looked round the room as if hoping to see his ward there; but the only things to be found were the glum disconsolate grey of his barrack walls and a resurgence of doubts he could scarcely ward off.

*What men are you talking about?*

*Doesn't matter . . . hurry . . .*

The novices selected by Cardinal Rivero for this mission were inside the building, and no more than fifty steps away. One was in the downstairs corridor of offices, and at this very moment was approaching the attic staircase. There he stopped for a brief second and felt the length of copper wire that lay coiled into a snare in his girdle pocket.

*Hurry, for God's sake*, the voice inside Schuster said. *Take the left-hand corridor. At its far end you'll find a door leading to a closet . . . if you want to stay alive, do as I tell you.*

It was dark in the corridor. Schuster could hear footsteps on the staircase, and the breathing of someone approaching. Twenty metres along the corridor, to his right, he found the door and slipped soundlessly into the space behind it. It was some kind of a storeroom, crammed full with Mass crucifixes and vats of incense.

*On the floor there's a carpet . . . roll it aside . . . you'll find a hatch . . . open it and climb down . . . they're coming closer.*

*How do you know all this?* he asked.

*I can see, no, feel it . . . so can you, if you try . . .*

But Schuster didn't need to try, because the voice, the phantom mind – hovering in a state between sleep and waking in the small area drafted between death and unconsciousness where a final step is so easily taken, but impossible to revoke – was still functioning. Irrespective of time or of space, through walls and hallways, through the meandering corridors of this stronghold, inside the walls of which Loyola had once observed a world he could no longer understand, for a second in time Julian Schuster connected with the consciousness of one of the young novices who'd been sent out to kill him. For the briefest of moments Schuster found himself inside the mind of the novice, discovering there a young man who, half a generation later, was to make a name for himself during the controversies surrounding the first Vatican Council and win over the Polish and Lithuanian officials in the decree of papal infallibility. Schuster didn't understand how he could possibly be aware of all this, since it belonged to the future. Nor could he understand how he knew that this man's sheer cold-bloodedness would one day make him one of the most feared men of his time. Furthermore, that he was of Polish origin, Wittold Kossak by name, but known to his colleagues as *"el Lobo"*, "the wolf". What he did know with absolute clarity, however, was that this boy, just as Hercule had warned, was out to kill him.

*My God*, he thought, scared stiff by this revelation, *where on earth are you?*

*Same place you left me . . .*

Exactly as the voice had foretold, Schuster found the hatch in the floor. Now he could hear distinct sounds coming from the corridor, someone tearing open the door to his room, then uttering a cry of disappointment. In only a matter of moments, they would go on searching the corridor, yank open locked doors and discover the room at the far end.

An iron ring had been screwed into the centre of the hatch. With an effort he managed to pull it open. Beneath him was a ladder fastened to the wall, leading down to a food lift.

*Climb down into the shaft,* the voice said*, crawl into the lift and unhook the cable . . .*

*And if it won't take my weight?* he wondered. *Will this be the last thing I'll ever remember?*

Footsteps were approaching from the corridor. He could hear men's voices whispering in the dark, followed by someone hushing them. With a prayer to the powers that be, he lowered himself down into the shaft, opened the repair hatch and crept into the lift-cage. Cold sweat breaking out on his forehead, he unhooked the cage cable and with a jerk felt the cage begin to fall, faster and faster, until the brake slides caught hold and levelled off its acceleration.

Landing gently against the springs in the cellar, convinced that it was thanks only to a pure oversight on Fortune's part the lift had borne his weight, he climbed out of the cage and half ran through a corridor dimly lit by tallow candles.

*There's a door at the other end,* the voice said. *There's a key on top of the door frame, open the door, and go up the stairs . . .*

By now Schuster had ceased to be amazed by the accuracy of the instructions he was receiving; he found the key in the specified place, and without asking any questions followed all further instructions to the letter. Climbed some stairs, turned left, retreated down a corridor, hid to order in a window-bay, held his breath, stood still when needed, until finally he found himself behind the back door leading into the examination room where he'd left his ward some four hours before.

On the other side of the wall he could hear someone knocking on the door, and then a voice – that of Kossak, the Polish novice – explaining that Schuster had vanished, was nowhere to be found, though they'd searched the entire building. The voices rose agitatedly inside the room, a door slammed, and the conversation continued in the antechamber.

*Go in*, he heard the phantom voice whisper, *take me away from this place . . . and then get out, as fast as you can . . .*

The sight that met Schuster made him think of the morning, scarcely a year before, when he'd found the boy in the madhouse cellar. Unconscious, bound, and seated in something reminiscent of a barber's chair, blood streaming from the open sores on the disfigured body. An awl, dug some decimetre deep into his flesh, stuck out from his back.

Schuster released him from the straps, carried the featherweight body in his arms over to the back door. In the antechamber the quarrel was still going on, he heard the Cardinal's agitated voice. It was only a matter of minutes before they would come back in the room.

He carried the boy a hundred steps before laying him down by a door which led out to one of the alleyways. Hercule was regaining consciousness.

Where is there any Divine justice for this creature? Schuster thought. Where was their God just now, when they needed Him the most?

He heard the boy panting like a consumptive. Saw him open his eyes and look vaguely about him before settling his gaze on him. Carefully, Schuster wiped away the blood with a handkerchief, and managed to get him on to his feet. Pointed to the back door. Limping, the boy ran off down the alleyway.

Later, Hercule Barfuss would reproach himself for not having used all his powers to prevent Schuster from going back to the examination room. But perhaps he'd already made up his mind?

Less than twenty-four hours later Schuster was found by a shepherd, in a vineyard out at Trastevere. Vultures were pecking at his eyes. Round his neck, as if drawn on in ink, was a very thin cord. In the carabiniere's protocol it was described as "the body of an unidentified male, strangled with a snare". He'd been found naked save for a small Indian amulet tied to a strap round his waist. Leaflets asked the general public to come forward with any information that might lead to the arrest of the murderer.

But by then Hercule, ignorant of Schuster's fate, was already far away, unaware that he too was being hunted or that there was now a price on his head.

IV

"**R**oll up! Roll up, ladies and gentlemen! Thrilling entertainment for only two centesimi! We've got just about everything you've ever dreamed of, and maybe more besides, some things being beyond the human imagination. What are the Seven Wonders of the World compared with the Eighth, and Ninth and Tenth? No-one ever leaves Barnaby Wilson's Roadshow disappointed.

"Pardon me, Your Ladyship, what did you say? What is it we have on show? Well, what don't we have on show! We've got Brutus' bloody dagger, Napoleon's confirmation suit, St Veronica's authentic Handkerchief, the golden dish on which John the Baptist's head was served up on a bed of crushed rice. We have several beasts and extinct species of animal, we have three of the infant Jesus' milk teeth, a bottle of the Mother of God's distilled tears at the price of ten lire a drop. A hydra, a dodo, as well as a great anteater from the Virgin Forests of Brazil, where no man has ever set foot, or at least, has not returned alive. Ladies and gentlemen! If nothing of all this takes your fancy, then at least have your portrait painted in the latest fashion from the East End of London – as a heliograph. In Hermann Bioly's studio your portrait will be drawn in light, your soul will be fastened to a glass pane by collodium, and you'll be immortalised. What, still not convinced? Well, then we've got something to suit all tastes. Do you perhaps suffer from some illness? The Moorish pharmacist Ibrahim, King of Liniments and Emperor of All Tinctures, whose mixtures are famous all over Christendom, has just joined our travelling show. The Grand Duke of Baden-Baden was himself cured by his famous ointments. The King of Saxony, whose eczema of the feet all but precipitated a war with the Austrians, was cured as if by magic by his incomparable footbath. In his apothecary shop Ibrahim the Moor can offer you love pills, invisibility pills, pills for virtuousness, pills for immortality, pills for consolation in nameless sorrows and pills for imaginary aches and pains; besides which, we have Professor Steinert's rejuvenation cure and Brown's infamous treatment by opposites, which cures everything from corns to inflamed heart sores. Welcome in to us, ladies and gentlemen, don't hesitate, the next show starts at a quarter past the hour . . ."

Here Barnaby Wilson pretended to lose his voice, coughing extravagantly just as a glass of water, filled to the brim, material-ised in his hand. Through a slit in his mask he drained it to the dregs, and at the same time as the liquid disappeared in little sips, the glass itself, strangely enough, also disappeared, centimetre by centimetre, before, after a loud burp on the circus director's part, it went up in smoke.

"Have you ever, ladies and gentlemen," he went on, "heard of the giraffe? Six metres tall, spotted like a fly agaric toadstool, with a dragon's neck . . .what are a steamboat or a locomotive compared with the sensations awaiting you at Barnaby Wilson's Roadshow?"

His monologue was suddenly interrupted by a violent explo-sion in one of the covered wagons parked in a circle of about a hundred ells in diameter beside the market place, thereby making the circus area invisible to the curious crowds. Feigning horror, he put his hand to his heart.

"What we have just heard an example of", he said in a con-spiratorial whisper, "is the Saxon phlogistonist Bruno von Salza's hair-raising experiment with lead sugar, arsenic butter and powder of zinc. With the aid of phlogistonised air he can blow a cathedral sky-high, make gold out of all kinds of base materials, get matter moving to the point where the dead will arise from their graves and cut and run for sheer horror . . . Allow me also to introduce Leopold the Savage, caught with a lasso in Numidia's endless desert, Gandalalfo Bonaparte, bastard son of the great Napoleon,

Miranda Bellaflor – the girl with four tongues – or the Ligurian omnivore Jean-Paul who swallows coins of various denominations and spits them out in any order you ask him to. Show us a sample of what you can do, Jean!"

With a discreet bow a tall, very thin gentleman, disfigured by a big outgrowth of hair covering half his face, took his place beside Barnaby Wilson on the little platform from which the circus director was addressing his public. In one hand he held a glass jar filled with live bees. Very carefully he unscrewed its lid. Placed his mouth against the opening – his gape was so wide he was said to be able to swallow cannon balls – and the public could clearly see the insects flying into it.

The Ligurian omnivore pursed his lips, replaced the lid, and then, calm as if it were a question of the apothecary Ibrahim's pills against nameless sorrows, noisily swallowed the bees, one after the other.

After which he, at a signal from Barnaby Wilson, reopened his immense abyss of a mouth so that the public could see with its own eyes that the insects were gone, and with another bow, to the crowd's undisguised delight, cleared his throat and spat out the bees, one by one, so that to deafening applause the tiny winged creatures flew away on the mountain breeze down to the bay where the town of Nice was bathed in the red of the setting sun.

Satisfied, through his mask Barnaby Wilson surveyed the gathering with his one eye. By now several hundred curious persons had congregated in a crescent around him: women, men, old folk, children.

A little further forward to his right, he saw an elderly gentleman, clad in a frock coat and with a funny-looking shock of thick grey hair falling in waves on to a pair of somewhat feminine shoulders.

"Good sir, step forward, and we'll reward you with a free ticket," he said in a honeyed voice, "and allow me to demonstrate yet another of our show's sensations: the Emperor of China's very latest fad, telekinetic fluid magnetism that works at a distance!"

The man appeared flattered at having been selected for an experiment with the Chinese Emperor's latest toy, and as he, proudly, if a trifle hesitantly, approached the platform, Barnaby Wilson took out a Leyden jar from the pocket of his baggy nautical waistcoat, had him stop right there on the steps and, in a flash, electrified him. "Fluid magnetism, the core of all secrets," he exclaimed, affecting a theatrical tremor in his childlike voice, all the while furtively rubbing a glass wand behind his back against a piece of chamois leather. And before the bashful gentleman in the frock coat had time to react, the circus director stood once more before him. Moving mysteriously as a mediaeval magician, mumbling formulas in an incomprehensible tongue that in fact was none other than Welsh from the islands in Cardigan Bay, he waved his hands over the man's head. Much to his pleasure, he heard his audience sigh raptuously as all manner of lightweight objects circulating in the air began sticking to the man's frock coat: leaves, particles of dust, scraps of paper, even two very-much-alive bees that the Ligurian omnivore had spat out a few minutes earlier. Little lightning flashes flew off the frock coat and a decimetre or so above the crown of the man's head his wig was hovering freely in the air like a greying halo, sparkling and electrified.

"Behold the Eleventh Wonder of the World!" Wilson exclaimed triumphantly. "The magnetic fluid known as electricity, the latest thing from the Emperor's court in China. By this singular power cities will soon be lit up, turning night into day, horses will be abolished in favour of electric cabs, messages be sent in a matter of minutes at distances of more than a hundred miles, and the face of God will be illuminated across the heavens as He looks down in amazement at the inventiveness of the being He once created at random out of a lump of clay."

Flushing red all over his face, the man made a grab for his hovering wig and disappeared at a run out of the market place. The audience shouted for joy and inside the nearest tent Lucretius III lit the lamps for his complicated phantasmagoria.

At a given signal, from out of the murky tent opening by the ticket window, to the genuine alarm of the public and the feigned alarm of Barnaby Wilson, now materialised a thirty-foot monster squirting fire to the accompaniment of the circus's ill-tuned brass band: the so-called Giraffe, so imaginatively described by the circus director a moment before.

The audience withdrew in alarm, but just as panic threatened to break out, the scene changed into a phantasmagoria of Marat's dreary bathroom with that famous revolutionary floating lifeless in an enamelled hip bath full of water.

"Ladies and gentleman," shouted Barnaby Wilson. "For a mere two centesimi the dead will rise again and archangels appear in reality . . ."

A new murmur went through the audience as Lucretius showed another spectacle, this time representing a deathly pale Robespierre who, a flintlock pistol in his hand, took a couple of steps towards the circus director and looked as if he was going to shoot him in the back. But at a sign from Wilson, Robespierre turned into a centaur and galloped back into the tent, to the accompaniment of two evil-sounding explosions from the phlogistonist Bruno von Salza's powder-stained tent.

"Have no fear, ladies and gentlemen," continued the smiling Wilson, "for two centesimi we promise you something more. You will be protected against any designs the ghosts may have on you."

One last presentation remained before the circus opened its ticket office to receive, this evening as on all previous evenings, hundreds of the curious to fill to the last seat its tent outside Nice. In the tent opening through which the centaur had disappeared stood an exceedingly pitiable being, scarcely three foot tall with a misshapen, outsized head disfigured by stony calluses. Stripped to the waist he let the audience take a good look at his furry back, at the little foreshortened arms that resembled roots, the cavities in his skin and the bones and condyles protruding criss-cross from his skeleton as if imprisoned in his body and struggling to escape. He was dressed in knee-length socks, a kilt from the Scottish Highlands, and his face was covered by a colourful Venetian-style cat mask.

"Allow me to present our latest attraction," Wilson said in a voice scarcely able to conceal his personal pride at this sensation which, in only a few months, had beaten all conceivable attendance records along the Ligurian coast. "Sir Hercules from the little known Barefoot clan, the monster from the Scottish Highlands who recites the Bible as fluently as a priest and can read your innermost thoughts!"


All that spring the Scottish mind-reader Hercules Barefoot, not knowing that the Cardinal's men were on his heels, had been fulfilling his duties as the circus's chief attraction. His telepathic powers were enabling him to reveal the colour of a lady's underwear, pull cards out of a tarot pack at will, treat the audience to mnemonic numbers that could only be explained by some dubious alliance with the supernatural, declare people's most intimate secrets and describe homes he'd never set foot in.

On a French clavichord Sir Hercules also played operatic airs that volunteers in the audience had been exhorted to hum under their breath, he meanwhile, to make assurance doubly sure, being sworn deaf and dumb by Barnaby Wilson, having put rubber plugs into his ear cavities and got down into a locked beer barrel – all to disperse any suspicion of fraud.

He also treated them to yet another sensation, playing with his feet, so vividly that the audience's collective longing materialised in the notes before dissolving in a tremolo of unrelieved yearnings that fell over them like a tearful cloudburst which all could feel but none could see.

On the circus poster that to Wilson's undisguised delight filled the tent to its last standing room seven days a week wherever they went, he was shown in his carnival mask, grasping a magician's wand between two toes.

His act was always the last to come on – after Lucretius III's Jacobin phantasmagories, after Leopold the Savage's breakneck trapeze acts, after Leon Montebianco's tales from a fabulous past, and after the Turkish poet who, scorning all pain like a fakir, had invited a member of the audience to use his scorching hot legs to light his cigar. At that point Barnaby Wilson, clad in a conjuror's coat spangled with the signs of the zodiac, would step into the ring and hold a brief discourse on the inner world of the deaf; about their sight, sharper than on those of us who can see; about their fantastic ability to lip-read and about Sir Edmund Booth's vision of the deaf and dumb one day having a state of their own in America.

It was to America Hercule had told Wilson he was headed when they had bumped into each other in a Liverpool pub. Hercule had a ticket to America in his back pocket and, at fourpence a sentence, had been just about to read the secret thoughts of a dressmaker's assistant. Only through a great effort and several hours' persuasion did Wilson induce him to postpone his voyage and instead take on a job with the circus where he could show off his wonderful gift in public, Wilson alleged to the crowd.

After his soliloquy Wilson would bow, the lights would dim and Lyra the Infant Harpist, climbing on to a stool that came up to her chest, stroked the strings of a harp five times as large as herself, causing the astounded audience to fall silent. When the lights went up again, Sir Hercules stood in the centre of the ring holding a pack of cards between his toes.

This was the beginning of a circus number that made the public suspect that higher powers were having an influence on show business. A trifle shyly the masked thought-reader would go up to someone in the front row, and Barnaby Wilson, two paces behind him, asked that person to take a card out of the pack, carefully remember its number and suit and replace it while Sir Hercules shut his eyes. After this the mind-reader would lean forward, put the pack on a small jacaranda table, straighten himself and turn the cards over, one by one, with his sensitive toes. Finally, with a movement as agile as it was nonchalant, he would hold aloft the correct one. This trick didn't arouse much enthusiasm in an audience still assimilating the Ligurian omnivore's ability to swallow coins of various denominations and spit them out again in any order he was asked to, or to Lucretius III's last phantasmagoria, so true to life, of the astounding Giraffe. What followed, on the other hand, aroused wonder even in the most confirmed sceptic.

Wilson asked someone in the audience to think of something, anything at all, an object, another person, a scent, a taste, a joke he'd heard, and to concentrate on this thought.

"I shall now permit Sir Hercules to use his clairvoyant powers to transfer this thought to me," he went on in his childish voice, with a sweeping gesture of his coat.

An intense silence descended on the ring. The Scottish mind-reader seemed to focus entirely on the chosen member of the audience, nodding to himself, as if memorising everything he could pick up on his magical wavelength, before turning to Barnaby with a humble bow.

The ringmaster, apparently affected by the tension, trembled and shuddered. Not until about a minute later did he raise his hand as if signalling that the message had been transmitted. Whereupon he turned to the volunteer and exclaimed, "Sir Hercules has transferred your innermost thoughts to me, as angels do!" And instantly announced what it was the selected person had just been thinking about. His fiancée, his daily bread, his hardships or his aches and pains. Nine times out of ten the volunteer – astoundingly – confirmed it. Or, in other cases, put up such a display of obstinate denial of his shameful secret that the audience, which only moments ago had been massively sceptical, saw quite clearly that Wilson was in fact telling the simple truth.

Sometimes he would have someone turn a book's pages at random, select a sentence and read it silently to himself before Sir Hercules transferred it telepathically. Similarly, he read off selected passages from the Bible, a psalm someone was reciting to themselves, a shopkeeper's receipt, or the precise contents of a fifty-year-old love letter on the person of an old crone in the audience. There was talk of a possible connection with the so-called heliograph that Hermann Bioly was demonstrating nearby in his studio. But others maintained the whole thing was a put-up job from start to finish, and that the audience volunteers were in fact being paid to feign or simulate their shame. Rumours spread that evil forces were at work, and in several of the villages where the circus pitched its tents the priest forbade his congregation to visit it.

Another of the acts that caused certain complications concerned what the audience carried about their persons. Wilson asked a volunteer to think of what he had in his trouser pocket or in his bag; instantly, using his toes, the kilted Scottish mind-reader set about chalking up the objects' names on a blackboard. More than once this sibylline tour de force gave rise to embarrassing situations when Sir Hercules showed up a piece of stolen silver in a policeman's pocket, pornographic cards in the brim of a chaplain's hat, or a bunch of billets-doux from a married woman, hidden in the knapsack of her blushing sixteen-year-old lover, who also, as it happened, was the nephew of her husband, the town mayor.

Usually he rounded off his act with a triumphant flourish on the French clavichord. In his unsatisfied longing for Henriette Vogel his renderings of the pieces Wilson had asked the audience to hum under their breaths (whether a lively quadrille or a bombastic march tune from the soul of an English colonel who was passing through the town) always sounded like love lyrics transposed as music, and unleashed in the audience such a surge of emotion that several men who had come to the show were moved to propose to their beloveds.

But by then the crowds were in ecstasy, and no-one was listening to Barnaby Wilson's concluding words about Lamarck's theories of humans having the same origins as animals, and that everyone could become a mind-reader if they wanted to, this having been at some point in the past the only means of communication before spoken language had been developed.

Meanwhile, Sir Hercules had left the ring, eager to get to his evening lesson in Wilson's carriage.

Barnaby Wilson's inexhaustible knowledge of the world's mysteries had brought the two together as teacher and pupil. For Hercule the little cyclops with whom he shared his gift became a ticket of admission to everything he had ever wanted to know. He could listen for hours on end to the extraordinary things Wilson, without even opening his mouth, would tell him about, or read from one of his four-language encyclopedias. The circus director was familiar with every intellectual tradition and every historical epoch; with technology no less than philosophy, with prose as much as poetry. But his predilection was for scientific speculation, especially if he thought it could improve the human condition. Surrounded by folios, tomes, books, sensational articles cut out of gazettes and gazette posters, in an ocean of circus tickets, plans, maps, letters from fans and heliograph portraits of his artistes, Wilson also told him about the ideas of Saint-Simon and Jeremy Bentham. To the minds of these thinkers, he explained, everyone was of equal value, the rich should give to the poor, there were no rulers, and if there were, they'd been chosen by the people. A woman was worth no less than a man, children were never beaten, and a heavy scent of blossoms was settling over the earth, just as in the dawn of Creation.

Wilson also gave him an emotive account of the ideas of Charles Fourier, the great visionary from Lyons, who had predicted an ideal world that would last for eighty thousand years, eight thousand of which were to be the perfectly harmonious era when mankind would live in peace and the deformed never suffer humiliations; when the North Pole would become milder than Mediterranean beaches. Then, Wilson assured him, the ocean would lose its saline quality and the lakes would fill with lemonade. In this ideal world, which, according to all known calculations, would actually fall within their own lifetimes, there would be thirty-seven million poets on a level with Homer, nine million mathematicians to match the great Isaac Newton and seven million dramatists worthy to bear the name Molière. Fourier's theories, Wilson thought, were of a lucidity of which history knew no parallel. Incorruptible in their stringency, they were divided up in an exemplary way into such sub-headings as Prelude, C#-lude, Citer-pause, Trance-Appendix and, not least, the daring Utter-lounge which with breakneck logic showed how in the future mankind would attain to immortality by taking reserve organs from animals. It was the best of all conceivable worlds, he assured him. People lived in phalangesteries, exactly 1652 persons in each, lived off the earth's produce, shared all property and held deliberations in the village market place.

Forgetful of time and space, Barnaby Wilson went on embroidering his pipe dream of a happier world, of Robert Owen's model factories in Scotland, of the socialist villages in Auvergne and the Bourbonnais, where the master's theories were already being put into practice; told Hercule about the Luddite revolt in England, where factory slaves together, sad to say, with eminent poets had trashed the machines they supposed to have been invented merely in order to render them superfluous, though this, the master assured him, was not the case. On the contrary, these machines held the key to a happier future by increasing prosperity and leisure time. The little cyclops spoke at length of the steam cars which, each containing a family, would soon run without need of rails, along paved streets, on endless Sunday outings to the mountains of Savoy. He described the fantastic animals in the African savannahs, which he was planning to gather into a menagerie next season and where the main attraction would be a striped horse called a zebra. He told of the houses of ice which undaunted explorers had recently discovered on the northernmost Atlantic islands, and the gigantic pyramids which giants had built in olden times on the banks of the Nile.

Further, he lost himself in thoughts about Maupertuis' theories of natural selection and Buffon's hypothesis of the creation of the world, so blasphemous it could only be whispered into people's ears where no priests could be listening, or else transmitted

130

telepathically. Wilson explained to an astonished Hercule Barfuss that the earth was ever so much older than the six thousand years the Wernerians had worked out with the help of the Bible. It was at least 75,000 years old, and Buffon, what was more, had provided evidence that man and ape had the same forefather, thus proving unequivocally that animals too have souls and that a man's diet should therefore consist entirely of vegetables.

In a carriage beside his own Wilson had also installed a laboratory for his numerous experiments with elements and automata. In this temple of scientific whims was an indescribable muddle of barometers, theodolites, reagent test tubes, dismantled machinery, horologia, stellar charts and clockwork dolls that could walk and talk. There were even copies of Leibniz's and Pascal's adding machines, as well as designs for Babbage's famous differential and analytical automaton, precursors of late-twentieth-century computers.

In a drawing made in his twilight years, Hercule would show Wilson in his laboratory, clad in a heat-insulating suit, puffing on his long Turkish hookah, a pendulum swinging from his other hand – a significant drawing of this brooding circus director whose zest for experiment knew no bounds.

In the past, Wilson had made serious attempts to construct a *perpetuum mobile* built on the same principles as a musical box. Moreover he had laid the foundations for a steam kitchen and was secretly polishing up an invention intended to illuminate the entire circus area with the aid of hundreds of Leyden jars connected to glass filaments. He would go on to make successful experiments with hot-air balloons, as well as inventing, quite by accident, dynamite, a formula he promptly destroyed when he realised its potential uses for warfare and bloodshed.

Hercule was dizzy with admiration. It was with a child's open mind he listened to his tutor, and this with only one ulterior motive: that education and these inventions were to be the path that should lead him to love's goal.


Henriette Vogel was still the centre of Hercule's life. It was for her sake he had withstood all those hardships, for her he had survived the attempts on his life, and it was for her he was searching as untiringly as any convert persisted in his new faith. In each village the circus came to he was on the lookout for her, always searching in the memories of people he ran into. He refused to accept his poor prospects, disdained the ever weakening odds, merely raising his eyebrows in reply to anyone who commiserated with him on his search, as if at a joke in extremely bad taste.

On the rare occasions when, even so, doubt beset him, it would be Barnaby Wilson who relit the flame of hope. For over and above his interest in modern science he too nurtured the cult of love inspired by the courtly poets. Love, he used to say, was not just the meaning of life, to the extent that it had spread its tentacles through existence, that it was the very precondition for the sun to rise and the stars to keep their positions in the sky. Proof of which he would declare was to be found in the works of the divinely inspired poets.

Many years later, Hercule Barfuss would remember Wilson as his saviour; for this was truly the right medicine. The poetry books he borrowed from him had opened the door to a world where love could be enjoyed undiluted.

He was flabbergasted that poets should be able to chisel out the most beautiful words from verbal granite, and in passing could fill even the spaces between the lines with meaning. He swallowed their poems whole, without a thought as to how he could digest them; sucked them dry of all content, ruminated fanatically on them, swallowed them again, and tenderised them in the seven stomachs of his own languishings. Heine he learned by heart, fell sick of Keatsian and Byronic fever, and read Jean-Paul's novels with a sense of their lifting the veils of paradise, if only slightly. On Wilson's advice he devoted a month to the libertarian von Kleist, and passed a harrowing night of love with Novalis. He suffered with Schiller, shuddered with Hoffmann, and was amazed at how de Musset could so convert pain into words that it turned into its opposite and became pleasurable beyond all reason. In Goethe's verses he discovered an excitement words could not explain, or only in the empty interstices where love lay in ambush, in the guise of blank pages. He wept buckets with Hölderlin, sighed with the Schlegel brothers and rejoiced ecstatically with Pushkin. Formed a lifelong alliance with Lamartine, and was so overwhelmed by emotions by Leopardi that it put him in bed for a fortnight with a migraine.

It wasn't unusual for Barnaby Wilson to find Hercule in his carriage half dead for lack of sleep after a night spent in the company of the poets, in a wild thicket of amorous trochees, ankle-deep in a flood of his own tears, sunk in one of Oehlenschläger's or some other poet's convoluted suites, just then in fashion. This, he'd say later, was the time when it became possible to find rhymes for his love for his Henriette.


Following in the same poetic footsteps as those he just then admired, tourists had begun to find their way to the Italian coast – Englishmen inspired by the travels of Lord Byron or Shelley, Germans by those of the great Johan Wolfgang von Goethe. Though it was still long before the mass tourism of the twentieth century, Barnaby Wilson, whose nose for profit was surpassed only by his insight into the sciences of the wise, decided that his circus should camp at Genoa. It was late August and the town was filled with travellers, among whom Hercule hoped to find some trace of Henriette.

Protected by the mask he, on Barnaby Wilson's advice, had begun wearing, he took long walks through the town, looking into the faces of northerners burned by the Italian sun, at the men in cotton suits holding forth in taverns, at the women in white crinoline dresses strolling along the promenade, fluttering like butterflies in the shade of their little parasols. Himself, unnoticed, he fumbled in a fog of thoughts formed in some unknown dimension within the passers-by, townspeople, tourists, craftsmen, burghers and shop assistants. He plumbed the girls' worries, groped merchants' inner accounts and overheard the plans of pickpockets. Turned inside out, the world bared its entrails. He needed a sign, however insignificant; just some memory preserved by someone who had once met her.

There were times when he really thought he was on her trail – the quiet rustle of her legs in some stranger's memory; air purified by her breath; her heartbeat, tremulous as an animal's. Then he would beat to windward through his cherished dreams, swim through the treacle of life's fragments, through history's murmur, like falling rain, until finally, in some market place, in an alleyway, in the great crowds, he realised it was all just his imagination playing tricks on him. In the same instant, he felt the ground slip from under his feet. The world, he felt, was far too big for him ever to find her . . .

Melancholia, the age's new malady, assailed him. For days on end he would lie on the bunk in his carriage, staring up at its roof. Sleep eluding him, he sought consolation in love lyrics. By the end of summer this had gone so far he had begun to neglect his circus duties. Not that Wilson had the heart to reproach him for errors that had their rootlets in his love. But when the audience noticeably began to fall off – either because Sir Hercules Barefoot was turning up too late or too early, or sometimes because he was reading poetry on a beach promenade with the moon for a lamp, and didn't turn up at all – then Wilson found it necessary to assert his authority and insist he bring his hot-air balloon down to earth. Whereupon Hercule returned to his duties, but this time firmly resolved not to rest for a minute until he had again found Henriette.

Never before had he performed with such authority. He could describe to an unknown member of the audience their whole life. He created a sensation with a new mnemonic act, writing down backwards the 180-digit numbers picked out of a book of mathematical examples that someone in the audience, at Barnaby Wilson's behest, had read silently to themselves, number by number. He even described other volunteers' repressed memories or ones that lay so far back in time as to have really fallen into oblivion; or else made up new ones for them, so plausible they could only assume they'd been forgotten and were grateful to believe they had now recalled them. Not for a moment did he relax his vigilance.

Perhaps it was this sharpening of his faculty, born of the need of his search, directed towards a single goal, that blinded him to all other dangers. At least that's how it would seem afterwards, when he became aware of how deeply he had flung those around him into misfortune.


Almost a year had gone by since the events in Rome, and still Hercule knew nothing of Schuster's fate. Sometimes the Jesuit haunted his dreams, but, if so, always faceless and mute as himself.

134

One morning, he was behind one of these merciful smokescreens when he found a message on his carriage steps. It lacked a sender, nor would it ever be cleared up who had left it there. The note described Schuster's fate; how he'd been found at Trastevere strangled with a noose. And it ended with a couple of words warning the addressee not to try to discover who had written the letter.

Embittered by the news, he wandered the city streets, beside himself with grief and the hatred he again felt stirring inside him.

Engulfed by this internal gloom, he failed to notice what was going on around him – that night was falling, that the stars had come out, and that the town had gone to its rest. Drifting helplessly about on the inland sea of his despair, blinded by weeping, he tottered about the empty streets, seeing nothing, feeling only this boundless sorrow and fathomless hatred. At the docks he tripped over rubbish, bumped against warehouse walls and crates, fell into holes in the paving, got up again cursing his existence and his fate. Tears coursing down his face he wandered through aeons of despair.

In this way, without noticing it, he reached the town's outskirts. Only as he approached a village where the dogs threatened with their barking did he pull himself together, make his way back to the circus and come to a halt on a hillside with a view over the town. It was a warm night, he would later remember. The heat, dripping with humidity, was like a massive block. The night's secrets filed past, the dreams people dreamed, the anxiety that kept the unhappy ones awake, the insomniacs' prayers for repose. Far below him he could see a lantern on Barnaby Wilson's caravan, and he wondered if his friend felt as uneasy as he.

The salt smell of the sea reached him, the somnambulistic waves grazing the beach and crashing against breakwaters, two fishing boats putting in at a quay, a schooner, sails reefed approaching at the speed of the dawn. But something else, too, was silently approaching in the dark.

Sensing this impending danger, he began running down towards the circus. But before he could get there he saw the night suddenly lit up by spurting flames as one by one the circus caravans were being set ablaze.

He felt his friends' mortal terror, how their souls passed before him before expiring with a last prayer on their lips.

He collapsed on the road. The Cardinal's men, he realised, were behind this, just as they had been behind Schuster's death. It was they who had hunted him, but it was fate that was immolating his friends.

All night he lay there on the road, shedding tears of grief and hatred, crying for himself and his atrocious fate, over his Henriette, over the castle in the air of their happiness and their house of playing cards, now in ruins. This was the end, he thought, never again would he be able to pick himself up. This time all hope was lost.

V

The world consists of tremors, vibrations that flow through the universe linking humans with brute matter. You don't believe me, but this is why you can comprehend my thoughts at this very moment, just as Swedenborg, in Lapland, could understand the thoughts of Madame de Marteville's deceased husband and was able to find her lost receipts there. Swedenborg, that great man, has himself explained all this. A long time ago, he writes, in the Garden of Eden, people had no need of speech to make themselves understood. Adam and Eve understood each other through their thoughts' 'fluidum'. What need of human speech in paradise? There were no grammatical misunderstandings, no double-bottomed verbal values, no stammerings, lispings or speech defects . . . Adam was the first telepathist! But after him came our Fall. When the serpent gave Man the apple he also gave him the spoken word. Long long ago, it was, we fell, my friend. But humans can again immerse themselves in intuitive knowledge. Swedenborg, the great visionary, also stressed the importance of respiration to being able to fall into magnetic sleep. We must let go of our surroundings, he writes, concentrate on prayer until the checks on our breathing set in, the fainting begins, and we are transported to the spirit world.

You can comprehend thoughts, Herr Barfuss. I know you're reading my thoughts at this very moment! I, as you know, speak with

139

*the spirits . . . In my youth, in Stockholm, that terrible Sodom, it was then Swedenborg personally initiated me into his doctrine of Correspondences: explained how the universe is made up of series and degrees between the interjacent determinators. There Anima, the soul's highest function, is to be in contact with our Lord God, the all-embracing* Fluidum Spirituosum . . .

Countess Tavastestierna, his prospective helper, straightened out her pillows and lit one of her perfumed black cigars. He comprehended her very clearly. She was making a real effort to get every nuance across to him.

*What are thoughts?* he had asked.

*Nothing but fluid undulations, my friend!*

*And what about speech?*

*Tremors conveyed to the mouth, which turn into air vibrations, which turn into sound. Believe me, thought is the real speech, infinitely more perfect than the larynx's coarse articulation. And that is why it can also be heard by the angels! You may well be an angel yourself, Herr Barfuss, though your earthly form is anything but angelic, but rather demonic, repugnant, in fact . . . But allow me to finish: the angels' speech to us, too, is pure thought. You know, Herr Barfuss, don't you, that I can hear the voices of the little angels, and even the voices of the spirits. I cannot hear the thoughts of men, apart from yours, of which you so generously allow me to partake. But I can hear an angel's speech as clearly as a peasant can hear a sermon at Candlemas. It's only at card games the angels refuse to help me. "That's where we draw the line, we can't help you, m'lady," they say. So that's where you come into it. You won't let me down this evening, will you? There's such a terrible lot at stake. And in return, tomorrow the spirits have promised to tell me where you can find your girl.*

*Please, oh please, do tell me where she is . . .*

*I'm sorry, you must think more clearly, sharply. I can't hear you all that well. On the other hand I can hear perfectly clearly the spirit voices in this room; like now! There's one sitting on my shoulder, can't you see him?*

He stared, but saw nothing. Only the Countess sitting up in her bed in her nightdress, on Østergade, here in Copenhagen, with the coverlet drawn over her though it was already afternoon. And further away in the room was Baptiste, her blackamoor servant, who had just come in carrying a tea tray.

*I can't see anything . . .*

*That's right . . . not everybody can see the spirits, or hear them. No more than little Baptiste is capable of hearing we two at this very moment. One has to have a special predisposition to it! But right now there's one of them sitting on my shoulder. I think it's a German, or possibly Dutch . . . In his last life he was a bricklayer. But in heaven he's a mason! That's right, a mason! There are some cracks appearing in the mosaic. They're laying new tiles, he says, and replacing the old ones.*

Hercule was doing his very best, but not even his gift could help him to hear the Dutch bricklayer's thoughts. Or to see him.

*A bricklayer in heaven?* he asked.

*Exactly! Earth is a copy of heaven, as I've already explained to you. There are bricklayers and carpenters in heaven, just as there are here. Think of how bored they would otherwise be, all those dead people! When the very best of men die, their souls go up to heaven and you can't imagine how amazed they are when they find that heaven is packed with services, functions, offices, workshops, even weaving mills, flax plantations, confectioners, coopers' workshops and breweries. Many of the new arrivals, you see, believe they're going to get away from all earthly toils and enjoy eternal rest. But they are soon relieved of that delusion. "Have you understood that eternal rest from labour is to sit and to lie for ever inhaling pleasures into your bosom and imbibing delights with your mouth?" they are asked on arrival. And when the new arrivals say, "Yes, that's how we've understood the matter," they're reminded that idleness merely breeds laxity, which is why it cannot be associated with lasting pleasure.*

The countess knitted her brow and listened again to the voice of the Dutch spirit that only she could hear . . .

*Wait, he's talking to me again . . . They've already found the girl, he says. But they'll know more tomorrow. That'll be fun, won't it, Herr Barfuss . . . just think! You're going to meet your loved one again, at last . . .*

Was it really possible? he thought: that he could find Henriette in this way, with the help of the spirits?

*Where is she?* he asked again.

*Come come, my little friend, you know we have an agreement. You'll have to wait until tomorrow. First you must help me with my game of cards with Lord Chief Justice Conrad. And to win it. Above all to win it!*

*How is she? She isn't ill, is she?*

*Perfect. That is, she's perfectly well. The Dutch spirit says she thinks about you non-stop, always. Can't get you out of her mind, though she sometimes wishes she could forget you.*

*Why would she want to forget me?*

*Maybe because she loves you even though you are such a repugnant little monster . . .*

*What does she look like? Has she changed?*

*Like the Queen of Sheba. Big-bosomed and stately. Her disposition is good. And her eyes are blue!*

*Henriette's eyes are brown . . .*

*Maybe the Dutch spirit is colour-blind. Everything that exists on earth is also to be found in the spirit world, even colour-blindness . . . Look, Herr Barfuss, can't you see! He's floating away from my shoulder now, like smoke, like steam from a small geyser; the spirit world is calling him back, the pearly gates need a new mosaic, the mortar is running out and the Dutch spirit has to sprinkle it with water from the spring of paradise. In heaven everybody's dreadfully busy . . .*

The Countess took a sip of tea and stubbed her cigarette in an ashtray the negro servant had laid out. For a while she searched among the objects lying scattered on the eiderdown – books by Swedenborg, letters, powder compacts, snuff, dice and a pack of playing cards – all before turning to Baptiste and asking him to fetch the box of healing crystals that, alongside games of chance and Swedenborg's spirit world, were her great passion in life.

*The heavenly speech,* she continued, noisily blowing her nose on her sleeve, *is brought out by the wonderful rings of heavenly design! Did you know that the angels' speech corresponds to all languages now spoken? Just like your own, Herr Barfuss. Isn't that why we understand each other so well, even though you're a deformed little German dwarf and I'm a Swedish countess, thoughts being a lingua franca? The angels' speech, the great Swedenborg tells us, starts by penetrating our inner vision where they instil lofty, scarcely comprehensible ideas; after which they develop like a deposit in the common language of human beings. Angelic speech is just as sonorous as if it had been formed with the tongue and the mouth, but usually it's much better articulated. It doesn't come through the air and the ear, but on an internal path to the organs of the brain!*

The Countess smiled, displaying her three remaining teeth. He smelled her odour of sweat, bad breath and old powder, for she never washed. In those northern cities no-one did. On the other hand, one didn't wash in the next world either. Smells, the Countess maintained, caused a great many problems in the spiritual world. Particularly unpleasant was the smell given off by demons. This was because they couldn't smell it themselves.

She picked up her pack of cards from the eiderdown. Not the marked deck she could fool her aristocratic women friends with, but a still-sealed Spanish pack.

*Just do me one last favour, my little deformed friend,* she said. *Be my saviour this evening. The Lord Chief Justice Conrad so badly wants a game of poker, and I'm in financial straits, but who is going to pay Baptiste if I don't? The blackamoor would starve to death if it weren't for me. And who would put a roof over your head, repulsive little monster that you are? Tomorrow the spirits will reward you . . .*

Countess Tavastestierna, who had promised him to find Henriette with the aid of the spirits, hailed originally from Sweden. But at that time the two of them were in Denmark, in Copenhagen, whither years ago she had fled from her creditors. How he had come to be here himself, Hercule wasn't quite sure. He must have arrived in the town in the course of his wanderings, and somehow or other the Countess, whose interest in the supernatural was matched only by her mania for gambling, had become aware of his qualities.

As others had too.

One morning some months before, he had suddenly come to his senses in London. How he arrived there he couldn't recall. Several weeks seemed to have passed since he'd last been lucid. He found himself standing naked on a demonstration table at the famous Athenaeum Club surrounded by a small group of inquisitive gentlemen. One of these, from the Teratological Society, was pointing out Hercule's abnormalities to the audience's mutterings.

143

". . . these disturbances occur as early as in the foetal phase. Why, we don't as yet know. Syphilis, or perhaps the mother's membranes were too narrow?"

Charts had been unrolled; pictures of other monsters were shown: albinos, duplications, craniophagi, microcephalics.

"Gentlemen, look at the cleavage in the face . . . this abnormal harelip is a sign of retardation. Moreover, our monster is deaf and dumb. The back has leaflike swellings. Not long ago I had the privilege of witnessing the dissection of a similar tumour at St George's Hospital. In it we discovered teeth, hair and cartilage, as well as a small, scarcely developed brain. What we see here is an autostisis with traces of parasitism. In some cases this deformity can develop in the foetal stage to become a full-grown parasite – another head, maybe even another body. It's not unthinkable that the swellings we see on the subject's back could reveal traces of a parasite that under more favourable conditions might have developed into a Siamese twin . . ."

Being deaf, all this had passed Hercule by, which as far as he was concerned was just as well. Instead, he had heard someone thinking: *an inferior form of life, but interesting from a racial point of view.* This made him feel sick, and by chance his gift enabled him to transfer his nausea on to the other man, and he laughed as the man rushed towards the exit to throw up.

This, then, was how he had been living the previous few years, he reflected; in a dream of lost love from which he never awoke. Adrift on an aimless journey where reality was nothing but poorly painted scenery.


It had been later that same winter, in Copenhagen, that he encountered this crazy Swedenborgian countess. From what she said, Swedenborg seemed to have been the prophet of a new church in London; proclaimed himself the Saviour who had come to let himself be crucified by the Jews; had thrown his clothes off in public, been stigmatised at Easter, had oddly taken to washing people's feet and had fallen into semi-delirious attacks while conversing for days and nights on end with the dead. He too had been a reader of minds.

The Countess, it was true, preferred the modern word "telepathy", and to put her point across she cited as an example the big fire in Stockholm seen in a vision by Swedenborg as it broke out, though he was a good three hundred miles away at the time. Then there was the celebrated story of how he had found Madame de Marteville's lost receipts by consulting her deceased husband, and the coffee party with Queen Ulrika Eleonora's brother, by then dead for more than a quarter of a century.

When the Countess herself had met Swedenborg in Stockholm in her youth, the old gentleman had been spending most of his time conversing with the dead and walking about in a trance in the spirit world. On one occasion when she had come to visit him she overheard him speak eagerly in Latin with someone in his study, laugh and call for a threefold toast. She had waited until the door opened and Swedenborg, bowing deeply as he accompanied his invisible guest out into the hall, had shaken hands with thin air.

"Who was that?" she'd asked.

"That was Virgil," Swedenborg had answered. "A devilishly decent fellow! We were discussing the antiquities of Rome."

Little by little, she maintained, his nestor's talents had rubbed off on herself. To take her at her word, she, too, mingled freely with history's most celebrated personalities; claimed to know Struense, the Danish politician who had been executed, but whom she admired for his attempts to introduce the spirit of the Enlightenment into Denmark. With Machiavelli she was in the habit of discussing the laws governing legal procedure – warfare with Crassus, the Roman field marshal – and how to murder queens with Henry VIII who remained deranged until the end of his days. With Pope Clement X she had long been in celestial correspondence. Joan of Arc was like a sister to her and St Birgitta treated her to an invisible array of sweets and chocolates. Naturally Swedenborg was her closest ally among the dead. With him she daily exchanged confidences.

Swedenborg, the Countess was fond of saying, had combined Leibniz's monist ideas with the hylozoistic doctrine of living molecules and the notion that some people were in contact with heavenly beings, even during their time on earth. These heavenly beings were called Amores and acted through the souls of men. In order to achieve balance in His Creation, and thanks to His fateful stroke of generosity in endowing man with free will, God had also

145

allowed certain genies, or evil spirits, to install themselves, which, the Countess explained, were in lively communion with the lowest parts of human consciousness. These genies shared the temperament of the person in question. Everyone was linked to two guardian angels and also to two of hell's spirits, the latter trying everything to tempt them to commit grievous sins.

The spirits also had their own worlds which could be either demonic or good, depending on how their occupants had behaved during their lives on earth. In the spirit world, the Countess explained, people looked precisely as they'd looked in their earthly existence, only slightly more translucent and anaemic. They consorted with their friends and relatives, worked as they had done on earth, were divided up among the same religious denominations, had the same nationalities, and lived in identical cities.

There were, for example, two Londons for Englishmen to come to when they died. In one of these Londons, not far from the Stock Exchange, could be found its spiritual governor and his officials. In the west dwelled those who were neither particularly good nor bad. The best lived in the east. And in the north, in the Islington district, lived those who were most intelligent. In Moorfields and the surrounding areas gangs of criminals were gathered as they arrived from life on earth, and in this way the city was continually being cleansed of its bad eggs. The Londoners' clothes, houses and food were all the same as in their contemporary London; the inhabitants drank beer, hot chocolate and tea, though punch was served only to the most righteous.

But where did people of other nationalities live? he had wondered.

In their own countries, naturally! the Countess had answered. Frenchmen in the France of the spirits, the Prussians in Spiritual Prussia, the Jews in a city called the filthy Jerusalem, where they roamed its streets littered with refuse and were tormented by the most excruciating stenches. They traded in all thinkable goods and occupied themselves with money-lending or selling precious jewels they had got hold of in some unknown manner in heaven, maybe with the help of the Cabal, and their existence in this Jerusalem was in fact so similar to the one on earth that they less than any other nationality noticed they had quit their earthly existence and were in fact in another.

According to the Countess, Swedes were by far the worst arrivals. The few good ones that existed lived in a town called Gothenburg, but the lowest of the low, the overwhelming majority, lived in a conglomeration of evil-smelling shanty towns which, apart from North Borås and Eastern Falun, included Stockholm, their abominable capital.

The Swedes' most outstanding feature, she was in the habit of saying, was envy, plus their craze for power and ambition. They were forever perniciously chasing titles, drinking vodka and copulating. Worst of all were the aristocrats. Just as they had done in their earthly life, they held meetings in the House of Nobility, and God's angels, who often sat in as spectators, could see they were incapable of telling good from evil, which was why they were gradually expelled from their positions of high office and ended up begging for alms on the streets.

These were the things Hercule pondered as the Countess waited for Lord Chief Justice Conrad to show up. He withdrew to the cubbyhole next to the bedchamber where she had been letting him live pending instructions from the spiritual world. There he was thinking about Swedenborg and this countess who could converse with spirits but had no mastery of "telepathy". That was why they needed each other: she to win money at cards, he to find his Henriette.

It was a little past ten o'clock when the Lord Chief Justice's carriage drew up outside the two-roomed apartment on Østergade. With a display of servile bowings the servant let him in, took his coat, top hat, gloves and scarf, and then led the way to the room where the Countess Tavastestierna sat enthroned in her bed amid her healing crystals. All was ready for their game. On the table lay the sealed deck of cards. A chair had been drawn up for her guest.

"Please excuse my being late," said the Lord Chief Justice amiably, "but affairs of State do not take other matters into consideration."

"You are forgiven, my dear Conrad," replied the Countess, holding out her hand to be kissed. "Duty always comes before pleasure . . ."

Apart from the bed, the gaming table and the chair the room

was devoid of furniture. A couple of paintings with flower motifs hung on one of the walls. There was a tiled stove, a small window with an extra winter pane of glass, looking out over a backyard, and a closet with a door locked on the outside.

After the two card-players had enquired about each other's health and business affairs, the Countess bade Lord Conrad be seated, broke the pack and shuffled it herself, leaving it to her guest to cut and deal. The game could begin.

The judge's hand consisted of a pair of kings, plus three cards of varying value. He kept the pair and bought new cards at the rate of ten dalers, which was the agreed price.

He was satisfied: one of the cards was the king of hearts.

The Countess replaced her whole hand, though her new cards weren't much better. All she had was a couple of fours. *What has the Lord Chief Justice got in his hand?* she wondered. And immediately was given the answer: *Three kings* . . .

Knowing there was no point in continuing, she threw in her hand even before the bidding had begun.

The second game went on the same lines. After his second buy the Lord Chief Justice had the luck to get three of a kind: aces. And the Countess, who'd been immediately informed about his hand, had only a pair of jacks. Once again she gave up before the bidding had started. Successive rounds all ended in the judge's favour, but the pots, as earlier, were meagre. It was, he'd recall, as if the Countess had known in advance when he was sitting on a strong hand.

At one point, when he'd been dealt two pairs of aces over queens, she gave up instantly, as if sensing she couldn't win. Another time she threw in her hand after he had bought a completely new one, where he found to his delight he had a straight, despite her having kept four of the cards from the deals, suggesting two pairs or possibly a full house. That he himself had got a straight after exchanging all his cards was hardly something she could regard as likely; she should have gone on with the game and thereto not have called him until after a longer bidding.

There followed a couple of amazingly easy victories for the hostess. Every time he bluffed she called him or bid just enough for him not to think he could afford to follow on.

He was an old hand at cards, and when the Countess

ostentatiously blew her nose he cast a quick glance over his shoulder.

The room was empty. The only place anyone could be hiding was in the closet, and that was so small it could hardly contain even a child.

Besides which, as for a possible peephole, he was sitting at such an angle that no-one could possibly see his cards. The cards – he'd made sure of this – weren't marked, nor had he heard any suspicious sounds, such as someone clearing their throat. Without guessing how right he was, he said, "You seem able to look right through my cards."

"Fortune favours the bold," she replied with an enigmatic smile.


Seen from the Countess Tavastestierna's point of view the game was proceeding exactly according to plan. Her hidden assistant was providing her with every bit of information she needed in order to win the decisive pot, and each time she had a bad hand, to lose as cheaply as possible. For it was through the judge's own eyes, if a little out of focus, that Hercule Barfuss was viewing his cards.

He was doing it half asleep, lying on the floor in the dark closet, half inside his own mind, half in the Lord Chief Justice's. But, taken up as he was by his dreams of meeting Henriette again, he failed to pay attention to the plans gradually evolving inside the Countess's head. Instead, at regular intervals, he was obediently casting a glance at the Lord Chief Justice's cards or answering the Countess's nervous questions. And in this way, a subtle piece of trickery that would have needed an all-seeing Swedenborgian spirit to expose it, the two players were winning about an equal number of pots, the only difference being that the Lord Chief Justice's were considerably smaller and more dearly bought. Before midnight struck he had lost all his cash.

"Will you accept promissory notes?" he asked, sweat running down the back of his neck.

The Countess regarded him with the graciousness that becomes a good winner.

"From you, my dear Conrad," she said amiably, "your un-tarnished honour is guarantee enough."

So the game went on, but now with IOUs for stakes . . .

It was getting on for two in the morning when the Countess looked at the wall clock, yawned a trifle exaggeratedly, and offered her opponent one last game. The Lord Chief Justice didn't hesitate, by now he was in the claws of his gambling devil and acting according to the law which says that the more hardened a gambler is, the more happily he persists in his humiliation, and that big losses simply incite him to run even greater risks. So he answered, "You're on, if you still trust my notes of hand."

The Countess nodded, cut and dealt.

Her opponent's first hand exceeded all expectations: three aces, the queen of hearts and the jack of clubs. After a brief hesitation, which was feigned, he kept the queen and the aces, and with a hastily signed IOU bought a new card.

To his disappointment he got yet another jack. I oughtn't to have abided by the rules of common sense, but according to the law of life's eternal injustice and got rid of the queen, he thought.

He bought a last card, placed it behind the ones he already had, and contemplated his hand. It was hard for him not to show some emotion or bat an eyelid or tremble involuntarily. He had a full house: aces and queens. If only I could tempt the Countess to go on bidding, he thought, I might be able to win back some of my losses . . .

The Countess's deal had been bad, and the only card she kept was the king of spades. But on her second buy something almost incredible happened; she had all the remaining kings. Of course, thanks to her hidden assistant, she knew exactly what her opponent's hand was. She was preparing to buy her last card, a mere formality, when she decided to put her plan into action.

"My dear Lord Conrad," she said. "I'll be generous. Even before making my last buy, I would like to give you a chance to win back what you've lost. The fact is, you look terribly upset. And I'm quite sure you will find it very difficult to explain to your wife where such a large sum as you've lost tonight has gone to."

She paused for effect, meanwhile, once again, just to be on the safe side, enquiring about her opponent's hand.

"I'm going to give you an opportunity to win back everything you've lost in a single game," she said.

Her partner looked at her amazed. "And what do you want me

to offer in exchange?" he asked. "An IOU for as much again?"

"My generosity must naturally be paid for at a certain risk . . ."

"Such as?"

"A blank cheque."

"A blank cheque? Do you want to ruin me?"

The Countess sighed.

"You're a gambling man," she said. "You can say no and we'll continue the last game in the ordinary way. But you can also say yes, because you're tempted by the excitement. Look, I'm going to buy one more card, I don't know what you've got in your hand, but you've just bought a last card, so your hand, at least up till now, hasn't been full. I too am going to buy a new card, but I'm giving you the opportunity right now. I'll put down two thousand . . . you call me with a blank cheque . . . Regard this whole thing as a lottery, double or quits!"

He hesitated. Not only did he have a full hand, it was also a very strong one. He wondered what she was hoping for, a straight or a suit. If she saw him with a full house, he'd win thanks to the three aces. After negotiating such a deal, it seemed unlikely that she had four of a kind. The simplest rough estimate told him he ought to win. But when it came down to it, he realised, it wasn't a question of algebra but, just as the Countess had intimated, of excitement for its own sake.

Beads of sweat were breaking out on his upper lip. He licked them away and, almost imperceptibly, nodded.

"I'm in," he said at last. "On condition you buy your last card for two thousand."

And while his hostess was putting the money in the pot, he signed a blank cheque, gulped down his frantic excitement, felt its tremors, the cramps in his stomach and the faint nausea that infallibly befalls a gambler when the stakes are high, be it in a game of poker or in affairs of State.

The Countess leaned back and looked at her last card, even though it was of no account: a jack.

"If you want to see me, put your cheque in the pool," she said. "Or if you're regretting it already, it's not too late . . ."

But the Lord Chief Justice had no regrets. He put the blank cheque into the pool and laid his full house on the table. The Countess cleared her throat.

"I've just ruined you," she said, displaying her four of a kind, all kings.


During the hours the game had been in progress, the Countess's hidden assistant had been dreaming of his reunion with Henriette. At the same time he was wondering whether it really was possible to find a missing person with the help of spirits. But hope, as we know, is the last travelling companion of the unfortunate. The great Swedenborg, he thought, had in any case been a remarkable man. And maybe it was true that everyone has his own guardian angel.

The closet was exceedingly cramped. But even here Swedenborgiana lined the wall: *Journal of Dreams*, *Arcana Coelestia* and *Divine Providence*. He wondered what would happen when he did see Henriette again, but couldn't even imagine that moment. After all these years of absence she had turned into a creature in a dream. Perhaps she had met someone else? Perhaps she wasn't even alive. But not so in his fantasies: there, just as he had never ceased looking for her, she was still waiting for him. And she was more beautiful than ever. And in one fell swoop her love would make amends for his whole life.

And in this manner, after the card game had come to an end and while Lord Chief Justice Conrad, in a state of shock at having lost his entire fortune, was making his way home from the two-roomed flat on Østergade, Hercule, fuelled by the stuff of his dreams, went on dreaming a pleasant dream in which, aided by the spirits, he was on his way to meet Henriette on a country road in Holland. It was spring. The lilac was in bloom. People were happy. His girl looked just the way she had in Königsberg all those years before; beautiful beyond words. On her left shoulder sat one of the spirits of the dead, and Henriette was talking with Swedenborg himself. Rushing up to her, he knew no time at all had passed since they'd been separated.

When he awoke it was morning, as he could discern from the light flooding through on to the closet's wainscoting. But on trying to open the door, he found it was locked. He pummelled it with his feet, but no-one came to open it.

In fact, it was not until twenty-four hours later that the porter found him by sheer chance, half dead of thirst, lying in a feverish delirium in the dark cupboard.

Otherwise the apartment was empty, the Swedenborg library gone, the bed, the few pieces of furniture, the Countess's playing cards and her healing crystals – all were gone.

When the porter threw him with a curse out into the bitterly cold Copenhagen street, he could only console himself with the thought that he was still alive. Life itself, he reflected, was now his last hope. Only life, in covenant with time, could help him find his Henriette.

He wandered for what seemed an eternity. Tramped hundreds of miles – across the great northern plains, through forests, beside rivers and along godforsaken coastlines. It mattered not which map he followed, always it was the same unhappy landscape.

Shamelessly exposing his deformed body in the cities, he lay outside churches begging, his feet holding out his begging bowl to the passers-by. *What kind of animal is that?* he could hear them thinking, *What kind of sins has his mother committed that God should punish her so . . .*

He laughed at them. He didn't believe in their God. For creatures like him there was no God. How would they look if they had made Him in their own image?

Hidden in the luggage compartment of a stagecoach he came to a town in the Brandenburg plains. Berlin.

In the shops he planted a faint scent of smoke in the guts of shop assistants, making them run into the storerooms to check whether a fire hadn't broken out, or else, as he slipped a piece of bread or a bit of cheese under his shirt, a non-existent voice ordered them to look the other way. Or else he got them running out into the street from a sudden notion that a royal carriage was passing by, sent them astray in long-forgotten memories, made them puzzle their heads over a riddle or an arithmetical conundrum, gave them a sudden urge to go to the seaside, run away with some woman, or start a new life in the colonies. So deeply did they sink into their broodings, he could make off with all the day's takings without their even noticing it.

His gift, he'd come to understand, was a weapon. One that could cause people to fall suddenly in love, render them oblivious to time and space, or make them burst into tears from some all-embracing sadness that, for no obvious reason or no reason at all, overwhelmed them and penetrated their minutest capillaries. Or sometimes he filled them with soundless music, wonderful harmonies that made them close their eyes in a pleasure beyond all explanation.

Once he was caught red-handed stealing a jug of gin from a liquor stall. The stall owner held him fast, shouting for the police. He responded with an itching that in a fraction of a second spread itself throughout his captor's body, until the man lay at his feet, a dreadful sight to see, screaming with fear, scratching his arms till they bled and praying to God for the torment to cease. Drunk on his omnipotence he left the man lying there . . .

By autumn rumours abounded in the city. Superstitious folk spoke of a wizard come to overthrow the Hohenzollern dynasty; of the Devil having sent out his minions to punish Prussia for the sins she'd committed during the Seven Years War. Satan was said to have appeared in the guise of a leprous dwarf. But no-one associated Barfuss with these legends.

Now he was sitting blindfolded in a great armchair in the legendary Madame Mendelssohn's salon on Wilhelmstrasse, describing the people in the room; where they came from, who they were, and their most secret thoughts. The officers were astounded when he wrote up their names and regiments on a blackboard. Women blushed when he exposed the identity of their admirers, a lieutenant-general left the room crestfallen when Hercule disclosed some counterfeit promissory notes he'd pawned with a relative.

He would write down the colours and shapes of objects kept hidden from him, as if holding them in his hand. People were astounded by his card tricks and his mnemonic faculty.

One evening he scribbled a verse on the blackboard and looked triumphantly round the room. A cry of amazement could be heard from a man in one of the front rows. It was the poet Chamisso who, in a dreamlike state, had begun the epigram that very morning and still had it in his mind.

So the rumour about the mind-reader spread. By Christmas the crowd at Madame Mendelssohn's had grown so big that she had to allocate tickets to her salon by lottery. That's when he grew tired of it all . . . and disappeared.

He was driven on by longing. Everywhere he searched through people's memories for just one trace of Henriette, but found none. Squandering his last few coins in Hamburg's red-light district, he could see the girls found him repulsive, recalled Madam Schall's establishment and understood that fate had sentenced him to repeat himself.

He wrote down Henriette's name on a piece of paper and showed it to people he fell in with, but no-one had heard of her. He searched surreptitiously through their minds, only to discover the losses in their own lives, the emptiness, the feelings of shame, thoughts benumbed by opium and brandy. Despair had driven him to buy himself a few weeks of tenderness. Only to be thrown out when his money came to an end.

All night long he would roam the docks. Girls shunned him like a disease. Pimps spat at him. Sometimes he was beaten up.

He slept in doorways with vagrants, heard their dreams through his own. He met the strangest characters, seamen who had been left behind when their ship had sailed, adventurers, an artiste who always performed in a swarm of yellow butterflies, a mad clairvoyant who ran away when he realised they were two of a kind. He felt he was soon going to die, though without knowing how or where.

Penniless, he returned to Berlin. He was in an atrocious state. People who saw him mistook him for a ghost. He expected nothing more of life than that it should soon come to an end. Death was a debt you paid only once.

It was as if he had become invisible. People scarcely noticed him. Considering himself to be already one of the dead, he slept in churchyards. Too weak now even to beg, he was beset by hunger hallucinations, thoughts that did not exist or that existed so far away he ought not to have perceived them.

Julian Schuster visited him. Inquisitor del Moro held a speech in Latin beside his grave. From Swedenborg's heaven the Countess Tavastestierna laughed down at him.

He saw an angel alight from a carriage beside where he lay in the gutter. She wore a white satin dress, held a parasol in her hand and wore yellow kid gloves up to her elbows. Radiant with light, she bent down and whispered:

"Hercule, is it really you?"

It was at that moment he felt life returning from a source beyond the universe. It really was her, the girl he'd been searching for for more than half his lifetime.

# VI

L et me be your ears, hear for you, just like when we were children . . . do you remember how I used to describe sounds to you? The girls' gigglings, the laundry fluttering on the line, the soughing wind that made the horses restless . . . now I shall ask time's memory: how did our footsteps sound when we ran through the house? How did the rain sound pattering against your hand, what was the sound of our heartbeat like? I'm hearing for you throughout time . . . hearing their voices calling through our past . . . my mother's voice, Magdalena Holt's voice, Madam Eugenia Schall's. The voices of the men, their oaths and compliments . . . I don't know if you're listening, Hercule, maybe you never could hear my thoughts, maybe only love has enabled you to understand me.

Shall I describe the emptiness to you? The emptiness when the lights go out and the last guest has gone, the emptiness when people disappear with a bit of one's life, and one is torn up by the roots . . . the emptiness when I met the magistrate, the emptiness in my mother's eyes during the last hours of her life . . . when did that happen? I can't remember. A street girl has no concept of time, and her algebra consists of the most elementary sums: how many bottles of eau de cologne she uses in a year, how many bodices she can buy with a rich lover's gratuity, how many post-stages away her next admirer is, how much train-oil her lamp burns up in one night . . . Oh yes, I remember you, you, my first admirer . . . How you comforted me

161

*when I cried, how you lulled me when I couldn't sleep, defended me, stole for me, how you sucked the blood from my finger when I cut it on a piece of glass . . . But now it's him calling in my memory, can you hear him, Hercule? The judge who laid waste our lives, Court Magistrate von Kiesingen . . . I shall describe it all for you . . . I'll tell you my life story . . . if only you'll be patient and don't prejudge me . . .*

*Be still! Heinrich is eavesdropping at the door, wondering why it's all so quiet in here. "I need to speak privately with Hercule," I've told him, but how can Heinrich be expected to understand how we can communicate?*

*"But the cripple's deaf and dumb, isn't he?" he laughed nervously as the servant fetched his pipe. "How do you do it? Does he read your thoughts?"*

*Yesterday, in the library, when I told you about my marriage, he didn't suspect a thing. He thought I was busy playing patience, when in fact I was laying him bare to you, my darling. You mustn't have bad feelings about Heinrich. It was he who took me away from that prison, brought me to this house with all its servants and caged birds, two dozen rooms and four carriages for various needs, its one cook, six housemaids, one chambermaid, one foreman, three liveried footmen and a coachman who speaks flawless French. He lifted me up out of misfortune, just as I lifted you up into our carriage.*

*What is love, my darling? What is it made of? I've read about it in Stendhal, I see it on artists' canvases, I can hear it in the composers' études; and I see it gleefully slip out of their hands just when they think they've captured it. Where have you been all these years? love asks me. Where have I myself been? In the kingdom of death, that's where I've been, until the nightwatch neglected its patrol and in an unguarded moment I managed to slink out . . .*

*Heinrich is standing at the door eavesdropping, maybe even peeping through the keyhole . . . let him be; after all, what can he see? Nothing could arouse his suspicions. His wife, seated on the chaise-longue, an heirloom from his mother . . . a little deformed man, his legs dangling from an armchair.*

*Outside the open window, the sun is shining, sounds float in from the garden, but the woman who is his wife, she's sitting quietly, eyes closed, nodding every now and then, as if in time with some inner melody she's listening to. Opposite her is the stranger she found in the*

162

*street, her half-brother so she claims, this odd mute gentleman who wears a silk mask over his face.*

*Why do you wear a mask, Hercule? You don't have to play a part for me, take it away and let me kiss you . . . no, not just now, not with Heinrich standing behind the door. Let's keep our story a secret just a little longer . . .*

*What are those two up to? my husband is thinking. What business has my wife with this cripple?*

*We were driving through the Royal Animal Park and had it not been for the right-hand horse being so lazy and the coachman not halting to let the mail coach pass, we wouldn't be sitting here now, and Heinrich wouldn't be eavesdropping at his own door . . . They both seem to be asleep, he thinks . . . As if on the verge of dropping off, the moment when dreams summon helpless humans . . . and he hasn't a clue that this is the way I speak to you, the way love wraps itself around us.*

*"Who is he?" my Heinrich asked me at dinner the other day. "Be so good as to answer me, Henriette. Is he really your half-brother? Do you intend me to believe that?"*

*But since last night the mote has gone from his eye. The story I told him made him blench.*

*"But good God, you can't be serious, why haven't you told me all this before?"*

*So he lives in the belief that we really are half-brother and -sister, Hercule. And after so many hardships along our separate ways, there is no Gabrielle Vogel left on this earth to denounce our kinship . . .*

*Climb inside me, Hercule, as you used to do when we were children . . . climb inside me and let me carry you behind my eyes. See yourself through my pupils . . . I'll carry you behind my eyelids, you're simultaneously in your own mind and mine . . . now I'm going to open my eyes and look at you, and your gift will enable you to see through mine . . . see yourself through me . . . and what do you find?*

*You find a deformed little man, not much more than three foot tall, wearing a green velvet swallow-tailed coat. My half-brother Hercule wears a grey ruffled silk shirt, has a French-style shawl around his neck and a triangular mask covering his face. On his feet are child-sized black shoes with silver buckles. He has become completely bald, black protrusions like forest snails reach down from his temples to the nape of his neck. His head is very large, and the doctors surmise that it's hydrocephalic. He has no arms. His coat sleeves are empty, but in the openings one might suppose there are two petrified tufts of seaweed – his useless hands, good for nothing but frightening off birds. On his back one sees a hump: or could this just be his shoulder blades grown awry? His chest looks like a plucked chicken's; but with his feet he can play the piano and make Baron Heinrich von Below gape in astonishment. He cannot speak, his cleft palate is too severe for that, and his tongue is forked like a snake's. Anyway, he doesn't know what words actually sound like, for he can't hear them as other people do with their ears, but intuits them with his soul. He is deaf, say the blind men, while others have a feeling of his comprehending something beyond the horizons of hearing.*

*You must tell me, Hercule . . . who are these secret men who are searching for you? Two months have passed since they were last here. I allowed Heinrich to converse with them. They showed him papers from influential men, and asked about a certain Barfuss, a dwarf and a monster, retarded and deaf-mute. When Heinrich asked them what they wanted, they reminded him menacingly that they have patrons in positions of power.*

*The first time they mentioned your name I knew you were nearby, Hercule. Inwardly I rejoiced, for it proved you were alive . . .*

*Why are people afraid of you, my love? Even the maids are afraid of you. Yesterday, when we returned from our outing, I heard them whispering . . . They are afraid of you, but I just laugh at them . . .*

*Imagine if they knew I was pregnant . . . Heinrich's going to thank God for this miracle.*

*Dr Herzl told him he was sterile . . . He'll never guess what's really happened.*

*I have so much to tell you, Hercule, about the last few years, about the church bells in Danzig, about the house where I worked, the sailors, the girls, about the angel of death who put me into the spinning house. And about Heinrich, my saviour, who rescued me and took me away to be his wife.*

*Listening at the door . . . and all he can hear is our breathing, the hum of his own wondering amazement, and the questions piling up. Is this cripple my wife found in the street and took pity on, and whom some people seem so keen to get their hands on, really her half-brother from a brothel in Königsberg?*

164

*I never forgot you, Hercule. How could I? It would have been like forgetting how to breathe. It was the hope of seeing you again that kept me going. In the end I saw you everywhere, even places you couldn't possibly be. There was only one thing I dreaded: that I would never see you again. But God has heard my prayers and the miracle has taken place. You must tell me everything, about the places you've seen, everything that's happened on your long journey. I want your memories, even the bitterest ones, I must catch up on my happiness . . .*

*Now Heinrich's left his sentry-go and is calling for the servant: "Get the carriage ready, Helwes, I have to go to Potsdam and attend to my business." When something baffles my Heinrich, he attends to his businesses: the mills at Dahlem, the property at Nicolasee, his estate, the brick kilns in Oranienburg. The weaving mill with its English machinery and the barge yard at Rostock. My husband is worth two million. All he lacks is an heir, a son to inherit the family's titles. Maybe our child will be a boy? That would put Heinrich in seventh heaven. And it would gain us time.*

*Don't be afraid, my love. Nothing will happen to you here. My husband's on our side. I've pulled the wool over his eyes . . . He would never hand you over to those men.*

*"If we have a boy," he said once, "he'll be named after the former Elector, and if a girl, she'll be named after the King's daughter Charlotte."*

*But what if the boy is born deformed, like his real father? Would he suspect something then? No, no, he'll listen to the maids and his aunts who'll blame the Evil Eye for a monster happening to be in the house when the missus got pregnant.*

*He's going now. Listen through my ears and you'll hear him . . . listen through me, Hercule: can you hear the horses down in the yard, can you hear the carriage wheels on the macadam as my husband leaves? Take off your mask, we're alone now, and nobody can see us. Let me kiss you. Can you feel the life in here? Don't be afraid, Hercule. No-one can harm you here. If they find you, we'll run away, with or without Heinrich. We've found each other. Nothing else matters . . .*

**H**alf a century later, when Henriette and Hercule's daughter, Charlotte Vogel, had been carried on fortune's trade winds to a house for impoverished widows on Helgeandsholmen in Stockholm, she would tell a friend, in broken Swedish, about the dreadful time her mother had been through in the Danzig spinning house. The path which had brought Henriette into Prussian court circles had been so lined with misfortune that a lesser person would have broken off their journey halfway. Life, her daughter would say, with its defective sense of justice, had punished Henriette far more than even her worst enemies could have wished.

Her story seemed so unlikely that at first no-one believed it, and many years were to pass before it came by chance to the notice of the feminist Frederika Bremer Foundation, which by and by published it as a pamphlet under the title "The Fate of a German Spinhouse Woman". That was in 1915, when not even the flowery crinolines of her mother's epoch remained.

On the afternoon Henriette and Hercule were reunited, thirteen years had already passed since their separation. The tale that she and her mother had started a new life with relatives in Saxony was mere hearsay which one of Gabrielle Vogel's suitors had invented out of despair. True, they had looked up a relative, but in far from happy circumstances.

Since the turn of the century Gabrielle Vogel's sister had been working in a run-down brothel in Danzig, and it was here that mother and daughter had headed for after Madam Schall's establishment had been closed down.

Mercifully, they'd been allowed to stay. They shared a room with two girls who had just arrived from Pomerania in the company of the owner of a vodka distillery, who ran the business with the aid of bribes to the public prosecutor. The establishment was a dreary one. Rats scampered across its tables in the dead of night, sicknesses raged and alcohol was God. Sailors who had jumped ship bought themselves a moment's love for a quart of beer, the girls gave themselves to tramps in exchange for food, and the distiller made the lion's share of his income by serving liquor in the front hall. The inevitable could no longer be held at bay: within a week of their arrival, Henriette had been taken on as a prostitute.

Never would she forget the man who robbed her of her virginity, the stench of his rotting teeth and a brutality that seemed unnecessary. Afterwards she had cried, but that, her mother tried to explain, was customary, just as it was customary that she should learn, in future, to brace herself against the men's repulsive ill-smelling breaths, their unwashed bodies, the lice feasting on the sweat in their armpits, their verminous souls and their mangy, vulgar bedroom conversation.

She had tried to blot all this out by thinking of Hercule. Over the next few years she did little else, falling into deep musings over where he might be, if indeed this unfortunate boy, so ill-equipped for the trials of existence, was anywhere at all. Despite the humiliations she never surrendered to despair. On the contrary, her sufferings fuelled her dreams. The deeper she sank, the closer she came in her imagination to Hercule.

Those first years in Danzig she would later recall as having been lived through as if sleepwalking. All contours had been erased, no faces remained, only bodies; an unbroken chain of strangers turning into a single male body with which she awoke and went to bed, unendingly, day after day, night after night.

By the fifth year she was awaking from one nightmare only to find herself deep in another. One winter night the distiller had taken her to a hotel in the town's outskirts. A servant in livery had led them into a smoking room furnished in Eastern style, with Turkish carpets on the floor, a hookah in front of an armchair, the walls covered in antique marine charts. The distiller withdrew to a room where she could overhear him loudly discussing her price with the well-to-do suitor who had placed an order for her. Then he left the hotel, promising to pick her up the following morning. Still unsuspecting, she sat down in the armchair and looked around her at a splendour of which she'd not seen the like since Madam Schall's heyday. Inhaling the smouldering tobacco fumes and contemplating a poster cross-section of a Havana cigar that explained in an incomprehensible language the difference between a *madurado* and a *claro*, she didn't even notice the man coming up behind her chair until, turning round to locate the source of the mysterious sound of human breathing, she was struck dumb with horror at the sight of him. It was the same court magistrate who had brought about the ruin of Madam Schall's establishment some years before.

Shortly thereafter, when the gendarmes had thrown her into the spinning house, she wondered whether the court magistrate, von Kiesingen, had had an eye on her ever since she had left Königsberg. But it seemed more appropriate to blame the incredible good luck of the unrighteous, and assume he, quite by chance, had come across her in the course of one of his journeys.

What he did to her that evening not only made her *want* to die. She had really been in mortal danger, only been saved by the diffuse intervention of her guardian angel. Never, except on one occasion, and that with Hercule Barfuss, would she speak about that night's events. Nor would it be in good taste to include it in this chronicle, not because of the offence it might give, but rather because the event as a whole, with its every macabre detail, scarcely lends itself to words.

The following morning, when the distiller returned to the hotel, he found her lying in a state of shock on a bunk in the servants' quarters, apathetic, pale and bleeding from several wounds. This was to be the overture to a far greater tragedy, whose first act would begin a month later . . .

Scarcely recovered from this abuse, she was called out again to the very same hotel to meet the very same suitor. The ensuing event soon became public knowledge and a topic of conversation for months on end all round the Gulf of Danzig. Some people sided with the girl, saying what she had done had been to defend her honour. Others took a more serious view, opining that the consequences must be severe, since it had been an act of violence against a representative of the Prussian courts who'd been appointed after all by the King, himself reigning by the grace of God, and therefore contiguous with it.

There was never any trial – a trial might have aggravated the scandal. Besides, the girl was not of age. Yet notwithstanding all the magistrate's efforts to keep the details of the drama secret, they leaked out anyway.

What was known was that a street girl had stabbed a high-ranking suitor from the civil service, his life only saved thanks to the speedy intervention of an able surgeon. According to one version a girl had tried to cut his carotid artery with a scalpel; in another she'd stabbed him severely in his groin. As time went on the former version became the more popular, though the latter was closer to the truth.

First to arrive on the scene of the assault had been the hotelier, drawn to the room by the terrible screams. He found the girl naked, standing in the middle of the room deathly pale, a bloodied razor in her hand. At her feet, curled in the foetal position, the magistrate was bleeding from the pit of his stomach. In the subsequent interrogations, the hotelier declared the girl to be not in her right mind. Fortunately a doctor happened to be on hand who'd managed to stop the magistrate's bleeding with styptic compresses, and had stitched up the cuts in a room hurriedly placed at their disposal.

Henriette, on the other hand, was taken to the spinning house without trial.

It was a nightmarish place where the overcrowding was so bad that the girls had to take turns to sleep on the floor. There were no blankets, no latrines, and they learned to fight over the evil-smelling slush that passed for soup.

Later, when Heinrich von Below looked into the circumstances surrounding the predicament of his wife-to-be, he came to the conclusion that her mother too, at the magistrate's express order, had been sent to the spinning house, since she'd arrived at the same institution only four days later, and had there been locked up in a wing away from her daughter. No documents existed to confirm his theory, but the events adhered to a logic suggestive of a plan.

It was said the judge had been so badly injured in the assault that he afterwards suffered permanent chronic pain. A couple of girls bore witness to his quirks and maintained that there was no way he could indulge in normal bedroom activities, wounded as he was. The revenge implied a slow death sentence.

That winter Gabrielle Vogel, scarcely thirty-five years old, died of malnutrition. Her body was discovered in a window-bay where death had overtaken her in a wretched state – a human skeleton clad in rags, toothless, bald, smeared in excrement and weighing scarcely more than a child.

Henriette had gone almost out of her mind with grief. Hadn't even been allowed to see the corpse, since it was removed at night and buried in some unknown place without so much as a cross to honour the deceased's memory. Most likely she would have met the same fate had Heinrich von Below, a young and successful businessman, not heard her story.


At the time of the scandal von Below happened to be in Danzig, where he had invested in a high-risk company that loaned money to sanitary contractors. The first gas lamps had made their appearance in Germany, likewise Herr Krapp's waterclosets, and water mains, which were now being drawn to the upstairs floors of houses and within only a few decades would revolutionise sanitation.

A business acquaintance had initiated him into the event the whole town was talking about. Maybe because he himself had been in conflict with the law in a matter concerning a patent where he had gained terrifying insights into the prevailing widespread state of corruption, the tale had stuck in his mind. He took it for granted that in a *cause célèbre* like this, involving a street girl, there must be a bone buried.

He couldn't get the story out of his head, it haunted him with a regularity that suggested some deeper meaning. What impressed him were the elements of the tragedy: poverty versus wealth, despair versus superior force, the twofold revenge, and evil winning out because power is all.

Chancing to spend the night at the very same hotel where the assault had occurred, he was shown the room where the girl had stabbed her suitor. There were still bloodstains on the floor. The hotelier told him in confidence that, in his opinion, the girl had avenged herself for some injustice.

Shortly after this von Below had gone to Bavaria, where the company had made commitments in a watercourse project, and almost two years passed before he returned to Danzig.

To his surprise, he still couldn't get the girl's story out of his mind. On the pretext of his company's readiness to invest money in new spinning machines and consequently also in prison care, he managed to get permission to visit the gaol where he made suggestions to its governor of ways to improve the sanitary conditions and so possibly minimise the abominably high death rates among the prisoners. But for him to do this, he said, it was important he should personally inspect the existing arrangements.

Shown around, he saw the workshop, where women sat chained to machines sixteen hours a day; also the kitchens, the prison chapel, the storage spaces and finally the so-called dormitories, where prisoners were locked up at night as in a crypt for the living dead. He didn't even need to have her pointed out to him. He knew at once it was she.

In the first letter he wrote to the prison governor asking for her release, he noted: "The girl has not even been sentenced, the accusations of vagrancy cannot be substantiated and, furthermore, the sorry calling of street girls cannot be prevented by enforced labour."

He didn't know why, but he had fallen in love, there and then, with no other reservations than those emanating from his own titles. Many years later, in a fever on the cotton plantation in German East Africa where, plagued by malaria and homesickness, he was to end his days, he would recall the instant sense of recognition that had struck him when first he set eyes on her. Guided by the governor, he'd found her sitting on the floor at the far end of a room, dressed in rags. Her feet were wrapped in paper. Her hair was tangled. Yet, in the midst of all this degradation, this filth, this darkness, this misery and stench of unwashed bodies, she was still the most beautiful woman he had ever set eyes on. She radiated a light, he thought, that lit up the whole of existence.

He managed to get her moved to the barracks where the female overseers lived. The owners promised to provide her with warm clothing and spare her the heavy labour at the machines. After that, he took measures for her release.

A letter to the city police chief was ignored and sent back to him by return of post. Later he realised that several people in the City Council had done everything in their power to put obstacles in his way. A remonstrance with the mayor, too, was rejected because of risk of infection – half the women in the spinning house had been detained without either trial or sentence, which was against the law, but served a moral purpose. One civil servant added: "And besides, it is a prophylactic measure: half of them are syphilitic!"

Obsessed by her, he rented an apartment near St Mary's Church and visited her whenever he could. It calmed him to think she was under his protection. In a room put at his disposal by the governor, he could visit her without their being disturbed, and at every fresh meeting his love for this girl, forbidden fruit for a man of his social standing, grew deeper. The poets had taught him that love which comes suddenly takes the longest to be cured of, and that there is only one palliative for heartache: to love yet more intensely. This didn't strike him as a problem, feeling as he did that he had always borne her within himself as a possibility, a potential not realised until now. He compared himself secretly to Edward in Goethe's *Elective Affinities*, stricken by a reckless passion for his Ottilia, a woman half his age.

He attempted to get her out by bribery, but failed. On another occasion he offered a prison warder two hundred thalers to help her escape, but the warder was removed before the plan could be put into action. Further letters to the authorities met either with cold answers or none.

Confident that she was at least temporarily out of danger, he went to Berlin to attend to business. In March a letter, unmistakably in her handwriting, was smuggled out to him. She was desperate. With no reason given she had been moved back into the prison. She was starving, freezing, sure she was going to die.

Returning, he'd found the prison management had been changed and he was no longer allowed to visit her. A new magistrate, too, had been appointed to the City Court: Klaus von Kiesingen.

Such is the nature of love, Goethe writes in his *Elective Affinities*. Alone in the right, it believes all other rights vanish before it. Not long afterwards, as he'd departed for Berlin with his wife-to-be, von Below had had occasion to remember this sentiment, for a new scandal, ironically, had contributed to her release.

In sheer desperation, he had confided the affair to a business acquaintance. One meeting with the judge had convinced him that this man was out to kill the girl. He had gone so far as to utter threats: if von Below insisted on poking his nose into other people's affairs, there would be an accident. This made him hate the man who, with a single word, could have set her free, but conversely was intentionally causing her time to run out.

It was the business acquaintance, a Polish share-dealer known for his unorthodox business methods, who saw a way out, via the mayor's Achilles heel: for some years he'd been having an affair with the British Consul's wife. Should this affair become known it would cause a scandal so immense it would raise mayhem in diplomatic circles. It was out-and-out blackmail, and within an hour of von Below's tête-à-tête with the mayor, Henriette was released.

Many years later, when Charlotte Vogel recounted her mother's tale to the emissary of the Swedish Frederika Bremer Foundation, she would explain in general terms that the magistrate had done everything in his power to get the mayor to change his decision, even planned to have Henriette kidnapped. He too, however, was to receive his just deserts, albeit not until much later and under the most extraordinary circumstances involving her one true love, the mind-reading Barfuss . . .

T he day in Berlin when Henriette had climbed down from her carriage on Grosse Hamburgerstrasse, and bent over Hercule, he was not sure if it was really happening to him or whether his befuddled brain was playing yet another of its ruthless tricks. He'd been lying, half conscious, in the gutter when a heavenly being laid its hand on his forehead and told the coachman to lift him into the carriage. Inside there was already a passenger: a well-dressed gentleman who gave up his seat and placed himself on the coachman's box. Not until the carriage was moving again did Hercule realise that reality had in fact surpassed imagination.

Henriette was living in a fairy-tale world that he could never have imagined had he not seen it with his own eyes. The baron belonged to a new class of people: manufacturers and industrialists who, after centuries of advances in technique and commerce, had stepped on to history's stage. Never before had anyone managed to make such immense fortunes in so short a time, and never before had there been such a wealth of luxury items on offer for them to enjoy, for Europe's colonisation of the world was in its initial, budding phase.

Any splendour he had hitherto seen paled into insignificance beside what he saw in the von Below palace. Chandeliers with prisms the size of ostrich eggs. Pilasters framing Italian landscape murals. Gilded cupids glancing down from the ceilings. There were closets with running water, a steam kitchen with hot-water radiators, and two portable baths in which von Below could spend half his days being massaged by his servant and reading newssheets in four different languages to keep up with the movements of the stock exchange.

All the rooms had modern lamps which lit up the darkness. Remarkable antiques adorned the shelves and chests of drawers. Stuffed beasts of prey scared him out of his wits as he explored unending corridors. Biedermeier furniture reigned in the salons. Yellowing elephant tusks held up gaming tables. There were Chinese vases, paintings by French masters, and an art gallery where von Below, in his Maecenas role, had collected art by German painters. For hours on end Hercule could stand transfixed before a landscape by Caspar David Friedrich or by Schinkel, whose buildings in the Prussian capital were springing up out of the ground like mushrooms.

There was the twenty-four-man brass band, hired for the extravagant dinners; larders filled with colonial foods from the East India companies von Below had invested in; coffee or cocoa was served in the afternoons, nameless tropical fruits adorned the waiters' trays. As for the baron, he could only make full use of all the garments he'd ordered from his French tailors by changing his suit three times a day. Theatrical performances were arranged, as were party games and readings featuring popular poets. Two outsized tortoises, their shells encrusted with jewels, crawled about the library – a gift from an Indian maharaja with whom von Below had clinched a deal for importing precious stones.

In the midst of all this opulence he had installed the magnetic pole of his love: Henriette Vogel.

Years later, when everything had changed, Hercule Barfuss would ask himself why von Below hadn't grown suspicious; not on one single occasion cast a sidelong glance at the barred door of the bedroom through which his wife, in a state of feverish excitement, stole stealthily at nights, nor even vented a rejected lover's frustration. Henrietta's clumsy lies certainly did not suffice as an explanation, nor their awkward game of hide-and-seek, nor that the baron was away on business, or the fact that he, Hercule, was so patently deformed as to be beyond all suspicion.

Hercule was shaken by the strength of the feelings they still had for each other after all these years of privation, the fire that made them seek each other out at midnight, their wordless conversations, the rays of pure energy that suffused his existence at the mere sight of her. Love was all, for love was greater than life. Henriette was the living incarnation of all the thousands of love poems he'd read in Barnaby Wilson's library, he dedicated all the composers' pieces to her, just as all roses had been created solely in her honour. She was all womanhood. The most beautiful creature he had ever known.

Their symbiosis was complete. At first they parted company only to sleep, or to dwell in private on the stories of the other. He would recall life at this time as a realistic application of Plato's idea about the origin of life in his *Symposium*. Each was the other's missing half, fusing together again.

But jealousy is every lover's nemesis, and this dark force he too must suffer. Just to see her talking to von Below threw him into fits of indescribable anguish. It didn't even have to be her husband, a visitor could trigger it off, or one of the servants, or even the attention she paid to the two tortoises as they lumbered with fossil-like slowness across the vast expanse of marble floor.

Then he would sink into a despair as fathomless as his love, until a glance from her delivered him and in a matter of seconds made him once again the happiest of mortals.

That summer they travelled to the family estate by Muggelsee, an old hunting-seat von Below had had restored with a view to his heir being able to spend holidays out in nature. It was by now quite evident that Henriette was expecting. The news had unleashed a fever of activity, with any number of receptions and parties where half of Berlin society filed past to offer gifts and congratulations. The baron was beside himself with joy, and the thought of becoming a father dimmed his wits. Hercule, on the contrary, aware of the true state of affairs, wasn't in the least surprised; everything he'd experienced recently had been so improbable that miracles no longer seemed impossible.

Von Below's business took him away on long journeys. Left to themselves on the estate, they lived in ecstasy, where neither future nor past existed. Hercule struck the servants with awe by playing the grand piano with his feet. With Henriette he went on excursions to the Brandenburg forests, or took the mail coach to Spreewald where folk floated down the canals on rafts. They visited Dresden and admired the city's architecture. To avoid attracting attention he dressed in a child's clothes and wore a mask. The present moment was all. But this made him careless . . .

Von Below had installed a model factory in one of the adjoining mansions. Everywhere in Europe factory workers were living in the most appalling conditions. Men, women and children toiled at the machines in sixteen-hour shifts, working in dark, filthy barracks, and when trade recessions reduced demand the workers would be immediately laid off. Schooled in the spirit of German idealism, von Below had begun experimenting with more humane methods of industrial labour. It didn't make sense that a whole family should starve to death simply because a tariff wall had gone up, or a rate of exchange gone down. In his new, model factories no-one worked more than a twelve-hour day, the premises were light and spacious, the company provided its employees with housing and medicine, and if they ran into hard times he intended to keep them on, unemployed, but with half pay. He also founded schools for the workers' children, none of whom were employed in the factory under the age of twelve. The adults too were taught to read and write. Much to the baron's delight, these measures actually helped raise output, doubling it within a few months. Hercule could not help but admire this rival who seemed scarcely aware of his existence, and whom he would never get to know, since Henriette made sure to keep them apart. If on some occasion they happened to be in the same room, the baron seemed to look right through him. Towards the end of his life, in correspondence with his exiled daughter, Hercule was to describe his rival as honest and kind-hearted . . .

Marriage doubles your duties, but halves your rights, the baron used to quip whenever his wife was mentioned. Adding Schopenhauer's words: "Time is truth's ally."

Hercule grew to doubt this sentiment, for what they were shortly to experience was that all our "nows" are different from future "thens".

Nothing is predictable, not even for someone endowed with

such a gift as our hero. Happiness was distorting his sense of reality, which was why he failed to heed the alarm bells. Had he been more vigilant, the catastrophe might have been averted. The foreman responsible for the factory in von Below's absence, for instance, had received several visits from mysterious gentlemen. But the closer Henriette came to her delivery, the more the two of them abandoned themselves to their imagination. Much later he would write to his daughter that they had formed plans to go to America, had even contacted a Bremen shipping company. Henriette had put aside some money and had begun to formulate a letter of farewell to her husband. She and Hercule had found each other again, and all the lost years entitled them to a future.

Late in autumn they returned to Berlin. By now Henriette was so big the midwife feared she was going to give birth to twins. Towards the end, Hercule saw little of her, since family duties and keeping up the semblance of being a good wife were taking up all her time. Jealousy plagued him. The irrational feeeling of being scorned by the whole world.

When first Charlotte saw the light of day, on the morning of November 9, he was alone in his room, but his gift enabled him to follow all that was going on in the house. He felt the baron's pride and joy as he paced the corridor outside the room in which the little girl was being born, he felt Henriette's birth pangs as if they had been his own, and even climbed into the state of non-verbal awareness to be experienced by his own daughter. The world is a wondrous place, he thought, it surpasses everything anyone can imagine . . .

On the same afternoon that the little girl was christened in a simple ceremony on the von Below estate, three men met up at the Golden Cockerel Inn, beside Berlin's Holy Trinity Church. The tavern was upstairs, and overlooked the graveyard. While two of the men were studying a plan of some building, the third was looking half-heartedly at a poster advertising an animal-baiting contest at the inn later that evening and marvelling at the idea of a mastiff set against a she-wolf, two cocks fighting to the death, and even something so extraordinary as an ape skinned alive by a lynx.

Though known as the "beggar monk" his real name was Johannes Langhans. He was adviser to the secret service built up after the Congress of Vienna by the Austrian Chancellor Metternich, a position to which he'd been appointed on the recommendation of the Italian cardinal Aurelio Rivero, also of a certain inquisitor named Sebastian del Moro. And as he sat in the inn he reflected on his divided loyalties, to Vienna on the one hand and the Vatican on the other. Like Hercule Barfuss, the Jesuit monk Langhans was able to pick up on other people's thoughts.

The other two gentlemen at the table were also clerics, although it didn't transpire from their outward appearances since they were dressed in civilian knickerbockers, overcoats and

179

broad-brimmed hats. One even wore, swinging in full view from a leather sword-belt, a military sabre.

Their names were Hans and Erich Malitsch, and they were brothers, orphaned during Napoleon's invasion of the Rhineland in the early years of the century. A Franciscan institution in Westphalia had taken pity on them, and they'd been recruited by the Inquisition, albeit indirectly. It was the younger of these two brothers who was just now in the act of inspecting the plan on the table.

"It has cost us four gold marks to get this drawn up," he was saying. "There are no honourable men about these days."

"How did you go about it?" Langhans asked.

"The foreman had gambling debts. We started by paying him visits on von Below's estate. As you know, he was an overseer in one of the factories . . ."

The plan was of a building surrounded by a garden, with a high wall between it and the street. The only way into the garden was through a gate. A short avenue led to the coach house. Where two wings flanked the courtyard, a row of fruit trees was indicated. Doors and windows were sketched in charcoal, as was every room and floor in the west wing.

"Which room does the monster sleep in?" Langhans asked.

"One in the west wing. Von Below never sets his foot in there. Only his wife and Barfuss. The foreman says it's the wife who keeps the two of them apart."

Langhans threw the younger of the two brothers such a sharp look that he lowered his eyes.

"We wouldn't need a foreman at all," he said, "nor a plan, if you hadn't insisted on going from door to door making enquiries about his whereabouts. That merely aroused suspicion. Now they're taking all possible measures to protect him and we'll have to break in like common thieves."

"It's not certain we'd have had more success if we'd gone about it some other way," the elder brother said. "They say the monster can make himself invisible. The maid swore she'd walked past him at least a dozen times without even noticing he was there."

"Let's stick to what we know and not to what silly people concoct to make themselves seem remarkable. Why didn't you do anything last summer when they were alone on the estate?"

"We did, but the monster must have a guardian angel. Twice we were about to go ahead, and both times they went away."

"You should have followed them." Langhans pointed to a broken line in an upper corner of the plan. "What's this supposed to be?"

"A secret door. A section of the bookshelves can be opened from a concealed space behind the bedroom. Only von Below and the foreman know it exists. It was the baron himself who had it installed, shortly after he bought the house, as an escape route. That was before the woman arrived on the scene. He'd made himself some enemies at the Ministry, and it seems there was an attempt to poison him. On another occasion he opted out of some duel or other, not very honourably. Any man of von Below's standing makes enemies and takes the necessary measures to protect himself."

"Duels are a barbaric custom," Langhans muttered. "Why do people have to kill each other for something so inglorious as honour?"

"Maybe because they haven't got any," the younger brother offered. "Von Below gets involved in shady business transactions. Besides his factories and railways, I've heard he deals in art stolen from churches. In my opinion, we should just take a walk over to the baron's bedroom when we've done with the west wing . . ."

But Langhans wasn't listening. Since his arrival at the inn he'd had a distinct feeling of someone watching them. Not that he'd noticed anything to corroborate his misgivings, but the premonition was there like an annoying tune one can't get out of one's head. Which was why, while he was laying aside the flyer advertising the animal-baiting contest and the brothers were marking a cross on the plan, he turned round to take a look.

The tavern was far from full. Further inside the premises some coachmen were playing dice. A group of guards officers were conversing loudly at a table. Two yawning women of dubious virtue were strolling between the bar and a separate part of the tavern, fitted out as a smoking room, where, to judge by the smell, you could also sink into opium dreams. At the far end of the tavern, the innkeeper, surrounded by half a dozen men, was busy demonstrating something. At regular intervals he let out a series of curses, unleashing general merriment.

Even so Langhans noticed nothing untoward, or outside the range of normal sensations. There were of course the usual chunks of longing and bitterness, undercurrents of love gone awry, short outbursts of joy or pain, tributaries of thought and streams of absent-minded images running aimlessly, without direction, one association merely hooking on to another, until nightfall and sleep, or inebriation, turned them all into dreams . . .

Johannes Langhans had acquired his gift during his time in Istria as a priest. That had been during the years when the Society was under an interdict and the house, which had become famous for the severity of its rules, had been surviving on charity on the outskirts of the Empire. Taking such banishment for granted, the abbot had proposed the novices go and live as hermits in the mountains. Langhans had taken a personal vow of silence. No-one had demanded it of him; but he was young, and impressed by the legends of the saints.

For nearly ten years he'd lived with no other human contact than the district's shepherds. By and by he discovered he had a natural inclination towards a hermit's way of life, impervious as he was to hardships, whether snowstorms or heat, hunger or thirst. It was during this time that he realised he had the gift. At first it was so faint that he put it down to the hallucinations brought on by hunger, but gradually, as it grew stronger, he'd interpreted it as his reward for the vow of silence he'd offered up to God.

He could sense the approach of another human being miles away. Had carried on a one-sided telepathic contact with the abbot and surprised him by sending letters via the shepherds, in which he described his superior's problems and gave him advice on how to solve them.

Eventually the heads of the house – ill at ease with this figure who, clad in rags, mute as a stone, emaciated beyond recognition, had more and more come to look like a tramp, and had an uncanny knowledge of what was going on in their minds – would absolve him from his vows; he was sent to the Vatican as a secretary to the bishops' congregation.

The connection between speech and thought having been all but severed, it had taken Langhans several months to recover his voice. He was convinced he was alone with his gift. No-one eluded him: he penetrated their souls. This wasn't imagination: he saw right through them, saw the secrets they thought well hidden, picked up the stench of their rotting souls, became shocked at the discrepancy between thought and speech among clerical officials, and had the insight to foresee that his gift might get him into trouble. Miracles were rarely rewarded by canonisation. On the contrary, the wars had created a surplus of icons and madonnas which shed tears of sacred oil in provincial chapels.

During his third year in Rome he'd been summoned before an investigating commission. The first time he met Sebastian del Moro he realised that it was this man who somehow or other had disclosed his gift.

The investigation established that it was not of a demonic nature, but he was forbidden to speak of it, and he heard from the corridor gossip that he, together with his prior, was on the list of clerics being considered for post-mortem canonisation. The rumour must have been put abroad by the Inquisition in order to protect him. That made him laugh.

Shortly thereafter he'd been placed in quarantine in an office specially invented for him. Two years later del Moro had him appointed to a post in what was to become the *sapinieri* movement. When his reputation had grown to the point where, on Cardinal Rivero's recommendation, he was offered the position of religious counsellor to Metternich, he'd gone on working in secret for the movement. The cases he was entrusted with were considered to have such high priority that only a man of his qualities could be called upon. Which was why he was just now in Berlin, under such clandestine circumstances that not even the Chancellor knew of his whereabouts.


Seated at the table in the Golden Cockerel, Langhans turned his attention to the brothers. They were intent on the job in hand: the drawings, the way into the house, any patrols, who was to do what. They had spent almost a year in Berlin, pursuing rumours that the monster was performing in salons as a mesmerist. But when they searched he seemed to have disappeared. All that remained was the eternal flora of legends in the making: that the boy could see into the future, pass on messages from the dead and ask favours of the Devil. There were people who swore blind they hadn't seen him though they'd walked past him only a foot away as he, at the expense of their sanity, tried out his faculty for rendering himself invisible. These rumours had been followed by others – that he was living in Brussels, in Copenhagen, in Hamburg and, finally, in Berlin, where he enjoyed the protection of a certain Baroness von Below.

This last rumour had proved correct. For almost two weeks now Langhans had been staying at a Catholic hostel by the Trinity Church graveyard while the final preparations were being made. And all the time he'd had this feeling of something not being quite right. Now it seemed as if his misgiving was being verified. He was picking up a most peculiar wavelength, sensing a flow of thoughts, or rather, a state of awareness, that he could neither understand nor locate.

Again he turned round to look. A squint-eyed woman smiled at him. The kitchen boy was blowing his nose like a trumpet and scrutinising its contents in his handkerchief. Over in the corner the innkeeper was swearing ever louder.

The consciousness Langhans was failing to locate was, however, in his immediate vicinity. He intuited it with a sense of urgency that was almost tangible, as if it had been rubbing itself up against his clothes and his skin. Over in the corner, he now noticed, the innkeeper had picked up a cane and was hitting out at something, though he could not tell what, since the men's backs formed a wall, blocking his view.

Some drunks were laughing. Someone else yelled:

"But she's worthless. What did you say you paid for her?"

"Three ducats! And I was told she was worth twice as much. When she first came here she could do tricks, walk on her hands, dance like a real lady. Truth needs few words, but lies can't get enough of them. I've been swindled by that damned gypsy who sold her to me."

The men around him moved aside to make way for the innkeeper, and now Langhans had a clear view.

It was a guenon.

The monkey, clothed in a dirty doll's dress and printed calico nightcap, was chained to a hook in the wall. The chain holding her was extremely short, giving her no more than a few feet to move about in.

"I bought this wretched monkey to perform tricks for my guests!" the innkeeper shouted. "But she's an idiot, won't do as she's told! Now all she's good for is bait."

The monkey did not utter a sound. Langhans wondered if someone had cut out her tongue. He perceived the crackle of some kind of language, mixed with hatred and bestial pain. It struck him that the conceptual world of a monkey was not wholly unlike that of a small child, and this insight filled him with awe.

Another fragmentary thought interrupted the horror of the guenon. It was coming from the elder of the two brothers: a doubt about Langhans' absent-mindedness.

He turned his attention back to them and asked, "Does von Below have any guards?"

"There's a gatekeeper at nights. But apart from the baron no-one is armed. According to the foreman he keeps two Dutch pistols in a casket in the library."

"No mastiffs?"

"No, the gatekeeper's our only snag. But look, here, further away, if you follow the garden wall . . . See, a blind corner? A lamplighter usually walks past just after midnight. After that, not a living soul."

"The kitchen entrance will be open," the younger brother added. "The foreman sees to that. The bottom of the secret staircase is behind a storeroom in the cellar."

But Langhans didn't need to ask for any more details of the plan the brothers had had drawn up, he went on building logically on the information he already possessed; besides which, he saw what was going on in their heads, the entire plan, in detail: how von Below and his wife slept in another part of the house, that is, if the baron was there at all and hadn't gone off to visit one of his factories. If he was staying in the house, he'd probably be sleeping soundly, although of course one could never be sure nothing unforeseen would occur. The plan prescribed how one brother was to keep watch outside the house while Langhans and the other brother climbed over the garden wall, entered through the open kitchen door – exercising every precaution so as not to wake the housemaids – descended to the cellars where barrels of wine and beer were kept, mounted the secret staircase the foreman had drawn their attention to, up to the wing's upper storey where the monster slept behind a locked door – maybe because he knew he was being hunted – lulled into a false sense of security, little knowing that a section of the bookshelf was at that very moment being thrust aside, and two shadows were entering the dimly lit room where one of them, probably Langhans himself, being responsible for the affair being brought to a satisfactory conclusion, went over to the bed, marked on the plan by the diligent foreman, pulled aside the curtains and, grabbing the deformed mind-reader by the throat, put an end to a life that, but for an accident of nature, should never have been . . .

"What about the woman?" he asked. "The baroness? Where will she be tomorrow night?"

"In her bedchamber, we think. Right under the baron's room."

"What do you mean, *think*?"

"It's rumoured that she's the monster's mistress. The foreman heard it from a chambermaid. It's said the monster is the child's father and that the woman visits him at night as soon as the house is asleep. It's said they have plans to go to America . . ."

Langhans laughed aloud. "That's absurd. The monster's utterly unfit to live. How could he sire children? And what woman would want a creature like that in her bed?"

Even so, it was quite possible, he later reflected: the gift could be used to gain almost unimaginable advantages.

"Wouldn't von Below have noticed that?" he said equivocally.

"He's blind where his wife's concerned. He'll do anything for her. The foreman says he drinks champagne out of her shoe, as the Poles do when they're besotted by a woman."

"God gave human beings two ears", the older brother declared, "to hear better. And two eyes to see better. But only one mouth, to not talk so much. The foreman's a braggart . . ."

But Langhans wasn't listening. His attention was on the chained monkey again. It occurred to him they might make use of a creature like that, Barfuss probably being on his guard.

At the other end of the room, the innkeeper lashed out at her with his cane, and she tried in vain to avoid the blows. She pulled and tugged at the chain, straining to get free, scratching at the metal and then, with no chance of escape, went to the attack and took the cane between her teeth.

"I'll teach you," the innkeeper shouted, "you damned brute!"

With a wrench he tore the cane out of the monkey's jaws and lifted it to hit back with full force. Langhans feared he would hear a crack, such as when someone strong snaps a dry twig across their knee, an explosive sound, as when an animal's limb is broken; in fact, he could already feel it, as if it had been his own leg . . .

Later, the innkeeper would recall a kind of whisper that had compelled him to let go of the cane and free the monkey from its chain for no obvious reason, unable as he was to grasp it. It was not his own will that acted, of course, but rather the taciturn guest sitting with two gentlemen at the far end of the room.

A shudder passed through the priest. The monkey was exceedingly aggressive, filled with hatred for all humans; a highly efficient weapon in the hands of anyone who knew how to wield it.

Freed of its chain, the animal, without a moment's hesitation, again attacked the innkeeper. It was all Langhans could do to calm it down, and, using his gift, to lure it to him, sit at his feet, whimpering guiltily.

The innkeeper was bleeding from two gashes on his leg and deeply shaken. Langhans turned to the wounded man, and said, "You've got all the animals you need for your baiting. I'll buy the guenon off you. Name your price . . ."

I n his dream he is walking through a forest, and his hearing is as keen as anyone else's. Birdsong, the wind in the treetops, the babbling of a brook, human laughter.

Looking at his arms he sees they have grown. The muscles are like a soft line of hills stretching from wrist to shoulder, veins protruding on the surface, a delta of blood whose effluents flow into two perfect hands lacking no fingers. And he has grown; the dwarf legs are long and muscular.

He mirrors himself in a watercourse. Gone is the cleft palate. His nose is proud, its profile as noble as a buzzard's. He sticks his tongue out, an ordinary pink tongue, not a snake's. His face is neither handsome nor repulsive, a perfectly common or garden face, and that pleases him.

There's a smell of autumn in the air, of rotting leaves, mush-rooms, damp moss. In a forest glade a young roe deer is standing. When a branch snaps underfoot, it sniffs the air cautiously but doesn't run away. He hums a tune and doesn't notice when his humming turns into song.

Is he singing?

Yes, he's singing and his song is exactly like the idea he's had of it, coming as it does from a piece he used to play on the organ; so the music in his head is the same as the music in his ear. The words stick in his throat through sheer amazement, but by and by he begins talking aloud to himself: "My name is Hercule," he says, "Hercule Barfuss. Once upon a time I was a dwarf, deaf and dumb, disfigured. But now I'm a fully grown man, I can talk, an everyday kind of person, neither handsome nor ugly, but well proportioned, as if I've been blown up to my full size."

The ground is drying out, the layer deepest down is sandy. The path winds its way onward among low pines, everywhere are sounds, the sounds of the forest, cracklings, little snappings of cones falling, birds. Not in his wildest fantasies could he have imagined the world as consisting of so many sounds, or that anything invisible can so fill existence. He sniffs in the odour of saltwater and seaweed. The path leads off to the west, takes him up to a hilltop. And there, in front of him, shining, almost at a standstill, is the sea.

Lazy waves nibble at the shore. Sea is all around him. He realises he is on an island.

The girl is sitting on one of the sand dunes. He calls her name, but she doesn't hear him. Again he looks at his human arms, the sinews at the wrists, the finger joints, not one missing . . . nails, more grey than pink, on the back of his hand he can see wormlike veins . . .

By now the girl has become aware of him and is beckoning him closer. He goes on along the sand dune, but the girl is still as far away as ever, as if she were being moved back at the same pace as his footsteps approach her.

An insect bites him in the back. As it's in a spot he can't normally reach with his feet, he tries to shrug it off. How many lice have bitten him over the years simply because of this, how often has the itching tormented him between his misshapen shoulder blades because it happened to be out of foot's reach. But then he remembers: he has hands! Carefully he draws his nails over his back. The growth of hair, too, he notices, is gone, as are the indentations and fossil-like protrusions. Out of sheer joy he starts talking again, quotes a French philosopher Barnaby Wilson had once drawn his attention to: "Happiness is a dream and suffering is reality." But the philosopher was wrong. "It's the other way around," he adds, in his own, somewhat squeaky, nasal voice . . . no, quite the opposite, in a soft baritone, reminiscent of the middle range on an organ: "I'm dreaming, I know, but when I wake up,

189

Henriette will be there, and I'll be even happier in reality than in this dream."

He saunters down the final sand dune on the shore of what he assumes to be an island. He trips over something: a tortoise with jewels set in its shell. It nods at him with its wrinkled old-man's head, and he senses it wants to communicate with him, but its way of thinking is so slow, so archaic, he can't translate it into his own tongue, and anyway the girl is waiting for him.

She's wearing a silk mask, he sees it now. His own. "Henriette?" he says, but she doesn't react; and suddenly he realises she is deaf, that in an act of self-sacrificing love she has taken his deformity on herself, along with his mask. Then he takes her mask off in order, once more, to exchange destinies with her, and when, a moment later, he opens his eyes, she is as endearingly beautiful as ever . . .


She is lying in bed beside him in his room in von Below's palace. The moon is casting a milky white light across the floor. Nobody sleeps as elegantly as Henriette, he thinks, like a temple dancer, with one hand on her forehead and her mouth formed into a kiss.

How long has she been there?

Since midnight, when she, cat-like, sneaked through your door and lay down beside you, Hercule, twice your length, twice your weight, infinitely more beautiful, though not more loving, since love, like silence, or come to that, eternity, cannot be multiplied.

Night broods over the house. Everyone is asleep except the tortoises who, with unending meekness, go on crawling across the floors downstairs. Henriette moans in her sleep, a tress of hair has fallen across her face and using two of his toes he brushes it aside and tucks it behind her ear. Whereupon she smiles in her angelic dream, in which he partakes, since if he concentrates hard enough, he is able to follow the series of dream images and finds to his astonishment that she is dreaming the same dream he has just dreamed. She too, is on the beach of an unknown island. He sees her, still wearing his mask, though in her dream he's the same as he always is, and she can hear and speak as usual. *Hercule*, she thinks in the dream, *why did you lend me your mask?*

There he sits in the night, unable to answer, still in phase with his unspeakable joy; dissecting it, examining a thousand wondrous particles spread before him on the quilt, reassembling them in the same pattern as before, or in a new and equally perfect one; a happiness beyond his wildest dreams, beyond anything he could ever have imagined.

But these last few weeks' restlessness has been a steady companion, so he gets up, rocks himself carefully from side to side until he has picked up enough momentum to roll over to the edge of the bed, turns on his axis, and slides, feet first, down to the floor, no mean drop for a man of his inconsiderable stature.

A beam of moonlight runs the length of the room. The light falls on to him like a weightless mantle. Now he goes and sits down at the desk by the window; a child's desk with a footstool for a chair. Carefully he opens the drawer, takes out a quarto sheet of paper between two toes and puts it on the desk. He eases off the top of the inkwell, picks up the quill between his big and second toe, dips the tip into rose-scented ink, wipes off a superfluous drop on the blotting paper, and writes: "I, Hercule Barfuss, am about to embark on a new life . . ."

A blot has formed beside the lavish initial letter he drew; never mind, he thinks, and goes on, words to the effect that he's just been born anew, is reborn along with his daughter, no, he corrects himself: the year before, when Henriette found him again, an unforgettable moment. Adding that all the years of hardship were as nothing compared with one second of happiness together with the woman he loves. He writes about the tickets to America, about their departure, only a week away, their plans and the precautions they have taken, the trunks packed in secret and the money they've set aside. Charlotte, his daughter, they will take with them. Everything is planned down to the last detail, they have rented a carriage which is to take them to Hamburg-Altona. They have a confidante, the squint-eyed Lisaveta, who runs their errands no questions asked, the baron must on no account become suspicious.

The thought of the baron makes his heart constrict. His happiness will be the baron's tragedy. He is a noble soul, he thinks, and he is indebted to him. After all, he was the one who rescued Henriette, wasn't he?

Yes, von Below's the last in a long line of this waning species and it hurts him to have to deprive the baron of the woman he loves almost as much as he himself does . . . Whereupon a pang of jealousy passes through him. He can't help it, for jealousy is ever love's morbid companion in funeral clothes, a death in miniature that leaves a taste of lead in one's mouth. The object of this emotion could well have been of a lower moral standing, but jealousy is non-negotiable. Love's inflamed appendix, it lives its own life, so he lets himself be placated by Henriette's assurances that although she is indeed most grateful to the baron for all he has done for her, it counts for nothing in love's omnipotent perspective.

The moon goes in behind a cloud and the room turns pitch black. Hercule gropes for the lamp with his feet, finds it, screws up the wick, lifts the glass and lights a tar match – all this with an orthopaedic elegance that would secure him a position in any circus. The lamp gives off a greenish glow, like some luminous aquatic plant, had he only been able to imagine such a thing. Again he dips his quill in the inkwell; writes the words symbolising his future: United States of America.

No-one knows what awaits them, but since no-one is able to recall their birth or envisage their own death, everyone already possesses a premonition of eternity and is already living now and for ever. America, he thinks, is a geographic eternity, a carto-graphic "for ever".

He gives a start, so violent he almost loses his balance. On the window ledge, by the trelliswork, sits a raven. It pecks lightly at the windowpane as if trying to draw his attention. Naturally, he can't hear the sound, but instead feels the vibrations. The bird, he surmises, probably sees its own image in the pane, and thinks it has found another of its own kind.

With an instantaneous act of will, Hercule does the most fantastic thing his gift permits: he puts himself inside the raven and looks at himself through its beady eyes. Then he climbs back into his own body again, grasps the pen and writes: "Does the raven see the world in black and white, or does this particular raven just happen to be colour-blind? The image is rough-grained, the mask especially, I forgot to take it off when I went to bed."

The bird takes flight and he with it, first over to the horse-chestnut tree in the yard, where an owl frightens it away with its henchman eyes, so it flies off again, with Barfuss inside it, ten fathoms up, twenty, forty, a hundred, straight into the dark Berlin sky.

He senses the city beneath him; the alleys, courtyards, stables, shopping streets, palaces and hovels. The stench is indescribable, rubbish is piled everywhere, dead rats float in the gutters amid human excrement thrown down from windows and balconies, but that's how nineteenth-century cities are: gigantic rubbish dumps, refuse tips for their budding civilisation.

The bird's consciousness, he notes, is no better than that of an imbecile, its thoughts are obsessive, scarcely distinguishable from instinct. For days on end, without cease, it repeats the selfsame thing: *rest, rest, rest*, or *thirst, thirst, thirst*. It sees everything with the same liberating air of indifference, nothing causing it to become unduly elated nor, for that matter, sad.

It's a dark night. The only visible sources of light come from a street lamp, or a window behind which a student sits studying, or a seamstress works late. Animals sleep in stables and sties. It is cold, the air extremely damp.

This last year he has been freer than ever before in his use of his gift. For hours on end he can travel with what he has begun to call his "carriers". A cat. A bird. Sometimes a mule or an ox. Only in exceptional cases, a human being, and then, preferably, a child. Sometimes he lets himself be carried several miles outside the city. It is easy for him to break off the journey and come back to his body whenever he wishes. But the night is long and he is restless, so he takes a respite behind the raven's eyes, gliding in ever widening circles above the von Below palace, feeling a little dizzy and seeing the world in black and white, until the bird descends and lands at the foreman's window.

A lamp fuelled with train-oil is alight, and the foreman, standing by a sideboard, is getting dressed. What's he up to at this late hour? By the look of things, some urgent business. He's trying to pull his boots on at the same time as he's frantically looking for a bushel for the light. *They've come*, he thinks, just these words, *they've come* . . . invoking the image of some serious-minded gentlemen whose faces Barfuss can't recall having seen before.

The raven, unaware of being steered like a kite on the string of a human will, lifts again and lands eight windows away at Lisaveta's, the housemaid of Russian descent. Distracted, a trifle unsure of its own motives, and maybe even a little sceptical about its own strength of character, the bird pecks at some seed on the windowsill. From here Hercule can intuit the girl's dream; something about money and her mother. Lisaveta's the only one of the servants who isn't frightened off by his appearance. Sometimes he has even felt feelings of sympathy emanating from her, and to Henriette she has always been as loyal as a daughter. She is almost twelve years old, and was bought by von Below at one of the workhouse auctions.

Again the raven takes off and lands in a tree outside the garden wall. The bird is as sleepless as he is, it has lost something, but can no longer remember what: his mate perhaps . . . or a chick? The moon reappears. Three men are standing outside the garden wall, one of them, oddly enough, has a monkey on his shoulder. But the bird, which has sighted a crust of bread on the ground, isn't interested in the remarkable group, and at the same moment as it lands before its booty, Hercule too loses interest and returns to the desk.

Death, he thinks, not knowing where the word has cropped up from so suddenly. Henriette, who has instructed him in life's complicated book of rules, has once told him about the city repository where von Below wants to be taken when he is thought to be dead. It's to Berlin's repositories doubtful cases of persons apparently dead are taken with a bell tied to one foot. Not until they have been there several weeks without once having rung the bell, and are already beginning to smell, are they carted off to the churchyard to be buried in Christian soil. Love's repository . . . he thinks, but doesn't pursue the thought, because now, on his extrasensory wavelength, he notices the foreman leave his room. Something has been bothering him for weeks now, but love, which makes Hercule less inclined to rummage about in other people's minds, causes him to throw caution to the winds. He has quite enough to cope with in the emotional landslide unleashed in him by Henriette and his daughter.

Lowering his pen, he looks around him. His girl is sleeping her cherubic sleep. She is beauty personified: her long, naturally wavy hair, her smile's touch of eternity, her noble profile, the triumphant arch of her nose, the almond eyes, her gait – like that of a timid gazelle – the perfect breasts, the profundity of her gaze,

194

the wise feet, the furtive ears, the sensitive temples, the holy vault of her forehead, the exotic fruit that is her mouth. He closes his eyes to avoid the thought of having to wake her up before dawn breaks, so that she has time to sneak back into her own room before the household awakes.

Will their daughter be as beautiful? For several months he had feared the worst, but the girl had been born without any deformities. In his mind's eye he sees them together in America. Unspeakably happy.

Then still sitting up, he dozes off. It's been a long week, filled with preparations for their journey. He dreams about a rat. Dressed in a frock coat and wearing a green mitre, the rat hands him a letter, warning him of something terrible about to happen. Then, caught out unprepared on this fateful night, he wakes up in a cold sweat, still seated in the same position he'd fallen asleep in: on the stool by the child-size desk, with a quill pen between his toes.

Henriette moans in her sleep. She needs her sleep, he thinks, soon enough she'll need all her reserved energy. He puts the pen down, wipes a blob of ink off his toe, walks silently over to the bed, climbs up into it by the steps the foreman has made for him. He strokes her cheek with his foot, and she emits another moan. It must be the moon- and lamplight that are troubling her, he thinks, and with amazing alacrity he takes off his mask and places it on her face to shield her eyes. She is curled on her side, her knees pulled up under her breasts. In this gloomy light, it occurs to him, they could be mistaken for each other.

He returns to the desk, but halts in the shaft of moonlight in the middle of the floor. The revolving antennae of his sixth sense are signalling some kind of movement, he focuses his attention and in his consciousness, so blurred by happiness, appears a single image. The monkey!

The monkey he had seen through the eyes of the raven shortly before was somewhere in the house.

How could it have got in? He doesn't know. Its mind is that of a child. It sees nothing in the dark and appears to be deeply confused.

He opens the door and walks out into the corridor to see if it's there. Nothing. All that's moving is the shadow of some trees lit up from behind by a sentimental moon. He carries on down the stairs, into the main building, coming to a halt outside the wet-nurse's door. She's dreaming a complicated dream in which someone keeps repeating the words: "It was on a Tuesday in April." Next to her, in a cradle, his daughter is sleeping. She, the newborn, is also dreaming, but kaleidoscopically, in blocks of colour mixed on an internal palette. Vague contours, hands maybe, appear out of a red backdrop. The dream is wordless. Suddenly, in her dream, he sees his masked face, perceives the memories she has of the wet-nurse's heartbeat, the rich flavour of breast milk, which makes her mouth water, and the memory of mother Henriette's smell.

Such is an infant's dream, he reflects, a fog in which the world is only very slowly acquiring any contours. No language, no feelings beyond those of hunger and thirst, a sense of well-being disturbed by colic pains. Good and evil are unknown, as are beauty and deformity. All this, life will teach her, little by little, and as always, of course, unasked.

He turns his attentions to those asleep in the opposite wing. Von Below's sleep, he observes, is tranquillity itself. The baron rarely dreams, and when he does, his dreams are of a practical nature and conform to a clearly defined grammar. But the foreman, where is he? Not in his room.

Perplexed, Hercule turns round.

Where, then, *is* the foreman?

Suddenly he knows it. By the kitchen door!

And somewhere in the house, in a space he doesn't recognise at all, is the monkey, together with a stranger. His heart beating wildly, he runs as fast as his dwarf legs will carry him back to the other wing, up the stairs, along the corridor where the trees perform their Indonesian shadow dance along the walls. Trips over the edge of a carpet, bumps into a chest of drawers. Something clumsy is moving about in a corner: one of the bejewelled tortoises.

His little lungs strain under the effort, in his throat a gurgle rises up, the closest his deformed speech organs can get to letting out a scream. The door is open, just as he left it. But the bookshelf, too, is open, exposing the passage leading to a secret stairway he never knew was there. On the bed, still wearing his mask, lies Henriette.

All this he sees in black and white, just as he had through the eyes of the raven, and for the first time in his life a real scream flies out of his throat, so blood-curdling it almost instantly brings the servants to the room. She's lying there, not moving, curled up into half her size, looking like a masked dwarf.

On the floor lies a razor blade. A monkey, senseless with fear, is climbing up the curtains.

The girl's throat has been slit to the bone.

# VII

CHRISTLISCHER ANZEIGER, Ratibor, January 14, 1837

# Tragic suicide or bestial manslaughter?

Over the last week a mysterious death has divided the citizens of this town into two factions and given rise to a furious debate about guilt and crime in our youthful epoch. On Twelfth Night, crofter J. Langenmüller found the corpse of an unknown male hanging from a tree in the churchyard of the neighbouring village, Jägerndorf. Deputy parish clerk Langenmüller, highly esteemed for his display of courage in the forest fire last year, summoned Constable Köhler who promptly arrived in the company of the parish dean, Heinemann. They were able to identify the deceased as being S. Moosbrugger, former watchman at the Ratibor lunatic asylum,

reported missing by his brother since the day after Christmas.

As our readers know, a post-mortem examination was carried out at the local mortuary. Barber-surgeon Jansen determined the cause of death as suffocation by noose, but also detected traces of external violence having been inflicted on the deceased's body. Before the moment of death, Moosbrugger's head had received several blows with a blunt instrument, which, however, according to Jansen, had in themselves not caused fatal injuries. Furthermore, his hand had been badly maimed: three fingers had been ripped from their joints, several lumps of molten lead had penetrated the bones of the hand, as also had a link from a heavy chain. Some signs resembling letters, deciphered by the constable as the words "seven years" were engraved into the deceased's back. The date of death has been determined as around the first of the month.

Constable Köhler initiated a door-to-door search in the immediate vicinity of where the body had been found, but as our readers know, no-one had anything of import to relate. With the aid of the graveyard's caretaker it was ascertained that the corpse had in all likelihood been hung up from the tree not more than a few hours before being discovered. It had not been there on the previous day when several people from the village had lit candles at the graves.

Because of the Twelfth Night festivities, the brother of the deceased and next of kin, K. Moosbrugger, was not summoned to a hearing at the Royal Gendarmerie until four days later. According to Constable Köhler he acted in such a nervous manner that a decision was made to take him into custody. The hearing was resumed in the presence of County Police Commissioner Brink, to whom Moosbrugger had in person reported his brother as missing at Christmas time.

According to the hearings held with Moosbrugger, the deceased had entertained notions of suicide ever since the brothers had been dismissed from the lunatic asylum last month following an anonymous letter – believed to be from a former inmate – which claimed that they had abused their charges, stolen their food, clothing and firewood, and through such cruel and neglectful treatment caused the deaths of many in their care. This scandal, as our readers may recall, has been reported in the *Anzeiger*.

On the day after Christmas, when K. Moosbrugger last saw his brother, the latter was deeply melancholic and had spoken about his imminent suicide. Moosbrugger maintains that he took leave of his brother at an inn before returning home for his supper.

According to sources at the *Anzeiger*'s disposal, Herr Moosbrugger is as yet not suspected of having committed murder, although certain information indicates that he may have knowledge of the villain's identity. Although it is quite clear that the body had been moved, the possibility of suicide, according to Constable Köhler, has not yet been excluded. According to the medical examination it is possible the deceased may first have committed suicide, then been maimed and moved to the graveyard by an unknown perpetrator. Meanwhile, the townsfolk are speculating about the motives for both murder and suicide. A sense of oppression has befallen us all. "This new era", Commissioner Rau is reported as having said shortly before this edition went to press, "brings us not only manufacturers and railways, but also ever more heinous crimes." The editor and the gendarmerie both welcome any information that may lead to the solution of this most tragic death.

202

# Moosbrugger under arrest

On Friday, County Police Commissioner Brink decided to take 42-year-old Karl Moosbrugger into custody, as reasonably suspected of the murder of his younger brother Stephan. As yet no admission has been forthcoming on the part of the detainee, but according to *Anzeiger*'s sources, witnesses have come forward with information pointing to Moosbrugger as a suspect. Constable Köhler has made a statement whereby he promises to keep the public up to date with any new information that can throw light on the tragedy. A man said to have been in the vicinity of the churchyard on January 6 is being looked for by the district public prosecutor. Should this person be one of the *Anzeiger*'s readers, we ask him to contact the authorities or our editorial office.

# Moosbrugger to be prosecuted

Over the last few weeks there has been much speculation in our town as to whether or not K. Moosbrugger is guilty of his younger brother's death. According to the sworn statement from the man under arrest, Stephan Moosbrugger took his own life as a result of being dismissed from the lunatic asylum last year. How Herr Moosbrugger can be so confident that this is so is a mystery to the editorial office, since he claims not to have seen his brother since Christmas, when he was alone and patronising one of the local inns.

When the *Anzeiger* spoke to County Police Commissioner Brink two evenings ago, Karl Moosbrugger had as yet not confessed. He maintains that his brother had entertained notions of suicide ever since the scandal at the asylum came to light. To all appearances this information has been contrived by the suspect in order to obstruct the investigation.

# Moosbrugger confesses to murder

After two weeks in custody Karl Moosbrugger has finally confessed to the murder of his younger brother Stephan. According to Police Commissioner Brink, the case is extremely delicate, the deed having displayed a brutality which "seems symptomatic of our times".

According to the minutes of the inquest, Karl Moosbrugger had, in fact, two days after Christmas looked in with his brother at the Three Anchors in our neighbouring village of Jägerndorf. A new witness recounts that a row had broken out about the thefts of firewood at the Ratibor asylum. At about ten o'clock, so the new witness reports, the brothers left the premises. What happened then was enough to shake any decent citizen in this part of the country. Nearby in a discontinued smithy Moosbrugger apparently knocked out his brother with a hammer before chaining him to an iron girder. The man under arrest then nailed his brother "through the tongue, to the wall", as well as melting down a pound of lead and pouring it over the unconscious man so that "he was by now not only nailed to the wall by his tongue, but also fused together by his right hand with the iron girder and chain". In this abhorrent manner Moosbrugger held his brother prisoner for four days and nights, submitting him to brutal torture, even going so far as to inscribe a "few words" in his back with a chisel. In the end, he strangled him with a noose, and then, under cover of night, carried the body to the nearby churchyard.

The suspect has as yet been unable to give a reasonable explanation for these acts of unprecedented cruelty. According to Constable Köhler he seems utterly confused and maintained throughout the interrogation: "It was the Devil himself who made me do what I did. He told me exactly what to do."

The admission is confirmed by the depositions of several witnesses. A seamstress of the parish, Fräulein Rachel Mandelbaum, is said to have met the two brothers on the road to the smithy on the evening in question. The innkeeper of the Three Anchors who previously claimed he had no memory of the brothers being there has now changed his evidence. A third witness, a child, probably a boy, who is said to have been seen around the smithy on New Year's night is still being sought by the prosecutor.

According to Police Commissioner Brink, the Moosbrugger case shows a clear indication of the dangers afflicting our modern era: "Corrupting publications are everywhere readily available, morals are dissolving, the move into cities is leading to divorces and anarchy."

The house was built in the Italian style and surrounded by an overgrown garden. A light snowfall had powdered the grounds, but being dressed in furs – a cat's dense fur, to be precise – Hercule didn't feel the cold. More importantly, he was availing himself of the cat's eyes.

Behind the windowpane the room lay in darkness. He could see so well in the dark that he could make out every detail. Large mahogany shelves filled with books lined the walls. Rows and rows of books like an unending keyboard: treatises, reference books, card indexes and legal documents. *Trials and Punishments of Animals*, he read on the spine of one tome bound in calf leather. *Delinquent Man* on another.

The cat's eyes swept over the English-style armchairs, the grand piano regally placed in the centre of the room, the desk covered with piles of documents. It was all that he could do to keep the animal under control. It was only by the force of his hatred, he thought, which held in its icy grip all other feelings, as if at bayonet point. A hatred which had kept him sleepless through endless nights of self-reproach, a hatred that never gave him a moment's peace, a hatred that compelled him to act.

At the far end of the room was a cabinet filled with naturalia. Engraved on a brass plate were the words *pantera unica*, or snow leopard. It was fastened to a plinth which was covered with sawdust that had been dipped in white paint, presumably to represent snow. The animal had been caught in an unnatural leap towards a stuffed Asiatic golden cat: *Felis temmincki*. A spotted hyena stood over something supposedly representing a carcass.

Where was his own body? Out in the overgrown garden, reclining in the dust. Snow was falling on his masked face; but his sleeping body was as unaware of the weather as of the contents of the natural history cabinet.

Above the bookshelves a couple of stuffed birds regarded the room. *Milvas milvas*: kite. And beside it, a black vulture the taxidermist had immortalised perching on a leafless branch. In its beak the vulture held a scrap of bloody meat. Just like the abbot in his cellar, he thought.

The door to the room opened and a housemaid entered carrying a paraffin lamp. Walking alongside the wall, the girl lit the lamps attached to it one by one and having done so crouched down on her haunches by the tiled stove, scraped out the ashes, put in more coal and blew life into the embers, opened the damper so that the fire would get going, then got up again and started walking around the room, curiously examining its contents.

From a ship's captain's table, superbly carved, she picked up a book and leafed carefully through its pages. Picked up a paperweight, and admired a porcelain ballet-dancer doll. Then she stiffened, her eyebrows raised in alarm, deftly replaced the objects in their rightful places. She smoothed her dress, checked the bow of her pinafore, quickly smoothed her hand over her hair and assumed a nervous smile at the very same moment as the door opened again.

A man came into the room. The years had deprived him of his hair, leaving a shiny tonsure in pledge. Locking the door behind him, he loosened his shirt collar and gestured absent-mindedly to the girl. She was very young, Hercule noticed, thirteen, fourteen at most.

Was this really the man he was looking for? He remembered him differently, from their single meeting long ago when the world had been in its cradle. And yet he was sure. He trusted in his hatred, this human emotion that cannot be clouded, that lives its own life beyond reason, and that is impossible to confuse with any other.

At a given sign the girl fell to her knees at the man's feet. Fumbling with his fly buttons, he dug into his trousers and took out what was left of his male member. A suture had been made just below the foreskin, which was blackened. The flesh surrounding the urinary orifice had turned into a necrotic callus.

The girl closed her eyes. Secure in the knowledge that he had locked the door, the man rocked his hips rhythmically to and fro as he thrust himself more and more deeply into her mouth. Her lips trembled, her eyes were tightly shut . . . The man's organ grew, he thrust harder still. Close to vomiting, the girl gasped. Tears welled up in the corners of her eyes. Breathing through his mouth, the man groaned, grabbed hold of her hair . . . dug his fingers into her hair knot and opened his eyes wide. Then he buttoned up his fly, smoothed the creases in his trousers and threw a quick glance at the wall mirror.

The girl, immobile, remained crouching. The man passed her a handkerchief. She spat into it. He dried off her mouth, went to his desk and settled down to his work.


Now the girl was gone and the red flush had disappeared from the man's face. Distractedly, he leafed through a few legal documents before, submitting to an inexplicable bout of restlessness, he got up from his desk chair.

The cabinet with its naturalia, its immobile fauna, triggered off another train of thought, and his glance passed his eyes along the bookshelves, to one of the volumes the cat had just been focusing on: *Trials and Punishments of Animals*.

It occurred to him that the criminal case he was just now working on, whose outcome he'd been summoned to witness the following day, had much in common with animal lawsuits of old.

His thoughts strayed on to a certain favourite uncle on his mother's side, the venerable Heidelberg district prosecutor Roes, dead this past decade, but vividly alive in his memory. In his youth, when he had been studying law at the university in Erlangen and had spent his holidays with him, Uncle Roes had told him about animal prosecutions he'd been personally in charge of some thirty years earlier, at a time when they still had fallen into the category of general prosecutions. On one occasion a sow and her piglets had been brought to trial for having caused the death of an infant. The sow had received a fair trial, Roes had smilingly assured him, her defender, a highly esteemed member of the Bar Association, had worn a pigtail wig. The interrogations had been conducted, not merely as a matter of form, but in a legally most correct manner. Questions of a personal nature had been put to the sow, which of course she had been unable to answer:

"What caused you to ignore the baby's cries for help?" and, "What made you take your piglets down to the common? Was there a motive for your action? Can you present us with any extenuating circumstances?"

The sow had replied by turning round in the witness box, where she stood like anyone else under prosecution, and stared in astonishment at her defender, a certain Court Delegate Lehr, who was just about to deliver his speech.

Further away in the courtroom sat an astounded public. Roes remembered the sow's master, a local crofter who, overwrought at his child's death, had screamed abuse at his pig, and applauded when the chairman had imposed the maximum penalty for infanticide.

Two days later the offender had been hanged on Heidelberg's gallows hill and her carcass buried in a field. Roes had found the fate of the piglets particularly amusing: they'd been acquitted on grounds of their tender years. Later, one of them had turned up on his dinner table.

Inspired by these recollections, the man now took out the volume, sat down in an armchair and began turning the pages. In Hamburg, AD 1601, he read, a cockerel had been sentenced to be burned at the stake for the heretical and unnatural crime of having laid an egg. Should a toad or a snake brood on such an egg, it could, according to popular belief, greatly endanger its surroundings: a basilisk might hatch out, with widespread death and disease as a result.

Backed up by the famous piece in Exodus 21:28, beasts had at times been considered no less responsible for their actions than humans: "If an ox gore a man or a woman, that they die: then the ox shall be surely stoned." Thus man and beast were equal in the eyes of the law, and by joining Mosaic law to Roman law, European man had laid the foundations of his civilisation.

Then there was a piece about murder and fornication committed by horses, bulls, oxen, dogs and even cats. A footnote told of how a stallion had been tortured to make him confess to having caused criminal damage. Magnanimity or an excellent defence had led to some of the animals being pardoned, or, as in the case of the piglets, because they had been minors at the time of the crime. Moles had been banished from two parishes in Swabia, and a goat had had to pay a fine of milk for pulling down a fence.

*Offensa cujus nominatio crimen est*, the man was thinking as he turned round and saw to his astonishment a pair of cat's eyes flash in the window. "Strays everywhere," he muttered. Like that cat out there. It was only natural if they sometimes caused injuries to humans, simple statistics could tell you that.

He got up and put the book back in its proper place on the shelf. Cautiously he went over to the window and looked at the cat. It was still sitting on the windowsill, absent-mindedly licking one of its paws. It seemed not in the least afraid of him, but looked him straight in the eyes, blinked, and resumed its grooming.

He tapped the glass with a finger. The cat didn't stir.

Perplexed, he went back to his desk. The case he had just put behind him in his judicial capacity might be compared in all its bizarre details to the animal trials of former times, he thought as he began to set his papers in order. Only one document was still needed before he could put the case aside: the accused's death certificate.


The lawsuit and execution the man was working on had drawn attention far beyond the limits of Danzig. The case was, as several of the jurors had put it, inexplicable. It was the motive, primarily, that was in dispute, subject to all thinkable interpretations. Sitting there at his desk, he reflected that he'd never in fact come across anything like it.

Two years earlier, the city had accepted a request from the Jesuit Order to found a house within the diocesan limits. The old one had been abandoned two decades earlier during the religious dispute between Danzig's German Lutherans and a minority of Polish Catholics. A certain Abbot Johann Kippenberg had been responsible for the work, a man who, as far as was known, was an exceedingly conscientious cleric who for years had successfully governed an establishment in Silesia.

The Order had purchased a building in the ancient part of the inner city. After less than a year its members had numbered about forty, half of them novices. The house had cottages where the poor could come and warm themselves, primary schools for indigent children and it carried on certain missionary activities among sailors. Half a dozen older clerics had come with the abbot from Silesia, but one by one, those men had disappeared.

Probably the matter would not have come to light – at least not until much later – had not one of the novices voluntarily reported the disappearances to the police. The boy, a convert by the name of Fischel, had grown suspicious when the abbot had responded to a query about the disappearances by asking him to keep the matter a secret so as not to damage the monastery's reputation. It was not until then, Fischel explained, that he had suspected that all was not as it should be.

The chief constable had set in motion a routine investigation. But when Kippenberg had been summoned for interrogation, he had broken down and, without further ado, confessed to having murdered five of his Order's brethren. The very same day he had pointed out the places where the bodies – that is to say, what remained of them – lay buried in pieces under the chancel of the monastery chapel. The crimes made no sense. The abbot was unable to give any plausible motive whatsoever. He seemed relieved at having confessed, as if an enormous burden had been lifted from his shoulders.

The man at the desk, who had been presiding judge at the trial, had been one of the first to read the shorthand minutes of the inquest, taken down in the new Gabelsberg system. Since that morning in December scarcely a year before when the prosecutor had handed the minutes over to him, he had read through them so many times that by now he knew them off by heart.

Above all, he was mystified by references to "the boy". Kippenberg maintained that he was governed by a voice that could not abide contradiction, a voice that had driven him to commit one bestial act after another. "The boy" was behind all this, he'd said. "The boy" was the real murderer, for it was he who had ordered him to kill his brothers. But when he'd been asked who this "boy" was, the abbot had answered evasively or merely burst into tears, saying the "boy" had forbidden him to tell what he knew.

On one occasion when the judge had visited the gaol incognito, the abbot had been sitting on his cell bunk in deep self-absorption, an imbecilic smile on his lips, and gazing into the distance. Though his lips moved incessantly it was impossible to hear what he was saying. The judge had to address him several times before he even reacted.

"Help me," he'd said in the end, and his voice had been so desperate that those gathered around him had come out in goose pimples. "It was the boy who made me do it. He told me exactly what I had to do."

The murders had been so savage that the newspapers had been reluctant to publicise any details. Kippenberg had imprisoned the monks in a cellar he had rented on the city outskirts. He had forced one of them to drink hydrocyanic acid and nailed another to the wall as if crucified, even thrust a processional crucifix up his anus. Two others he'd turned into living torches, and then eaten them up piecemeal, "grilled and superbly spiced", as he admitted under cross-examination, without so much as batting an eyelid. The fifth one, whose head was still missing, he had carved up, alive, into little bits: a toe, a finger, the genitals, the ears. After that he'd locked a starved stray cat in the cellar. The monk, he had confessed, was still alive when the animal started feasting on him.

"The boy tells me exactly what I have to do," Kippenberg had repeated on being asked for the reason for these excesses. "The boy is driven by a hatred beyond belief. He's avenging himself for what we did to Schuster."

"What boy?" they had asked again. "And who is Schuster?"

"The mind-reader," had been the abbot's cryptic answer, "Schuster's deaf and dumb protégé." Whereupon he'd fallen into a fit of hysterical weeping.

The name Schuster had cropped up so many times during the interrogation that the police felt impelled to make certain enquiries. Schuster, it turned out, was an old Jesuit priest who, years earlier, had disappeared under mysterious circumstances on a pilgrimage to Italy. "We sent him to his death, knowingly," had been Kippenberg's comment. "Myself and the other five . . . the ones the boy instructed me to kill . . . it was we who had

Schuster sent off to his death, that's why the boy's avenging himself . . ."

One of the experts summoned by the court came up with the hypothesis that Abbot Kippenberg was a pyromaniac, since the police investigation showed that he, together with two brethren, had burned some of the house's collection of books, and that this, according to one witness, had apparently given him a "dispro-portionate sense of satisfaction". It was not impossible that behind the abbot's weird actions lay a combination of perversions.

In his report this expert had had the sexual offenders classified in a spirit almost worthy of Linnaeus. Apart from pyromaniacs, the list had included sodomites, pederasts and exhibitionists. Then there were perversions the mere mention of which sent shudders up the spines of the members of the court: gerontophiles, perverts with a predilection for having intercourse with the very aged; zoophiles and zooerasters who preferred animals. Further, presbyophiles who raped the blind, and gynecomasters of both sexes, united in the worship of men with matured female breasts. Then there were the so-called invertites who were prepared to pay a small fortune for one night with a hermaphrodite, not to mention dysparaneutics, men who favoured females who suffered agonies of the womb during sexual intercourse. It might well be, the report concluded dryly, that several of these perversions are indulged by the abbot.

The similarity with animal trials of bygone days, the judge was thinking, lingered on in the starving cat the abbot had let loose on his fifth victim. In his uncle's day and age, might not the cat have been brought to trial as an accomplice to murder?

The crimes, moreover, were of such a kind that Kippenberg's brethren had denied him absolution on the eve of his execution. Even the prison chaplain had refused to bless the condemned man, while no fewer than eight Catholic blacksmiths had offered to fashion a broad axe. It was unprecedented: a Catholic, an abbot no less, denied unction!

A rumour was going the rounds that the abbot's hair had turned white as chalk during his last week, and that his fear of the "other side" had driven him out of his mind. According to information received from the prison governor, he'd spent his last hours staring at the crucifix on the wall of his cell, his body in cramps and convulsions, as one possessed. He'd screamed at the prison guards that they'd better watch out, because, although the boy had made himself invisible, he was right there, close at hand. Several times he asked whether they could hear his voice. Himself, he could hear it loud and clear, the boy was "laughing" at him and "mocking" him.

"The abbot ain't waitin' for hell," one of the prison warders had observed to the prison governor, unable to contain his malicious pleasure, "him's there already."

Sitting at his desk, the judge thought he didn't much believe in mankind's spiritual profitability, least of all in his own. He cultivated the thought that morals have no intrinsic values of their own; they need tasks to endow them with meaning. The Jesuits were most likely prepared to agree with him, though naturally they would have condemned him had they known his motives.

He recalled the counsel for Kippenberg's defence, who had rounded off his speech with a few words well worth considering: "Our verdict on a deed is never the same as the verdict for the aspect of the deed that God punishes or rewards."

God alone knows the true nature of a deed. But if God existed, he would also know the true nature of the judge, and not only his own moral shortcomings . . .

The clock had just struck eleven when he laid aside the minutes of the trial. A branch was tapping the window. Turning round, he saw the cat was still there.

It must be sick, he thought, or deeply confused. Why else is it still sitting on that windowsill?

He repressed a shudder. Under cross-examination the abbot had told of the stray cat he'd let loose on his last victim. "A mottled tom-cat," he'd said in a tone of voice one might use about some much-loved family pet. "It had lost an ear in a fight, and had a white patch on its forehead."

The judge got up and walked over to the window. Confusedly he wondered if this could possibly be the same animal. This creature too, had an ear missing, though the patch on its forehead was more grey than white.

Next day was a Saturday. The judge rose early so as to be in good time for the abbot's execution. His wife, the aristocratic Rosalinda von Kiesingen, with whom he had not been intimate for the best part of a decade, since the unfortunate maiming incident, about the details of which she still remained in doubt, regarded him with sleep-dazed eyes from her bedside as he did his morning toilet.

He poured water from the enamel pitcher, lathered the soap and took out a razor. As he shaved himself he pondered whether it was fitting to wear eau de cologne to an execution. He reminded himself of his duties. It was he, together with the doctor, who would ascertain that death had occurred. A death certificate would be signed, and a receipt issued for the doomed man's last possessions. In view of all this he laid aside the aftershave lotion.

Dusting his armpits with talcum powder, he put on his starched front shirt, the loose collar with the silver button, the waistcoat and his dark official suit. Just as he was about to wind up his pocket watch, his wife sat up in bed.

"There's someone out there," she said. "Someone's spying on us."

"You're imagining things," he said.

But she insisted. "There's someone outside that window! Please go and take a look."

The judge went over to the French windows and drew up the blinds. What he saw made him start so violently that he almost lost his balance: at eye level, only a couple of inches away, was the stray cat. The animal's breathing on the windowpane had misted it over. It was hissing quietly and baring its teeth. Heart pounding wildly, the judge looked into the spots in its amber-coloured irises, the almond-shaped pupils, and the red scar where there'd once been an ear. It hissed again, with hatred, so it seemed to him, before vanishing into the garden in three bounds.

"Something ought to be done about them," his wife said, worried. "A cat-plague seems to have broken out."

"Must be a good year for rats, then," he answered.

"In that case the rat killers should be doing better. What did it look like?"

He described the cat; the mottled fur, the patch on the forehead, the missing ear.

"Must be the same one," she said. "It's been hanging around the house for almost a week. Yesterday morning it went for the gardener."

The judge nodded, parting his hair down the middle with his comb.

"The servants have attempted to catch it," his wife went on. "But it's a sly one. By the way, there have been some more cases of hydrophobia reported from Pomerania."

He cast a hurried glance through the window. The cat was nowhere to be seen. Instead, seeing rainclouds piling up, he looked in the cupboard for an umbrella.

"Will you be gone long?" his wife asked.

"Until dinnertime."

"How awful to have to witness an execution."

"It's all part of the job."

"For the masses it's just a bit of entertainment. I wish we could kill that cat instead of a Jesuit."

"Kippenberg's a murderer," he retorted. "He deserves his punishment!"

"Who knows but that cat isn't just as vile an assassin? Hydrophobia is every bit as serious a matter. It hissed so at the gardener it scared him. I'm worried for the girls. What if they get bitten?"

He nodded solemnly.

"You're right," he said. "I'll have a word with the mayor. The rat killers must be given greater resources . . ."


A little later, on entering the dining room, the judge again saw the cat. This time it was perched in a tree outside the kitchen door. The coachman and one of the maids were trying to frighten it away. The girl was throwing stones, the coachman brandishing a rake. But the cat showed no signs of fear. Baring its teeth, it spat and hissed as if considering attacking them.

The housemaid, the young one he'd been diverting himself with this past month, served him his breakfast. She blushed and refused to meet his eye.

"Know anything about that rascal?" he asked, indicating the scene outside the window.

"It came here a week ago, sir," she answered.

"Why haven't you tried to scare it off earlier?"

"It ain't so easily frightened, sir."

"What do you mean?"

"It bites if you gets too close."

"I want you to speak to the gardener," he said. "Tell him to set a trap, or shoot it if that's more expedient. And make sure the girls stay indoors until I get home."

He ate quickly, glancing through the incomplete death certificate. Two attestations missing, he thought, and anyway the Kippenberg case would be added to the records without in fact having been properly solved. Still no motive, nor was there an answer to the riddle about "the boy" or "the voice". He cut short his ponderings and looked at his pocket watch; if he didn't hurry now he'd be late . . .

When he came out into the yard, the coachman had already brought the coach round. The cat was no longer anywhere in sight.

"Scooted off down to the woods," the coachman explained. "But I swear to God, sir, it'll be back any moment. Seems to me it's looking for something."

"And what might that be?"

"Don't know, sir. But looks like it's lost something, and if you bothers it, it gets mad."

The air was still heavy with impending rain which the judge hoped would soon start to fall. A downpour might keep the crowds away from the place of execution.

"The gardener will have to deal with it," he said. "A couple of traps should do the trick."

"Don't think as how it will, sir. There's something eerie about that cat. A proper witch's cat, if you ask me."

The judge was just about to climb into the coupé when he again saw the animal, this time over by the garden gate. He asked the coachman to wait a moment.

Armed with his furled umbrella, he approached the gate where the cat was sitting, motionless, on the gravel. He threw some stones, but it didn't budge. Just went on looking at him, exactly as it had done yesterday evening, very calmly, without averting its gaze.

Now he was no more than three feet away from it. The cat put its back up and looked intensely at him, straight in the eyes. Cautiously he lifted the umbrella. A single forceful blow, he thought, and that would be that.

But, in that very same instant quite another sensation overwhelmed him. This cat that was staring him in the eye, he felt, was trying to tell him something. Of course it was absurd, but he couldn't explain it any other way. It felt as if the creature was trying to whisper something to him, inaudibly, though he didn't know what.

Suddenly he felt giddy. Could it have something to do with the execution, he wondered; all this unending work he'd recently done supervising it? He felt an irresistible urge to touch the animal, put out a hand and stroke its fur. And when he listened, he felt that this was precisely what the cat was whispering: *Touch me, touch me!*

He did. The cat looked at him. Bewildered by his own behaviour, he stretched out his hand. Cats can't talk, he thought, or whisper, or think. At that moment, he felt a sharp pain in the back of his hand. The cat had scratched him. Frightened, he let out a cry, and at that same moment the monster, with unnatural swiftness, vanished into the undergrowth.


By the time the judge arrived at the site of the execution, a large crowd had already gathered, men and women of all ages, also a few children. Women in particular would come to executions, stricken by some sort of sinister bloodlust. If one wasn't careful, it could all degenerate into a riot. He had heard them howl with suppressed passion as a murderer was led away to the headsman. And then seen them vomit when the broad axe fell. A company of recruits had been ordered out to form a rank of fixed bayonets as the doomed man approached.

At the witness stand the judge greeted the persons of authority presiding. A secretary from the mayor's office, the doctor, the county police commissioner, the parish constable and the prison governor.

Ignoring their enquiries about his bandaged hand, he muttered, "Nothing worth mentioning. Accident with a stray cat."

A young medical student had obtained permission to examine the murderer's head immediately after decapitation. Science wanted to ascertain whether any living reflexes were left after it had been severed from the body. "Blinking," he'd divulge expertly, "eye movements, lips still twitching . . ."

Over by the scaffold the executioner was passing the time with his assistant. Only once before had the judge met him, but his appearance was hard to forget. The headsman, himself a pardoned criminal, had had both his ears cut off for stealing cattle.

At the command of the county police commissioner, the recruits shoved the crowds aside in order to leave the scaffold free. Hoping to gather up a few drops of the murderer's blood while it was still fresh, some of the women had equipped themselves with cups and tins. It was said to help against eczema and epilepsia.

As the prisoner's cart appeared round the bend in the road, an excited murmur rose from the crowds. The recruits fell into line and the police commissioner quickly read out the sentence. As Kippenberg climbed down from the cart, silence fell once more. The doomed man was clad in prison garb, shackled and was wearing a black scarf. Fear had robbed him of his sense of balance. He reeled along like a drunk between two prison wardens. The judge noticed that the rumour was true: his hair had indeed turned white as chalk. The prison governor offered him a dram, but the abbot seemed no longer aware of what was going on around him. He collapsed and had to be dragged the last few metres to the block. By now, weeping openly, he was trying to postpone the inevitable with kicks and blows. Forcing him down on to the block, they took off his scarf, but let the shackles remain. The executioner tactfully averted his gaze.

"The boy!" Kippenberg screamed. "The boy's laughing . . . at you too, Your Honour . . . You're next in line!"

To all appearances the headsman had been drinking. The first blow cut into the doomed man's shoulder. The sound of a collarbone cracking could be heard loud and clear by everyone. Kippenberg didn't make a sound, but his eyes rotated in their sockets so that only the whites showed. The headsman struck again, this time striking Kippenberg in the back. After this, the mob began to jeer at the executioner. A woman in the front row fainted. Not until the third attempt, by which point Kippenberg had already lost consciousness, did the headsman succeed in decapitating him. The blow fell aslant, separating the upper part of the abbot's head from the lower, the lower jaw still hanging intact on the neck, its line of teeth in a perfect horseshoe. The fountain of blood spurted from the carotid artery.

218

Von Kiesingen looked the other way. The prison governor, he noted, was leaning over the platform, vomiting straight down into the crowd. The young medical student, on the other hand, appeared to be in fine fettle. Fifteen metres away, the judge saw him standing with the severed head in his hands. It made him think of an insane Hamlet, wildly shaking a bloodied skull in the hope of making it blink.

Seen from the perspective of a stray cat, the garden was simply one part of a vast nature. The house was of no interest to him, nor were its people. For more than an hour he'd been lying in wait by a molehill on the slope leading down to the woods. Now, without forewarning, the animal was filled with a dark power which had of late been coming and going from its consciousness at will. A power that extinguished its own intention and, seemingly imprisoned within itself, turned the cat into an obedient instrument, as if obscure reasons were investing its body, never asking why. Thus, the cat relinquished its plans to go hunting and left the garden slope.

Creeping through the undergrowth and rose-hip bushes, it threw a disdainful glance at the cat-trap hung up by the head gardener in a tree some hours before. Still on the alert for any humans who might be about, those beings who, screaming insanely, had not long ago chased it, it made its way down into a ditch, slouched onwards, came suddenly to a halt and looked out over the woods. There, in the fork of a tree and all but hidden by its foliage, was a stunted man with a mask on his face, seemingly asleep. Leaves and pine cones had fallen on the little fellow's clothes, and he was sitting so still a spider could have begun spinning its web between his feet. But a moment later the stray cat, soon tiring of what it saw, availed itself of the natural protection afforded by the screen of a fountain to stand by the house in front of an open cellar window.

A smell of mould and damp arose from inside. Opening the hatch slightly with its paw, the cat crept in and with an agile leap jumped down on to the floor. For a moment it stood there, a little unsure as to what had actually impelled it to enter this building, with its hostile inhabitants who had just spent hours chasing it, even trying to shoot it. But once more the alien will took over and, with an authority it had to yield to and in a tone that brooked no arguments, drove it silently on through the dark into a confined space filled with foodstuffs, barrels of beer, herring and pork, and where an assortment of hams and sausages hung from rafters in the ceiling making the poor stray's mouth water. Not spoiled with such facile delicacies, his legs ignored an impulse to halt and make a meal of this extravaganza, and had not its short-term feline memory been so dependent on a continual flow of sensory stimulae in order to survive in the world – the heartbeat, for instance, of a mortally terrified prey, or a field mouse's desperate squeakings from its half-metre-deep subterranean nest – had it not been for this flagrant shortcoming in the make-up of a cat's memory, it would doubtless have rebelled against this super-ordinate power that was driving it on.

With a hunter's stealth it made its way up a flight of stairs.

Someone, the housemaid perhaps, had forgotten to close the door properly. A crack of light seeped through. The cat nudged the door. Saw it open.

Now it came into an illumined hallway. A corridor, infinitely long, ran the length of the house, with doors on either side. No movement, no sign of life.

Crouching low, the animal prowled on, hugging the walls as it went, spying, picking up scents, without knowing what mission it was on. From one room, laughter could be heard, from the kitchen a clatter, again the smell of food, inexorably censored by the alien will, driving it on towards another staircase covered in a thick oriental carpet, up to another floor in this strange house where stray cats normally never set a paw.

Then, at some inaudible signal, it halted. By now it was on a dark landing on the building's top floor. A noise made it slink under a sideboard, there unprotestingly to await fresh instructions.


When the judge got home that afternoon he was met by a cacophony of agitated voices. Amid a swarm of servants gathered in the salon he saw his wife. Drawing her aside, he asked her what was going on.

The gardener had had his eye torn out, she explained excitedly, by the same beast that had attacked him that morning. No question about it, the cat was rabid.

The gardener lay outstretched on the floor, his face bandaged. A doctor was bending down over the poor man, shaking his head. "Jansen will be blind in one eye, I'm afraid," he sighed. "There's nothing I can do."

His wife went on to give him a detailed account of what had happened. Following her husband's instructions the gardener had set a trap, which the cat had simply ignored. Whereupon the gardener had attempted to chase it off the grounds. But no matter how he tried, it had refused to leave. In the end all the servants, and even she herself, had taken part in the hunt. But time and again the cat had outwitted them, taking refuge in trees or among the boxhedges' dense growth and every other conceivable hiding place. At last the gardener had gone to fetch his fowling piece. For two whole hours that elderly man had lain on the roof of the coach house waiting for the cat to reappear. Two shots he'd let off, without hitting his target; and the cat, hissing and spitting, had disappeared into the wood that bordered the grounds. Everyone had returned to their duties, in the hope that they'd succeeded in scaring it away.

But later on in the afternoon, when their teenage daughters had ventured out into the garden, it had shown up again. By now, according to the judge's wife, it had become so enraged that it was foaming at the mouth, "more like a dog than a cat", and had attacked the girls, who'd only just managed to take refuge in the house, though one of them had had her knee scratched, and the younger girl, Maria, had twisted her ankle and thereto lost her silver necklace in her flight. Once more the gardener had gone out with the fowling piece; but it was as if the cat guessed what he was up to. The earth seemed to have swallowed it up.

Then, only an hour ago, his wife confirmed, it had turned up again, this time inside the house! No-one could explain how it had got there. There was something unsettling about the animal, as if it could make itself invisible.

Irritated by this intermezzo, which looked like spoiling his day, the judge followed his wife up to the top storey.

In the smoking room reigned a terrible disorder. Shattered glasses and china lay all over the floor, some paintings had been ripped to shreds and two armchairs had been overturned. There were bloodstains on the carpet. The place looked like a battlefield.

One of the housemaids had found the beast, his wife told him, when she'd gone up to get the table linen for dinner. Bold as brass, the cat, perched up on the bookshelf, had hissed, frightening the girl out of her wits. Instantly she'd called for the gardener who, armed with a cane, had gone upstairs to the smoking room.

When his wife came to this part of the tale she dissolved into silent sobs. It was as if the cat were insane, she insisted, arching its back and spitting. The gardener had chased it to and fro in the room, tipping over vases, glasses and furniture in the tumult. Then, driven into a corner, the beast had suddenly attacked, throwing itself with an unnatural leap at the gardener, and clawing him in the eye. The gardener had collapsed on to the floor, shouting that he could no longer see. The cat had disappeared in the commotion.

"Where is it now?" the judge asked.

"Somewhere in the house," said his wife. The housemaid had heard it moving about in the attic, but no-one had dared go up there. Clearly it was out of its mind.

He and his wife went down to the salon. The servants had gone back to their duties. The gardener was sitting in a chair as the doctor felt his pulse. The judge asked where the fowling piece was and was told that it was hanging on a hook in the tool shed.


A little while later the judge was up in the attic. Though the light falling through the gaps in the ceiling was enough for him to see where he was going, he tripped over an old travelling trunk and swore loudly when he hit his hand against a beam in the roof. The scratch had begun to ache, and the thought that his wife might be right, that the animal was rabid, made him shudder.

The room was noiseless. All he could hear were subdued murmurs from downstairs where the evening meal was being prepared. The cat, he thought, had probably managed to find a way out. Tomorrow he'd summon the forester.

For a little while he stood there, eyes closed, imagining the sort of things he could get up to with the young housemaid up here. She wouldn't protest, he thought, no matter what he did to her.

She was too young, too frightened, too powerless. He could even kill her.

He was just about to turn back when he heard a noise coming from the roof. Further along, one of the skylights stood ajar. Beneath it was a ladder. Feeling strangely dizzy, he climbed out on to the roof. The city lay sprawled out below him, St Mary's Church, the Town Hall with its spire, the Artushof, Lange Gasse and Langer Markt. In the harbour the boats looked like toys. In the background gleamed the River Weichsel and the sea.

Then, without forewarning, he began hearing voices in his head: the voice of a ten-year-old girl he'd once drowned, the wheezing sounds made by a prostitute as he'd cut her breast off in a Königsberg brothel, the wailing of the girl who had stabbed his genitalia with a knife in a Danzig hotel years ago. All followed by guffaws, hysterical laughter, the hissing of a crazed cat and the abbot's whining as he'd climbed down from the prisoner's cart at the place of execution.

Was he going mad?

On the furthest ridge of the roof, he saw the cat. It was standing up on its hind legs like a human being – and laughing at him. A wholly human laugh, with the corners of its mouth upturned. It was talking to him now, unimpededly, inside his head, in a flat, terrifying voice. *Come closer*, it said, *see how close I am, come closer*. And he himself was shivering inexplicably. I've gone mad, he thought. I've lost control of myself.

Yet something made him go on walking across the roof. It's the cat making me do it, he thought, making me move my feet, step by step across the ridge – slippery though it is after the rain . . .

Fifteen metres below him, in the garden, he caught sight of his wife. She was calling up to him to take care, to come back down; but the voice, or rather the voices, hundreds of them, forming an enormous choir in his head, were screaming at him to keep moving, no matter what, impelling him to continue. Unbearable, incessant, the screams urged him towards the edge of the roof where the cat was standing on its hind legs, smiling at him – a wholly human smile.

Then he felt a completely novel sensation, a terrible itching in his maimed sexual organ. Never before had he experienced anything like it, it was as if thousands of lice were rummaging about down there, biting and tearing at his crotch making it itch in a way he didn't believe possible.

Afterwards his wife, the venerable Rosalinda von Kiesingen, who was following his perilous balancing act from her seat in the stalls down in the garden, would remember his movements as like those of someone submerged in water, as if he'd been trying to swim his way across the roof and, when he fell, how he'd done so with abnormal slowness, in a wide arc over the stone-paved terrace.

From the perspective of a stray cat, all this looked quite different. All it saw was a clumsy, staggering human animal with a panic-stricken look on its face, like one of its prey fleeing from some real or imaginary pursuer. At most, the cat, erect on its hind legs with its mouth curled up in a human leer abhorrent to and utterly out of keeping with nature, was amazed by its own unnatural stance.

# VIII

I n the village of Fossa, in the Abruzzi hills, a man is opening a wardrobe. Momentarily, on the wall behind the clothes hangers, a demonic face comes into view. An horrific sight, for the face is sorely maimed. The nose has been cut off. An eye plucked out. And both ears have been drawn out from their roots.

The man gasps, shuts the door, and collapses on the floor, pulled downward by earth's implacable gravity and by the fear that has been pursuing him now for weeks on end. But his faith helps him get a hold on himself – faith, this thing humans so unhealthily confuse with remorse and fear of a life they've never even asked to be born into, but which imperceptibly takes possession of them and drives them on even so.

Knowing full well what lies in store for him, he reopens the door. This is how it has been these past few months; surprises recurring until they no longer surprise, only fill him with an icy fear, which is why he knows the maimed face will now have gone. Apart from the bag of mothballs on a hanger, the bag filled with his equipment, the black, leather-trimmed coat he wraps himself up in at night against the cold and the dreadful dream visions, the wardrobe is empty.

The nightmares, he thinks in despair, looking at the surface the face had just peered out from, these very real nightmares that haunt me and make me shun sleep.

But no-one can survive without rest, and in the end, at day-break, the body, his unreliable body that doesn't give a fig for his will and exposes him to the demons who climb uninvited in and out of his dreams, snatches an hour's slumber for itself.

True to his motto that Satan's cunning tricks are as manifold as mankind's sins, he tries to brace himself. My faith will help me, he thinks, condemning this room that has ended by becoming a prison – a prison he daren't leave, even in the daytime, because the demon is watching over the door, a room for travellers in a god-forsaken village he has come to on a great quest, or, to be more exact, challenge. But his challenger has proved himself stronger than anything he could ever have imagined, for he has never before experienced delusions of this calibre.

He lies down on the bunk and closes his eyes. These sudden visions in broad daylight have been happening more frequently the past few days, as have the dreams that are no longer dreams, but journeys into an horrific landscape.

He wonders if he is nearing a settlement that can be at the end of this long journey to the Tropic of Darkness. An hour earlier, for instance, the room had filled with the pungent smell of smoke, a smell of burning human flesh, the crackling of something on fire. But when he'd turned round he could see nothing burning. Soon afterwards he, quite distinctly, had heard someone call his name, and when he'd answered automatically in a voice that for the last twenty-four hours had failed to speak, he'd been met by a caco-phony of mocking laughter. Ordeals of this kind are continually assailing him. Woken by knockings on the wall, when he asks in anguish, "Who's that?" he is answered with a sigh or someone teasingly whispering his name.

But that's not all. At any moment he can be assailed, possessed, by music. His body becomes an acoustic chamber in which someone is everlastingly arranging concerts. He's an organ made of flesh and bone on which someone is playing fugues, whole cantatas on the keyboard of his fears; pumping air through his fear's organ pipes. He lacks words to describe the experience; the notes threaten to blow him up, they are playing so loudly inside him he's afraid his eardrums will burst and the stagnant water inside come splashing out in a triad intoned with the Devil's tuning fork, bringing on a fit of the shivers. He is terrified these delusions will drive him crazy. It is Satan tempting him, and he escapes into morbid broodings.

Is all this simply a delusion? Just like suffering and illness, he wonders, which perhaps only make sense if seen from the lofty viewpoint of the Creator? But if man is unable to see it all from this divine point of view, both the Creator and His creation can only appear to be evil.

God is one with His creation, say the theologians. But since evil is everywhere apparent in creation, is not then God, too, evil?

The demons tempt him with this thought. Because if it is true, equally in the murderer and in his victims, what is left for man to worship?

Satan exists, and he exists within himself. Creation isn't perfect, and therefore neither is the Creator. Those people he knows in the Vatican . . . the learned theologians . . . they're wrong when they maintain that evil isn't really evil, only a lower level of goodness, or for that matter, an absence of goodness . . .

Now twilight is falling swiftly beyond the windowpanes where the demons, regular as clockwork, have been appearing. He looks out towards the mountains. The sky is monochrome. The trees leafless. He wishes he could leave the room, but doesn't dare to.

Is evil an absence of good? he pursues his line of thought. Just as saltiness is a lack of sweetness, sorrow a lack of joy or black a lack of white? Attempts to save God's honour suddenly strike him as laughable. What was it St Augustine wrote: "Evil is but goodness reduced to the point where it no longer exists." But if that was so, how did the God he had served all his life relate to what he was being forced to experience now; to the trail he'd followed through the villages, to the disfigured face he'd just seen in the wardrobe, to Satan who was tempting him now as never before, who was trying to make him confess: "Yes, since my Lord doesn't intervene, you are more powerful than He."

He wonders whether God is indifferent to his trials? Or simply irresponsible? But a failure to intervene is also to adopt a standpoint.

He is nauseous with fear. If he opens the front door he will encounter the flames of hell. He wonders how it is that fire has been made so hot it can mutilate a human being. Why didn't God hold back a little on the potential for suffering? "If God hadn't created suffering to its extreme limit," his old prior had once said, "neither would His creation have been complete." In a perfect world there must be room for everything. A limited world disputes the principle of the generosity of creation. Thus also fear.

Cold sweat is running in a furrow between his shoulder blades, carrying with it the pungent smell of fear. Again he smells smoke, followed by a voice calling eerily from inside his chest: *Del Moro, my dear inquisitor, I'm not frightening you, am I?*

He falls to his knees, his body jerking like an epileptic's. Violent convulsions are shooting through him as each hell-pitched chord leaves its imprint in his flesh. Sounds from an organ being played by some invisible demon, shrieking with laughter, about to drive him mad.


Exhausted by his horrific recollections, Sebastian del Moro lies asleep in the travellers' guest room here in the village of Fossa. He is awakened by the sound of someone clearing their throat. Opening his eyes, he discovers on his chest a diminutive figure. A man, no bigger than a thumb, busily examining the hairy landscape of del Moro's torso. The figure is wearing glasses, the black garb of the Dominican Order and a soiled kaftan. Del Moro realises this must be a miniature version of himself. But this double, who seems not even to notice him, lacks ears and a tip to his nose. In his hand he is holding a bag. An exact copy of del Moro's own, over in the wardrobe.

*Sebastian, my exorcist,* whispers a childish voice that seems to come from all directions at once, *you didn't expect this, did you? We're inside you already. We are legion, as they say . . . and if you want to get rid of us you'll have to resort to your most advanced rituals . . .*

Rotating his eyes in their sockets, del Moro looks around the room. No-one there. He suspects he may be dreaming, but then reminds himself that the status of his conscious mind is neither here nor there, the nightmares having recently penetrated so far into his waking hours, and, conversely, his nightmares of his waking hours having pursued him into his dreams.

"Who is it?" he asks, with this in mind. But as he expected, there is no answer.

On his chest, his double has opened its miniature bag of demonological equipment. He chooses slowly between various instruments, until he decides upon one of the sharp awls in the outer compartment. To del Moro's surprise, and still apparently unaware of his existence, he takes out, from the same bag, two false ears and a false nose, which he then with some difficulty proceeds to attach to his face. That done, he takes out a small but perfectly formed human tongue, which he sews into his mouth with the aid of a needle and thread thin as a spider's web.

*Del Moro!* the voice repeats, but more challengingly this time. *You wonder where we are since you can't see us, neither when you're asleep nor awake. That must be making you wonder!*

*And what state are you in? Let me make this quite clear: you are asleep, but soon you'll realise that it makes no difference whether unnatural things happen when you're asleep or in broad daylight, because, in your case, sleep and waking are two sides of the same coin . . .*

His catatonic state has begun to let up a little. Much to his relief he can turn his head to one side. He looks about him. On the table by his bunk someone has lit a branched candlestick. Meanwhile, on his chest his diminutive double has grasped one of his awls and is busy jabbing it energetically into his skin just under his left nipple, making a rhythmical sound as the instrument digs painlessly into his flesh.

*Listen to me*, the voice says. *You can't see us, and yet the most rational explanation doesn't occur to you: namely, that we are talking inside you. Maybe we've possessed ourselves of your body, the way we sooner or later take possession of all evildoers . . . How? you ask yourself. And when? In an unguarded moment of course . . . through the first accessible bodily aperture . . . through your disgusting anus, let's say. We detest you! But how to get rid of us? Flush us out with an enema of holy water?*

The demon voice gives a mocking laugh, and del Moro understands with a shudder that it is true: the demons have indeed taken possession of his body.

He tries to gather his thoughts into a prayer, but is distracted by a tune. In his head he hears a piece by Clementi, played on an organ, which turns into another piece by Bach, before, strangely enough, being played backwards, note by note.

231

On his chest, his double has succeeded in boring a small hole in his skin using the awl. Now he can hear the minute figure cluck its newly sewn tongue and then burst into a lengthy tirade in a nonsensical language. A drop of blood wells up on his chest like a red bead, before coming loose from its mounting and spilling down into the cavity formed between his ribs. His miniature wipes the sweat from its brow with a handkerchief bearing a papal monogram. The work has fatigued him.

While del Moro stares bewitched at this remarkable scene, a pillar of steam rises from his other nipple.

*Del Moro, you ass*, says the demon voice. *The time has come! It's time for you to cast us out!*

The music in his head stops playing. Out of the nipple where the pillar of steam had just arisen, a demon's face appears and then, quick as lightning, vanishes, once more withdrawing its ethereal, greenish body. His little double, too, has vanished, but on del Moro's stomach, immediately above his navel, the bag still lies open, leaving all its instruments in full view.

The bag swells as if someone were blowing it up, or as if del Moro himself were inflating it with his navel; it grows ever larger, until arriving at its full-scale shape.

*The time has come for you to perform the duties of your profession*, the demon voice whispers inside him. *Time to look for us inside yourself by all available means . . . this, truly, is your last hope.*

Opening his eyes del Moro thinks he has been dreaming. But only for a split second, for resting on his stomach is the bag. Unaware of having himself put it there, or of someone having made him sleepwalk over to the wardrobe and fetch it, it seems to him he is gaining a clearer grasp on his predicament and what to do about it.

I'm possessed, he thinks with lucid insight. The demon is already inside me. I must expel it.


By the window a small domestic altar has been put in order. The tools are neatly arranged on a white cloth: a flask of holy oil, a crucifix encrusted with relics, a syphon of holy water. The greater Roman ritual, or Rituale Romane as it is called by demonologists, is a ritual reserved for exorcising serious cases of demonic possession. Del Moro has carried it out before, but never yet on himself. Now – in this ghostly room – he prepares the ceremony in its every detail.

Just as he is about to embark on the introductory prayer to the archangel Michael, the demon's voice pipes up inside him, *You fool! I hope you know what you're doing . . . exorcising evil spirits can kill a man . . .*

The voice is stronger than before, and with a feeling that time is running out del Moro hastens his recitation, "*Sancte Michael Archangele, defende nos contra nequitiam et insidias diaboli esto praesidium.*"

As prescribed by the liturgy, he strews salt on the floor, lays a purple linen cloth over his shoulders and kisses the chalice of sacramental wine.

"*Exorcizo te,*" he chants, "*omnis spiritus immunde, in nomine Jesu Christi Filii ejus, Domini et Judicis nostri, et in virtute Spiritus Sancti.*"

He puts the sacramental wafer to his lips, lets it dissolve on his tongue. Inside the back of his head he hears the demon laughing, followed, this time, by another, more childish voice, that says, *What use is a host against my sheer hatred? You have no idea what hatred can drive us to. An eye for an eye, a tooth for a tooth. We have a debt to settle . . .*

Prayer, del Moro thinks as the demon's voice peters out, prayer will give me strength, for in prayer mankind has been given a divine power.

"*Ut descedas ab hoc plasmate Dei,*" he mumbles, "*quod Dominus noster ad templum sanctum suum vocare dignatus est, ut fiat templum Dei vivi, et Spiritus Sanctus habitet in eo.*"

The voice in the back of his head giggles, as if the demon had become tipsy on the sacramental wine. Unaffected, del Moro goes on, "*Per eumdem Christum Dominum nostrum, qui venturus est judicare vivos et mortuos, et saeculum per ignem. Amen.*"

By now the room is quite silent and for a brief moment del Moro cherishes a hope the evil spirit has gone away, frightened off by the sacred words. At the same time, he knows from experience that the powers of darkness will resort to every kind of stratagem to nullify an exorcist's ceremony.

So he bows down to the crucifix, kisses it, spits on the tips of his fingers, genuflects, wetting first his left ear, then his right, with his saliva. "*Eppheta, quod est, adaperire,*" he prays. "Open up!"

Another wafer dissolves on his tongue as he touches his nostrils.

"*In odorem suavitatis. Tu autem effugare, diabole; appropinquabit enim judicium Dei.*"

The demon is beginning to feel worried. He can hear it muttering something, but cannot grasp the words. From the depths of his chest comes something del Moro initially believes to be a new voice, but which he finally recognises as organ music. Again he kisses the crucifix, lights two mass candles and asks himself solemnly, "*Abrenuntias satanae.* Do you abjure Satan?"

"*Abrenuntio,*" he answers, "I abjure!"

His face is visible in outline on the surface of the sacramental chalice. The sagging cheeks, his greenish, blotchy skin, the hairs of his beard: matted together in dirty tangled knots, they frighten him.

"*Et omnibus operibus ejus?*" he asks himself: And all his deeds and doctrines? "*Abrenuntio!*"

He takes the syphon of holy water and splashes a few drops on his clothes.

"*Et omnibus pompis ejus?*"

The demon remains calm. But from the wardrobe there comes a rustling sound. And the wind from the mountains, del Moro observes, is gaining momentum.

He opens the flask of holy oil and rubs a drop of it into his forehead.

"*Ego te linio,*" he continues, "*oleo salutis in Christo Jesu Domino nostro, ut habeas vitam aeternam.*"

As the ritual nears its end del Moro is filled with wonder that the demon isn't putting up a fight, that it should submit so passively to being exorcised. And he is just about to begin the final prayer when it starts talking again: *This is all most amusing, del Moro . . . you can't see me . . . not even in your past . . . do you really not remember me? After all, we've met before, under very different circumstances. But as we all know, in the realms of the blind the one-eyed king rules . . .*

Del Moro raises his voice, continues, "*Credo in Jesum Christum Filium ejus unicum . . .*"

*You don't believe in anything, not even in human beings. Anyway, you think I'm dead . . . you, and your superiors . . . belief*

234

*makes a fool of a man . . . and your God never did come to my assistance, though I've more than once sorely needed Him to . . .*

While del Moro exchanges the purple linen cloth around his shoulders for a white one that symbolises the soul's purity, and uses all his strength to resist talking back to the demon – something the ritual strictly forbids – he hears him laugh mockingly; and a moment later, when he has knelt down to read the praise, he is sent reeling to the floor by a triad from one of hell's organs.

*Can you really not remember me?* the demon voice shouts, to make itself heard above the din. *I've played the keyboard for you before, remember?*

Del Moro staggers to his feet. Inside him the organ music is playing another piece by Clementi with a force he'd never have thought possible.

*"Credo in Jesum,"* he shouts, taking off his garment and smearing holy oil on his chest in the sign of the cross.

The organ music turns into a slow improvisation. His intestines cramp in fear. On the spot where his double, in the dream, had chopped a hole in the skin immediately under his left nipple, a small green-coloured viper sticks out its tail. Panic-stricken, he claws at it, but the monster manages to slip back into his body as a new peal of demonic laughter fills the air.

He is on the verge of vomiting. Everywhere on his stomach and chest little holes are opening up where worms, larvae and reptiles' spawn rear their heads. From his body he discerns a strong stench of putrefaction rising, as if he were already dead. And again the demon starts screaming at him.

*So much sin gathered in your breast . . . so many evil deeds, so much horror . . . are you really seeing all this? Or am I distorting your vision? Come on, you can remember me if you want to . . . your little organ virtuoso . . .*

*The awls!* another voice breaks out inside him. *Expel him with your silver awls!*

Imagining it to be the archangel Michael coming to his rescue at the last moment, del Moro reaches out gratefully for one of the awls in his bag; the ones he uses to ascertain whether the possessed can still feel pain in warts and witches' marks.

The voices are merging inside him now, a whole chorus, a cacophony of devils and angels, or so it seems to him, fighting for the mastery of his soul. Once again, in the hole under his left nipple, a demon rears its repulsive face, but much to his relief it flees back into his chest when he prods the silver awl at the cavity.

Before him in the room, or perhaps in his overheated mind, driven to the very edge of madness, weird visions are appearing. Cardinal Rivero materialises before his eyes, but del Moro realises with a vertiginous sense of clarity that he is in fact under the fatal influence of his enemy, who has intentionally set him this trial, enticing him yet further up into the mountains so there shall be no witnesses to this final struggle. The Jesuit priest Schuster, too, appears, perhaps to his inner eye, and now del Moro knows that he, soon a dead man like Schuster, like the cardinal and all the others who have led him, step by step, to this place, is nothing but a common pawn in a higher struggle between cosmic forces.

The demon grovels and squirms in the hole under his nipple and again he hears the voice he had taken in his confusion to be that of the archangel Michael, *Drive out the demon with your awl, Sebastian, it's your last chance!*

In the instant that del Moro puts the tip of the awl to his chest, at precisely the point where a few minutes before the demon face had shown itself and which is just over his heart, the door of the wardrobe at the other end of the room opens and he recognises the figure that, illuminated by the mass candles, steps out on to the floor. It's the deformed boy he had once, years ago, examined in the Vatican.

As the exhilarating tones of Clementi's organ music fill him, he fully understands it, but the realisation that this is an act of pure revenge comes too late. Someone blows out the candles, the room falls into total darkness. In a last attempt to drive out the demon, he has driven the awl into his own heart.

Dear Father Confessor,

It will not be long before malicious rumours will be reaching you, by some roundabout way, in Naples, and I hope to forestall your worries with a calming letter, which also bears good tidings concerning your nephew Gianfranco. Place no confidence in what you hear about me, Ildebrando, my reputation is, and will remain, untarnished.

Apart from recent tragic losses in our ranks, such as have caused considerable confusion, and of which I know you have already been informed, this spring has gone under the sign of consolidation. By the grace of God and a hitherto well-documented good fortune in the pontificate's political concerns, we have arrived at a consensus in the important matters to be discussed this summer in the Klerus congregation and our steadfast Cor Unum council. The fear of God, alas, does not always fill our dear brethren when national affiliation comes up for discussion. But then, none of us is perfect.

Now for the good news. After much deliberation, Lorenzetti, the prefect of the Pontificate Academy, has recommended your nephew Gianfranco for the position of next nuncio in Geneva, a bit of news that I presume has not yet reached you. Still further to add

237

to his good fortune, I have given him the honorary task of hosting the multitude of visitors to Ad Limina Apostolorum this summer; the Swiss bishops seem to be somewhat over-represented in these obligatory pilgrimages to Rome this year. And this ought to fit in well with Gianfranco's ambitions.

With best wishes to you and our brethren in the Campania province, I conclude this hastily dictated letter, and ask you yet again to place no trust in rumours.

Your most faithful and obedient servant
Cardinal A. Rivero


Sant Angelo, Ischia, the XXIV April MDCCCXXXVII

Dear Aurelio,

Your letter dated the XX reached me today at the thermal baths in Ischia, where it roused me from the ruminations of old age. The hot springs on this island are, as you know, most beneficial to my rheumatism, and I thank divine Providence that thus far, my health not being what it used to be, I am nevertheless in good spirits and of sound judgment.

As you so rightly guess, I could not but help hearing of your supposed doings, though until now they have come to my attention only in furtive subordinate clauses and abstruse allusions. Naturally, I do not take them *ad notam*, at least, no more than to the degree where I am forced to ascertain what I have already known for a long time: namely that you have a rather unenviable flair for making enemies.

Otherwise, as you know, life in Naples is a somewhat modest affair. The exalted intrigues up in the Cardinalate and Bishops' boards pass us by as a matter of routine, and what an archdeacon in Rome thinks about Mandatum Docendi for free-thinkers does not even come to our knowledge. I therefore thank you most humbly for all your confidences concerning high-ranking ecclesiastical matters, which undoubtedly satisfy my profane curiosity, but even more so for those of a private nature which do not enter into personal confession.

How I miss you here sometimes, Aurelio, the evenings in the

library, our walks in the mountains, the work with the poor. Just now, reading your letter, memories of our first summer come back to me with all their sentimental force and demand to be drawn in bright colours.

Believe me, such things grow more difficult with the years. Our memories progressively withhold from us all that is unpleasant, lifting only the most beautiful moments up to the light to comfort our souls. The toils, hardships, bygone years of famine, increasingly assume the form of a marred dream.

I hope to see you here in the not too distant future. Not in the shadow of the Lateran Church, but here, in the South, your former and my present home.

The good news about Gianfranco particularly pleased me, and I ask you to pass on my sincere congratulations when next you happen upon him in the corridors of Borgo Santo Spirito. As for the deplorable losses in our ranks within the secret association, I must concur with the misgivings apparent between the lines of your letter. Notwithstanding the Restoration, the brethren still have some powerful enemies, and with this in mind I beg you to be vigilant.

Hoping for a speedy reunion, your aged teacher and confessor,
Ildebrando Montelli

Borgo Santo Spirito, the XVI May MDCCCXXXVII

Dear Ildebrando,

I am writing this letter in all haste, but lacking a secretary to take dictation, as you may notice from the handwriting. Recent events, of which I fear you will by now have been made fully cognisant, call for an expeditious explanation and likewise rigorous discretion in order that my reputation not be still further sullied. I assure you, Ildebrando, there is an explanation for everything that you are hearing about me. Do not jump to conclusions!

First of all, I must inform you of yet another death in our ranks, since it is quite possibly connected with the campaign directed against me. This time it concerns our most revered and, among some, dreaded inquisitor the Dominican monk S. del Moro. He was found in the Assisi district the week before last, with an awl driven into his heart. As yet my servant, Silvio, who has gone there in order to form some idea of the tragedy, has been unable to confirm the theory that our enemies – whoever they may be – are involved. Nor has it been possible to determine the actual cause of death. It could be murder or, God forbid, suicide. As you know, I considered Sebastian to be one of our most trustworthy colleagues. May God have mercy on his soul. The event troubles me deeply, and I can draw no conclusions other than that some person, or persons, want to damage the inner structure of our Association. Can it be I am next in line? Without exception these deaths and disappearances have befallen our key personages. Some time ago the two Malitsches, our brothers from the Rhine, vanished without trace. Last winter another of our faithful fellow workers, Pirandello, responsible for recruiting our Order's laymen, was found dead off the Ligurian coast, drowned. This is a brief account of what appears to be a planned campaign against the movement that I, but also to a certain extent you too, Ildebrando, have sponsored.

Now to the rumours that have most surely come to your knowledge. These lines I write to you as being my most long-term confessional father, and this ever since my novitiate: never forget the ties thus uniting us. I have recently, to put it mildly, not quite been myself, perhaps because of the pressure I've been under since these inexplicable deaths began to occur in my immediate vicinity. The suspicion has crossed my mind that these actions (the scandals and blasphemies), of which I am guilty, have in some way been caused by an external source. But on my honour, I assure you what is happening seems more portentous than it in fact is. Outwardly viewed, my actions might be seen as injudicious, unjustifiable or outright scandalous. But allow me to explain them to you when we meet, they are not suited to being put into writing in a letter.

It is therefore first and foremost concerning this matter that I am writing to you. To the end, my oldest father confessor and spiritual guide, of making a complete confession of my sins in regard to these recent events, I have decided to come down to Naples. But my duties – not least to defend my present position, strongly questioned as it is – keep me in Rome for at least another month, or four weeks from the time when you receive this post. Until then, pray for me with all the strength and love I have so long admired in you.

Your Aurelio Rivero

PS Our intercessions during the immediate future ought to be for our deceased inquisitor S. del Moro.

Naples, the XXVI May MDCCCXXXVII

Aurelio,

Through my friends at the Prefecture I have been able to follow your exploits in Rome more closely than you believe, and with the new information that has reached me I find the situation alarming. Do not lie to me! Do not attempt to shirk responsibility for what you have been doing of late! Also, spare me the cowardly excuses and measureless euphemisms in your letters: "not quite been myself", "what is happening seems more portentous than it in fact is", "injudicious", events "caused by an external source"! Given the information I possess, I am seriously worried about the state of your soul. I hear rumours about you that I can scarcely bring myself to put into words: blasphemies, profanations of all sorts, fits of uncontrolled anger, scenes in public before dozens of witnesses, all highly respectable men. It is said that you have behaved with gross indecency, and that you on two occasions have struck a public official. Further: acts of dishonesty; failure to attend Mass; two nuncios have written to the Academy, complaining, and – I pray to God this is not true – that you, Aurelio, formerly my favourite pupil, are guilty of unmentionble blasphemies inside a church, of polluting it with excrement, acts the nature of which I neither can nor wish to formulate in words. I demand an explanation, in writing, before your arrival in Naples, which is thought by some to be a feint, inasmuch as it is said you are in reality planning to flee the country.

I have also asked my nephew, Gianfranco, to keep me updated on your doings over the next period of time. The Association, if I have understood it aright, no longer wishes to run any risks on your behalf. I would recommend that you pray and practise self-denial, and that you take a leave of absence from your already sadly neglected duties. Maybe fasting would bring you to your senses, likewise a routine medical examination. I expect a letter by return of post.

Ildebrando Montelli


Rome, the XI June MDCCCXXXVII

Dear Confessor!

I beg you: do not take your hand from me, not now, when my despair equals my guilt.

This morning I received news of our Rhineland friends, the Malitsches. Apparently they have poisoned themselves. By mistake? The circumstances are wrapped in obscurity. No witnesses, no farewell letters, no-one able to tell us anything about them since their mysterious disappearance last Easter. Pray for their souls, Ildebrando, as I hope you will pray for mine, when the time comes.

A terrible suspicion has begun to haunt me: that, somehow or other, it is the deformed boy who is behind all this. The thought that somebody wishes to revenge themselves for the boy's death leaves me no peace. As you know, the boy was got rid of, but all the people who have recently met with accidents were in some way involved in that business. I am deeply confused. In my darkest moments I fear a terrible mistake has been made, one so inconspicuous that we have quite overlooked it. For this reason I have written to our loyal colleague J. Langhans in Vienna. When last we met, in November, he assured me yet again that the mind-reading monster was well and truly out of the way. Is there any reason why he should lie to me, or, for reasons unbeknown to us, hold something back?

These thoughts have been haunting me to such a degree that I have still not been able to reply to your last letter, in which you, so rightly, reproach me for my actions.

With these words I seal this letter, for now my new secretary is beckoning to me on some urgent matter. Hopefully, I shall be able to start writing a fresh letter to you this very afternoon, answering all your questions.

May God keep you in good health,
Your obedient servant,
Aurelio

Dearest Ildebrando,

I continue now where I left off this morning.

I am in despair, and I beg to be forgiven for what I have done and for the damage I have caused to the Secret Association. In the light of what has happened I know these explanations will seem too late, but – for lack of a better simile – it is as if I have been possessed by an alien force; or to put it more precisely, by alien thoughts and will-power such as I had never believed it possible to entertain.

I do not know how to express these feelings, for they are as frightening as they are bewildering. Things are happening that are beyond my control. For every hour that passes I act more and more in defiance of my faith, in conflict with my convictions and all the obedience I believed myself to have embraced ever since I entered the Order. Just putting these lines in writing calls for an extreme act of will, my pen hardly obeys me, not in the physical sense, but spiritually: it wishes to write words that are not mine.

Yes, that is how it is: my pen wishes to humiliate me, and you, too, my dearest Ildebrando. What force is this that will not leave even my words in peace? The accusations being brought against me are, as you of course understand, true, and I cannot explain my actions in any other way: it hasn't been me! But who then, I ask myself, is it?

Can you see how hard it is for me to formulate these notions on paper, how angular my handwriting has become, how it tilts and heels over in a style you have never seen before, as if I were writing with my left hand? Can you see the ink blots, the thwarted initials; how I, with all the will I can muster, and rigidly clasping the quill, struggle to bring one single lucid sentence to an end? It is as if an external force scarcely allows me to formulate these words.

Nor can I allow myself to dictate this. For my words, Ildebrando, are like faeces. I think one thing, but emit something else, something despicable, something vulgar and gross comes out of my mouth causing those around me to back away. I am no longer responsible for my language, even less so for my actions. Pray for me, Ildebrando, pray for my salvation, it is under dire threat.

Had it not been for my newly appointed secretary, the situation would long ago have gone to rack and ruin. He has of late relieved me of my daily duties, holding visitors at bay, admitting only my closest associates for an audience.

You must believe me, Ildebrando, when I tell you that this is the fourth draft today of this letter. I've had to burn the others, since to my horror I've seen them imbued with sentiments that are not my own: abuses, curses. Sentences that are not of my making worm their way into the text, words I didn't even know were thinkable, nor even how to spell. I think: write this, Aurelio! But when I follow the movements of my pen and hand, I see quite other words take shape on the paper. Even my handwriting is not my own!

Everything you have heard about me, Ildebrando, is true: all these immoral acts, blasphemies, excretions, profanities. It is as if I were transported, wildly out of control, as if I were but an automaton, the creation of an evil-minded maker of dolls. Only the strength of my position and the help given me by my secretary have enabled me to stifle the scandal. The alien voice speaks within me, this obnoxious voice that wants to harm me, drives me to do all this, wishes to scandalise me and wreck my life. The voice that has spent the last few hours convincing me I must commit the ultimate mortal sin . . .

My mental faculties are running out, Ildebrando. I finish here before the evil force starts in earnest dictating what I write.

Rivero

Naples, the XXII June MDCCCXXXVII

Dear Aurelio,

I send you this letter poised between hope and despair since I've received no answer to my last. Give me a sign of life, that is all I ask. Answer me by return of post.

Your Ildebrando Montelli

Aurelio!

I beg you once more: answer my letter at once. Give me, at the very least, a sign that you are well! This silence on your part fills me with the most ominous forebodings. Only this morning my last letter was returned. I have had my friends search for you, but you have been unavailable. Gianfranco informed me by messenger that you no longer give audiences. It is said he has spoken with your new secretary, who announced that you were "indisposed". What does that mean, Aurelio? And who is this new secretary? I beg you, give me a sign of life!

Ildebrando

Naples, the VIII July

My dearest Aurelio!

Still no sign of life from you, and yet another missive returned with its seal unbroken. I've decided to send this letter by courier to assure myself that it at least reaches your secretary, who rumour has it is intractable, furtive and not of our ranks. Who is he, this stranger, Aurelio, who forestalls visitors on the very threshold of your office's antechamber? I've heard rumours too outrageous to be true. No-one has seen you this past month, only this remarkable secretary, short of stature, who makes known in writing that you are not "passant" or are "indisposed for conversation", and whose appearance – apart from his insignificant stature and peculiar mask – no-one seems able to describe. I do not expect a reply to this letter, your correspondence with the outside world having come to a total standstill. Unless I get some sign of life from you within ten days, I have decided to come to Rome and personally demand a meeting with you. Gianfranco has tried to find you a dozen times to date. There is growing concern within our ranks. Some say you have gone over to our enemies, that you are in some unknown place outside Rome, conspiring against the Society. Until I have spoken to you in private, I cannot know what to believe. My greatest fears now are for your health, if indeed you

245

are still alive. God willing I hope to see you again or to soon receive some word from you.

Your Ildebrando Montelli


Sabine Hills, St Peter's Day MDCCCXXXVII

To my brethren in Jesus and in particular my oldest confessor, the most honourable and God-fearing Ildebrando Montelli, my mentor and Christian guide since the days of my novitiate, as well as to my colleagues at the Secretariats and Congregations and my sisters, Anna and Ricarda, and to all those who may find my imminent end to be of interest.

I write these lines in a state of acute anxiety, with the greatest effort, being as I am at the mercy of forces over which I have no control, and no longer capable of fighting off the inevitable. There is nothing left for me but to relinquish myself into the hands of the Good Lord in the hope that He will receive an undeserving soul. All that I, Aurelio Rivero, can hope for, is that someone will be able to decipher this epistle, since I am no longer master of the hand that writes it.

This place is a deserted farmstead in what appears to be the Sabine Hills, whither in early June of this year I was taken against my will by my secretary, who has complete control over my actions     I write this letter with his gracious permission; anything else would be impossible, since he controls my every step and has complete insight into my soul, my thoughts, my mind and even into my innumerable sins     my handwriting shifts violently and I beg my reader's patience     Nor are all of the words my own!     news has reached me about Luca S. and all the others in Rome who were involved in the death of Julian Schuster, our brother of the Order Wittold Kossak too has been     but for the providence of Our Lord escaped when he was lured by two children to a place outside Regia     all, all has to do with my scribe who holds me prisoner here     may this letter reach those who seek knowledge of my terrible fate!

Forgive me for the evil-doings I am guilty of in the chapel of St Maria Maggiore in the church of John the Baptist, in St Luigi dei

246

Francesci, where I in my confused state was allowed to
must finish now secretary calling me and I can do nothing but
obey because of his terrible power.


Sabine Hills, the VIII after Trinity Sunday

I dispatch this letter in secret, my custodian having left the
building in order to carry out his errands and get some food for me
– for he wants to keep me alive to torment me        I am a prisoner
here, locked up like a common thief        God is no longer with
me in my darkness, only the cup of poison, so that I shall commit
the ultimate sin.

It is only through an extreme act of will I can refrain from
blaspheming against Our Lord and my loved ones in this letter.
        a faint streak of light is breaking through a window
hatch six ells up on what I believe to be the western wall of my cell.
Apart from that, nothing! No furniture, no lamps, the floor is bare,
stone walls, a raw cold in the mornings as the tower faces north
        my personal secretary and gaoler has used his cunning and
power to lure me here, exploiting my weakness, my sorely
disturbed mind        even enticing out of its dark corners long-
forgotten events from my earliest years here voices hear within me
very clearly, even hallucinations of a strange kind        he sees
into my soul, exploits my weaknesses, my fear of mortal sin,
deeply impressed on me since childhood, hence death by my own
hand, which he is trying to force me to commit, using illusory
powers, offering practical assistance        no furniture or comfort
in this cell, only the cup of poison, a snare made of pure copper
wires, a sharp pair of scissors        A ladder attached to the wall
leads up to the gallery, there's a single window hatch, if you look
through a crack there's a backyard with an almond tree        in
the background, I think, the silhouette of the Sabine Hills
must finish he's coming back

Sabine Hills, August or September

May this letter reach a Christian soul! I, Cardinal Aurelio Rivero, am slowly going out of my mind, voices pursue me incessantly, my secretary-cum-enemy has chosen this path to drive me into taking my own life    He even makes himself invisible, only to reappear, laughing, out of nowhere!

this is a desolate region, no-one lives here. I have lapsed into complete silence, lost my faculty for speech, my secretary poisons my drink, bringing on hallucinations, scenes from hell worse than those depicted by Dante, this is a dead place, the morning comes slowly, imperceptibly to overpower    me hear sounds from the locked room next door: chairs scraping, music, someone playing a piano my scribe, the deformed boy, speaks to me through my thoughts    May God have mercy on my soul when I appear before His throne.

hoping this letter by the grace of God finds an addressee willing to pray for my salvation I go to my doom

IX

S o it was. Driven by hatred, Hercule had cultivated his gift to the point where he could appear unnoticed, managing to blot out the idea of him in people's minds by pinpointing where in their grey brain-matter it had initially appeared, and transforming it into something else.

Some might say he had made himself invisible, but in that case he would have had to correct them: nobody can make themselves invisible, only unnoticed, such as is often the case with the lonely.

The apprentices in the slaughterhouse yard where he was standing, for instance, didn't notice him, even though he was right in their midst. Possibly they apprehended him as a breath from death's angel (always present in such places), or from some dead animal's carcass, a pig about to be stabbed, or some caged beast.

Beside him, a butcher's apprentice was flaying a sheep. To him, he didn't exist, other than as a vague presentiment that every now and then made him look reluctantly over in his direction. But without noticing him. Until, finally, these repeated premonitions which never came to anything tired him out, and were therefore added to the dormant pile of non-essentials that people daily surround themselves with in order to be able to concentrate on their work. Consumed by a stifled repugnance coupled with the low-intensity bloodthirstiness characteristic of every butcher, the apprentice flayed the body until its skin hung loose like a bloodied skirt from the sheep's vacantly staring head.

The acrid odour of entrails had caused Hercule momentarily to forget what he was here for. When the apprentice opened up the sheep's belly and tipped out its clustered bowels, the youngster stared as if bewitched, proceeded to plunge his hands into the reeking abdominal cavity, withdrawing the liver, lungs and stomach, before very carefully lifting out the bag of taut, moist membrane. He then laid them out with utmost care on the ground, as if they were a fragile bundle. Using the tip of his knife, he opened the membrane, and it was only when the parcel burst open, steaming in the cold morning air, that Hercule understood what was in it: two unborn lambs, about to be slaughtered for the sake of their precious fleeces.

That, he thought, was exactly how he would now slaughter his final victim – among other beasts, like the beast he was . . .


Hatred it was had driven him to this macabre lookout post at the slaughterhouse yard, there to refuel himself with a hatred so potent it could only be measured against the love whose hub had gone for ever, there to fertilise it and nurture it for higher purposes.

Hate was his only friend, his armour bearer from moment to moment. It had a stench of carcasses, sodden earth, cold sweat and excrement, an odour of dying gasps and the blood of a thousand slaughtered animals. Hatred even emitted a sound of its own. A ringing sound which never ceased. The tinnitus of hate. An incessant hum, it reverberated through him, buzzing like a moth against the glass of a lamp; forever keeping him awake, the only sound he'd ever heard, reminding him of the vengeance he must exact. It wasn't his life they'd taken, but its meaning, and here vengeance could only be paid out in the same coin. Revenge as a monetary standard. Death pays for death; these were the two sides of his equation.

Hate even has its own taste, he thought, looking over to the tavern on the yard's far side. His oral cavity had been filled with a sweet dough spewed up, ruminated, then parboiled in his hatred's stomach, but impossible to spit out, grief having sewn his lips together.

His hate could also be touched: it was a razor blade his toes could grasp with all their strength, and which could be swallowed, an icy blade that cut throats and sliced open stomachs, cold as ice, hot as burning coals.

There, alone in the inn on the other side of the yard, sat the man who had unleashed these passions. At one of its windows, sitting bent over a mug of beer, looking through some papers, was the final, but also the most powerful object of his hatred, had it been quantifiable. But the hatred would not let itself be quantified. All objects of such hatred were of equal importance, he'd noticed, and he found this confusing. He didn't hate this man any more than he had hated the others. He hated them all to the same extent, but limitlessly. Hatred had no chronology. It stretched away in all directions into infinity. Not being conceivable from any other perspective than infinity, it had always been there, and always would be. It abrogated all sense of time. It was Being itself.

But with this man at the inn table he had to be careful, for he possessed a gift not unlike his own. Which was why he now raised his eyes from his papers and looked about him, as if aware of being watched.

Hercule read the man's emotions. His thirst had been quenched. His premonitions had made him wary. In a moment he would get up and leave.

To a deaf person, in this city of a million inhabitants the carriages slid by on soundless wheels. The frantic animals in the slaughterhouse yard, the bellowings, the howls and death rattles from throats choking in their own blood went unheard. The apprentices talked and laughed without him noticing them, mouths moving like fishes' mute gobs.

Having made up his mind not to let the man out of his sight, Hercule left the slaughterhouse and went into the alley, where a cab almost ran him down, its driver swearing at his suddenly rearing horses. Only the horses notice me, he thought, and perhaps also those children who, somewhat astonished, are looking over in my direction.

Overhead the sun burst through the cloud. It was morning, but already very hot. He waited for the inn door to open and his enemy to appear. This man is the last, he thought. Only when he too was gone would Hercule at last have avenged his love.

253

But hate made him careless, as love had once done. Inside the inn, Johannes Langhans was beginning to track down the deformed man's tinnitus of desire for revenge. Then, taking care to let his thoughts go in a misleading direction, he left the premises through a back door and hailed a cab.

It took a while before Hercule realised his enemy had gone. Not that this troubled him in the least, since he already knew where to find him. He'd only followed him to the inn in order to strengthen his resolve. But his plans for the Jesuit were already formed. And any moment now he would implement them.


When Johannes Langhans got back to his office, only his immediate superior, Secretary Wohlrat, was still there. After enquiring about a couple of appointments, all having to do with the paperwork he'd been looking through in the tavern, he withdrew to his own office room, a gloomy chamber at the end of a dark corridor.

Next to the pile of documents which had heaped up during the week, lay a note. Sealed and stamped, the letter was addressed to him personally. He opened it and read:

> Most honourable head of division! A messenger will be coming this afternoon to deliver information of a delicate nature concerning Count Kollowrat. In order to avoid any unauthorised persons gaining cognisance of this material we would like to meet you on neutral ground.

There followed some directions to an address in the suburbs. The letter had been signed with a scarcely legible signature, and lacked a sender.

Langhans remained seated, held the note. There was something about this communiqué that wasn't right.

After having thought over the ins and outs of the matter awhile, it struck him that the envelope had not been stamped by the office, and in order to elucidate this mystery he went back to the office where the secretary was standing bent over a pile of books.

"Do you know who handed this in?" he asked, holding out the letter.

Wohlrat looked up from the books, which had just been delivered from the censorship.

"Came by internal post," Wohlrat answered. "No-one else has been here today. They've all been given the day off. This afternoon the Secret Association is holding a meeting behind locked doors. The Emperor's indisposed again."

"You wouldn't happen to have seen the internal post arrive?"

Wohlrat gave him a weary look.

"The letter has not been stamped," Langhans clarified. "You haven't seen any private messengers? Or visitors?"

"You know as well as I do that no visitors are allowed. Secrecy, Langhans, is the only protection we have in a land of intrigues! And believe you me, apart from you, myself and the caretaker there's not a living soul has set foot in here today. The copyist is off, just like everyone else, and I've been sitting five metres from the entrance since eight o'clock this morning. The internal post came at ten. Same errand boy as usual. Your letter can't have flown in here on wings, can it?"

"Is the Emperor really indisposed?" Langhans asked, to cover up his unease.

"Epilepsy. Our monarch sets the tune for the bureaucracy, nothing works any more. Look!"

Wohlrat waved a folder across the desk. "I'm having to deal with censorship even though I, like yourself, have been educated in religious matters. The cutbacks have gone too far . . ." Wohlrat spat into an over-full spittoon, before sitting down at his desk. "Besides which, you have the authority to work in whatever way you see fit," he said. "And if it's a question of secret missions, you know where you must turn to."

Langhans settled for this answer and returned perplexed to his office.

Once installed behind his desk, he unfolded the letter again and read, once, the three sentences' forty-three words; then once more, to make sure he had understood it aright.

He couldn't detect any messages between the lines, nothing that appeared to be out of order considering the nature of the errand. Receiving sensitive material from anonymous sources was part of his work, but his recent sense of being watched had made him suspicious. Officials, he thought, were pitched against each other in the

255

power vacuum arising from the Secret Association's court intrigues. Loyalties tended to shift, depending on whose protection they happened to be enjoying. Not even a man in his position was safe.

That someone wished to secretly hand in information about Count Kollowrat didn't surprise him: an emperor who preferred book-learning to writing decrees, and charity to replenishing war funds paved the way for many possible intrigues. Vienna was astir with rumours. The Emperor's marriage was childless, and his sister-in-law – or so it was said – was trying to induce him to abdicate. A secret court group with Metternich at the helm was ruling the land however it saw fit, but the Council was made up of enemies who spent most of their time conspiring against each other. Count Kollowrat was secretly attempting to have Metternich deposed and was seeking support from the third most powerful member of the council: Archdeacon Ludwig. With a political agenda like this, Langhans reflected, the letter ought not to arouse his suspicions. Yet it did.

Having completed some written recommendations concerning the day's routine affairs, Langhans put his files aside. An hour remained before his meeting with the anonymous letter-writer.

Through the only window in the room he looked out over the afternoon traffic. On the other side of the street a coupé was parked. The coachman had fallen asleep on the box, but the curtain in the coach window stirred. It occurred to Langhans that whoever it was who had been following him might be in this particular coach, and watching him from there. But the longer he looked at the carriage, the less he felt this to be the case.

By now it was obvious that whoever had sent the letter must also be involved in the attempts to discompose him, and might, therefore, also be the same person who, without making his presence known, had been watching him at the inn. It was imperative that he find out why, and who it was.

One thing that still puzzled him was how the letter had found its way on to his desk. He was quite sure it hadn't been delivered by internal post – the obligatory stamp was missing, and so was the caretaker's pagination. Of course Wohlrat was correct in saying the letter couldn't have flown in by itself. But it had not been lying there when he'd left the office earlier that day. The rest of the staff had been dismissed, and unless somebody had made themselves invisible and managed to walk into his office unseen, only one possibility remained . . .

He was interrupted in his ruminations as the object of his suspicion came into the corridor. Unable to hear the secretary's footfall he became aware instead of the contours of his own thoughts. Something was bothering him, and this he confirmed on entering the room.

"Don't you have an appointment in an hour's time?" Wohlrat said.

"You're well informed about my daily schedule."

"Spare me your ironies, please. I've just received a report from the Ministry. They know you're going to receive information about Kollowrat from a secret source, and the archdeacon's delighted."

"It said so in the letter I showed you."

"What letter?"

"The one you said arrived by internal post . . ."

Wohlrat appeared unaffected by this insinuation. Instead he sighed and sat down on a chair.

"This work is tiring," he said. "The circumstances demand discretion. We take great care not to find ourselves at loggerheads with anybody, but it's impossible when the land's being ruled the way it is."

"It's not being ruled, it's being 'managed'."

"I know about your double loyalties, with Metternich on one side and the Vatican on the other, and that's precisely why you ought to be more on your guard."

Langhans did his utmost to track down what was going on in his superior's head, but much to his surprise, and maybe dismay, he couldn't pick up anything at all, only a dull weariness with his work, possibly with life itself.

"Considering the political situation", Wohlrat went on, "and your vulnerable position, I was merely wondering whether you might not need an escort?"

The secretary was referring to a body of guards which for some time now had been at the disposal of the officials. This offer calmed Langhans somewhat. Maybe, he thought, the letter had in fact come by internal post, and they had simply forgotten to stamp it.

"That won't be necessary," he said, "but I'd appreciate it if I could order a carriage."

Wohlrat proffered one of his rare smiles.

"Send the coachman back when you're done with this. And then take a few days off. You look awfully tired."

In his thoughts Langhans accompanied his superior back to his office, where he sat down in front of the dismal pile of paperwork. But not even now, when the secretary ought to have eased up on his vigilance, did his consciousness revolve around anything but work, the Emperor's indisposition, and the task of censor he considered ill-placed on his desk.

The address given by the letter-writer was near a market area on the northern outskirts of the city. A group of high-spirited people was crowding in front of an enclosure made of rough planks. No-one seemed to be waiting for Langhans.

He asked the coachman to hold the carriage. Got out. Went over to a drinking fountain where he'd be in full view and waited for the informer to appear.

He felt safe. The driver had been given orders to come to his rescue should anyone threaten him. But the minutes went by without anybody revealing themselves. Just as he had decided to abandon the rendezvous, he again got the feeling of being watched. But though he turned this way and that, he saw nothing suspicious.

Instead, without being able to explain why, he walked over to the area enclosed by the plank fence. A poster advertised animal contests. The crowd, he now realised, was in fact a sort of queue.

An inner voice whispering that the letter-writer wouldn't make himself known until he was inside the enclosure, he bought a ticket, on impulse, or so he told himself.

From his position on the stand he looked out over a makeshift arena. A rough fence separated the audience from the show ring. Not far from where he was standing, next to the stalls selling drinks, were some caged wild beasts. The animals were frightened out of their wits, he could feel their mortal anxiety as clearly as if it had been his own.

The impresario was wheeling and dealing with folk placing bets

258

on the sanguinary spectacle they were about to witness. People were arriving in hordes. The stands were near filled to capacity.

Langhans let his gaze wander over the sea of people. Over and over again it came to a halt in a place near the wild boars' cages; an empty patch, scarcely a square metre in size, where, oddly enough, there was nobody.

The crowd's excitement was growing. The impresario, a man with a duelling scar on his cheek and a patch over one eye, was leading a real-life grizzly bear into the compound. The beast had an iron tether through its nose, and the tether was fastened to a metre-long chain. The beast's nostrils must have been very sensitive, Langhans could find no other reason why it followed its master with such acquiescence.

In the middle of the arena the impresario affixed it to a metal hook on the ground. The lead was so short that the bear was unable to get up on its hind legs without tugging on its nose ring. It was going to have to fight on all fours.

Now another man was bringing in a pack of bloodhounds. The bulldogs were seething with excitement, baring their teeth and tugging at their leads, almost causing their owner to lose his balance. The man let them loose in the enclosure. A shudder passed through the crowd.

Dust whirled up when the dogs attacked. One of them sunk his teeth into the bear's abdomen and tore off large tufts of its fur. Another hopped to and fro in front of the bear's nose, feigning an attack, then withdrawing. The two remaining animals approached it on either side.

The bear flailed wildly, but the moment it struck with its paws in one direction, a dog would attack it from another. Again and again the tether stopped the bear from getting at its tormentors.

Then one of the dogs lost its balance, and with a movement which seemed unnaturally swift, the bear pinned it to the ground. A sound like a piece of cloth being ripped could be heard as the beast tore the dog's belly open. The animal tried to drag itself away, its intestines trailing in the sand.

Foaming at the mouth, the bulldogs kept throwing themselves at the bear, as if to avenge their dying friend. The bear's ear was ripped off, blood gushed from an abdominal wound and sinews lay exposed on a front paw.

Then, once more, something happened to change the scene. One of the dogs lunged at the bear's back leg, feinted and withdrew; the bear tried to attack it with one paw but failed to notice the dog approaching from the side; with a single bite it tore off the bear's nose.

Thick streams of blood welled out, as from a fountain. The beast gave a scream of pain, but now that the nostrils were completely gone, so was the tether. The bear reared up on its hind legs, snorting out its own blood.

Blood pumping from the open wound, the bear went on the attack. The dogs tried to escape, but the arena gates were closed. A sweetish smell of blood and intestines descended over the area.

The bear flung one of the dogs to the ground, and tore off its lower jaw. The animal was still alive when the bear turned round and went to attack its next tormentor.

The bulldogs' owner was shouting out, calling for an end to this performance, it had gone too far, too much blood had already been spilled; but the audience held him back. Bloodlust, Langhans thought; ravenous for the suffering of others. They all bore within them a desire to witness others' pain, to feel on their cheeks the breath of others' deaths, the horror of a life so easily extinguished, the tremor that went through them all when one of them, for no good reason, almost nonchalantly, was snatched away simply because life was abandoning them . . . At the same instant, he again got that feeling of being watched. He looked around at the crowd, but as before, no-one stood out.

People's thoughts were easier for him to pick up than they had been for a very long time. Over by the wild animals' cages he saw the one-eyed ringmaster who had led out the bear. He was in a cold sweat of excitement, inebriated by the scent of blood. His consciousness was that of a drunk, and inside him someone was whispering, though Langhans couldn't grasp exactly what.

The sun blazed down over the compound, and he was overcome by an intense thirst.

A little way off he saw a drinks stall, but the crowd was now so dense he couldn't budge. Once again he picked up on the thoughts in the one-eyed man's mind, or rather, the thoughts of someone else speaking to the one-eyed man and making him walk over to the cages of the last remaining beasts.

This is what happened. In response to some inexplicable inner command the one-eyed man, owner of an entire menagerie of wild animals, began walking towards them, towards the cage containing a highly aggressive wild boar. All this the one-eyed man did in a kind of a trance, little knowing it wasn't his own will that was controlling his every action, but that of a small figure he couldn't even see, even though he'd been standing less than a metre away for the last few hours, on a vacant spot in this human sea, vigilant of every step he took, but so unnoticed he could have been taken for thin air. And it was the wild boar's cage, constructed of high-grade timber, that he now, inexplicably, opened, as panic broke out in the arena.

While the one-eyed man, believing he had temporarily lost his self-control having maybe had a drop too much to drink, was engaged in carrying out the invisible man's will by releasing the wild boar, the bear, pain-crazed, had managed to break out of the compound, smashed through the fencing, and with blood splashing out of the open wound that formerly had been its nostrils, charged into the audience.

Langhans shuddered. Out in the arena he could see three of the bulldogs in their death throes, their bellies gashed open and intestines bared. The white corrosive sunlight illuminated this macabre scene. The bear flailed wildly. People fled in all directions. And in the midst of this chaos, this orgy of death, he became aware of how someone else, someone with a gift similar to his own but infinitely stronger, was planting his legionary will in the wild boar: driving it to rush out of its open cage, into the crowd of humans, and, ploughing ahead with Homeric force amid the horror-stricken onlookers, move with a speed only a wild boar can muster, until, to Langhans' horror, it stood in the very place where he too was standing, pinned against a wall by the immense force of the panicking crowds.

*You think you live a life*, he heard a voice hiss inside him, *but it's life living us, and when we're used up it carries on without us.*

Apt final words, he thought, preparing himself for the horrific coda. The crowd had locked him into a sitting position, on a level with the beast's tusks, sharp as awls. Confronted with this raw power his gift had little worth. At the very moment the bear avenged its humiliation, with one deft blow of its paw decapitating her one-eyed master, the wild boar, taking Langhans to be its enemy, went on the attack.

For such was the power of the man he couldn't see, it could create something out of nothing, and carry a trick of substitution to its extreme. A beam of pure energy lifted up Langhans' face, a concession, or so it seemed, to a sudden desire to look up at Vienna's blinding white sky, but which in fact bared his throat to the wild animal's tusks.


Where Hercule Barfuss was standing invisibly, or rather, unseen by the terrified crowd, it occurred to him that no man can imagine his own end, with the result that he dies astonished.

In order to fully enjoy the Jesuit's imminent death from the inside, to pay him back for the loss of his one true love, he had placed his mind in the front row of Langhans' consciousness. Yet, at the very last instant, something stopped him.

Langhans would subsequently recall how the wild boar had stopped short in mid-onrush, as if someone had commanded it to halt. Then, turning round, it had gone calmly back to its cage. And, almost instantaneously, right there in front of him, as if appearing out of thin air, was the deformed boy.

Never before had Langhans experienced anything like it. The boy seemed to have made himself invisible, then materialised before his very eyes.

He sensed Barfuss inside his mind and knew all about him. Yet at the same time, he, Langhans, was inside Barfuss and knew all about him, too. They were inside each other, were each other, as if their souls had changed places. Never would he be able to account for how long this went on, whether for an eternity or for only the briefest of moments. But inside the boy he heard a girl's voice. And it was the girl, he heard, who bade the boy contain himself.

For Hercule Barfuss this moment altered his life for ever. Inside him he heard Henriette Vogel speaking. And it made him a changed man.

It was indeed her voice, reaching out to him from the brink of the abyss; clearer, more tender than ever before. Beyond all human language, beyond life and death, it was the voice of love itself speaking to him from within; pure, undiluted love, its very ideal, its essence spread warmth through him, banishing the force of hatred that had threatened to destroy him. Suddenly he was engulfed in a tenderness he had never before felt, so strong it obliterated everything else: abhorrence, bloodlust and what he had believed to be unremitting sorrow. No longer aware of his surroundings, he was carried away from the macabre place where he was, on an inner journey. The priest Langhans, the wild beasts, the crowds – everything vanished in the face of this experience of unalloyed purity. A final capitulation to a love that defied the laws of nature. From some place on the other side of time, he heard the girl explain that these acts of cruelty were pointless and would poison him if he did not cease. He heard her pledge her undying love, saying death isn't the end, only the beginning of a new existence where they would one day be reunited.

It wasn't people, she explained, which were his most powerful enemy. It was hatred. The hatred he had lived with half his life and which, having driven him to a dead end, the limit of what a man can endure, would erode him. Hate, she continued, was meaningless; it gave nothing, only took. Forever placing new demands for more nourishment, more blood, more loathing, hatred demanded to be satisfied. Only love could replace it.

Amid the screaming crowd, the dying animals and trampled people, he fell to his knees. Unaware of his surroundings, all he was conscious of was the voice of his beloved reaching out to him over distances inconceivable to the human mind: *I'm with you*, she whispered. *Always with you, until we meet again . . .*

Johannes Langhans, too, was to remember this day to the end of his life in the Age of Steam. Pushed up against a wall, he saw Barfuss' contours clarify, as if distancing himself from his invisibility. He saw the boy's eyes sparkle with love for the girl he'd lost: a love as great as the Creator felt for His Creation, a love for love's sake, a hold-all of existence, preventing the universe from losing all meaning.

Then he disappeared, vanishing on his dwarf legs through the panic-stricken screaming crowds: happy, Langhans knew, infinitely happy that the girl had made her presence known, had banished hatred once and for all.

M any years later, Hercule Barfuss would describe this event in Vienna as the watershed of his love and his life. He'd thought he had reached the end, when in reality he was on the brink of a new beginning.

Until the end of his days he was to remember every little step that had taken him to the bear-baiting, his plans for Langhans, and how, when love at last had been avenged, he was shortly thereafter going to take his own life. That wasn't the way it had turned out. Instead, love triumphed over hatred. Henriette had spoken to him from somewhere in the unknown, and this had changed him for ever. He had gone out among people again, one among others, without hate, without bitterness, as one of their kind, grateful to life, to his fate, to existence in all its infinite wealth.

All that day he'd walked through the imperial city, along its streets, through market places, along alleys and into parks. Fully visible, without his mask, he'd walked, a deformed person, a dwarf, but proud and, beyond belief, happy. He'd noticed how people smiled at him, how he infected them with his love and his happiness in the knowledge that death isn't the end, but the beginning of a new existence. For the first time in his life he understood what freedom implied; knowing no limits, causing people to rise high above their own earth-bound selves: it was identical with being.

That same summer, also in Vienna, he ran into Barnaby Wilson in the market place by the Danube canal, not far from the Augarten Palace. He was in a crowd of folk on an exhibition area, watching a hot-air balloon rise skyward.

*Did you know, kind sir, that it's the phlogistonised air that makes the object rise?*

The little cyclops was standing close by him, holding a telescope to his one eye. Hercule could hardly credit his senses. He'd thought Wilson was dead.

*No, Hercule, I survived . . . the others didn't, but my mission, whatever it may be, is still awaiting its accomplishment.*

They went off together. The cyclops told him all about his life and plans. How Cavour's and Garibaldi's nationalistic ideas had taken hold of him. Since the dissolution of the roadshow he had been working for a new and better world. Socialism, he claimed, was the future; new thinkers were planning a better world: they called themselves communists. The world would become an improved place to live in, even for deaf people. In Paris, he expounded, there was a school for the deaf that was subsidised by the French state. He had been there himself and studied its methods. The teaching used a new form of sign language based on French grammar. The introduction of various forms of inflection and conjugation marks, formerly the missing link, now made it possible to develop a complete language. All the teaching was done in sign language. Hercule ought to go there, he said; their own way of communicating via thoughts was clumsy, since others found it frightening. True, the practice of burning witches at the stake had died out on the European continent, but science would never accept their way of conversing. He really ought to pay the school a visit, sooner or later he would have to learn a language that others could understand. Sign language should suit him, with his sensitive feet he could easily learn to make the signs.

Barnaby Wilson smiled. The world, he assured Hercule, would soon be a paradise to live in. Everything was going in the right direction; progress was unstoppable. Within a few years the railway would cover the whole of Europe, linking up people in a way not formerly believed possible. Disease, cancer and the pox, as well as famine, crop failure and war would be eradicated. If only factories and manufacturing were properly managed, goods could be produced at cost price and everyone would receive according to their needs.

In America, Wilson went on, there was a place where deaf people were in the majority and where they led their own lives in the spirit of freedom. This was on an island off the coast of Massachusetts called Martha's Vineyard. Their society consisted almost exclusively of the deaf. They all addressed each other in sign language; even those who could hear learned to sign first. Spoken English came as a second language. Hercule ought to go to America as soon as he could save up enough for a ticket. Could Martha's Vineyard be his special place in the world?

They parted company that same afternoon, Wilson on his way to Sicily where he was to attend a meeting with Italian nationalists to whom he was to teach the new socialistic ideas by which they could build a better state, based on justice and basic human worth. As they said farewell, they knew it was for good.


In September that same year Hercule Barfuss took the stagecoach to Paris. He'd decided to look in on the Institute for the Deaf in Rue des Moulins, the school Wilson had told him about.

At that time this Institution Nationale des Sourds-Muets was the world centre for methodical sign language. Hercule arrived at the end of the month with a written recommendation from Barnaby Wilson, and was immediately taken on as a student.

It was during his stay in Paris that his lifelong conviction about the superiority of the visual teaching technique as compared to the oral was founded. In no time at all he learned French sign language, though signing with his feet complicated the grammar. All his life he would be an embittered opponent of the German School, where the emphasis was on teaching the deaf to lip-read and use their speech organs. One event in particular made a deep impression on him. Twenty years later he wrote of it:

During one of my first lessons I witnessed the following: a teacher, trained by the grammarian Sicard, was to prove the excellence of the visual method for a representative of the French Academy of Sciences. Standing at the teacher's desk, he dictated a text – I think it was a poem by Victor Hugo –

using methodical signs for the students, who were seated in the classroom in such a way that they couldn't see each other's papers. There were five of them: four lads and an exceptionally beautiful girl. As the teacher dictated to them in sign language they wrote down what they "saw" him say, and this in no fewer than five languages, one for each student. The girl wrote in Latin. The boys in French, German, Italian and English. The representative for the Academy was stunned by the result. Of course he knew that sign language uses neither letters nor words, but concepts, which – on condition you know them – can be written down in whatever language you are familiar with. But what really amazed him – and me too – was the level of language education among the school's students, far above the average at a French *lycée*.

It was also during his time in Paris that he began to understand that grammar is universal and can be adapted to the eye as well as to any other sense:

The teachers, as well as the students among themselves, used depictive signs ("fire" and "horse" were the first two I picked up), signs depicting movement, indicative and arbitrary signs. Plural was indicated by a repetition of the basic sign, the definite form was signed by a slight indication after the sign, the verbs were bent to all the various tenses in French by the addition of different signs to the present – all of this grammatical usage I was of course already familiar with through reading, but now it took on new meaning and greatly widened my horizons. It even occurred to me that dialects could arise within sign language, and that the idiom used by non-hearers was the universal language man had dreamed of since the beginning of time.

It was in Paris, too, with the school chaplain and headmaster, he said his first prayer in sign language, the Lord's Prayer.

He remained at the Institute half a year. He maintained contact by corresponding with some of the teachers. The school's destiny continued to be close to Hercule's heart until the end of his days.

He left in March 1838, having by then laid the foundations for a perfect understanding of sign language. Love was the fundament his life rested upon; love for the dead girl who no longer belonged to any place in particular.

A new continent awaited him, and a new existence. In Martha's Vineyard.

A postscript for Miss Vogel and other initiates

L	ove, in early Egyptian poetry, is symbolised by a peculiar
	three-part hieroglyph. It consists of a hoe, a mouth and a
	male figure holding his hand to his mouth. The first Egypto-
logists wondered if Pharaonic love was a kind of labour demanding
tools and a gardener's patience. Or perhaps love didn't exist before
there was a way of expressing it? Some asked themselves jokingly if
love's dwelling was in the chest? And, for fear it might fly away with
a careless word, the man was holding his hand to his mouth.

Perhaps, Miss Vogel, there was something to that point of view,
since the Egyptians also happened to be the first to equate love
with the heart: "My brother seduces my heart with his voice", a
poet has a woman exclaim. So love's abode was in the heart, and
the voice was the tool to unlock it. On terracotta vases and papyrus
scrolls people lose their hearts, or feel them break from unrequited
love, and the pain is unbearable.

In his twilight years, when Hercule Barfuss concluded the long
educational journey that had brought him all the way to the
drawing rooms of the learned in America, he was to write a letter
to one of his grandsons who was at that time involved in taking a
licentiate examination in classical languages at Harvard:

Hieroglyphics are, as you know, the foremost of all written
languages, being capable, in one and the same symbol, of

271

reproducing an image and expressing abstractions. Hieroglyphics are the true alphabet of the deaf.

In one of his work journals Barfuss makes the observation that sickness as a metaphor for love first appears in the "Song of Songs". "Refresh me with raisin cakes, comfort me with apples." But the theme persists like a scarlet thread throughout the history of love poetry. Together with Plato's thoughts, it forms the basis for our experience of passion.

In Plato's *Symposium* the following story is told about love's origins. In prehistoric times there was neither man nor woman, instead there were various blends of the two. They had two faces, four arms, four legs, four feet, and so on; they were attached back to back and therefore able to go both backwards and forwards. Some consisted of two male parts, others of two female parts, and a third group, the largest, was half-male, half-female. These four-legged primaeval beings, Plato says, were so power-mad that they constituted a threat to the gods. So Zeus decided to divide them into two, thereby diminishing their power. Thus man and woman were created.

But once their original form had been divided, they were driven by a longing to be reunited. Thus Plato, and later on Barfuss, describes love as the desire to merge and grow together.

"Each and every one of us is only half of what used to be a human being," he was to write. "The pleasure of romantic love is not in itself enough to account for the strength of lovers' feelings. Love is the search for the lost half, and the striving to merge with it. For ever."

For our ancestor, Miss Vogel, this was a truth whose incontestability could measure itself against the greater laws of nature. During his last year in Europe he'd heard Henriette Vogel speak to him, and this had been his life's pivotal moment. The conviction that love continues beyond death had changed him. His hatred and lust for revenge had disappeared overnight, as had his unfathomable sorrow.

On several occasions my father, John Barefoot, retold the story for me in sign language, using the gesture for love in which both palms of the hands are pressed lightly against the heart, and the sign for eternity, the right forefinger drawing circles horizontally

272

from left to right. He explained that Barefoot was convinced he would meet her again in an existence beyond our earth-bound one. Nothing could shake him in this belief, and until his dying day, he lived with the conviction that love, no less than matter, is indestructible. "Just as matter can be converted into energy," he observed, "and energy into matter, so love persists, indestructibly, throughout eternity."

His experience in Vienna he ascribed wholly to love as a force powerful enough to overcome death. But his certainty that he would meet his beloved again didn't make life on earth any the less meaningful. On the contrary, he lived his remaining years to the full, as if each and every one might be his last.

The revelation had also influenced his decision to leave Europe. In March 1838 he left Calais on a steamship bound for Liverpool, and on his arrival there booked his passage through a Belgian agent to New York. The price was thirteen pounds and included third-class board and lodging on the schooner *St Mary*. Like so many other travellers to the Americas, he overnighted in a hotel on Duke Street, while waiting to sail.

On the evening of April 24, a final divine service was held on the quayside, and the day after, at dawn, the ship lifted her anchor. From where he was standing on the foredeck he saw the English port spread itself out, the last glimpse millions of people were to have of the Old World, before it was enveloped in a mist as the ship headed out across the Irish Sea.

This was the same year the paddlewheel-driven Atlantic steamship, the *Great Western*, accomplished the crossing in a record-breaking fifteen days, before Samuel Cunard founded the first passenger line for regular crossings between England and the United States, before the era of mass emigration some decades later, when Iman, Dominion, National and the White-Star shipping companies all competed for the crossings of millions of Europeans leaving everything they possessed behind them in order to make a new life for themselves in "the land of opportunity".

But Barfuss doesn't seem to have noticed the lack of comfort or dreariness of a crossing that took six weeks, or the dead calm on the fortieth degree of latitude, neither seasickness nor the unpalatable food. Instead, in his diary entries made during the crossing, he writes enthusiastically about life on board. He is captivated by the sea, admires the ship's technical equipment, its deadeyes, blocks, square topsails and their tackle, he makes sketches of masts and spars, and tries to familiarise himself with procedures involving log lines and charts and other navigational instruments.

The schooner was a reconstructed brig, launched in Hull in the 1810s on behalf of a slave-trading company. It had four masts. The passenger count was 240. They came from all corners of Europe and comprised no fewer than seventeen different nationalities.

In the ship's logbook the captain wrote about an epidemic of jaundice and a few cases of scurvy among the Irish. Most of the passengers were plagued by seasickness, as well as scabies and lice. The ship's rats behaved shamelessly and stole food from the hands of careless children.

The men, among them Barfuss, slept in hammocks on the 'tween deck. Astern was a department for women and families. The areas were screened off with hanging drapes.

Barfuss seems to have made a friend in the *St Mary*'s carpenter. He writes about "my new-found friend Richards who has taken me under his protection and shown me around the ship". A sailmaker, by the name of Waddington, too, seems to have taken pity on him. Perhaps they thought he was a handicapped child? Nothing is said about how people reacted to his appearance, his deafness or his eating and writing with his feet, nothing about the thoughts he picked up from his fellow travellers. Maybe they simply were all too caught up in the excitement to adhere to old patterns of behaviour?

His longing for the new country grew with each sea mile they put behind them. He writes about the "new life" which is about to start, and his faith "in a better future".

The *St Mary* must have sailed before favourable east winds. In his logbook, the captain records a maximum speed of seventeen knots. Barfuss spends a lot of time on the poop, looking out at the horizon surrounding him on all sides. Of the sea he heard nothing, nor did he hear the flapping of sails and ventilators, or the wind and the sea birds that began appearing as they approached the east coast of America. But his other senses, he felt, were wide open.

On May 27 the ship put in to New York harbour. The journey had been normal by the standards of the day. From the original figure of 240 passengers, 238 were alive. One child and three old people had died during the crossing, but a Scandinavian woman had given birth to twins. Nothing of this is mentioned in Barfuss' notes. Nor, it's true, is there any mention in the ship's logbook of deformity or deafness and dumbness. Just the births and deaths. And a sailor who had been washed overboard in a storm just south of Iceland.

When Hercule Barfuss arrived in New York the stream of immigrants had not yet reached the level that some two decades later would cause the still-young American state to set up an immigration authority. Several decades more would come and go before the buildings on Castle Garden and Ellis Island were built in order to facilitate the administration of the enormous hordes of people arriving daily in the new land. When the schooner SS *St Mary* cast anchor in Upper New York Bay at dawn on May 27 there were no persons in authority waiting for her passengers. The travellers were transported in small steamboats to the harbour, or, more precisely, to the small area on the southern tip of Manhattan nowadays called Battery Park.

It was a very hot morning, a heatwave having swept in from the west. The health inspectors and passport-control officials were as yet but a dream nurtured by suspicious bureaucrats. There were no waiting rooms or delousing halls, no chalk lines drawn on the trunks or, much to the distress of latter-day immigrants, labels pinned to their clothes by uniformed officials. A few lodging houses flanked the quayside. Some "runners" from various hotels and routes met the passengers on the gangway, holding out tickets to the riverboats and contracts for mining concessions in the great lakes up north.

In the ship's passenger list, preserved at the Ellis Island Immigration Museum, Hercule Barfuss is listed as passenger #67. His name is written in capitals. There is no mention of nationality. What is noted is that he lacks an emigration passport from a European authority and that he is deaf and dumb.

That is all. He is simply a name in an anonymous mass of travellers, and the thought cannot be avoided that had he arrived two decades later he would almost certainly have been refused entry.

He spent a few nights in Manhattan. In his diary he wrote about the "spirit of freedom" pervading the city. With the help of the dockside authorities he acquires his identity papers. At the same time he anglicises his name to Barefoot.

In mid-June 1838 Hercule arrived at Martha's Vineyard. This we know from his own notes and from the population register for Tisbury County, where he is entered under the name D.H. Barefoot. What the letter D stands for isn't clear. "Deaf" maybe? He would tell my father how happy he had felt to be surrounded by others with the same hearing handicap. No-one seems to have reacted much to his physiognomy. As usual he wore a mask, but by that time only covering the lower part of his face. He had been told in Paris he had exceptionally beautiful eyes.

Inspired by his stay at the Institution Nationale des Sourds-Muets, he picked up the local sign language in record time, and wrote English almost as quickly.

The Rev. Robertson, clergyman in Chilmark parish, got him a secretarial job. He translated documents and religious writings from German – that same year some sixty deaf people arrived on the island from Austria. Alongside his everyday duties he worked as a stand-in organist. No-one questioned the fact that he could play the instrument despite his handicap, or that he did so with his toes.

During the last few years of the decade he solitarily developed a sign language for feet. This was a simplified form of French sign language for hands, worked out dialectically, and used on the island. Within a very short period of time it was comprehensible to those in his immediate vicinity, and was later to spread among others with similar handicaps.

I recall from the days of my childhood how he would write down anything he wanted to say with a chalk on a small blackboard which he always carried around with him. When he wanted to add something, ask questions, or give an answer, he would rub out the previous sentence with a sponge and write down a new one. I remember how fascinated I was by the dexterity of his feet and what perfect control he had over his toes, every bit as elaborate as a normal person has over their fingers.

One thing that puzzled those around him, were his financial

means. In some way, prior to his departure from Europe, he must have come across a large sum of money. He lived well, better than most on the island, but never commented on his economy. My father assumed he had received a grant, from von Below, perhaps, with whom he had shared the tragedy of losing a much-loved woman. Or perhaps it was money he had put aside with Henriette Vogel. It is not inconceivable that by using his gift he had embezzled a sum of money from someone he considered deserved such a fate.

In 1841 he had a house built in Chilmark, not far from the vicarage. It still stands; a solidly built two-storey whitewashed building, testifying to considerable wealth in the owner. This building contract he gave to a local company whose craftsmen and carpenters were, without exception, deaf.

That same year he met a woman, Sonya Pereira. They lived together without getting engaged. Less than a year later she gave birth to a daughter, Charlotte, christened after Barefoot's daughter with Henriette Vogel. At that time he had no contact with his daughter in Europe. It wasn't until the 1890s when, quite by chance, he got news of her through a Swedish immigrant who had moved to that country.

He had two more daughters with Sonya, both of whom died in early childhood. At that time, the late 1840s, he had already become famous in sign-language circles in America.

He worked as assistant editor on the first American journal for sign-language grammar while taking an MA examination in English at Boston University. In 1847 the Baltimore publisher J. Cooper published his book about the history of the deaf: *History of the Deaf and Dumb*, a three-hundred-page illustrated folio publication. He wrote in chronological order, starting with hieroglyphics and Plato's "Kratylos" in which, for the very first time in literature, sign language is mentioned. Famous deaf people are presented, from Roman Quintus Pedius, whom Pliny mentions, to the Spanish court artist El Mudo, the "Iberian Titian" who, together with Lope de Vega, was considered to be the most cultured of all men at the court of Philip II in Madrid.

A quote from Leviticus 19:14 serves as the book's motto: "Thou shalt not curse the deaf." The underlying sentiment is that of Christian humanism and the notion of the equal value of all men, as expressed in the American Declaration of Independence. In a lengthy passage St Augustine, who asserted "the ear is the gate to salvation", is pilloried for despising the deaf, as too is Samuel Heinecke, the German oralist, who had been feuding with Barefoot's number-one idol the Abbé l'Epée, founder of the deaf school in Paris.

Barefoot wrote about deaf people's pantomime theatres in ancient Rome and the first methodical deaf teachers: John de Beverly, Archbishop of York in the 700s, and Rudolf Agricola of Gröningen, philosopher in Heidelberg in the late Middle Ages. He translated sizeable chunks of Hieronymus Cardanus' *Paralipomenon* in which that renowned Italian physician points at the possibility of educating the deaf through the written word. He also refers to Jean Marc Itard's "Discourse on ears and hearing ailments", at that time a sadly neglected work, in which various types of hearing handicaps are, for the first time, medically classified. The book is illustrated with woodcuts. One of them, Juan Pablo Bonet's famous leather tongue, shows how he taught his deaf students the positions of the speech organs in the formation of various sounds. Another shows John Bulwer's Chirologia, a collection of manual gestures in pictorial form, paving the way for modern-day sign language.

The book never became the standard work Barefoot and the publisher had hoped it would. It came out in a modest edition: three-hundred copies, of which half never left the stockroom. In the only copy Barefoot owned, which was later inherited by my uncle, I particularly recall the reproduction of George Delgarno's glove – in which the alphabet was painted in different areas of the palm of the hand. With a deft touch of the finger on the different letters it was a practical way of communicating with the deaf. Delgarno's intention was that this system should be widely spread and that the glove, once one had learned the position of the letters, would no longer be needed. It was, so to speak, a kind of organic typewriter. My father claimed that at one time Alexander Graham Bell had had plans for mass-producing the invention and introducing it into American schools for the deaf.

A particularly critical chapter in the book is dedicated to the Swiss Johann Konrad Amman's books, *Deaf People Can Speak* and *Dissertatio de Loquela* – two works which formed the basis for the German oral method in which emphasis is laid on getting those with hearing deficiencies to use their speech organs and to lip-read, which Barefoot opposed. In postscript, as a furtive allusion to his gift, Barefoot criticises Defoe's novel about the deaf prophet Duncan Campbell: "Both", he sneers disdainfully, "strike me as charlatans."

In March 1848, ten years after his arrival, Hercule suddenly left Martha's Vineyard. No reason for this break-up is to be found in his writings and diaries, or gained from asking his nearest and dearest. Maybe it was grief over the loss of his two daughters. Or maybe, as some say, he was driven on by a spirit of adventure. My grandfather, who was the offspring of a later relationship with the seamstress Josephine Smith, believed the departure to have been precipitated by an illicit affair with his mother, who was at that time working in Barefoot's household. The reason for his leaving, so my grandfather said, was that he didn't want to make the scandal worse than it already was. Personally, I believe he was motivated by other reasons, such as Henriette Vogel.

Leafing through his diaries from that period of time, it is apparent that she is ever more on his mind. He longs for her to appear again, to "speak" to him from the other side. He misses her and longs for her more than he has done for many years. It was Henriette he had loved since early childhood, and her he would go on loving until the end of time. The other women in his life, Sonya Pereira and, later on, Josephine Smith, could never measure up to Henriette. He appreciated their friendship, and treated them, as mothers of his children, with the greatest respect. But it was Henriette who continued to be the meaning of his existence. Under such circumstances it is not impossible he was beset by restlessness or felt claustrophobic in the company of women who craved his undivided love.

He travelled by paddle steamer across Lakes Ontario and Superior to Minnesota, and from there on by caravan with a company of settlers via North Dakota, Montana, Idaho and Oregon, until he reached California and the Sacramento Valley in the autumn of 1848.

He is said to have been lured by rumours of gold deposits. With childlike pride he would afterwards claim to have been one of the so-called "Forty-eighters", that is, to have arrived with the first wave of gold seekers to San Francisco; not with the larger group which came in '49 when the gold rush was already a fact.

He stayed in north California for a year. Together with a Danish

279

adventurer he bought a mining concession outside Sonora. After only a couple of months, however, their collaboration was on the rocks. In a letter to his daughter (addressed, from a conventional point of view, to a seven-year-old girl, but equally directed to the abandoned Sonya Pereira) he wrote that the Dane complained increasingly over the manual workload he single-handedly had to carry. Given the nature of Barefoot's handicaps, he could hardly be of much help with the heavy toil of panning, digging and ditching. But it was he who had financed their investments and paid for their keep. The Dane, he wrote, had also been trying to cheat him out of his money.

That winter he acquired another mining concession at Diamond Springs, El Dorado County. Now he had six contracted Indians working for him; but the concession proved poor in gold and the men left when he had difficulties in paying their wages.

There are several more letters to his daughter over the following years. He resided in rural Los Angeles, and for some time in Tennessee. In the Southern States he was deeply upset by the cruelty of the slave trade, and sent letters to acquaintances in Washington pleading vehemently for its abolition. In New Orleans he worked for a while in a newly established school for the deaf, where even black children with hearing handicaps were included among the students. After a while, though, he looked northward; the American railroads were being extended along the east coast and it was this route which carried him onward.

For the second time in his life he came to New York, and set about writing a love story of which only fragments remain. The novel was never given a title and according to his own testimony he wrote only five of the planned twenty chapters before abandoning the project for lack of motivation. The story, he told my father, was of Henriette Vogel's life, written in a style reminiscent of Stendhal, and having the Frenchman's "crystallisation" metaphor as its basis. In the fragments that remain, a total of ten pages from two chapters, there is not a trace of sorrow over the girl's horrific fate. Instead, the text is saturated with a feeling of warmth, confidence and blind faith in love as a power of good that triumphs over evil.

Then in March 1853 he returned to Martha's Vineyard having been away for five years. After that he only ever left the island twice during the rest of his life.

*

I know Barefoot was happy and continued to be so until his death. The mildness he exuded was drawn as much from human wisdom as from the sense of harmony he felt within himself and in those around him. In his old age he was a patriarch surrounded by a family of loving women, children, grandchildren and great-grandchildren.

His attractiveness to the opposite sex was an enigma. After all, his appearance had, for most of his life, frightened women off. But love, as is well known, can crop up in all manner of guises. Maybe it was his sense of security that drew them to him. Or a longing for something he couldn't give them: namely the wholehearted love he'd reserved for Henriette.

Over the years he became an institution on the island. He was regarded as a wise old man to whom one could turn for help, whatever the problem. Never once did I hear anyone describe him as deformed or as a monster. To everyone on the island, he was Hercules Barefoot – a master and a diplomat of high standing.

As far as his gift was concerned, he kept it a secret from all but his immediate family. Besides which, he used it less and less frequently. It was as if he had learned to consciously switch it off. Perhaps he endeavoured to attain some kind of normality, to be merely one among others, and this is just what he could be in Martha's Vineyard, in a society of the deaf which he'd made his own. On the island there had always been a greater degree of tolerance towards those who were different, even among those who could hear. Besides, Barefoot had an almost masterly grasp of English as a written language, and his understanding of sign language, too, was exemplary. Seated, he used his feet to make signs. Thus his gift was no longer of vital importance, he had other idioms. Now that he at last belonged somewhere, he managed better without it.

Yet there were still occasions when he made use of it. Sometimes, jokingly, he would whisper something inside us, or reveal what was in our thoughts, just to score a comic point. But he was discreet, and avoided anything too personal. I remember that there were rumours about him being able to make himself invisible, but only to people in positions of authority, methodist clergy or the Irish police constable. Even after his death he was still an object for all kinds of tales. Like Störtebecker in north Germany or Dick Turpin in England, he has become a part of local folklore.

As far as his gift for making himself invisible was concerned, I myself witnessed this phenomenon on a couple of occasions in my childhood. It was exceedingly strange. All of a sudden he would be standing right in front of you, though you'd swear the room had been empty just seconds before. It was as if he could decide when he was ready to be detected. You could be somewhere for several hours, in his study for example, or in the garden outside his house, before discovering that Barefoot too was there. The sound of someone clearing their throat might come from the armchair, or from the desk, and only then would you discover his presence. Innumerable are the accounts of people who maintain they passed right by him on a road or in the aisle of a church and only noticed him afterwards. It is impossible to find an explanation and, in my opinion, some things are best left unexplained. But perhaps the fact of the matter is that his gift taught him how one can eradicate the idea of oneself in others.

To me he was mainly great-grandfather, a relatively ordinary old man, stocky, and with the lower half of his face hidden by a mask, but for those of us who knew him, he was part of our everyday life. We all loved him dearly and admired him for his goodness and generosity; and the grief we felt when he died was not of this world. He was one of the kindest and most loving people I have ever met, always close to laughter, but also to despair over the sorry state of our world.

Among the photographs which remain of him there is one I often take out and look at across the illusory distance to a moment in our existence we call time. It was taken one morning in August 1908 in Martha's Vineyard. My grandfather's father, Barefoot, is sitting in the arbour at a table laid for breakfast, surrounded by grandchildren and great-grandchildren. He is looking straight into the camera and one almost discerns a smile beneath his mask. His eyes, those dark, beautiful eyes, radiate a happiness that can only be communicated by the sign language of the deaf, where the look in the eyes is so important a part of the idiom.

I can see what that look in his eyes expresses: blind faith in love as a power so strong it can overcome death, and that he himself will soon, very soon, be reunited with Henriette Vogel, his beloved.

Tisbury, 1994
Jonathan Barefoot